ADVANCE ACCLAIM FOR *THE CANDIDATE*

"*The Candidate* is a political thrill ride. It's like being thrown into the middle of a presidential campaign, but with some major—and terrifying—twists. Never has the corruption of power been more chillingly portrayed. This book is a spellbinding trip into the heart of darkness. I couldn't put it down."

—RITA COSBY, EMMY-WINNING TV HOST, RADIO HOST, AND BESTSELLING AUTHOR

"Lis Wiehl's latest thriller *The Candidate* opens a number of windows for the reader. Can an ambitious reporter keep her soul while fighting her way to the top of the TV news industry? That intense conflict will keep you turning pages."

—BILL O'REILLY, FOX NEWS ANCHOR

"*The Candidate* is quite a yarn. It takes you deep in the intrigue of a presidential campaign with savvy and authority, and the twists and turns are unpredictable, spooky, and so relevant. It will keep thriller fans and political junky readers up late into the night!"

—ALAN K. SIMPSON, U.S. SENATOR, WYOMING (RETIRED)

ACCLAIM FOR *THE NEWSMAKERS*

"This book is distinctive, with a terrific plot and an imperfect main character who is spellbinding. Kudos to Lis Wiehl for imaginative, yet absolutely believable in this 'me' world, great writing. Wiehl has distanced herself from the pack with this one."

—*SUSPENSE MAGAZINE*

". . . Wiehl is more than up to the task in crafting a superb page-turner as provocative as it is scary."

—*PROVIDENCE JOURNAL*

"Wiehl's insider knowledge of the television news industry gives this novel credibility and excitement beyond the everyday tale."

—*RT BOOK REVIEWS*, 4-STAR REVIEW

"*The Newsmakers* is sure to grip readers and open their eyes to the intense field that is journalism."

—*CBA Retailers + Resources*

"*The Newsmakers*—introducing a compelling new character in cable-news star Erica Sparks—is a twisty, suspenseful adventure with the ring of authenticity that only an insider could provide. Wiehl and Stuart bring us into the world of major-league broadcasting with verve and thrills."

—William Landay, *New York Times* bestselling author of *Defending Jacob*

"A heart-pounding thrill ride from someone who knows the news business inside out. Lis Wiehl's *The Newsmakers* is not to be missed!"

—Karin Slaughter, author of *Pretty Girls*

"A page-turner from the word 'go'! Completely entertaining! Outrageously readable! This quick-cut action-thriller spotlights television's cutthroat deal-making, unholy alliances, and lust for success. Gotta love Lis! As always, she nails it."

—Hank Phillippi Ryan, Agatha, Anthony, and Mary Higgins Clark award-winning author of *What You See*

"*The Newsmakers* is a stunning debut thriller in a new series by one of my favorite authors. Lis Wiehl casts her insider's eye on the intrigue and drama of high-stakes television journalism. Terrorist attack? Murder of a presidential candidate? A reporter whose own life is at risk? This thrill ride has them all. Wiehl has crafted another bestselling winner with this powerful crime novel."

—Linda Fairstein, *New York Times* bestselling author

"Lis Wiehl is a seasoned journalist who knows the news business. Here, she's fashioned a tantalizing story that takes full advantage of her insider status. It's a fascinating thriller, which poses a curious question: What happens when reality is not quite good enough? The answer is going to shock you."

—Steve Berry, *New York Times* bestselling author

"*The Newsmakers* is sensational—taut, troubling, and terrifying. With Erica Sparks, Lis Wiehl has created her most memorable character yet: a reporter who has smarts, drive, heart—and a dark past that threatens to pull her down. Waiting for book two won't be easy."

—KATE WHITE, NEW YORK TIMES BESTSELLING AUTHOR

ACCLAIM FOR *A DEADLY BUSINESS*

"The second Mia Quinn mystery is action-packed from the first page. Layers of lies and deception make for a twisting, turning story that will keep mystery lovers entranced. This is a thrill ride until the very end, so hang on tight and enjoy the trip!"

—PUBLISHERS WEEKLY REVIEW, 4 STARS

"Wiehl's experience as a former federal prosecutor gives the narrative an authenticity in its depiction of the criminal justice system. Henry's expertise in writing mysteries and thrillers has placed her on the short-list for the Agatha, Anthony, and Oregon Book awards. The coauthors' . . . fast-paced detective series will keep legal thriller readers and John Grisham fans totally engrossed."

—LIBRARY JOURNAL REVIEW

"Wiehl has woven a wonderfully multi-layered story that will have readers on the edge of their seats . . . *A Deadly Business* delivers everything we love in a massively good mystery."

—CBA RETAILERS & RESOURCES REVIEW

ACCLAIM FOR *A MATTER OF TRUST*

"This suspenseful first in a new series from Wiehl and Henry opens with a bang."

—PUBLISHERS WEEKLY

"Wiehl begins an exciting new series with prosecutor Mia at the center. The side storyline about bullying is timely and will hit close to home for many."

—RT BOOK REVIEWS, 4 STARS

"Dramatic, moving, intense. *A Matter of Trust* gives us an amazing insight into the life of a prosecutor—and mom. Mia Quinn reminds me of Lis."

—MAXINE PAETRO, *NEW YORK TIMES* BESTSELLING AUTHOR

"*A Matter of Trust* is a stunning crime series debut from one of my favorite authors, Lis Wiehl. Smart, suspenseful, and full of twists that only an insider like Wiehl could pull off. I want prosecutor Mia Quinn in my corner when murder's on the docket—she's a compelling new character and I look forward to seeing her again soon."

—LINDA FAIRSTEIN, *NEW YORK TIMES* BESTSELLING AUTHOR

ACCLAIM FOR THE TRIPLE THREAT SERIES

"Only a brilliant lawyer, prosecutor, and journalist like Lis Wiehl could put together a mystery this thrilling! The incredible characters and nonstop twists will leave you mesmerized. Open [*Face of Betrayal*] and find a comfortable seat because you won't want to put it down!"

—E. D. HILL, FOX NEWS ANCHOR

"Who killed loudmouth radio guy Jim Fate? The game is afoot! *Hand of Fate* is a fun thriller, taking you inside the media world and the justice system—scary places to be!"

—BILL O'REILLY, FOX NEWS AND RADIO ANCHOR

"Beautiful, successful, and charismatic on the outside, but underneath a twisted killer. She's brilliant and crazy and comes racing at the reader with knives and a smile. The most chilling villain you'll meet . . . because she could live next door to you."

—DR. DALE ARCHER, CLINICAL PSYCHIATRIST, REGARDING *HEART OF ICE*

ACCLAIM FOR *SNAPSHOT*

"The writing is strong and the plot is engaging, driven by the desires (both good and evil) of the characters and the reader's desire to know who killed a man decades before, how it was covered up, and whether an innocent man has been charged and imprisoned. The book offers a 'snapshot' of the civil rights movement and turbulent times."

—PUBLISHERS WEEKLY

"A pitch-perfect plot that tackles some tough issues with a lot of heart. *Snapshot* brings our world into pristine focus. It's fast-paced, edgy, and loaded with plenty of menace. Lis Wiehl knows what readers crave and she delivers it. Make room on your bookshelves for this one—it's a keeper."

—STEVE BERRY, *NEW YORK TIMES* BESTSELLING AUTHOR

"*Snapshot* is fiction. But it takes us along the twisted path of race in America in a way that is closer to the human experience than most history books."

—JUAN WILLIAMS, BESTSELLING AUTHOR OF *EYES ON THE PRIZE: AMERICA'S CIVIL RIGHTS YEARS*

"Inspired by actual historical events and informed by Lis Wiehl's formidable personal and professional background, *Snapshot* captivates and enthralls."

—JEANINE PIRRO, BESTSELLING AUTHOR OF *SLY FOX*

"Riveting from the first page . . ."

—PAM VEASEY, SCREENWRITER AND EXECUTIVE PRODUCER

THE CANDIDATE

ALSO BY LIS WIEHL

NEWSMAKERS NOVELS

The Newsmakers

The Candidate

THE MIA QUINN MYSTERIES (WITH APRIL HENRY)

A Matter of Trust

A Deadly Business

Lethal Beauty

THE TRIPLE THREAT SERIES (WITH APRIL HENRY)

Face of Betrayal

Hand of Fate

Heart of Ice

Eyes of Justice

THE EAST SALEM TRILOGY (WITH PETE NELSON)

Waking Hours

Darkness Rising

Fatal Tide

OTHER NOVELS

Snapshot

THE CANDIDATE

A NEWSMAKERS NOVEL

LIS WIEHL
WITH SEBASTIAN STUART

THOMAS NELSON
Since 1798

Published in Nashville, Tennessee, by Thomas Nelson. Thomas Nelson is a registered trademark of HarperCollins Christian Publishing, Inc.

Thomas Nelson titles may be purchased in bulk for educational, business, fund-raising, or sales promotional use. For information, please e-mail SpecialMarkets@ThomasNelson.com.

Publisher's Note: This novel is a work of fiction. Names, characters, places, and incidents are either products of the author's imagination or used fictitiously. All characters are fictional, and any similarity to people living or dead is purely coincidental.

Library of Congress Cataloging-in-Publication Data

Names: Wiehl, Lis W., author. | Stuart, Sebastian, author.
Title: The candidate / Lis Wiehl with Sebastian Stuart.
Description: Nashville: Thomas Nelson, 2016. | Series: A Newsmakers novel; 2
Identifiers: LCCN 2016018974 | ISBN 9780718037680 (hardcover)
Subjects: LCSH: Women journalists—Fiction. | Reporters and reporting—Fiction. | Presidential candidates—Fiction. | Conspiracy theories—Fiction. | Political fiction. | GSAFD: Suspense fiction. | Mystery fiction.
Classification: LCC PS3623.I382 C36 2016 | DDC 813/.6—dc23 LC record available at https://lccn.loc.gov/2016018974

Printed in the United States of America

16 17 18 19 20 21 RRD 6 5 4 3 2 1

For Dani and Jacob. With unconditional love always and forever.
—Mom

PROLOGUE ——————————————

CELESTE PIERCE ORTIZ WINCES AS the needle slides into her forehead. She should be used to it—after all, she's been Botoxing for, what is it, six years now? Of course it's worth it, but there's just something about the first sight of that hypodermic that makes her afraid—just for a moment. Celeste is never afraid for more than a moment. Fear is for weak people. Little people. Tragic little people. Lily taught her that. And so much more.

"All done," Dr. Martin says, withdrawing the needle.

Celeste looks out her dressing room window. The mansions of Pacific Heights march like gilded bullies down the hillside to the Marina, the Presidio, and the waters of San Francisco Bay. Looming above the scene is the Golden Gate Bridge. This morning the iconic orange span is shrouded by fingers of fog that creep up its foundation like the tentacles of some ghostly sea creature. Celeste loves the fog. It slinks in silent and silvery, obscures things, hides them in plain sight. Under the cover of fog all manner of deeds can be done, safe from prying eyes. And when the fog lifts, plans are in place and no one is the wiser.

"I don't think you need any filler touch-ups today," the doctor says.

Celeste looks in the mirror—her face is as smooth as a plate. "No, I think we're fine," she agrees. She clasps the doctor's hand. "Thank you, Phillip. How's the family?" She rarely gets into the whole family thing with employees. It can drag on forever, and does she really care that so-and-so's daughter made a goal at her last soccer game? But her dermatologist ranks right up there with her lawyer and her husband's top donors as people she needs.

And the media, of course. But they're in a separate league, a big league, and they have to be cultivated and stroked and wooed and, yes, manipulated. Because no one gets to the White House without having the media in their corner. But you can't trust them. They can turn on you. And start digging, rooting around in your darkest corners. They're dangerous. They have to be watched. Like a hawk. Like a hungry hawk. And if need be, stopped. By any means necessary.

The doctor leaves, and Celeste walks into her small private office adjoining the bedroom. She switches on the TV to GNN, her preferred cable news network. Newscaster Erica Sparks is on, delivering a special report on the thousands of earthquakes that have rattled states where fracking is used to extract gas. Celeste watches carefully. Sparks is good. Really good. Beautiful and charming, yes, but also serious and thorough. As well as powerful—she's host of the highest-rated news show in the country. As she watches, Celeste is intrigued by Erica. There's something in the newscaster's eyes that hints at hidden depths, at some secret she keeps from the world. What could it be—and could it possibly be used to the campaign's advantage? Celeste makes a mental note: *It's time to begin investigating—and wooing—Erica Sparks.*

The latest polls are out today. Why hasn't Samantha called? Not a good sign. Celeste picks up her phone and dials her public office, which is in a separate wing of the mansion.

"I'm just on my way up with them," Samantha says preemptively.

Celeste gets down on the floor and does a series of core-strengthening exercises. Not that her core needs strengthening. It's steel. Always has been. Hasn't it? She could have just coasted through life as the Princess on the Bay, as that story in *Town & Country* labeled her two decades ago. Going to parties and benefits and sprinkling her vast inherited fortune on various worthy causes. That's what her mother wanted—her silly, shallow socialite mother. How insulting. To Celeste. To all women. Of course she ignored Mummy's wide-eyed admonitions. Celeste went to Stanford and then Stanford Law and then the Harvard B-school, and then into international banking where, armed with her fluency in Mandarin—and her friendship with Lily— she became Wall Street's go-to person for navigating the Byzantine byways of Chinese finance, making her *own* vast fortune in the doing.

And now. *Now.* Now she is married to Senator Mike Ortiz, who stands a very good chance of becoming the next president of the United States. Which will make Celeste the most powerful person in the world. With Lily Lau—who will be named President Ortiz's chief of staff—by her side. Sometimes, usually in the early-morning hours as the world sleeps, she imagines what they'll do with that power. And it won't be half measures. It will be a tectonic shift. They will do nothing less than remake the world as we know it.

There's a knock on the master suite door. Celeste stands up. "Come in."

Samantha Baldwin enters. Celeste can tell instantly from the expression on her pudgy face that the polls bring bad news. Samantha is such a homely girl, with those porcine features and that lank hair. Celeste likes to hire unattractive girls; their pathetic insecurity makes them putty in her hands. A single inflection in her voice can make them squirm or jump, which is always such fun to watch.

She takes the pages from Samantha's hands and scans the poll results. There are only two Democratic candidates left fighting for the nomination, her husband and that folksy Fred Buchanan. He and his drab wife, Judy (she really should change her name to Mousy), with their lack of charm and charisma, make these latest results doubly hard to swallow. Buchanan is gaining on her husband, is up six points in the last two weeks. Measures must be taken. Celeste walks over to the window and looks out. The bridge, which on clear days looks almost close enough to touch, is barely visible through the thick fog. The fog of war.

Without turning from the window Celeste says, almost casually, "Samantha, that gardener you hired last month chopped down the peony hedge."

"He says he didn't recognize them."

"Don't they have peonies in Mexico?"

"He's Ecuadorian."

"Tell that to the peonies. I'm afraid he has to go. I've been paying for his daughter's tutor. I'll continue that for six weeks and give him a month's severance."

Samantha looks stricken. She didn't hire the gardener; Celeste did. But that's a piddling detail—Samantha was in charge of the search.

"But—"

Celeste whirls around. "Don't bore me with your *buts*. Go and do your job."

Samantha turns and is just about out the door when Celeste says, in a whole new tone of voice, "Samantha . . ." The poor thing turns and Celeste goes to her, takes her hand, and gives it a squeeze. "I'm so sorry about your father's diagnosis. I've donated ten thousand dollars to the Pancreatic Cancer Foundation in his honor."

Samantha looks like she might burst into tears. "Thank you."

"We're all in this together."

Alone again, Celeste's wheels start churning, churning. These poll numbers are unacceptable. She feels her anxiety skyrocketing, that awful claustrophobia that strikes when she senses control slipping away. Celeste *needs* to be in control. She slips off her robe and stands there in her bra and panties, then walks into the dressing room and looks at herself in the full-length mirror. Thanks to a combination of genes, discipline, and the very best doctors, she still has the body of a teenager.

She walks into her office and over to the console that connects her to the rest of the house. She clicks on the gym. As expected, she sees her husband, Senator Mike Ortiz, exercising—right now he's on the rowing machine, wearing nothing but gym shorts, his muscular, nearly naked frame covered in sweat. He's an amazing specimen. And he's hers. She has him on a strict regimen of campaign events, policy tutorials, and exercise. She and Lily take care of strategy.

She clicks on her own cam. "Hello, darling."

Mike Ortiz looks up at the camera and smiles. That smile.

"I need you to get up here as soon as possible."

"I have a Middle East policy session in fifteen minutes," Mike says in that earnest way of his that voters mistake for sincerity. Celeste knows better.

"I'll postpone it," she says.

"What's up?" he asks.

Celeste reaches behind her, unhooks her bra, and lets it drop to the floor.

"I'll be there in a flash," Mike says, leaping off the rowing machine.

A half hour later, after he's performed his husbandly duties to Celeste's satisfaction, she sends him off to his policy session and slips back into her robe. The thought that he could even begin to understand the political and strategic complexities of the Middle East makes her smile.

She walks back into her office, picks up her secure line, and calls Lily. Her heart is racing and she feels that surge of exhilaration, adrenaline, and power that is her drug of choice.

The call is brief, just long enough to set things in motion. When she's done, she looks out the window. The fog is lifting.

CHAPTER 1 ──────────────

IT'S MONDAY MORNING AND ERICA Sparks is in the elevator at GNN headquarters in New York—going up. She's on her way to a meeting with Mort Silver, the head of the network. Silver called her yesterday and scheduled it. She isn't sure what his agenda is, but she suspects it has to do with her hopes of moderating one of the presidential debates in the fall. With her nightly news show *The Erica Sparks Effect* dominating its time slot, and her reputation as one of the best in the business, Erica is searching for new challenges, and the prospect of being part of America's quadrennial exercise in democracy—messy and imperfect as it is—excites her.

She feels a little shiver of expectancy as the elevator shoots skyward. Erica loves mornings—when the world is still fresh and her mind clips along, almost tripping over itself with plans, ideas, and inspiration. Her life, so tumultuous over the past few years, is finally settling down. She's achieved her two great goals: success in the news business and gaining custody of her daughter, Jenny. Yes, things get edgy at times—Erica feels like she still has the training wheels on her mothering skills—but they usually manage to work it all out. Jenny means more to her than anything in the world.

The only piece missing from her life is Greg, the man she loves. He's a world away, in Australia, working insane hours helping to launch a cable news network. It's an amazing opportunity, and Erica was supportive of his seizing it, but not having him around has been tough. There are nights—after her daughter has gone to bed, as she goes around the apartment turning off lights—when she feels almost overcome with loneliness, with a yearning to have a man by her side during these exciting and fulfilling times.

The elevator doors open on the fortieth floor and Erica gets off. She takes a deep breath. She likes Mort Silver, but his leadership style can be a little intimidating. After Erica's investigation sent GNN's founder Nylan Hastings to jail for the rest of his life, several large media companies vied to buy the network. Google was the winner, and CEO Sundar Pichai has turned out to be a demanding if distant boss. He was smart enough to hire Silver, a seasoned broadcast pro, to run the network—these men play to win, and the company's results prove the wisdom of their ways. But they're known for pushing employees to deliver—and if they don't, well, sayonara.

Silver's receptionist gives Erica a deferential smile and says, "Mr. Silver is expecting you."

Erica walks down the wide hallway and into Silver's large corner office. Unlike Nylan Hastings, who filled the space with modern art, Silver's taste is more traditional—one wall has been lined with mahogany shelving that holds his three Emmys and other awards, and the other walls are home to numerous framed articles about Silver and his successes in the news business. Modest the man isn't.

"Erica!" Mort Silver says with a big smile, leaping up from his chair and coming to greet her. He's around fifty, tall, and a little bulky, with an avuncular manner that borders on the overbearing.

"Nice to see you, Mort."

He ushers her into the office. "Can we get you something to drink, something to eat?"

"I'm fine," Erica says, sitting down opposite his desk.

Mort sits back down and leans forward, elbows on the desk. "It's always such a pleasure to see you," he says. He works hard at being charming, but it always comes across as just that—work.

"Likewise," Erica says.

Silver grows serious, lowers his voice. "Sometimes, in the hurly-burly of our daily efforts, we forget how important journalism is to our democracy, indeed, to the world." He looks Erica in the eye. "It truly is an honor to work with you."

Erica's bullcrap alarm begins to sound—platitudes have a way of setting it off.

"Thank you."

"But as crucial as our role is in uncovering the truth and exposing injustice and criminality, at the end of the day, GNN is a business." Silver pauses, looks out the window as if he's searching for his next words—but Erica can tell this has all been rehearsed. He turns back to her. "As you know, *The Erica Sparks Effect* is very important to the network's bottom line. Which is why we're so concerned."

Erica is thrown. After her work in exposing Nylan Hastings as a psychopath bent on world domination, her celebrity was transcendent, and for months her show had a firm grip on the number one spot in the ratings. Erica knows it has slipped a little since then, but she avoids tracking the ratings race. She's a journalist, not an entertainer, and she's seen integrity compromised in the hunt for higher ratings. She's not about to let that happen on her show.

Silver stands up and starts to pace, his whole demeanor changing as his jaw sets and his eyes narrow. "Last month FOX beat you three times and CNN twice. That's five weeknights out of twenty-two. There were six other nights where your lead was miniscule." He stops abruptly and turns to her. "These numbers are unacceptable."

Erica knew she'd lost a few nights, but she didn't realize that her lead all month was that tenuous. And Silver's ultimatum is so stark and brutal. She feels the fiery demons of insecurity that have haunted her for her whole life flare up. She hears her mother's mocking voice.

Ha-ha, smarty pants, got a little too big for your britches, didn't you? And then, after the taunts, comes *Slap! Slap-slap! Take that, you little brat!*

Erica feels a bead of sweat roll down from her left armpit. She crosses and uncrosses her legs. Mort Silver has taken a step closer to her, seems to tower over her.

She's starting to feel a little bullied, and Erica has never liked bullies. She sits up tall and says, "I'm proud of the show, Mort, proud of my team. I think we've become a consistent source of superior journalism. We're taken seriously across the country and around the world."

"That's a given. And your being in the top spot *used* to be a given. Now it isn't. And that's a problem. For me. For Sundar. For our shareholders. And for you."

"If you think I'm going to start chasing sensational stories just to give my ratings a temporary boost, you've got yourself the wrong woman."

Mort looks at her—or is that a glare? Maybe he didn't expect her to respond so forcefully. In any case, he seems to switch gears; his face softens and he sits back down. "We all have the same goal. To see *The Erica Sparks Effect* firmly on top. Any thoughts on how to make that happen?"

"The presidential campaign is heating up. We may well have the first woman *and* the first Latino nominees. This is history in the making. I want to be a part of it. Moderating one of the debates would put me in the spotlight in a whole new way and take my reputation to the next level. Let's make that happen."

Mort nods. "We'll put your name forward to the Commission on Presidential Debates. You do have a rep for being nonpartisan, which should help your chances, but there are no guarantees. Both of the eventual candidates have veto power."

"Lucy Winters has a lock on the Republican nomination," Erica says. "The Democrat will be either Ortiz or Buchanan. I'll do my best to let all three candidates know I'm interested and impartial."

"Debate moderator or not, I think we have to address the underlying cause of your slippage."

"Which is?"

Silver drums on the desktop with his fingertips and takes a deep breath. "You've lost some of your mojo, Erica. Sometimes you seem to be gliding through your show. Other times you seem distracted. You're not as hungry as you used to be. You have to stay famished in this business."

Erica feels anger rising up in her. "I'm the top-rated cable newscaster in the country, and you're telling me I've lost my mojo?"

"*I'm* not telling you; the *numbers* are," Silver says forcefully, harshly.

Suddenly Erica's position at GNN feels, if not quite precarious, far less secure. And if her career is uncertain, so is every other aspect of her life. She feels the sweat spread to her forehead, and suddenly the room feels close and airless. Her breathing grows shallow.

Silver leans back in his chair and tries to contain his smirk. "Have you caught any of Sara Kenyon's show over on CNN? She's interesting. Bright. Driven. Incredibly self-possessed for a twenty-six-year-old."

Sara Kenyon is the new flavor of the month. Yes, she's smart and watchable, but she began her career as a meteorologist; she has no journalism training. And there's a rumor going around that she had plastic surgery—to look more like Erica Sparks.

"I'll give her a look," Erica says.

"*Her* ratings keep going up," Silver says, standing up, signaling that the meeting is over.

Fifteen minutes ago Erica was walking on sunshine. Now it feels more like quicksand. As she walks back down the cold white hallway, she has one thought: *I need a story. A big story.*

CHAPTER 2 ———————————————

ERICA IS SCRAMBLING EGGS FURIOUSLY. She has no time, no time. It's two days since her meeting with Mort Silver. Her flight to Cleveland leaves in ninety minutes and she hasn't packed. And she still has so much prep yet to do for tonight's show. "Jenny!" she calls. If they don't hustle, Jenny will miss her school van and Erica will miss her flight.

She plates the eggs, adds a piece of toast and a slice of cantaloupe, and puts it down on the kitchen table just as Jenny walks in.

"Why the long face, honey?"

Jenny sits and looks at her breakfast without touching it.

"You have to eat, sweetheart."

"I'm not hungry."

"I have a very busy day."

"You have a very busy day *every* day."

Not this again. Erica bites her tongue. She wants to tell Jenny that her hard work is what pays for this beautiful apartment on Central Park West, for her tuition at Brearley, for the camp in the Adirondacks Jenny is going to this summer. Her job is what gets them invited to the movie premieres and Broadway opening nights Jenny loves. And that if she doesn't push and sweat and put in long hours, it could all disappear.

Mort Silver made that pretty clear. But more than anything, she wants Jenny to understand that she *loves* her work—she loves the platform her nightly news show affords her; she loves the power she has to uncover the truth, to stand up to the high and mighty, to shine the light of fairness on injustice and inequality.

But she's explained all this to Jenny before—and it doesn't make up for all the late nights at the network, all the missed dinners and broken dates, all the weekend plans upended by a breaking story. Jenny feels neglected, and she can be resentful. Her transition to New York and living with Erica has been a little rocky. No doubt she sometimes feels like a fish out of water in the competitive and ultra-wealthy world of Brearley, and it's only natural that she misses her father and her old friends up in Massachusetts. And then there are those other, darker things . . . things Erica can't blame her daughter for having trouble forgiving.

Erica hears that haunting echo, that mocking voice—*You'll never be a good mother; you're a fraud, a fake, a pretender.* And it spreads like a toxic spill deep into her psyche. Some nights she bolts awake at three a.m. in a cold sweat, gripped by intense fear and a certainty that something terrible is going to happen. The slip in her ratings and the driving pressure she feels to deliver a big story have only exacerbated her night terrors.

Erica exhales with a gush, puts the frying pan in the sink, and sits down across from Jenny. She reaches out and strokes her hair. "Yes, I'm busy, but there's *nothing* in the world more important to me than you are."

"I don't believe you. You won't even raise my allowance. Morgan Graham gets *twice* as much as I do."

Oh—so *that's* what this is about. A little bit of emotional blackmail as practiced by a smart eleven-year-old. Erica feels a surge of relief—allowance disputes she can handle.

"No, Jenny, I'm not going to raise your allowance. I don't care how much Morgan Graham gets. I think twenty-five dollars a week is more than enough for a girl your age. You know that if there's something special you want, you can come to me and we'll discuss it."

Jenny looks Erica in the eye, and Erica smiles. Oh, how she loves this little girl! Jenny picks up a piece of toast and takes a bite.

"Did you get all your homework done?"

Jenny nods as she digs into her eggs.

"You remember that I'm flying out to Cleveland today to cover the final Democratic debate."

"Who do you root for?"

"Well, as a journalist, I stay neutral. But between us, I do think the prospect of a Latino candidate is exciting."

"So do I. We talked about the election in class. Senator Ortiz was a marine who served in the Iraq War. Then after he was elected to Congress he went back on a humanitarian mission and was kidnapped by Al-Qaeda and held hostage."

"And then he escaped from Al-Qaeda."

"Yes, the escape was like in a movie."

"But it was real, Jenny. He's a brave man."

"He's cute too."

"Yes, he is cute, isn't he?" They smile at each other. "Yelena will make you dinner."

Yelena is Erica's part-time housekeeper, a middle-aged Russian woman. She's dependable and a terrific cleaner, but her English is limited, making it tough for her to engage with Jenny.

"I hope she doesn't make those potato dumplings again. They're a carb-a-thon."

Erica laughs. Her cell rings. It's Eileen McDermott, her lead producer.

"Good morning, Eileen."

"We're setting up a temporary studio at Case Western, but it's across the quad from the debate hall, and neither Ortiz or Buchanan will commit to an interview."

"If they won't come to me, I'll go to them. I'll be on the ground in front of the hall as they arrive, and I'll grab each one for a few questions." Getting out of the broadcast booth—which is where the other anchors will be—will create exciting television.

"Perfect," Eileen says. "It's a big night. See you at the airport in a few."

Erica hangs up and stands. "Your van will be downstairs in fifteen minutes, and my car will be here in twenty. We're a couple of busy girls. Now, I better go throw a few things in a suitcase."

"This is our only time together all day and you're leaving."

"Oh, honey . . ."

"Never mind." Jenny pushes away from the table, pops in her headphones, grabs her knapsack, and heads out of the apartment.

Erica strides back to her bedroom and opens her closet—but she can't concentrate. All she sees is the expression on Jenny's face as she walked out of the kitchen. She imagines her daughter's lonely evening, filled with homework and indigestible dumplings and incomprehensible Yelena.

Snap out of it, Erica. You're doing the best you can. Erica grabs a simple, never-fail peach dress. Nancy Huffman made it for her, and it fits like a glove. She also pulls a black suit as a backup. But her mind—and heart—just won't let go of her daughter. The demands of her job are staggering—it's a pressure cooker in a minefield—but it's what she wants to be doing. What she hasn't figured out is how to carve out enough time with Jenny. She needs help.

Erica has a terrific staff at the network, but she's resisted hiring a personal assistant, someone who would bridge her professional and personal lives. She prides herself on being able to handle it all, but the stark truth is she *isn't* handling it all. Not well, anyway. Pride can be a dangerous thing. Maybe it's time to relent. It would be such a relief to have someone who could handle the thousand prosaic details that clutter up her life, someone who could tie up odds and ends, engage Jenny, and hopefully anticipate both Erica's and Jenny's needs.

But it has to be the right person. Female. Young. Bright. Takes initiative. And most important, of course, clicks with Jenny. Erica has several interns on her show, kids just out of college trying to build their resumes. She runs through them in her head. There's that super-organized one—Amanda, Amanda Rees. She's a hard worker, a self-starter, upbeat. *Hmm*. Certainly worth talking to.

Erica calls Shirley Stamos, her amazingly efficient, dry-witted secretary, on whom she has come to depend. "Can you get me Amanda Rees's resume?"

"Will do."

"I've decided I need a personal assistant. What do you think of her?"

"I think she's terrific, a real go-getter, heading for big things."

"I had the same impression. If you think of anyone else, let me know. Maybe put out the word that I'm looking."

Erica hangs up. She'll contact Amanda Rees in the next couple of days. Right now it's time to concentrate on tonight's debate. The candidates have fought to a near draw in the primaries and delegate count, and—as the final round of primaries looms—this debate could be the deciding factor. It also gives Erica an opportunity for face time with the candidates and their staffs—the more comfortable they become with her, the more likely it is they'll consent to her moderating one of the general election debates. Which would be a career coup.

There's *a lot* at stake. As her focus sharpens and her juices flow, Erica tosses a pair of heels, a light sweater, and a half dozen pairs of her clip-on earrings into her suitcase. Then she grabs it and races out the door.

CHAPTER 3 —————————————————

THE SCENE OUTSIDE THE VEALE Center at Case Western Reserve University is a raucous testimony to a vibrant democracy. There are crowds, contained by police barricades, on either side of the walkway that leads from the curb to the sleek, low-slung glass building. On one side are the Ortiz partisans, on the other are Buchanan's supporters—there are hats and flags and signs and cheers and chants; everyone is pumped and primed and passionate. Erica finds it all energizing, thrilling. She has zero respect for people who don't vote, are cynical about our system, or take our freedoms for granted.

She is standing near the entrance to the center, between the two sides, ready to go live. She's still working with the same pod—cameraman Derek, soundman Manny, and associate producer Lesli—that was assigned to her on her first day at GNN, which seems like a lifetime ago. They've been through the crucible with her—Derek and Manny risked their lives that terrifying day in Miami—and her loyalty to them is unshakable.

Just as Erica is getting her game face on, there's a small commotion down by the curb. Lo and behold, it's CNN's Sara Kenyon arriving with her crew and taking up position just where the candidates' cars will be pulling up. Sara looks over to Erica and feigns excited surprise. Then she dashes over. She's pretty and perky, but her green eyes have a hard edge.

"Be still my heart. It's an honor to meet you, Erica."

"It's a pleasure to meet you, Sara."

"Well, I better go *woman* the battlements, the candidates will be arriving any minute. Can we do lunch?"

"Of course."

Sara mouths *Call me* and dashes back to her crew. She still has a lot to learn, Erica thinks. First of all, she made a freshman error by positioning herself where she has. When the candidates first get out of their cars they'll be engulfed in cheers and outstretched hands. They won't turn their backs on their supporters to grant an interview. Erica, by placing herself in front of the entrance to the hall, has increased her chances of snagging at least a few words.

"All set, Erica?" Lesli asks.

Erica nods. Like all newscasters, Erica has had to master the art of peripheral vision. She looks right into the camera when she speaks, but keeps half an eye on a monitor below the camera that shows what's on-screen as seen by viewers. Now she sees Patricia Lorenzo, the GNN anchor in New York. In her earpiece Erica hears Lorenzo say, "Now let's go to Erica Sparks live in Cleveland."

"Thanks, Patricia. This is Erica Sparks reporting from Case Western Reserve University in Cleveland, where the final debate between the two remaining contenders for the Democratic presidential nomination—Senator Mike Ortiz of California and Pennsylvania governor Fred Buchanan—will begin in just under an hour. As you can see, the crowd outside is divided into the Ortiz and Buchanan camps, and passions are running high. The candidates themselves are expected to arrive at any minute. They're both fighting for the right to take on the presumptive Republican candidate, Minnesota senator Lucy Winters."

A great cheer goes up as a caravan of black SUVs pulls up to the curb. A Secret Service agent leaps out of the first car, rushes up to the second car, and opens the door. A blond woman of about forty, with perfect makeup and hair and wearing an exquisitely tailored suit, steps out—she has show-stopping presence and a dazzling smile that is at once both welcoming and off-putting.

"It looks as if Mike Ortiz has just arrived. That's his wife, Celeste Pierce Ortiz, we see getting out of the vehicle first. She's a powerful and intriguing woman in her own right—heiress to a car dealership fortune, an international banker specializing in China markets. She has put her own career on hold to work for her husband's campaign, to which she has donated over twenty million dollars. And here comes Senator Ortiz."

Mike Ortiz steps out of the SUV to frenzied cheers from his supporters. He's in his midforties, handsome with close-cut black hair and a powerful build that looks like it's barely contained by his expensive suit. He breaks into a broad smile that could melt the darkest heart. Standing side by side, the couple is blindingly glamorous.

They ignore Sara Kenyon's entreaty for a few words, and as they make their way along the police line, touching outstretched hands, patting babies' cheeks, signing autographs, Erica can't help but be a little starstruck—and she's seen her fair share of stars. They reach the end of the line, and when Celeste sees Erica she turns into a heat-seeking missile and steers her husband over.

And now they're in front of her. "Senator Ortiz, can I ask you a couple of quick questions?"

The senator shoots a glance at his wife, who, without missing a beat, says, "Anything for you, Erica."

In spite of her tough reporter's hide and professional neutrality, Erica is flattered. "What do you need to accomplish tonight, Senator?"

"The American people are looking for answers, and I want to make sure they know what I stand for and why."

"How do you respond to criticism that you're relying too heavily on your admittedly powerful capture and escape from Al-Qaeda?"

"My experiences in Iraq shaped the man I am today. During my tour as a marine I saw unimaginable suffering. After I was elected to Congress, I was determined to return to Iraq to help the civilian population. Then I was kidnapped. I knew that if I made it back home, I would redouble my commitment to the common good. And my escape taught me that anything is possible." He speaks with heart—making the words sound like he's never said them before, when in fact he repeats them at every opportunity. Like a great actor, he makes the stale sound fresh—the man has enormous political talent.

Celeste Ortiz leans in and squeezes Erica's hand. "We'd better get inside, Mike has some last-minute preparations."

As they enter the arena, another phalanx of black vehicles pulls up, and a great cheer goes up as Fred and Judy Buchanan step out of their car. They are the anti-Ortiz—they both have gray hair, Judy is in a plain cotton dress, and her husband's suit is wrinkled. There's art to their homey image—Buchanan is running as the champion of the working and middle classes. They too ignore Sara Kenyon, who gamely smiles into her camera and chatters away.

Watching the Buchanans, Erica is struck by their sincerity and warmth. There's nothing rote about the way they're greeting their supporters; they seem to genuinely listen and connect. Their lack of polish is refreshing, but Erica isn't sure it will carry Buchanan to the White House. Americans want their presidents and movie stars to be idealized versions of themselves—better looking, smarter, richer. The Buchanans look like a couple of bird watchers you'd strike up a conversation with on a hiking trail in Vermont. Thoughtful, compassionate, and a little dull.

Still, they seem like lovely people, a reflection of Americans' core decency. As they approach the end of the police line, a young mother hands Judy Buchanan her baby and Judy holds it up and makes a funny face—the baby smiles in delight.

Then there's a flash of light and a deafening boom and Erica's world goes black.

CHAPTER 4 ——————————————————

ERICA COMES TO A MOMENT later. She's lying on the ground, an intense pain shooting through her right shoulder, which took the brunt of her fall. But otherwise she's in one piece. Screams and cries for help fill the air. Erica looks over to where the Buchanans stood, now a scene of horror and carnage. Bodies and body parts lie bloodied and mangled. She stumbles to her feet, afraid she's going to vomit; she suddenly feels cold, frigid, and realizes she's going into shock. But people need help; they're crying and screaming. Erica sees a teenage girl lying on the pavement—all that's left of her right leg below the knee is the jagged tip of her shinbone. The girl is frozen, looking down at the place where her leg was thirty seconds ago. Erica races over to her as the wail of ambulances is heard in the distance. The girl is wearing a belt, and Erica swiftly takes it off and wraps it tightly just above the girl's right knee. Then she lifts the thigh, angling the leg up, and the blood flow diminishes. Two EMTs arrive and take over.

As the first responders flood the scene, Erica realizes she's just in the way. She stands up, and that's when she notices the twisted, lifeless bodies of Fred and Judy Buchanan. A terrible sadness washes over her, grief for the loss of these two sincere people who clearly loved their country and each other. Then fear takes over. If she'd been standing ten feet closer to them, her own body would look like that right now. Her hands start to shake.

She goes back over to her pod—who were just far enough away from the blast to escape injury—and picks up her mic, sucking air, willing herself to stop shaking and do her job. "This is Erica Sparks reporting from the campus of Case Western Reserve University, and a bomb has just exploded near the entrance to the Veale Center, where the final Democratic primary debate was scheduled to start within the hour. Both Fred Buchanan and his wife, Judy, have been killed. As you can see, the scene here is one of carnage and chaos. First responders have arrived in force, and the injured are being taken to local hospitals. We have no count of the casualties and fatalities yet, but I would esti-mate them in the dozens. This is simply horrific."

Erica sees a campus security guard standing nearby, his uniform covered in blood. She goes over to him, her pod following, taping.

"Did you see anything suspicious before the bomb exploded?"

The man is fighting back tears. "I was over there on the Ortiz side. When Buchanan was shaking hands, I thought I saw a teenager, or maybe he was a young man, pushing forward to get close to him. Next thing I knew the bomb went off. Oh, this is terrible, just terrible." The man turns away from the camera, unable to continue.

"Once again: a bomb exploded less than five minutes ago here at Case Western Reserve University in Cleveland."

A man and a woman, both in dark suits, approach Erica. They flash FBI badges and signal for her to stop taping.

"This is Erica Sparks reporting. I'll bring you any updates as they happen. Now back to GNN headquarters in New York."

Manny turns off the camera. The female FBI agent says, "We'll need that footage." Manny looks to Erica and Lesli, who both nod assent.

"Let us know if there's anything else we can do," Erica says as the agents take the camera and walk away. "Get the backup camera, Manny."

Erica grabs her bag, takes out her cell, and turns it on. There have been three calls from Jenny in the last five minutes. She ducks inside the Veale Center and calls back.

"Mommy, Mommy, I saw it on TV, are you all right?" Jenny is sobbing.

"Yes, I'm fine, honey. I'm *fine*. It's a horrible thing that's happened but I'm fine."

"When are you coming home?"

"I'll be spending the night out here. I have a job to do. This is a very important story."

"I don't *care*. I don't want you to have that job anymore. It's too scary."

"No one said it was an easy job, Jenny, but it's an important one." Erica takes a deep breath—just talking to Jenny is grounding her. She's still a mom. "Can you please ask Yelena to stay over tonight?"

There's a pause and then Jenny says, "Yes."

Law enforcement is swarming around the arena, and Sara Kenyon and other newscasters are delivering live on-the-scene coverage. GNN isn't. That's unacceptable.

"I better get going, honey." Out the glass doors, Lesli is gesturing to let Erica know they're ready to go. Erica walks back outside. All of the dead and injured have been removed, but their blood remains, staining the concrete like a demonic Rorschach test. Evil. There's so much evil in the world.

Erica flashes back to the Staten Island ferry crash that launched her career. Is it possible this horrific act was also orchestrated by unseen forces who want Erica to be on the scene? No, that's ridiculous. No one except a few people at the network knew where she would be positioned. And she can trust everyone at GNN. Can't she? She's being paranoid. Isn't she?

Erica takes the mic from Derek, and as she opens her mouth to begin reporting, she wonders if it's all really worth it.

CHAPTER 5 ————————————————

THE NEXT MORNING ERICA IS sitting at her desk in New York. She was on the air for another four hours anchoring GNN's coverage of the bombing, and then she crashed for a few hours at an airport hotel. The network's plane flew her back to New York and she came straight to the office, where she showered in her private bathroom and changed into a clean dress.

Fifteen people died in the bomb attack, forty-two were injured, eight are in critical condition, and the country is reeling. Cell phone and network footage clearly show a young man—first described to Erica by the campus security guard—pushing his way forward in the crowd in the moments before the explosion. He was wearing sunglasses, had a ski cap pulled low on his forehead, and was carrying a backpack. Some anchors at other networks—eager to get ahead of the story— are already speculating that he's an Islamic terrorist. Erica refuses to engage in that kind of inflammatory reporting. It's irresponsible, demagogic, and just plain lousy journalism. She'll wait until identification can be made and the facts uncovered. She's told Eileen McDermott that she wants to stay off the air until there's a break in the story.

Something from last night has lodged at the back of Erica's mind, but she can't remember exactly what it is. It happened before the bomb blast, and with the ensuing panic and pandemonium she can't bring it up. It's like an itch she can't scratch, and it's driving her a little nuts. But she pushes her frustration away—if it's gone, it's gone.

Her phone rings.

"Great job last night, Erica," says Mort Silver. "We topped the ratings."

Erica understands that the news is a business, but the obsession with ratings at a time like this, when the nation has lost an admired public servant and been traumatized by an act of terrorism, makes her uneasy.

"I'm glad to hear it, Mort."

"Let's stay on top," he says, and there's an edge in his voice, subtle but unmistakable.

Erica isn't ashamed of being ambitious, but she never wants it to cross the line into ruthless. Since she helped nail Hastings and his cohorts, she's enjoyed a unique status among American journalists. She even got a call from the president, asking her to become chief of the Broadcasting Board of Governors, the state department agency charged with delivering accurate news to strategic audiences overseas and serving as an example of a free and professional press. It's an important job, but she turned him down because it would have demanded too much of her time. But just to be asked was evidence of her stature. And she's definitely earned that most coveted of American titles—she's a *celebrity*! A fact she does her very best to ignore. Erica refuses almost all requests for interviews; she shuns parties, benefits, and photo ops. Over the last eight months, since Hastings was sentenced, she has waited for the hoopla and buzz to subside. She wants to be *less* famous, wants to return to her roots as a journalist who is in it for the long haul. And if she loses the ratings battle to FOX or CNN now and then, so be it.

With her vast office—complete with kitchen, bath, and closet/dressing room—and staff of writers, directors, producers, and researchers, Erica is in a position of enormous power. She wields it gently. She hates diva behavior—everyone at *The Erica Sparks Effect* is treated with respect and integrity. No games, no backbiting, no bull.

Erica spoke to Jenny a little earlier. Yelena stayed overnight and got her off to school. Erica hopes she can make it home for dinner, but everything depends on the Buchanan bombing story. If there are any developments, it could be a very long day. Which would mean Jenny will be alone again for another night. Just when Erica thinks things will quiet down, an important story breaks and Jenny suffers. Erica calls Shirley.

"Can you tell Amanda Rees I'd like to see her in my office?"

"Amanda left the network today."

"You're kidding. Why?"

"Some videos of her just surfaced. Apparently she worked her way through college via the world's oldest profession, or at least its latest online iteration."

"Didn't she know how risky that was?"

"You would think so. She disguised herself, black wig, exotic makeup. You know, I've heard girls can make thousands a day on those sites. With all their crippling student loans . . ."

"Who are we to judge? Poor girl—but I bet she lands on her feet. Do we know who leaked the video?"

"No, it was sent anonymously to Mort Silver yesterday. Amanda may have an enemy out there."

"Has it gone viral?"

"It's gaining traction, but we're hoping her swift departure will nip it in the bud."

"Let's hope. I can't afford that kind of publicity. Meanwhile, I'm back to the drawing board on the personal assistant."

Erica hangs up and feels a sudden stab of loneliness. She misses Greg. His light touch with Jenny, his concern, his pragmatism . . . his kisses. He's left her several messages since last night and she's called back, but they keep missing each other.

Erica pulls up Skype and calls him. He answers immediately, and his handsome face fills her screen. It's eleven thirty p.m. in Sydney and he looks exhausted, but in that tousled, stubbly way that Erica finds irresistible. She feels a surge of tenderness and want.

"How are you?" he asks.

"It was rough but I'm okay. I think being knocked out for those few moments was a real blessing. I missed seeing people blown apart. The poor Buchanans."

Part of her wants to cry, wishes Greg was with her so he could wrap his arms around her shoulders and she could rest her head on his chest and weep. For the Buchanans, for that little baby Judy Buchanan was holding up, for the girl who lost her leg, for the world and all its lost innocence.

"The coverage over here has been wall-to-wall. Do you have any sense of who might be behind it?"

"I honestly don't, and I'm not going to speculate."

"How's Jenny?"

"Moody. Feeling neglected." There's a pause. "How are you?"

Greg lowers his voice. "I'm lonely, Erica."

She reaches up and instinctively touches the screen, as if she could reach across time and space and touch Greg. "I'm lonely too."

"Didn't you and Jenny promise to come down and meet some kangaroos?"

"We did. We will." But Erica knows a trip halfway around the world would be a bad idea right now. It would risk disrupting Jenny's shaky adjustment to living in New York. And the bombing has upended the presidential campaign, which won't be over until the votes are counted on November 4, just over six months away. Erica needs to stay at home, on top of the story, ready to hop on a plane at a moment's notice. "But now is probably not the best time, with Jenny still settling in and the campaign heating up. Any chance you can come stateside for a visit?"

Greg runs a hand through his hair. "If only. But I'm working twenty-hour days and will be for at least the next couple of months."

There's a pause. "I understand," Erica says.

"Are you sure you're okay, Erica? Maybe you should take the day off."

And do what? Go home and be lonely in the huge empty apartment? "This is a fast-breaking story. The FBI, the CIA, Department of Justice, they're all trying to identify the bomber. I want to be ready when they do."

"I guess we're both married to our work."

There's another pause, and Erica isn't sure how to fill it. When they first met, the words just poured out; they had such an easy rapport. Skype is fine as far as it goes, but it's a poor substitute for the chemistry that sparks when they're face-to-face. Erica knows how hard Greg is working, but he's sometimes hard to reach for several days at a time . . . Australia is full of bright, beautiful women . . . They've been apart for almost three months . . . Men are men.

Erica, stop it! You don't jump to conclusions as a journalist, do you?

"I'm going to go now, Greg."

"Stay in close contact."

The call leaves Erica feeling even more distant from him.

She again tries to recall what it was that stuck in her mind from last night, before the explosion. It was something to do with her interaction with Mike Ortiz. But what? She needs to move. She stands up, walks into her sleek galley kitchen, and turns on the teakettle. A small plate is on the counter, covered in tinfoil. Erica removes the foil, and there sit a half dozen homemade muffins and a small folded note.

Erica unfolds the note and reads:

Erica—

I'm so sorry you had to go through that. Your actions were inspiring. Please let me know if there's anything I can do to make your life easier.

All best—Becky Sullivan

Becky Sullivan is another one of the interns. She's competent enough, but insecure and self-effacing, she doesn't make much of an impression. But what a lovely gesture, above and beyond. Maybe she rushed to judgment on Becky. Throwing carbs to the wind, Erica tears off a piece of muffin and takes a bite—it's corn blueberry, not too sweet, just delicious.

She makes herself a mug of green tea and takes it and the rest of her muffin back to her desk. But instead of sitting, she walks into her outer office, where Shirley Stamos sits behind her desk. Shirley, who is around forty, is plump, has short gray hair and a round face, and wears a turtleneck every day. She's one of those women who looks and acts as if she skipped adolescence and went straight from studious sixth grader to efficient adult.

"What do you think of Becky Sullivan?" Erica asks her.

There's a pause and then Shirley says, "She has a lot of potential."

"Maybe not ready for prime time?"

"You never know, she might rise to the occasion."

"Could you send me her resume?"

By the time Erica gets back to her desk, Becky's resume is in her in-box. She's from Norton, Ohio, a town outside Akron, and she went to the University of Ohio on a full scholarship. Then something leaps out at Erica—Becky worked at Burger King during high school. Just like Erica did. This is a young woman who has had to earn every step up the ladder. Erica calls her extension.

"This is Becky Sullivan, is this . . . ?"

"Yes, Becky, it's Erica Sparks."

"Oh . . ."

"Could I see you for a minute?"

Becky Sullivan appears in her office doorway moments later. She's a reasonably attractive young redhead in her early twenties—chubby, freckle-splashed—who would be a lot more attractive if she stood up straight and looked Erica in the eye.

"About those muffins . . . ," Erica begins.

"I'm sorry, was that inappropriate? I was just so upset and felt so terrible for you. I remember when you went through that Staten Island ferry crash, and now this. I just wanted to do *something* to help, or just even show how much everyone here cares about you, but I know I shouldn't have come into your office and kitchen without asking. I'm sorry."

"Whoa, Becky. Slow down. Please, come in; have a seat."

Becky makes her way to a chair, grimacing at one point.

"I just wanted to thank you. The muffins were a thoughtful gesture. And guess what? They *do* make me feel better."

A tiny smile of satisfaction flits across Becky's face, so quickly that Erica almost misses it. Then she reverts to flustered. "I can't believe Erica Sparks likes *my* muffins."

"Do you want to be a journalist, Becky?"

"That was my childhood dream—or should I say delusion?—but I think maybe I'm more suited to being behind the scenes. I like to make things happen and to take care of people. I'd love to try producing. Not now, of course, I'm nowhere near ready—*duh*—but I mean later, when I've had some experience. I'm just trying to soak up everything. You know how grateful I am to be here."

Yes, she's obsequious, but there's something interesting about Becky Sullivan. She's empathetic, bright, enthusiastic, but there's also a depth and even mystery that flashes in her eyes. Erica senses she could be a lot of fun once she relaxes. Might be a good match for Jenny.

"Well, you're doing a good job, and I appreciate it."

Becky exhales and actually smiles. "I meant what I said about doing anything I can to help make your life easier. You can call on me, twenty-four hours a day."

Erica considers a moment. Clearly Becky Sullivan is a mixed bag. But Erica sees her younger self in the girl and would like to help her. "As a matter of fact, Becky, I'm considering hiring a personal assistant, someone who could help me at work and at home with my daughter. It's going to be a very glamorous gig. Especially if you like picking up dry cleaning."

Becky lets out a little gasp of disbelief. "I would *love* to be considered for the job. I know I'm gushy, but I have so much . . . *respect* for you . . ." She finally looks Erica in the eye and says, with a hint of confidence, ". . . Erica."

Erica is hesitant. Does she detect a note of instability in Becky? Or is the young woman just understandably nervous? "I'd like you to meet Jenny before I commit to anything."

"Of course."

Erica looks down at the yellow legal pad that holds her to-do list. It must have a dozen items on it, at least half of them relating to Jenny and the household. She tears off the page and hands it to Becky. "In the meantime, how would you feel about tackling this list?"

"Delighted."

With Becky gone, Erica takes out her well-worn playing cards and deals herself a hand of solitaire. The cards always relax and center her, freeing her to think. As she plays the hand, her mind goes back to her short interview with Mike and Celeste Ortiz last night, just before the bombing. Something was disconcerting about it, but what was it; what *was* it?

As she puts a red queen under a black king, it hits her—when she asked Ortiz if he would take a couple of questions, the senator looked at Celeste before answering. It was almost as if this man, this war hero, this possible next president of the United States, needed his wife's permission to speak.

CHAPTER 6

IT'S ONE WEEK LATER, A little past nine thirty at night, and Erica is walking home after her show.

Pretty much the whole show was taken up with updates on the search for the Buchanan bomber. Since there were no breaking developments, she had to go over the same ground again and again, trying to find new spin. She interviewed a law enforcement expert, several politicians, a psychologist specializing in trauma, personal friends of the Buchanans. It's called grasping at straws.

So far the FBI has been tight-lipped. Erica replayed footage of the young man in the moments before the bombing a dozen times. He seems to appear out of nowhere, slithering through the crowd like a snake, getting about six feet from the Buchanans, slipping off his backpack, letting it slide to the ground, turning, and disappearing back into the crowd. Blink and you miss him. His face is virtually obscured by the ski cap, dark glasses, and a full beard, but his skin tone is pale and the FBI has determined that the beard is fake. Between twenty and thirty years of age. Approximately five feet nine, weighs about 150. In the sketch released by the FBI, he looks baby-faced, unremarkable, like an assistant bank manager. Forensic analysis has determined that the bomb was homemade, primitive, detonated by a timer, a cousin to the one the Boston Marathon bombers built.

Until he's identified and caught, the country is on edge, and stories that would usually get a lot of coverage—yet another deadly weather event, the ongoing refugee crisis, a controversial bill in front of Congress—are barely touched on. Erica had to repeat the same information so often she was afraid she would lapse into gibberish. But she kept it fresh and interesting and found perceptive guests. Still, the effort has left her exhausted, and she is savoring this chance to walk and unwind.

It's twenty blocks from GNN to her apartment—up Sixth Avenue, across Fifty-Ninth Street to Central Park West, and then up to her building at Seventieth Street. With her makeup washed off and a base-ball cap and nonprescription glasses on, she's unrecognized. Erica loves the anonymity, the chance to watch the parade of tourists and fellow New Yorkers—yes, she considers herself a New Yorker now—as they stroll the nighttime streets. She feeds off the city's energy, the sense of light and movement racing fearlessly toward the future, a drive that seems to slip into a lower gear after dark as workday stresses lessen and the streetlamps and neon signs cast a comforting glow on the side-walks. She can't imagine living anywhere else.

Erica reaches Sixth Avenue and Fifty-Sixth Street. There's a crowded bar and restaurant midblock, and she notices that the patrons seem frozen, riveted, with their heads turned toward the three tele-vision screens above the bar. They're all turned to GNN and *Breaking News—Buchanan Bomber Identified* is scrolling across the screen below newscaster Carl Pomeroy, who has the hour show following Erica's. She races into the restaurant in time to hear Pomeroy say, "The FBI has just announced that it has positively identified the lead suspect in the Buchanan bombing at Case Western Reserve University. The identi-fication was accomplished using DNA found on a scrap of fabric from the backpack that held the bomb."

A mug shot of a pale, slightly pudgy man fills the screen.

"His name is Tim Markum. He's twenty-eight years old, a trained accountant with two prior arrests, one for fraud and one for impersonating a law enforcement official. Markum's last known address was a post office box in Tucson, Arizona, which has since closed. That is the only information the FBI has released, and according to knowledgeable sources, that is pretty much all the information it *has*."

Erica feels an enormous surge of relief, though IDing the perp is just the first step. But at least she has something fresh to report. Erica leaves the restaurant. Out on the sidewalk people have stopped, alone and in small clutches, glued to their smartphones—the whole country, the whole world, is sharing the news in real time. The new normal.

As Erica switches direction and heads back down to GNN, she remembers that she promised Jenny she would help with her book report on *To Kill a Mockingbird* tonight. She stops in her tracks and takes out her phone and calls home.

"Jenny, they've identified the Buchanan bomber."

"That's big news."

"Yes, yes, it is. I think I should get back to the studio."

There's a pause and then Jenny says, in a voice tinged with loneliness, "I do too."

"So you're all right with it?"

"Do I have a choice?"

There's another, longer pause.

"I'll ask Yelena to stay until you get home."

Erica pockets her phone, and as she races down to the network on a wave of adrenaline, she feels herself pulled backward by a fierce undertow of guilt.

CHAPTER 7

BASMATI RICE. HOW DIFFICULT CAN that be? But when Erica takes the lid off the saucepan the rice looks soggy, and there's still a quarter inch of water in the bottom. Does that mean she should turn off the oven so the salmon doesn't dry out? And what about the broccoli, which is boiling away? Is it going to be green mush by the time the rice is done?

It's Saturday, two days after the bomber was identified, and this was supposed to be a nice evening at home for her and Jenny. And it's an important night—Becky has dropped by before dinner to meet Jenny and see if they have any chemistry. The two of them are in the living room—Erica didn't want to be a hover-mother so she retreated to make dinner.

Great idea, Erica. Takeout was invented for a reason.

The whole world is avidly following the manhunt for Tim Markum, but he seems to have disappeared into a black hole. Erica selfishly hopes he isn't found for at least the next couple of hours; she would hate to be called to duty tonight of all nights.

Becky appears in the doorway and smiles shyly. "I'll leave you two alone."

"How did it go?" Erica asks.

"Pretty well, I think. We talked all about school. She loves history and hates French, and sometimes she feels stupid because the other girls talk about things like skiing in Switzerland and having three houses, and she wonders if they're only nice to her because you're famous."

"You got a lot out of her very quickly," Erica says. "Sometimes I feel like I'm pulling teeth."

"I've always been the kind of bland, nonthreatening type people feel comfortable opening up to."

"Becky, you shouldn't sell yourself short."

"It's just kind of a knee-jerk thing. I'm sorry. Old habits die hard." She stands up a little straighter, as if willing herself to be confident. "I do think I clicked with Jenny. She's wonderful."

"Most of the time. This dinner, on the other hand, is a disaster. The rice isn't cooking."

Becky does a quick assessment. "May I?"

"Please do."

Becky takes the lid off the saucepan of rice and turns up the heat. "Colander?"

Erica hands her one, and she drains the broccoli and puts it in a bowl.

"Lemon, mustard, butter."

Erica retrieves all three from the fridge and Becky adds them to the broccoli, mixes it, covers the dish with tinfoil, and puts it on the warming element. Then she takes the salmon out of the oven.

"Spices?"

Erica points to the spice cabinet. Becky opens it and takes out three jars that Erica has never opened—cumin, shallot pepper, and a blend called Turkish—mixes them with a little olive oil, and spreads the mixture on the salmon. Then she sticks the fish back into the oven on broil.

Jenny walks into the kitchen. "What's going on in here?"

"Big doings," Erica says.

"Can I help?"

"Is the table all set?"

"We still need glasses," Jenny says, grabbing a couple. "Is Becky staying for dinner?"

There's an awkward moment. Erica hadn't wanted to make the commitment of dinner. What if Becky and Jenny had zero chemistry? Then they'd all be stuck together through a clumsy meal. But now that things are going smoothly, should she tender a last-minute invite? But she was looking forward to one-on-one time with Jenny.

"Oh, I can't stay. I have a lot of research to do tonight. I'm putting together those dossiers you want on Mike Ortiz and Lucy Winters."

"Anything leap out at you?"

Becky looks down and nibbles the corner of her lip, as if wondering if she should open up. "Celeste Pierce Ortiz is an . . . *interesting* woman."

"Say more."

"Well, she's from one of San Francisco's wealthiest and most socially prominent families. But she's had an amazing career in her own right. Until she took a leave, she was one of the world's most successful international bankers, specializing in China. In fact, the president named her a special trade ambassador to Beijing. She's also written a couple of business books, is on at least half a dozen nonprofit and think-tank boards, and is worth an estimated 1.7 billion dollars."

"She's a powerhouse, no doubt about that. I'll see her on Monday at the Buchanan funeral."

"Will you have a chance to interview her?"

"Doubtful. But I'm fascinated by her too. And her relationship with her husband."

"Plates?" Becky says to Jenny, who hands her two. Becky deftly plates the now perfectly done rice, the broccoli, and the glistening salmon.

Erica is impressed—Becky rolled up her sleeves and dived in. The girl is a worker, no doubt about that. She salvaged dinner without breaking a sweat. And her insecurity, which could be off-putting at times, was starting to look more like a becoming modesty.

"You didn't learn to cook like this at Burger King," Erica says. Becky looks at her in surprise and Erica says, "I'm a fellow alum."

"Wow, small world."

"I can still smell the grease," Erica says.

"Me too. Say what you will, though, Burger King taught me discipline, and compared to home it was a safe haven." Becky immediately adds, "I'm sorry. That was too personal. I just meant that we didn't have a lot of money, and there were other . . . issues."

The two women look at each other—they share a similar past, a similar struggle. They're not spoiled rich girls, not middle-class or even working-class girls. They're girls who've worked their way up from nothing, from less than nothing. Erica feels a wave of respect and affection for Becky.

"I'll leave you two to dinner," Becky says, gathering up her bag.

Erica walks her to the front door. "Thanks for coming over."

"It's my pleasure, and privilege, really. I probably shouldn't say this, but I just have so much admiration for you, Erica. You saved the world from a madman. You showed real courage and integrity."

"I'm going to stop you right there, Becky. I appreciate the kind words, but I'm not interested in being put on a pedestal."

Becky looks like she might burst into tears. "I'm sorry."

Erica puts a hand on her shoulder. "I think we're both well advised to focus on our work. Burger King taught us that."

Becky's eyes open wide and she nods her head, looking like a schoolgirl. "Gotcha. I'm sorry. I've only been in New York for a couple of months and I'm still—"

"I *forbid* you to ever say 'I'm sorry' to me again."

Becky makes a zipping-my-lip gesture and Erica laughs. Then she leaves and Erica shuts the door behind her. *That girl has a lot of growing up to do.*

"This salmon is de-lish, Mom," Jenny says as Erica sits down at the kitchen table.

"Becky's a whiz in the kitchen."

"No more potato dumplings for moi."

"So you liked her?"

"I did. She's really nice and smart. And I think she'll probably spoil me."

They laugh. Erica has noticed a growing confidence in her daughter, an opening out. In spite of her troubles at Brearley, the school is good for her. The girls are bright and the teachers challenge them, and Jenny is rising to the test. Her classmates may be privileged, but a little bit of privilege can be a good thing, especially if it's backed by hard work.

"I guess I'll hire her, then."

"Can we go to the movies tomorrow?"

"Depends on your homework situation."

"That's under control."

"Is there anything you're dying to see?"

"The new Ryan Gosling."

"I smell a crush."

"Oh please, Mother, I'm not just some drooling fan. I'm his future wife."

They laugh again, and for a brief moment Erica feels suffused with happiness. She did it; she really did it—she brought Jenny home. To a good home. A place where her daughter can feel safe and nurtured and can blossom. Has Erica finally been able to free herself from the legacy that defined her own childhood? All those frigid Maine nights spent shivering under a Dollar Store Elmo blanket that felt like it was woven out of recycled six-pack holders, listening to the drinking and drugging and screaming on the other side of the prefab's cardboard walls?

And for her part, is Jenny finally forgiving her mother for all those times she saw her stumbling around in a vodka haze—and then that terrible dark night when it all came crashing to a head.

"There's a new *Dateline* murder mystery on tonight," Jenny says.

"I'm not sure I like you watching those shows, honey. They're morbid."

"I think they're interesting. I might want to be a lawyer."

"Really?"

"No, I just said it so you'd let me watch those morbid shows. Come on, Mom, admit it—murder is fascinating."

"It can be. But you know as well as I do that it's *always* the husband who did it."

"I've seen a few where it was the wife. Women can get weird too."

"Women *can* get weird, can't they?" Erica's phones rings, and she glances at the caller ID. "This is Moira."

"Say hi for me. I'll put the plates in the dishwasher."

"Thanks, honey . . . Hi, Moy."

Moira Connelly is Erica's best friend, a fellow reporter who stuck with Erica during her slow, sad fall and her final blackest hours up in Boston—and drove her to rehab on her day of reckoning. Moira now works as an evening news co-anchor on a local LA station.

"How are you, amigo?" Moira asks. Just hearing her voice has a calming effect on Erica—she'd trust the woman with her life.

"Hanging tough. Or trying to. You?"

"I'm good. Any thoughts on the bomber?"

Erica stands up and walks down the hall and into her office—she doesn't want Jenny overhearing any of this. "Aside from the fact that he's a coward and a psychopath? He's a smart cookie, evading capture this long. I just hope they find him soon. Then the big question becomes, did he act alone? You hearing anything out there?"

"Nobody wants to say it out loud, but people are asking who gained the most from Buchanan's death."

"You don't mean Mike Ortiz?"

"It cleared the field for him. That was a poor choice of phrase, but . . ."

"I suppose it's the truth. But it's pretty farfetched."

"So was the idea that Nylan Hastings poisoned Kay Barrish. Erica, we're journalists. Speculation can be the first step on the road to the truth. And it's not *Mike* Ortiz people are whispering about."

"Celeste?"

"Bingo."

"What's the word on her?"

"Once you get past that charming overbred exterior, she has a reputation for being an icicle, a ruthless icicle. And she's tight as glue with a woman named Lily Lau who runs Pierce Holdings, the company that manages Celeste's assets. And Celeste has *a lot* of assets."

"Say more."

"Lau is also Ortiz's chief fundraiser and a key campaign strategist. She and Celeste are considered the powers behind the throne. Power can do strange things to people."

The words hang in the air a moment—*power can do strange things to people*—and then Erica says, "You know, Moy, I think I'd like to do a segment on the candidates at home. Try and get up close and personal, see what I find."

"I smell a reporter's instincts kicking in."

"We *are* journalists."

Erica's work in nailing Nylan Hastings led her into the heart of darkness. Man is capable of unthinkable acts of evil and depravity. She walks over to the window and looks out at the glittering lights of Central Park, their radiance turning the leafy canopy into a sea of iridescence. "Meanwhile, I'm consumed with the bombing story. Every federal law enforcement agency is working 24/7 to find this guy. Let's hope there's a break this week."

Erica hangs up and flashes back to the moments before the bombing, the look in Mike Ortiz's eyes when he turned to his wife for permission to speak. Her short hairs stand up. Suddenly she feels chilly. Has the temperature dropped outside? She walks out to the foyer to grab her favorite red scarf from the row of hooks on the wall beside the coat closet. She always puts her scarves there when she walks in the door. But she doesn't see the red scarf. She fingers through them. Definitely not there. She opens the coat closet. No scarf.

She walks down the hall and into the kitchen. "Jenny, honey, have you seen my red scarf?"

"Uh-uh."

Erica scans the living room and her office, then heads into her bedroom. No scarf. A certain neurotic compulsion kicks in when she can't find something, especially something she was sure she knew the location of. She distinctly remembers putting the scarf back on one of the hooks when she wore it the day before yesterday. She walks quickly back to the front door and checks again. Nope.

Scarfs don't just dematerialize. What is going on?

Erica takes a deep breath and wills herself to cool it. It's only a scarf. She must have left it at the office. Of course. That's what happened. Right?

Then she triple-checks the locks on the front door.

CHAPTER 8 ———————————————

IT'S MONDAY, AND ERICA IS in the temporary broadcast booth that GNN has set up outside the Cathedral Basilica of Saints Peter and Paul in Philadelphia, where the funeral of Fred and Judy Buchanan is being held. With the president and First Lady due at any moment, security is massive. In spite of that, Erica feels a wave of anxiety. She likes to think of herself as a battle-toughened pro, but the truth is the Buchanan bombing has unnerved her. It happened so suddenly—a boom, a flash, the blood, the bodies, the children, the thin line between life and death. Erica keeps seeing the crumpled, twisted corpses. Followed by Tim Markum's bland, round face—such a benign mask for evil. She's been having trouble sleeping, she jumps every time she hears a sudden noise, and she has begun to worry about Jenny's safety on the streets of New York.

But no matter how sleep-deprived and spooked she is, Erica knows she has a job to do.

And today it's an important one. The nation was convulsed by Buchanan's murder; he's the most prominent politician to be assassinated since JFK. And the horror has been magnified because it was broadcast live, caught on scores of cellphone cameras, and seen by billions of people around the world in the last five days. This day of mourning matters to the nation, to the people of Pennsylvania, and most of all to Philadelphia, where Buchanan was born and raised and is revered. The streets surrounding the brownstone cathedral are jammed with thousands of people who feel compelled to join in this public sorrow.

Because she was there when the bomb went off, Erica is a part of the story. Today she wants to be part of the soul-searching that Americans are going through. How do you make sense of such horror? How does the country respond? Leaders from hard left to hard right are pouring into the cathedral—no matter what ideology, there's no place for assassination in a democracy. Erica hopes that this coming together will have a ripple effect and Americans will start to see that what unites them is far greater than what divides them.

She checks the monitor under Derek's cam—midday anchor Patricia Lorenzo throws it to her.

"This is Erica Sparks reporting from outside the Cathedral Basilica of Saints Peter and Paul in Philadelphia. The joint funeral of Governor Paul and Judy Buchanan is scheduled to begin within a half hour. We are awaiting the arrival of the president and First Lady."

There is a camera inside the cathedral, a feed used by all the networks and also broadcast on a jumbo screen outside the cathedral, and GNN goes to it as Erica says, "As you can see, the cathedral is filled. Two former presidents are present, as well as over sixty members of Congress and fourteen governors." GNN goes back to a shot outside the cathedral, panning the tear-streaked faces. "Perhaps more impressive are the many thousands of ordinary Americans who are lining the streets around the cathedral. Their shock and grief is palpable. Reflecting our nation's mood, this is a city in mourning."

The other half of the story—the search for Markum—can't be ignored, even today. "To bring us up to date on the search for the bomber, let's go to Washington where Craig Bergen, GNN contributor and former head of forensic psychology at the FBI, is following every development."

Erica goes to split screen with Bergen, who is rumpled and intense. "Craig, is there anything new?"

"My sources inside the Bureau tell me that progress is being made."

"Do you have any sense of how real that progress is?"

"Believe me, nobody over there wants to raise false expectations."

"As a forensic psychologist, do you have any thoughts as to where Tim Markum may be hiding out?"

"Psychopaths are more comfortable operating in familiar surroundings. Markum was raised in Montana, went to the University of Arizona in Tucson, and seems to have remained in that state. I know that tremendous manpower has been focused there."

"Do you have any sense of whether Markum acted alone or is part of a cell or a radical organization that may now be sheltering him?"

"No terrorist organization has taken credit for the bombing. It's only been five days, but they usually claim credit immediately."

"Can you tell us anything about his personality?"

"This is a confident, single-minded individual. We can see on the video that he knew just what he was doing; he doesn't seem to be nervous. In fact, I'd describe his affect as casual. Whether he acted alone or not, that young man is a cold-blooded killer."

"So there is no remorse."

"Quite the opposite. He's feeling very powerful right now. Omnipotent even. I have no doubt he is watching today's funeral and gloating."

"That's a spine-chilling thought." A squadron of black SUVs pulls up in front of the cathedral. "Thank you for your always fascinating insights, Craig." Erica goes back to full screen. "The vehicles we see approaching the cathedral are not the presidential motorcade. Let's see who it is."

The back door of an SUV opens, and Mike and Celeste Ortiz get out.

"It's Senator Mike Ortiz and his wife, Celeste. They look very somber, as if they're still in shock."

Celeste Ortiz is stunning in a black suit, but she looks ashen, even a little unsteady on her feet, almost as if she's tranquilized. There have been rumors fed to the media—which seem to originate from Ortiz allies—that Celeste feels it could just have easily been she and her husband who were killed in the bombing, and she's having second thoughts about his campaign. She slips her arm through his as they make their way up the front steps. Then he looks over to the crowd—and smiles that magnetic smile.

Erica is brought up short. How inappropriate and even bizarre. Celeste gives his arm a jerk—the tranquilizers seem to have worn off in a flash—and they proceed into the cathedral. That image of the two of them—Mike's behavior and Celeste's reaction—sears itself into Erica's mind.

"Even in the midst of this tragedy, politics continues, and Mike Ortiz is now the presumptive Democratic candidate for president. His likely Republican opponent, Minnesota senator Lucy Winters, is already inside the cathedral."

Suddenly Erica hears pulsing music through her earpiece as *Breaking News* scrolls across the monitor. Then: "Throw it to New York, Erica, there's a break in the bombing case!"

"We're now going to GNN headquarters in New York, where there is breaking news in the Buchanan bombing."

Erica watches as Patricia Lorenzo reports.

"Surveillance video taken this morning at Philadelphia International Airport appears to show Tim Markum, identified by the FBI as the Buchanan bomber, arriving in the city on a flight from Houston, Texas."

The airport footage shows a young man who certainly looks like Tim Markum exiting a plane. He's wearing dark glasses and a baseball cap pulled low on his forehead.

"Without positive identification, the FBI is referring to this individual as a 'person of interest.' According to reports of eyewitnesses, he left the airport and got into a taxicab. That's all the information that has been released. Now let's go back to Erica Sparks in Philadelphia."

Erica looks out at the scene around the cathedral. People huddle over their phones. As the news of the sighting sweeps across the crowd, there are exclamations of shock and alarm. The unanswered question is obvious: If the bomber is in Philadelphia, will he strike again? Here and now? Fear races like a wildfire through the crowd; there's a sense of impending chaos; parents scoop up their children and start to run.

"As you can see, the news of the bomber's possible presence in Philadelphia has unnerved the crowd of mourners. There seems to be a growing panic, which we can only hope won't lead to a stampede."

Just at that moment, the presidential motorcade pulls into view. It stops abruptly before reaching the cathedral. Then it speeds up and roars past.

"The presidential motorcade has left the scene," Erica reports. "We can presume they heard about the suspected arrival of Tim Markum in Philadelphia and for security reasons are not going to attend the funeral."

GNN goes to the pool feed inside the cathedral. The organist has stopped playing. There is agitation among the mourners; silenced phones are turned on; heads are bent over them, reading avidly, tense, afraid. Are they in danger? Is another bomb about to go off? Time seems suspended—and no one is in charge. People turn and whisper, their faces filled with questions and fear. Some start to move out into the aisle, to head to the exits. There's a feeling of an imminent unraveling.

And then a young man in the front row stands up and walks to the pulpit. He seems remarkably composed. Everyone freezes, and those who have started to leave turn and watch.

"Hello, everyone. I'm Jeff Buchanan, Fred and Judy's oldest child." His voice is strong and steady. "I think many of you have heard that the suspected bomber may be in Philadelphia. I think the best way to respond is to move forward with this service. It's what my mom and dad would want."

The cathedral grows hushed; people return to their places; a calm seems to pass over the pews.

"My parents had boundless faith in the American people, in all of us. If we cower or panic, fear wins. Surrender wins. Evil wins. We're better and stronger than that." He looks up toward the heavens. "Aren't we, Dad?" And now his eyes fill with tears.

As the organist strikes up "Amazing Grace," the mourners put away their phones, take their neighbors' hands, and sit up straight as a serene resolve takes hold. Outside, as they watch on the jumbo screen, the crowd has a similar response—people stop running and grow still, rapt, children are hugged, hands are held, shoulders sway, voices are raised in song, eyes grow moist, and for a moment the crowds both inside and outside the cathedral become one—a unified sea of humanity defying mankind's darkest impulses.

Erica's own eyes well up—and she knows that the most eloquent way to convey the mood in Philadelphia is to remain silent.

CHAPTER 9 ———————————————

THE PLANE BANKS LOW ACROSS San Francisco Bay as it approaches SFO. Erica has flown west to tape her "The Candidates at Home" segment with Mike and Celeste Ortiz. It's been a week since the Buchanan funeral. It was confirmed that Tim Markum—using highly sophisticated false identification—did fly into Philadelphia that morning, but he has since slipped away. His presence was a taunt—a sick head game with the mourners, the media, and law enforcement—an act of terrorism that left the whole nation fearful.

Some progress has been made in tracking Markum's steps, but he remains a cipher. For the six months before the bombing, he'd been living in a bland, furnished studio on the outskirts of Tucson. A search of the apartment yielded almost no insight into his motives or history. In fact, the place was devoid of any revealing idiosyncrasies—except one. The bookshelves were empty, the kitchen almost bare, the closets hung with a couple of shirts. Even though Markum had no known source of income, his rent and utility bills were paid on time, by money order. There was no computer, although a forensic investigation found an e-mail account—but it held little but spam. The websites he visited were banal: Kohl's, a few news sites, a Celine Dion fan page. The one eye-opener was his taste in pornography. He spent hours at sites featuring Asian mistresses who abused and humiliated willing men.

There's no evidence that links Markum to any terrorist organization or cell. But would a stand-alone crazy be able to seamlessly engineer such a horrific crime? And forge the high-tech fake ID that enabled him to fly into Philadelphia?

While the search for Markum remains a hot story, time moves on, and it is no longer the lead every night on *The Erica Sparks Effect*. With the candidates decided—although not formalized at the parties' conventions—the nation's focus is turning to picking its next president.

Erica has spent the flight studying her file on Mike Ortiz—his working-class upbringing in Oakland, his early years as an activist and community organizer, his tour of duty as a marine in the second Iraq War, his subsequent election to Congress and marriage to heiress and banker Celeste Pierce, and, most dramatically, his capture and incarceration by Al-Qaeda while on a humanitarian mission to Iraq. His subsequent escape made him a national hero and propelled him into the Senate. It's a compelling story—one that, coupled with his raw political talent, may carry him into the White House.

Erica will have her preliminary meeting with the Ortizes this afternoon, and the taping is scheduled for tomorrow. There's nothing more telling than getting inside someone's house and taking a peek, albeit sanitized, into their private lives. Often, the more people try to conceal, the more they reveal.

What most fascinates Erica about Mike Ortiz is his power dynamic with his wife. Celeste Ortiz exerts an extraordinary level of control over him. And she's a . . . *strange* woman. Yes, she's brilliant and driven, but it goes beyond that; there's something feral in her eyes, and when her jaw sets, Erica senses rage lurking just below the polished surface. And her body, coiled and freakishly fit—she's a snake about to strike. Erica can't wait to observe this reptilian creature in her native habitat.

Last week Erica spent two days on an expansive farm in rural Minnesota with Lucy Winters, the presumptive Republican nominee, and her family. Erica found Winters down-to-earth and sincere with enormous ambition, intelligence, and charm. Her husband, who runs the farm, stayed mostly in the background, but Winters wasn't shy about using her three well-mannered teenagers to bolster her image as America's Mom in Chief, in contrast to the glamour and wealth of childless Mike and Celeste Ortiz. Winters has been able to thread a tough needle, using her warmth and charisma to compensate for some of her more moderate positions with the party's base. Polls show her trailing Ortiz, but the race remains fluid and she has plenty of time to make up the gap.

The plane lands and Erica retrieves her luggage and gets into the waiting car. It's a bright, sparkly California day and the driver takes her to the Huntington, a quiet luxury hotel that sits atop Nob Hill. She prefers the relative anonymity of small hotels—fewer distracting fans to chat up and selfies to pose for. Erica's room has a view of Grace Cathedral, the Union Club, and Huntington Park. This is her fourth trip to San Francisco and she's always enchanted—the city is like Paris or Venice, a cliché until you get there and its sheer charm and beauty disarm you.

She unpacks and changes into slacks and a blue oxford and goes down to her car. Her driver heads north through Russian Hill, then turns west on Broadway until they reach Pacific Heights, which Erica has never visited. The neighborhood is perched on a hill overlooking the bay, and the streets are lined with one enormous, perfectly tended mansion after another. Flowers sprout in dazzling displays; exotic specimen trees bloom and sway; there isn't a single crumpled candy wrapper on the sidewalk. To Erica it doesn't seem quite real somehow—it feels like a movie set or a fantasy sprung to life or even a parody of extreme wealth. She knows she has driven into the heart of the buffered bubble that the one-tenth of one percent calls home. Then they pass an ambulance and she sees an old man—skeletal, his eyes wide with fear—being wheeled out of his house on a stretcher. All the gold in the world can't keep decay and death at bay.

The Ortizes live in a towering redbrick Edwardian that looks like it could shrug off a drone strike with barely a broken window. As Erica's car pulls up to the portico, Mike and Celeste appear from inside. They're both casually dressed in a sort of tossed-off lunch-at-the-country-club way—he's in chinos and a denim work shirt; she's in slacks and a blouse, with a sweater draped over her shoulders and knotted in front. In spite of it all, Mike retains a certain working-class virility, while Celeste radiates casual ease and confidence. But Erica knows that under her smooth surface the woman is paddling like mad. Fine. Erica admires ambition.

Celeste lets Mike take the lead—holding back as he steps forward and extends his hand. "Welcome."

"It's nice to be here."

Now Celeste takes her turn, grasping one of Erica's hands in both of hers and saying in a low-key way, "We're not usually this upbeat. Blame it on the Erica Sparks effect."

Erica musters a smile at the pun.

"Seriously, I'm a big believer in the importance of a free press—passionate journalists have saved this country more than once. Present company included."

Erica follows them into the house. It's like stepping into a glossy real estate brochure—rooms seem to stretch on forever, and everything is immaculate and glistening and looks unlived-in. They're halfway across the foyer when a mixed-race teenage girl appears with three straining dachshunds on leashes.

Celeste says, "This is Alicia. Alicia, meet Erica Sparks."

Alicia looks starstruck. Erica puts a hand on her shoulder and says, "What a pleasure."

"Yes. For me too," Alicia says with a shy smile.

"Alicia is my mentee. We connected through a wonderful program Mike and I support called A Hand Up. She's only been in this country for eighteen months. Her mother is struggling to raise six children on her salary as a hotel maid."

"You're a lovely young woman, Alicia, and you're going to do very well here," Erica says.

Celeste puts a hand on Alicia's lower back and says, "Have a nice walk."

They head past the kitchen and through several living rooms before coming to a sun porch that offers one of the most spectacular views Erica has ever seen—the city, the bay, the bridge, the boats, Alcatraz. Again, a sense of unreality prevails—it's almost too beautiful, and to live like this every day seems like an impossible dream. But under it all Erica senses something darker—a drive that knows no bounds, a pitiless hunger.

"This is breathtaking," she says.

"We don't even notice it anymore," Celeste says. A rolling cart is topped with a plate of sandwiches, one of cookies, a teapot, a coffee pot, and a pitcher of lemonade. "Would you like some coffee, or a sandwich? We have PB&J."

Erica is brought up short—in an interview with Robin Roberts last year she admitted that her favorite midnight snack was a peanut butter and jelly sandwich. This is the part of being a celebrity that she hates—this loss of a private life, this intrusion, right into her kitchen. What do her eating habits have to do with her work as a journalist? She regretted doing the Roberts interview and hasn't done another since.

"I'm fine," she says.

Mike Ortiz sits on an ottoman and leans forward, elbows on knees—it's an engaging pose and he seems eager to talk. Celeste sits on a chaise and crosses her ankles, trying her best to look casual.

Erica was hoping to have some time alone with Mike but sees that's probably not in the cards. Today anyway. She's going to insist on a one-on-one tomorrow when the cameras are rolling.

"I'd love to hear how you two met," Erica says.

Mike shoots a glance at his wife, whose expression doesn't change. "I was a congressman from the East Bay. Celeste was a major Democratic donor. We met at a fundraiser for my 2006 campaign."

LIS WIEHL WITH SEBASTIAN STUART

"You obviously come from very different backgrounds. What was it like for you to adjust to Celeste's lifestyle?" Erica asks.

"It was difficult at first. My father worked for Caltrans; my mother was a waitress. I felt uncomfortable around Celeste's friends and family. As if they were judging me." Again he looks to his wife, who is smiling in approval. "But we were in love. And we still are. And that's more important than any differences."

"I think our first Thanksgiving was a little rocky," Celeste says.

"Yes, my mother cleared the table."

"And *my* mother let her!"

They both laugh, in a rehearsed kind of way.

"I've always wanted to make a difference with my life, but with Celeste by my side, I feel that anything is possible."

"I find that so touching," Celeste says. She swings her legs to the floor and perches on the edge of the chaise. "Mike had nothing to prove to me. He was a great congressman, a fighter for those who need a champion. His experiences as a marine in the Iraq War gave him a strength and a perspective that I felt the country needed."

"You can't see death and destruction up close and not be affected by it," Mike says. "The innocent victims, wounded children, the orphans, seared themselves into my soul. That's why I led that humanitarian mission back to Iraq as a congressman in 2008. I was determined to secure congressional funding for schools and orphanages."

"But you were captured by Al-Qaeda," Erica says.

Ortiz nods. He looks down; his voice softens; his tone becomes intimate. "The months I spent as an Al-Qaeda prisoner changed me. Deeply. I went days without food or water. I was tortured. Threatened with beheading. I thought I would never see my family again. There was more than one dark night of the soul. But then I decided to fight, to escape or die trying." He looks Erica right in the eye and contin- ues. "And once I made that decision—*to fight*—everything changed. I had purpose, a mission. And I accomplished it. I want to inspire *every* American to join me in the fight, the mission to make this country a more perfect union. A house divided will not stand. My America is a house united."

He seems sincere, and his magnetism is seductive. Celeste is watching him with a reverent expression. Maybe Erica was wrong about these two. Maybe under their ambition they are caring and compassionate and would be able to bring the country together.

As if he's reading her mind, Mike says, "You know, Erica, all of this"—he gestures to the house and view—"means nothing to me. What matters is what's *inside*. The *heart*."

Celeste beams. "Mike has a vision for this country." She leans forward and lowers her voice. "*You're* a fighter too, Erica. You fought Nylan Hastings and you won. You saved this country, the whole world in fact, from a very dangerous man."

"I was just doing my job."

"I don't believe that for a second," Celeste says. "Most journalists would have turned the investigation over to law enforcement. You didn't. At great personal risk."

"There must have been times when you were afraid for your life," Ortiz says.

"And even for your daughter's," Celeste adds.

They're both leaning toward her with warm, encouraging expressions, and for a moment Erica forgets where she is, even who she's with, and she's back in Miami on that terrifying day. "I had help. I had my colleagues . . . but, yes, I was afraid."

"You must miss Greg Underwood a great deal," Celeste says.

Erica nods and looks down, thinking of Greg and Moira and Manny and Derek and all the people who got her through that terrifying time. She feels a swell of emotion and wishes she were back in her hotel room so she could call Jenny.

And then—with a jolt that makes her sit upright—she realizes something: the Ortizes have effortlessly, artfully succeeded in making this visit about *her*. She looks at them with wry admiration. They're world-class charmers, and she waltzed right onto their dance floor.

Then she notices Celeste noticing her realization—it's a fleeting moment between them, but unmistakable. Celeste Pierce Ortiz doesn't miss a thing. *Well, guess what, Celeste, neither do I.* Something shifts in the room, in the mood.

And then, from the front of the house, come cries and sobs and commotion. Mike and Celeste jump up just as Alicia runs in, distraught. "I am so sorry, so sorry. He ran away; he pulled away and pulled the leash out of my hand and ran into the street! I tried to catch him; he ran into the street. I am so sorry."

A stout older woman, whom Erica assumes is the housekeeper, walks in and says simply, "Jasper was run over."

Celeste gasps. "Not my Jasper!"

"I am so sorry, so, so sorry; he ran away from me," Alicia sobs.

"Is he dead?" Celeste asks.

The housekeeper nods. "I called the vet. They're on the way over to pick up the body."

"What about Molly and Adrian?"

"They're fine. A little upset, but fine. I put them in their crates."

Celeste stands stock-still. "I've had Jasper for eleven years . . . He was my first dachshund." She looks down—when she looks up, her eyes are filled with tears.

"He was a wonderful little fellow," the housekeeper says.

A pall comes over the room. Celeste is disconcerted. Alicia is terrified. The housekeeper is resigned.

And Mike Ortiz is blank. Nothing. No affect. Just blank.

Erica feels out of place, and the whole scene creeps her out somehow. "I'm very sorry about your dog. I'm going to go now. Call me when you're ready to continue, but let's wait until at least tomorrow."

Celeste looks a little embarrassed by her momentary loss of control. Then she takes a deep breath and shoots a look at Alicia—it's a fair bet this mentor/mentee relationship just went south. Then Celeste says "Mike" and nods toward the front door.

Mike escorts Erica out to her car. The driver opens the door for her.

"I'm sorry this happened while you were here," Mike says, but in a detached way, as if a pipe had sprung a leak or dinner had burned. Then he extends his hand to the driver. "Mike Ortiz." Then he smiles. That blazing movie star smile.

As Erica heads back to Nob Hill, she's reminded again that there are some things money can't protect you from. And there are some people who aren't what they seem.

CHAPTER 10 ————————————————

AN HOUR LATER CELESTE IS sitting at an outside table at Gott's in the Ferry Building on the Embarcadero, waiting for Lily Lau to appear. As soon as Erica Sparks left, she called Lily. The two met in a Chinese history class their freshman year at Stanford, where the professor's passion for the subject—coupled with Lily's brilliance and beauty—ignited Celeste's fascination with China. And Lily was hardly averse to having smart and socially connected Celeste in her orbit. That first day they went out for lunch after class and bonded immediately, kindred spirits. Their relationship has since evolved into something profound. Transcendent. And they're just getting started.

The restaurant, famous for its mahi-mahi sandwiches, is thick with tacky tourists; it's loud and chaotic, and just blocks from the office of Pierce Holdings. Celeste finds the hubbub amusing—it's fun to observe the masses in their element.

She spots Lily as she approaches the restaurant—she's hard to miss. Tall and striking with jet black hair and pearly skin set off with glistening red lipstick, she's wearing a white shirt, a thin black men's tie, and a dark suit that fits her toned body like a second skin. Her limbs are long and she moves with a lithe, powerful grace. The stupid little tourists stop and watch as she walks by. They're not used to Chinese superstars in Loserville, Indiana.

Celeste and Lily smile at each other, and Celeste feels that frisson of excitement that Lily always elicits in her. They're partners in . . . what would you call it? Rewriting history? *That sounds so immodest,* Celeste thinks. But it's the truth.

Lily sits down. "Would you like something to eat?" Celeste asks.

Lily waves off the suggestion—she and food have a tenuous relationship. "How did it go with Sparks?"

"It was going well. Then my mentee took the dogs for a walk, and Jasper was run over and killed."

"I'm sorry, Celeste. I'll send you a replacement."

"I'll stick with two for the time being—the yapping was getting on my nerves. So Sparks left early. But not before leaving an impression. She's *very* smart."

"Intelligence is a two-sided coin."

"And *very* curious."

"Another mixed blessing. Look what happened to that poor cat. Speaking of mice, how is Mike doing?"

"He's behaving."

The two women exchange tight smiles. They were in their early thirties, their plans already hatched, when Mike came into their sights. They'd been casting around for the right figurehead—someone attractive, electable, and *malleable.* A modern-day Ronald Reagan. Someone they could nurture and . . . mold. Congressman Mike Ortiz seemed like the perfect vehicle for their ambitions. And so Celeste went to that fateful fundraiser. She wore a tight black dress and just enough bling to make her sizzle, and introduced herself, wide-eyed and admiring. Of course he knew who she was, what she could do for his career with her wealth and network, but no one was faking the chemistry. They made a dinner date for the following night. It was the shortest dinner on record—why, they practically ran from the restaurant to Celeste's Russian Hill penthouse, desire pulsing between them. The following morning, when he left for some dull community meeting in his district, Celeste immediately called Lily. The trap had sprung. And the rest, as they say, is history. No, *her*story. No, no, *their*story. Lily and Celeste. Celeste and Lily.

"That suit is sharp. Tom Ford?" Celeste asks.

"Tom Ford is for wannabes. Dries Van Noten. I flew him over to fit me. I ordered three."

"I wish *I* could get away with an outfit like that. But I'm not sure it would fly at my next Iowa pig roast."

"Aren't you going to have to come up with some recipes for deep-fried hot dogs?"

The two women laugh, a secret shared laugh, a laugh filled with scorn and dark corners. Hidden corners. They sit in an easy triumphant silence for a moment.

"So, what are we going to do about our feline friend?" Celeste asks.

"We need her and want her—up to a point. But we have to watch her carefully. Closely. The eyes—and ears—have it." Lily stands up and scans the scene with a look of bemused noblesse oblige. Let them eat mahi-mahi. "Give me twenty-four hours."

Celeste watches her as she strides away. Celeste hates weak, emotional women. Quivery little cows. They disgust her. Lily, on the other hand, she idolizes. Her sangfroid has sangfroid. Even though they're the same age, Lily is really her mentor, her teacher. She took Celeste by the hand and led her into . . . a brave new world.

Then some obese creature in a sparkly sweatshirt approaches.

"I *love* your husband!" the woman screeches.

Please, dear God, don't let her touch me. Celeste wants to say: *Get off the feed bag, you oinker.* What she does say, with a warm smile, is, "So do I."

"He's going to be *pressss*-ident!" the woman cries, a small chunk of half-chewed French fry flying out of her mouth.

Celeste smiles serenely and says, "Yes. Yes, he *is* going to be president."

CHAPTER 11 —————————————————————

WHEN ERICA GETS BACK TO her hotel, she heads to the fitness center and does a half hour on the treadmill and then takes a quick dip in the pool. As her body moves, her mind stays fixed on the Ortizes—she feels her concerns about them growing into an obsession. Mike Ortiz's reaction to the death of the dog was bizarre. It was as if he had no emotions to draw upon, almost like a robot. But even a robot would be programmed to at least *display* emotion. And Celeste, equal parts charm and calculation. And their life in that huge empty house—how many rooms do two people need? It's all so antiseptic and ordered and controlled—but in the end, no matter how hard we may try and wrestle it into something pretty and predictable, life is messy, nasty, and brutish.

Erica goes back up to her room and orders a salad for dinner. She could go down to the dining room, but that would mean sitting there alone—the object of whispers and stares and intrusions. As if she were on display. She would feel self-conscious and even lonelier. She calls Jenny.

"Sparks' residence."

"Becky?"

"Hi, Erica."

Erica's not sure how she feels about Becky's answering the phone that way. "Listen, there's no need to say 'Sparks' residence.' I prefer a simple hello."

"Oh, I'm sorry. I just thought it sounded classier, more grown-up or something."

Girls from poor backgrounds often overcompensate like that. Erica used to do it all the time during her difficult first year at Yale—mimic a phrase or inflection that she heard come from a rich classmate's mouth. Becky is trying so hard.

"Not a big deal. May I speak to Jenny?"

"Of course, she's right here."

"Hi, Mom."

"Hi, sweetie. What are you doing?"

"I'm playing Scrabble with Becky."

"That's terrific. Who's winning?"

"I am. But I think Becky is *letting* me win."

"Not true," comes Becky's protestation in the background. They both laugh, and Erica feels a tinge of jealousy. But mostly she's glad that Jenny sounds happy and stimulated. And how cool that they're playing Scrabble.

"Where did the Scrabble come from?"

"Becky bought it. Listen, Mom, can I take tennis lessons? My friend Lisa from school is taking them and she invited me."

"Of course you can, honey."

"The first one is on Saturday, so you can come and watch."

"Can't wait."

"I better go, Mom. It's my turn and I think I have a big word."

"I love you."

Erica hangs up. She doesn't know which is worse—having Jenny lonely and missing her, or having her engaged and treating her mom like an interruption. She smiles to herself—being a mother is a complicated dance. And Erica has never been the most graceful hoofer.

As soon as she hangs up, Erica's mind goes back to Mike and Celeste Ortiz. What was it Mike said: *The months I spent in that Al-Qaeda prison changed me. Deeply.*

Erica gets up and strides around her suite. She's got a pebble in her psychic shoe, and she knows she won't be able to rest until she can shake it out. She wishes she could hash it out with Greg. Everything was easier with him around. She'd call him, but it's the middle of the night in Sydney.

To feel some connection with him she picks up her iPhone and checks his Twitter feed as she paces. There's nothing recent, so she checks the Australian Global News feed. What she sees makes her stop in her tracks. There's Greg, in what looks like a nightclub, standing next to a beautiful young woman. Erica can't quite make out if his arm is around her waist. He's definitely had a few drinks. The tweet reads: LAUREL MASSON AND GREG UNDERWOOD CELEBRATING OUR FIRST TRIAL BROADCAST #PSYCHEDINSYDNEY.

Erica feels her stomach hollow out. She sits in the nearest armchair and studies the picture. Both Greg and this Laurel Masson are smiling broadly, exuberant—from success, yes, but there's more. Their body language is unmistakable, their shoulders touching, heads leaning toward each other. Erica's shock gives way to hurt. Greg is clearly attracted to another woman. How far has that attraction gone?

Or is her imagination running away with her? It could all be completely innocent. The network has reached a milestone, and they've all earned a few drinks. *A few drinks.*

Erica looks over to the bottle of champagne the hotel left next to the fruit and chocolates. She walks over and picks up the bottle, runs her hand down it. It's not fair, is it? Greg and *Laurel*—what a stupid name; was she named after a tree?—can have a few drinks and stop there. Erica can't. She can't. Once she starts, it's off to the races—to morning nips and midday cocktails and midnight shots and impulsive acts and crushing hangovers and shame and self-hatred and regret.

But maybe that's all behind her. She's been sober for almost four years. She could probably handle one glass of champagne. The gold foil surrounding the cork is so bright, so lively, so fun and full of promise. All she has to do it take it off, ease out the cork, pour herself a glass— just one glass, in the civilized flute—and she'll be soothed, cocooned in a sweet cushioning haze. Laurel Masson won't matter.

There's Jenny in the backseat of the car that terrible night, crying, asking what is happening, afraid and in danger. In danger from her own mother.

Erica's body flushes with prickly heat and she puts down the bottle. She sits down at her laptop and Googles Laurel Masson. Sure enough, she's the network's star reporter. *I guess Greg has a thing for star reporters.* Innocent or not, he could have been a little more discreet. The tabloids could pick this up. The tabloids *will* pick this up. Should she call Greg and demand the tweet be taken down? Or is that shrewish? Or embarrassing? She can't live her life in fear of social media and gossip websites.

Erica feels a headache coming on. Under her confusion and anger is hurt. Pure, simple hurt. It's too painful. She starts to pace again, trying to get away from the pain the way an animal does, by moving, moving—*Keep moving, Erica, keep moving forward.* The plush hotel suite begins to feel like a cage, a gilded cage. She'll call Greg, yes, in a couple of hours when it's morning over there. She'll call him and confront him, get this all cleared up. One way or the other. But what if it *is* the other? What if he is having an affair with Laurel Masson? What if he's falling in love with her? What if he's going to leave Erica?

Stop it! There's nothing you can do right now! You're just torturing yourself.

Erica grabs her worn deck of playing cards, sits on the bed, and deals a hand of solitaire. As she plays the cards she feels her blood pressure go down, her head clear, and a sense of control, of mastery of her emotions, returns. Work. Work has always been her salvation. As she draws an ace, her other obsession returns, and now she welcomes it.

The months I spent as an Al-Qaeda prisoner changed me. Deeply.

. . . changed me. Deeply.

Erica abandons the cards midgame and returns to her laptop. She Googles Mike Ortiz and then hits Videos. She finds what she's looking for: a video of Ortiz giving a speech before his humanitarian mission to Iraq and his months as an Al-Qaeda prisoner. Then she finds a video of a recent speech. She goes to split screen and watches them both simultaneously with the sound muted. Yes, he's changed physically. In the recent video he has more wrinkles and less hair. And his face is slightly less animated and expressive, although that change is subtle. But the biggest change is in his eyes. In the older video they sparkle with life. In the recent video they look oddly blank—like empty vessels waiting to be filled.

CHAPTER 12 ———————————————

ERICA AND JENNY ARE APPROACHING the Sutton East Tennis Club, which is housed in a white plastic inflatable structure that sits under the Williamsburg Bridge at Fifty-Ninth Street and York Avenue. Jenny looks adorable and stylish in her sky-blue tennis outfit with white piping. Becky took her to Bloomingdale's—which Jenny now calls Bloomies—yesterday to buy it.

Becky also took it upon herself to reorganize the apartment's kitchen, which—in keeping with Erica's cooking skills—lacked a laundry list of culinary essentials, e.g., a decent spatula. Erica loves that Becky takes initiative this way—when she's at work she feels like the home front is covered. She's even begun to let Becky take over managing Yelena, who now comes in just two days a week.

Erica's interview with the Ortizes at home was disappointing. After the segment with the two of them, she taped her one-on-one interview with Mike, but Celeste stood just off-camera the entire time—tense, watchful, encouraging, even mouthing answers and generally behaving like a stage mom at a preteen beauty pageant. When it was all over, Erica made a vow to get Mike Ortiz on-camera when Celeste wasn't in the same room, preferably not even in the same state. Meanwhile, she hasn't let go of her suspicions, unformed as they are, and is taking steps to confirm or disprove them. She's asked one of her researchers to put together a tape showing Mike Ortiz in a variety of situations before and after his time as an Al-Qaeda prisoner.

They walk into the tennis club and there is Lisa Walters, Jenny's classmate, and her dad. Lisa is lovely and well-behaved, and Erica feels a swell of pride that this is Jenny's world now.

"Josh Walters, so great to meet you," Lisa's father says. He's definitely not a buttoned-down Upper East Side type—he has a curly mop of reddish hair and is wearing cool black linen pants, stylish sandals, and a black T-shirt embossed with an image of a Calder mobile. His eyes are twinkly, his smile is dazzling, and although he looks to be in his midforties, he radiates a natural boyish enthusiasm.

The tennis coach leads Jenny and Lisa onto one of the courts. Erica and Josh move to a small seating gallery.

Lisa misses a ball, and Josh calls out, "You almost had it, honey." Then he turns to Erica and adds, "I don't think Venus and Serena have anything to worry about."

"Has Lisa been taking lessons for a while?"

Josh nods. "Her mother is all about tennis and Southampton and getting into Harvard."

"And what are you all about?"

"Hmm—flea markets and mystery drives and Catskill swimming holes."

"Sounds like a mixed marriage."

"Oh, the marriage lasted about as long as it takes to eat an ice cream sandwich in August. Is that a strained metaphor?" He smiles in this self-deprecating way that Erica finds appealing. "I'm all for Harvard, if that's what *Lisa* wants. I went to City College and loved it."

"May I ask what you do?"

"I make things. Big things. Like huge pencils and coffee cups and shoes. I mean really huge."

"For . . . ?"

"Fun. For fun. They sell well enough to keep me in flea markets, mystery drives, and Catskill swimming holes. And Brearley tuition."

"So you're kind of a latter-day hippie."

"I prefer to think of myself as a man who loves people, loves adventure, and loves being his own boss."

"Unfortunately, in my business that's not an option."

"You've done pretty well under the circumstances. By the way, you're much prettier in person."

Josh Walters is just so sincere, and he's bursting with life—there's no holding back, no game playing, no hidden agenda, no male ego, no self-conscious irony, just an outpouring of goodwill. It's simple but hardly simpleminded—and so refreshing after the countless complications of Erica's life and career. This is a man she feels relaxed with just a few minutes after meeting him.

Josh takes out his phone and shows Erica a couple of pictures of his wares—they're enormous, yes, but also charming, whimsical, and slightly surreal. What a fun way to make a living.

"Very cool," she says.

"I think you're kind of cool too."

"I've been called a lot of things in my life, but I think this is my first *cool*."

"Hey, why don't the four of us go out to lunch after the lesson?"

Erica is a little thrown by the invitation. Clearly there's some chemistry between them—but lunch? This soon? She's not a free woman. Is she? Then she flashes on that picture of Laurel Masson and Greg.

Just then Jenny slams a ball across the net, nailing a shot. Erica leaps up and cheers—"Way to go, Jenny!"—pumping her arms in the air, surprising herself with her outburst.

Josh is laughing, loud and loose and free. "That was a great mom moment!" he says.

I had a great mom moment!

"Hey, lunch sounds wonderful!" Erica says. Then her phone rings.

"I have to take this. Be right back." She moves away a few steps and answers.

"Erica Sparks? This is Dr. Martin Vander, the Chief of Neurology at Columbia-Presbyterian Hospital. I'm returning your call. You said it was important."

CHAPTER 13 —————————————————

"SO I WAS A LAWYER at a fancy midtown firm, making a small fortune, on my way to partner, married to Lisa's mom, Park Avenue apartment, place in the Hamptons—put it all together and I was miserable and bored out of my mind."

Erica, Josh, Jenny, and Lisa are sitting in a nondescript coffee shop that Josh picked because they make "awesome" omelets sautéed in olive oil. The girls are deep in a whispered conversation—Erica loves seeing Jenny engaged with her classmate, forming an easy friendship.

"And?" Erica asks.

"One spring day I went out to lunch in Central Park. The whole park was blooming around me—and I was wilting. I couldn't face another real estate contract. Sitting there eating my tuna fish sandwich, I had the mother of all *aha!* moments. And I never went back to the office. Best decision I've ever made."

As much as Erica loves her work, she knows the feeling—there are days when she'd just like to walk away from GNN and reinvent herself. Pack Jenny and a few things in a car, drive out to Colorado or New Mexico, and get a teaching degree. In the time it takes to have the thought, Erica realizes how ridiculous it is. In spite of the overwhelming stress at times, she *adores* her work.

"And then you founded your own company?"

"I did. Making absurdly enormous objects. Japan is my biggest market."

Their omelets arrive. Erica ordered spinach and asiago, and it's sublime; the subtle flavor of the olive oil gives it a savory and surprising finish. Josh digs into his food with unrestrained pleasure, looking like a little kid.

"Are you working on any particularly exciting stories now?" he asks.

Erica is tempted to tell him about Mike and Celeste Ortiz, but holds her tongue. She's going to consult with Martin Vander on Monday, and she'll have a better sense of things after that meeting.

"The Buchanan bombing case, of course, is front and center. It's intriguing. Tim Markum is almost a nonperson. He's left virtually no fingerprints, physical or psychic. I have a hard time believing that he acted alone."

"I know. I'm following it closely. It's fascinating—and deeply creepy. We all know evil exists, that it's around us at all times, but on some level I find murder and terrorism incomprehensible. Getting inside the mind of the killer and thinking about committing a crime, yes. But actually carrying it out . . . I just can't imagine it."

"That's how most sane people feel," Erica says.

"I know some of your story, of course," he says. "You've witnessed a couple of serious traumas. How do you bounce back from something like that?" Josh's face is filled with concern and curiosity. He's gone from little kid to empathetic man, and Erica feels her attraction to him deepen.

"You know, I'm a professional. It's what I signed up for. Of course it's tough to see death, especially gruesome deaths . . ." She struggles to find the right words. She lowers her voice and leans into the table. "It's hard, Josh. Sometimes when I'm struggling to fall asleep at two a.m., I hear their screams and see their faces. They're mothers and fathers and daughters and sons and friends and lovers . . ."

Josh reaches out and squeezes her hand. His hand is slightly rough, and strong.

"When I knew we would be meeting today, I Googled you," Josh says. "I read about your background, about your childhood up in Maine, your mother's arrests, your struggle. That was really rough stuff, Erica. I think you should be very proud of yourself." He lowers his voice. "*Bon courage*, young lady."

His words touch her deeply. "Thank you," she says, looking into his gray-green eyes.

"Dad, can we go to Serendipity for sundaes?" Lisa asks from the girls' end of the table. The mood is broken, and suddenly Erica is back in a lively Manhattan coffee shop on a Saturday afternoon.

"Yes, we *can* go there, Lisa, but it's such a gorgeous day, how about we all walk over to Central Park, get ice cream pops, and then check out the zoo?"

Jenny looks expectantly at Erica, who says, "Sounds good to me."

As they walk across the East Side to Fifth Avenue, Josh eagerly points out architectural and cultural highlights. When they reach the park entrance, the girls run ahead of them. Josh turns to Erica—parent to parent—and they both break into big childish grins.

That's when Erica remembers that she's still engaged to Greg.

CHAPTER 14

BECKY SULLIVAN WALKS INTO HER soulless Second Avenue studio sublet in a circa 1960s white brick building—the bricks look like they haven't been washed since. It's one small room that barely fits a queen bed, and its window looks out at the back of another building, so close she could almost touch it. Still, it's home for now. A place where she can be herself.

Becky spent the morning at Erica Sparks's apartment, organizing her books alphabetically. Erica dressed incognito and then went off on some mysterious mission. Becky tried, discreetly of course, to pry some details out of her, but none were forthcoming. It's not that she's nosy, in general that is; it's just because it is *Erica*.

Their relationship is going so well. It's meaningful, isn't it? On both sides. Just as Becky hoped it would be. She felt terrible about sending that video of Amanda Rees to Mort Silver. She bought a phone with cash, used it once to send the video, and then threw it down a storm drain. She couldn't let Erica hire an assistant with that sort of sordid background. Really, exposing Amanda was a selfless act.

Becky locks the door behind her, crosses to her bed, kneels down, and pulls a small suitcase out from under it. It's a vintage suitcase she found at a thrift shop. She runs her hands over it gently, her anticipation growing. Then she snaps it open and lifts the lid. Inside sits Erica's red scarf, neatly folded. Becky brings the scarf to her face and inhales the faint trace of Erica's perfume—Chanel No 5 (Erica has so much class)—and imagines the scarf draped around Erica's long shapely neck. Then she reaches into her purse and pulls out a bar of soap wrapped in tissue paper. She carefully unwraps it. It's Erica's shower soap, half worn down, translucent, unscented. She replaced it with a new bar, of course, from under the sink. Erica probably won't notice. And if she does, she'll think Yelena did it.

Becky imagines Erica in the shower, lathering up her body. She gently strokes the soap. Then she places it in the suitcase, on its bed of tissue, next to the scarf. That's when she notices a long gleaming strand of Erica's hair on the scarf. She reaches down with her thumb and middle finger and delicately grasps the single blond strand. She lifts it up in front of her, where it catches the light and glistens like a dream come true.

Then her phone rings, and her reverie is broken. She picks up her phone with her free hand—it reads *Unknown*. Should she answer it? She has to—she told Erica she would be on call 24/7.

"Yes?"

"Hello, Becky." It's a woman's voice. Is there the faint trace of an accent of some kind?

"Who is this?"

The woman laughs, a low laugh, a flippant, mocking laugh. Then she says, "It's natural, you know."

"*Who is this?* And what's natural?"

"Why, Erica's hair color, of course."

CHAPTER 15 ——————————————

ERICA DECIDES TO TAKE THE subway up to Columbia-Presbyterian Hospital in northern Manhattan. Fame can be a bubble of chauffeurs and first-class flights, and she cherishes opportunities to break out and get a dose of a grittier reality. With no makeup on, and wearing a baseball cap and large sunglasses, she attracts just a few second glances as the 2 train barrels through the black tunnels drilled deep into the city's bedrock.

She gets off in Washington Heights, a vibrant Dominican neighborhood—Latin music blaring from stores and car radios, outdoor displays of exotic produce, dress stores selling neon-hued satin dresses, families laughing and arguing, old men and women sitting in folding chairs watching the passing parade. Erica inhales the sheer pulsing humanity of it all. As immigrants have done since our nation's founding, these people have come to America and made it their own, creating a cultural fusion that lifts her spirit and her heart.

Erica walks west to the vast campus of Columbia-Presbyterian, one of the country's leading research hospitals. It's a throbbing, thriving urban hospital, and the hallways are filled with doctors, nurses, patients, and support staff, all of them looking fully engaged in their work. She follows a labyrinthian corridor and finds Dr. Martin Vander's office. Vander is considered one of the country's leading neurologists and has written several popular books about exotic neurological disorders. The door to his office is open, and the doctor is sitting at his desk.

"Knock, knock," Erica says.

"Come in, come in," Martin Vander says, standing. He's a tall, lean man in his sixties with a slight Dutch accent.

"Thanks so much for seeing me on such short notice."

"Your call intrigued me." Vander shuts his office door. "Please, sit."

Erica does.

"So, tell me a little bit more about your concerns."

"This is all confidential?"

"Absolutely."

Erica tells the doctor about Mike Ortiz's inappropriate responses, including the incident with the run-over dog.

"You know, some people just don't like dogs very much," Vander says with a gentle smile.

"It's not just that. His affect in general seems . . . flat. And he doesn't seem to pick up on emotional clues. At Fred Buchanan's funeral he smiled and waved to the crowd."

"He's a politician, Erica. He's also a man who underwent profound physical, psychological, and emotional trauma. An experience like that changes a person."

"Well, maybe my imagination is running away with me. That's why I came to see you. One of my researchers has put together a tape showing Ortiz before and after his time as a prisoner in Iraq."

"I'm eager to see it."

Erica takes out her laptop, puts it on Vander's desk, and pulls up the tape. It follows Ortiz from his early political career through today and includes clips of him at a congressional hearing, at the ribbon cutting for a new public school, being interviewed at the start of his humanitarian mission to Iraq, and again after his escape, and it ends with some footage from Erica's recent interview.

Vander watches intently. When the tape is over he sits silently for a moment. Erica can barely contain her expectation.

"Fascinating. There do seem to be subtle changes in his demeanor after his time as a prisoner. A certain flattening. But as I said, trauma on that scale changes a person. I hardly have enough evidence or information to make any sort of definitive diagnosis, or even to speculate with confidence. I'd have to meet and examine the man personally, put him through some tests."

"That's obviously out of the question. You saw his wife in several of those clips. Did you notice anything strange in their relationship?"

"She certainly seems to keep him on a tight leash."

"I'd call it a harness."

"There does seem to be a profound psychic connection between them. Of course, they may just be in love."

"My concern is that he seems to be under her control in an unnatural way. You've done a lot of writing and research on cults and mind control. Do you see any similarities here?"

"That's a big can of worms, and as I said, I just don't have enough information. It's true I have studied cult members. You see a similar flattening of affect, although Ortiz's is much less pronounced. However, with cult members there's also a lack of personal willpower, a complete surrender of control to the cult leader. I don't see evidence of that here—Mike Ortiz is a driven man. The changes in him are more nuanced."

"Can you tell me a little more about what happens to cult members?"

"After indoctrination they become less animated. They feel no attachment to their past. Without familiar touchstones, they lose their sense of self and their ability to reason and make decisions for themselves. They become unable to think independently."

. . . unable to think independently.

"Over time, the brain actually becomes rewired. In many cult members we see a physical manifestation of this, a slowing down of movement and motor reflexes. I'm not seeing that in Ortiz. If his intellectual skills are compromised—which is by no means certain—it may be the result of an organic brain injury suffered during his captivity. After all, he was tortured. But even there, he's functioning at a very high level."

"Doctor, Mike Ortiz may well be the next president of the United States."

"I understand your concerns. And I think the tape demonstrates that they have some validity. The case intrigues me. I'd like to pursue it. Conduct something of an investigation. Paramount would be an opportunity to observe him up close."

"Ortiz will be in New York next week for a fundraiser. Robert DeNiro is hosting it in his apartment in Tribeca. Is there any chance you could attend?"

"There is a great deal at stake here. And this is a fascinating case. I'll go to the fundraiser."

"You understand how critical confidentiality is."

Vander nods solemnly.

Erica puts away her laptop and stands. "I can't thank you enough."

As she is walking out of the hospital her phone rings, and she sees Eileen McDermott's name on the caller ID.

"Erica, I heard from one of our sources in the FBI that they've just captured Tim Markum in Detroit. Attempting to cross into Canada. He's going to be arraigned before a federal judge tomorrow morning. The FBI hasn't released the news yet because they don't want this to turn into a circus. But they won't be able to keep it under wraps for long."

"Still, we're a step ahead of the competition. I'll head out to LaGuardia right now. Book us a private jet if the network's plane isn't available. And grab a couple of outfits from my office closet. See you at the airport."

As Erica steps off the curb and hails a cab, she thinks, *This is just the kind of break I need to get firmly back on top.*

CHAPTER 16 ———————————————

ON HER WAY OUT TO LaGuardia, Erica calls Becky.

"Hello, Erica," she answers. She doesn't quite sound like her usual overeager self. She almost sounds a little spooked.

"Is everything all right?"

"Oh, yes, yes, fine. I was just . . . doing my laundry. Down in the laundry room. I might be a bit winded. I heard the phone from out in the hall and ran to answer it."

Funny, it only rang twice.

"Okay. Listen, I have to fly out of town for a breaking story. Can you spend the night at my apartment?"

The apartment has a spare bedroom—originally the maid's room— behind the kitchen. This is the first time Erica has asked her to sleep over, but Becky has earned her trust.

"Of course. That's exciting about the breaking news. Where are you flying to?"

"Detroit."

There's a pause and then Becky asks, "Does this have to do with the Buchanan bombing?"

Erica wonders how much she should tell Becky—loose lips sink scoops. She probably shouldn't even have told her *where* she was going.

"I should keep that confidential for now."

"Of course, I understand. But you're going to Detroit?"

"Can you make dinner? If not I can ask Yelena."

"No, I can handle dinner for sure."

Erica looks out the taxi window and sees a mother herding her three young children across the street. "Becky?"

"Yes?"

"How do you think Jenny is doing?"

"I think she's doing well, all in all. She does worry about you. The danger you put yourself in."

"If she brings it up, can you please reinforce that it's my job? And that I'm very careful?"

"Of course. I tell her how important your work is."

"Thank you. I shouldn't be gone more than a day. Call me if anything comes up, anything at all."

"I'll take care of everything. Don't worry."

CHAPTER 17 ──────────────────

AS SOON AS SHE HANGS up, Becky reaches for the secure phone, the one that was handed to her on the street by a stranger an hour ago. Just as the lady who called told her it would be: "Go downstairs and walk around the block. A man will hand you a package. Be a good girl. Don't screw this up, Becky. If you do screw it up, we'll have to tell Erica that you stole her scarf and her soap, and what you did with them."

Picking up the phone fills Becky with some weird combination of fear and excitement. She would never, ever, *ever* betray Erica, but she has to be a good girl. Or else they'll punish her and tell everyone that she's a bad girl—*bad girl, bad girl*—and she won't be able to help Erica take care of Jenny anymore and that's *so* important. Erica and Jenny *need* her.

The phone is so strange and fancy, as thin and light as a wafer, and it can only dial one number. In a way, it makes Becky feel important. She presses the dial button.

"Yes?" The woman's voice is so strong it sends a shiver down Becky's spine.

"Erica is flying out to Detroit. I think it's related to the Buchanan bomber."

"You *think?*"

"She wouldn't tell me, but I could tell by the way she wouldn't tell me that it was, probably. I'm sorry. Was that a bad sentence?"

"Anything else?"

"She asked me to take care of Jenny and sleep over tonight."

The voice softens into a purr, an icy purr. "Good girl, little Becky girl. You spend the night with Jenny."

"I'm a good girl? You won't tell on me?"

The voice goes cold again. "Keep your eyes and ears open."

After Becky hangs up she sits on the edge of her bed and rocks back and forth . . . back and forth . . . back and forth.

CHAPTER 18 ————————————

EILEEN IS WAITING TO GREET Erica at the network's jet, which is parked beside the private plane runway at LaGuardia. Eileen is tall and thin, with glasses and dark spiky hair, a little nerdish and gawky, pretty much unable to sit still, a natural-born detail-obsessed producer.

The plane takes off, and Erica studies her file on Tim Markum. She's fascinated by his nonlife—the fact that his apartment was bare, that he had no visible means of income, that he paid his bills with money orders. He grew up middle class outside Missoula, Montana. Even then he was the kind of kid who blended in—when his former teachers and classmates were asked what they remember about him, many drew a blank. In fact, his most distinguishing characteristic seems to be his total lack of impact.

He went on to the University of Arizona but dropped out after two semesters. That was three years ago. Where has he been since? And what compelled him to commit such a horrific act? Surely not his obsession with Chinese fetish porn. Which has created a bit of a challenge for the news media—how do you delicately describe an addiction to videos that go way beyond everyday fantasies into disturbingly hard-core practices? The tabloid websites suffer no such inhibitions, and they're having a field day with clips of Mistress Anna May Wrong and her colleagues in full whip-snapping action.

When analyzing behavior as shocking and evil as Markum's, Erica keeps an open mind. His motive could have been political, but there's not a shred of evidence that it was. In fact, the man has never registered to vote. It could have been a personal vendetta against the Buchanans for some irrational reason, but there's no evidence that they ever met. It could have been self-aggrandizing, the product of a deluded and paranoid mind. Is Markum schizophrenic? Again, there's no record of hospitalizations, ER visits, or previous psychotic episodes. Or, just possibly, was he under the command of someone? Someone who ordered him to commit the crime? Someone who had taken control of his mind? As Martin Vander said, cult members who are in effect brainwashed become unable to think independently.

It's a fascinating and horrifying case, and Erica is glad she made the decision to fly to Detroit—there's no substitute for being on the ground. She wants to get a firsthand look at this monster, who was apprehended at the Canadian border by an eagle-eyed TSA agent in spite of a beard that disguised his baby-face features and a false Canadian passport.

The plane banks in for a landing. Erica has never been to Detroit—has anyone?—but even from the air she can see its graceful old office buildings, haunting vestiges of its days as an industrial powerhouse. It's hard not to root for this classic American underdog.

Eileen has booked them into a Hyatt near the courthouse. The room is generic to the point of parody, but Erica finds the muted hues and no-frills design strangely calming. And she needs to slow down a little. Markum's arrest is a big break and an important story, but Erica can't let go of her meeting with Vander and his words about Mike Ortiz's affect. Or the fact that Markum seems similarly robotic. Somewhere, way in the back of her mind, a suspicion is taking shape—could the two stories possibly be related?

After a swim and a workout and an early dinner with Eileen, who seems incapable of talking about anything but work, Erica heads up to her room and calls Jenny.

"Hi, Mom."

"How's it going there?"

"Fine. We had ravioli for dinner. I helped make the mushroom sauce."

"And homework?"

"All done. I'm just watching *48 Hours*."

"Jenny, you know I worry about you watching all those murder shows."

"I worry about you being blown up by a bomb."

How can she answer that? "Where's Becky?"

"She's in her room, on her phone."

Her room. "Jenny, that's the spare bedroom, the guest bedroom." And why does Becky have to go back there to take her calls? "Can I speak to her, please?"

"She seemed like she wanted to be alone."

"What do you mean?"

"When the call came in, she started to talk in, like, a whisper. Then she went into her room and closed the door."

"Well, please go knock and tell her I want to talk to her."

"I don't want to bother her."

"Do what I asked, please."

Jenny sighs and Erica can hear her padding through the apartment. Then there's a knock.

"I'll be out in just a minute, Jenny."

"Mom wants to talk to you."

"Oh, okay." Erica hears the door open, and then Becky says in a rush, "Hi there. We had a nice ravioli dinner, and then I checked her homework and it looked good, so we bargained for a TV show."

"I don't like her watching those true-crime shows. And I'm okay with you making personal calls, but please keep your door open. You just never know."

"I'm sorry. I won't do it again. It was just that it was a . . . um, a fella, a boy, a guy I've gone out on a couple of dates with. I'm sorry. I'll tell him not to call me again when I'm here. I mean, I won't talk to him again when I'm here."

Erica sighs and reminds herself how young Becky is. Dinner went well; homework is done; what's the harm of a little phone flirting? "Not a big deal."

"Are you in Detroit?"

"I am."

There's a pause and then Becky says, "I saw that they caught the Buchanan bomber there."

"Yes, they did."

"I guess his arraignment is going to be tomorrow."

Erica pauses before saying, "Your guess is as good as mine."

Erica hangs up and looks out the window at the lights of the struggling city. Something about Becky's tone was unsettling, almost as if she were dissembling. And she's grown so curious about Erica's schedule, about her every move. Erica brushes away her concerns—after all, Becky wants to be in the news business, where curiosity is a must. And Erica has probably been throwing too many personal—and not enough professional—chores at her. The bottom line is that she's doing a good job.

Erica closes the curtains and gets into bed with her laptop, intending to work on her coverage of Markum's arraignment in the morning, but she has a hard time concentrating. She gets out of bed and does a half hour of Tae Kwon Do, working up a good sweat. Erica first started to practice Tae Kwon Do when she was a freshman at Yale, and she found it helped her deal with the anxieties triggered by the high-pressure, high-privilege school. She learned how to defend herself—both literally and figuratively: the practice stresses courtesy, integrity, perseverance, self-discipline, and invincibility. She saw her early classes as lessons in adulthood, and she's kept up her practice ever since. When she's done, she feels a sweet fatigue spread over her limbs. She climbs back into bed.

But sleep doesn't come. What do come are images—haunting, almost fun-house images of Mike Ortiz flashing his spectacular smile.

CHAPTER 19 —————————————————————

ERICA IS IN THE SOARING lobby of Detroit's Levin Courthouse, a stately Art Deco building. By not announcing the time of Markum's arraignment until an hour ago, the FBI has been able to avoid the media circus. The Bureau did alert the victims' families immediately after Markum's arrest, and many have come to Detroit to witness the arraignment. Security is tight. Erica and her crew passed through metal detectors, were patted down and wanded, and were finally issued passes to wear prominently around their necks. In addition, the building's main entrance has been closed, and there are at least a dozen uniformed federal marshals present. The only other broadcast media present are a crew from a local station—Erica has definitely scooped the competition. There are about a dozen print and online journalists. All the media are contained behind rope barricades. Around them, lawyers, clerks, and defendants come and go, preoccupied with their own cases. The law grinds on.

Markum is going to be driven from the city jail, where he spent the night, to the back of the building and brought up through the basement. The mood among the reporters is somber and hushed. Erica feels tense and very curious. She wants to get a look at this killer. And she wants to throw him a question. Just one: "Why?"

She watches the monitor just below the camera, the feed from GNN in New York, where anchor Patricia Lorenzo says, "We now go to Erica Sparks, who is live inside the Levin Courthouse in Detroit."

"That's right, Pat. I'm in downtown Detroit, where Buchanan bombing suspect Timothy Markum is going to be arraigned before federal magistrate Deborah McGivern. Markum is being represented by prominent defense attorney Jeremy Munson, who is known for his flamboyant style and fierce tactics. Markum is expected to enter a not guilty plea and Judge McGivern will then set a tentative trial date. We are told that among those waiting in the courtroom are Paul and Judy Buchanan's four children, as well as relatives of the other victims of the brutal bombing, which convulsed our nation just four weeks ago."

Down the hall an elevator door opens and Markum, surrounded by US marshals, is led out. Handcuffed and shackled, he shuffles along, his eyes trained straight ahead, devoid of any emotion.

"Here is Timothy Markum now, being led out of an elevator and escorted to the courtroom." With that round baby face, slouchy posture, and chubby body, he doesn't look capable of killing a bug, let alone committing an act of terrorism that killed fifteen people and wounded dozens more.

"Mr. Markum, why did you do it?" Erica shouts.

He turns his head and looks at her, dead in the eye—and Erica sees a lost soul who doesn't know the answer to her question. It's almost as if he has one foot in this world and the other in some parallel universe, some dark, unfathomable place where none of the rules of civilization apply. The marshals tug him along.

Then a print journalist—a young man standing near Erica—pulls out a handgun and fires three shots into Markum's face, which explodes in a fusillade of flesh, blood, hair, and brains.

Erica's dress and face and hair are covered with splatter. She drops the mic, leans down, and heaves up a thin stream of bile. Then she sucks air again and again, filling her lungs. *You have a job to do!* She grabs a handful of tissues and wipes off her face, picks up the mic, and stands up just in time to see the shooter put the gun into his own mouth and pull the trigger.

CHAPTER 20

THERE'S A SUSPENDED MOMENT OF shock and silence in the Levin Courthouse. It's an eerie, skin-crawl silence. Many bystanders look away from the horror, but others stand riveted, unable to avert their eyes. The federal marshals are frozen, trying to figure out what to do. But there's really nothing *to* do. The bodies speak for themselves—the danger is over.

Eileen has GNN cut away to the newsroom in New York. Erica collapses on a nearby bench and her first thought is, *Thank God Jenny is in school and not at home watching.* She wills herself to take deep, calming breaths. Handling this kind of trauma doesn't get easier, but she has learned some tricks for managing her own response.

Then her reporter's mind kicks in. With Markum's death, it's going to be next to impossible to find out the truth about his motives, his actions in the weeks and months before the bombing, and whether or not he acted alone. As with Lee Harvey Oswald, the ultimate source has been shut down. The whole story may never be known. And what about the bogus reporter who killed Markum and then himself? Who is he? Who put him up to it? What are their motives? How did he get his fake credentials and then through security—with a gun no less?

The unanswered questions start careening around in Erica's head like runaway bumper cars.

Eileen comes over and sits next to Erica. She's ashen, trembling slightly, her tough-gal producer veneer peeled back to reveal a deeply shaken woman.

"Are you okay, Eileen?"

"I honestly don't know, Erica. I didn't sign up for this."

Erica wants to tell her that as a journalist, she did in fact sign up for this. It's their job to walk into war zones, to report on horrific events, to delve deep into the heart of darkness. But she holds her tongue, because she knows Eileen will figure all that out on her own.

"The shock will wear off," Erica says, giving Eileen's hand a squeeze. "In the meantime, we have to get back on the air."

CHAPTER 21 ————————————————

ERICA ARRIVES HOME THAT EVENING, walking in the front door to the smell of sautéing garlic and herbs. Then suddenly, from the end of the hall, Jenny is rushing toward her, a look of love and concern on her face. She races into Erica's arms and squeezes her tight. Jenny smells fresh and clean and innocent. Her baby girl.

"Oh, Mom, Mom, I'm so glad you're all right."

"I'm fine," Erica says, hoping she sounds more convincing than she feels. Still, it's so good to be home, to walk into a house where food is cooking and soft jazz is playing.

Jenny takes Erica's hand and leads her into the apartment. "Becky and I are making chicken Provençal-ish with asparagus and wild rice."

"That sounds *so* good."

They reach the kitchen and there's Becky at the stove, wearing an apron, looking very much at home. Erica feels a stab of jealousy—the easy rapport between Becky and Jenny is what she hoped for, but now that she has it, she doesn't want them to get *too* close.

Becky turns and looks at Erica with urgent empathy. "We thought it would be nice for you to come back to a home-cooked dinner." She has a glass of white wine on the counter and indicates it. "Would you like a glass?"

That's a little bit strange—Becky must know Erica's history; it's public record, for goodness' sake. Erica shakes her head. And Becky seems a little too at home. It's almost as if this is her house, and Erica is the guest.

"We're just about ready here."

"I'll help you plate," Jenny says.

They all sit at the dining room table, which is candlelit and set with linen napkins.

"This is delicious," Erica says, savoring a bite of the melt-in-your-mouth chicken.

"We invented it," Jenny says proudly. "Becky never uses recipes. She says that's copying, not cooking."

"Does she . . . ? I mean, do you?"

Becky nods with a sheepish smile. "Growing up we never had cookbooks. My mom hated to cook, so I just started to make things up."

Jenny grows serious. "I was so worried about you, Mom. I wish you had a job that wasn't dangerous."

"You know I love what I do, honey."

"I get so scared sometimes. I had a bad feeling about this trip. I woke up in the middle of the night sure that something terrible was going to happen. And it did."

"Yes, it did. But not to me. I'm still here."

"I couldn't get back to sleep."

"You did eventually, didn't you?"

"Only later, when Becky came in."

"What do you mean—when Becky came in?"

"She came to sleep in my room."

"In your *bed*?"

Jenny nods.

Erica puts down her fork. It's a queen bed and she's sure it was all completely innocent—right?—but it's just so . . . intimate. Erica herself hasn't slept with Jenny in years. She looks at Becky, who is busy eating—maybe a little too busy eating.

"There was new polling released today—Lucy Winters is gaining on Ortiz," Becky says abruptly.

"I like her," Jenny says.

"So do I," Erica says distractedly.

"Oh, I forgot the rolls," Becky says, getting up and going through the swinging door into the kitchen.

Erica leans into Jenny and asks in a whisper, "Did Becky get under the covers with you last night?"

"*Nooo.* Silly. She had her clothes on, and she slept above the covers."

Erica exhales with a sigh. "Would you like me to sleep with you tonight?"

"I don't worry when you're home."

Becky returns with a basket full of warm rolls. Erica's phone rings.

"This is Greg calling from Sydney. I'm going to take it. Be right back." As Erica walks into her bedroom, she can't shake a creepy feeling about Becky climbing onto Jenny's bed.

"Hi, Greg," Erica says, closing the bedroom door behind her. The darkened room is bathed in a noirish glow from the city lights outside.

"Are you okay?"

"I'm okay, yeah. How are you?"

"Worried about you. You've had a traumatic day."

"I appreciate it."

"Any updates?"

"The shooter's been identified. His name is Peter Tuttle. Twenty-six years old. His press credentials were forged. They think the gun was planted in the courthouse yesterday. They found adhesive-tape residue under one of the benches."

"Sounds like they're moving fast on this one. But I think you should put it on the shelf for a couple of days. Witnessing something like that takes a real toll. Try and pull back a little."

"I'm trying." Erica sits on the edge of her bed and wonders if now is the time to bring up Laurel Masson. She notices that her bedside clock is running fast. She picks it up and adjusts it.

"Are you back in New York?"

"I am. Having dinner with Jenny and my personal assistant, who is turning into Jenny's best friend."

"You don't sound like yourself, Erica."

Erica can feel an enormous wave, a tsunami of emotional exhaustion heading her way. Today in Detroit she was hoping to come closer to the truth and she ended up further away, covered with bits of bone and brain. She's in no mood to dissemble or play cute. She stands up and starts to pace, steeling herself as she says, "I saw that tweet of you and Laurel Masson."

There's a long pause. Too long. Finally Greg says, "She's doing a terrific job."

"Assuaging your loneliness?"

"That's unfair, Erica."

"I'd say seeing another woman is unfair."

"Boy, one tweet and you're off to the races."

"One picture is worth a thousand lies."

There's another pause, and Greg lowers his voice. "We need to talk."

"I thought we were." And then, in the pause that follows, Erica knows: Greg *is* having an affair with Laurel Masson. She feels a stab of hurt and betrayal, and then a terrible cosmic sadness washes over her. "I'm going to go now, Greg."

"Okay, Erica."

"Good-bye."

Erica sits in a chair she never sits in. She had thought Greg was the one, her one and only, for always and forever. A bitter little laugh, a snort really, comes out of her. *Ain't life grand?* And then, in spite of herself, she pictures Greg's green eyes, his lopsided smile, his arms around her. Her career wouldn't be where it is today without his savvy and unwavering support. She arrived at GNN a rookie from a small station in New Hampshire, rebuilding her life after it shattered like glass—a glass full of vodka at ten in the morning. Greg took her by the hand, fought for her, gave her brilliant advice, protected her. Loved her. Did he love her? Does he love her? Is he lost to her? Loss. And love. Love and loss. Are they inseparable? Erica looks around her. The beautiful room is empty.

And now?

Now she knows she'll never be able to trust Greg again. She went through this with Dirk, her first husband, Jenny's father. His Internet date that turned into an affair with that perfectly nice, deadly dull office manager. Her smell on him. His transparent lies. *Never again.* Erica feels anger rising up in her and she welcomes it, wants to embrace it, step into it like a coat of armor—Greg, that creep, that sleazy little Lothario who can't keep it in his pants.

But as she stokes her rage, it's extinguished by something greater. Pain, hurt, loss. It grips her body like a vise, squeezing out anger and reason. The truth is she's still in love with Greg Underwood. She still wants him. And he's in the arms of another woman.

Erica walks over to the bed and throws herself back on the pillows as her eyes fill with tears.

She lies there for a long time. She can hear muffled sounds out in the apartment, but it all seems a million miles away.

Then there's a tentative knock and a soft, "Mom? Are you all right?"

Erica struggles to pull herself together, to make her voice sound normal. "Yes, honey, I just have a little headache. Did Becky go home?"

"Yes. Can I come in?"

"Of course." Erica quickly sits up and leans against the pillows.

Jenny comes in. Her face is side-lit by the hallway light, and Erica can see that her brow is furrowed, her mouth turned down. Erica manages a little smile, but Jenny's expression doesn't change.

"You know how I said I don't worry about you when you're home?" Jenny says.

"Yes."

"That's not true."

CHAPTER 22 ———————————

IT'S THE NEXT MORNING AND Erica is back in her office at GNN. Eight hours of sleep helped, but she's still feeling shaky and trying to sort out her feelings toward Greg. In the cold light of morning she feels much more in control. And more humiliated. And more angry. The milk has spilt and taken trust with it—and all the apologies and hurt and regret in the world won't restore it. But it's a sea change in her life, and in the way she thinks about her future. In fact, it's close to overwhelming. Thank God for the demands of her job.

The television networks have agreed not to replay footage of the assassination and suicide—it's easy enough to find it online, but the consensus is that it's just too grisly for general viewing. But the tape of Erica reporting before and after the shootings has been shown endlessly, and GNN's ratings and her profile have both skyrocketed. A few more details have emerged about the shooter: Peter Tuttle was a former divinity student from Woodstock, New York, who was working two jobs, struggling to support his wife and two young kids. He flew into Detroit from Albany the night before last. That's all that law enforcement has released so far.

Mike Ortiz has suspended his campaign for three days, and he and Celeste have released a statement decrying the horrific act and calling for a national period of prayer and healing. Their fundraiser at Robert DeNiro's apartment will mark the resumption of the campaign.

Shirley appears in Erica's doorway, holding a bouquet of flowers filled with exotic blooms in neon colors—gaudy and playful.

"These just arrived for you," she says. "Someone has a wild imagination."

Erica stands up and takes the bouquet into the kitchen to find a vase. Then she opens the note:

> Hope you're in one piece after yesterday. I'm around if you want to talk. Thinking of you and hoping we can have some fun again soon.
>
> Your pal—Josh

Erica arranges the flowers in the vase—they're a welcome reminder that in the midst of all of life's danger and darkness and heartbreak, there is exuberant life. She puts them on her desk and texts Josh: THANK YOU.

He quickly texts back: ARE YOU OKAY?

Erica: SHAKY BUT STEADY. BUT CHEERED BY THE BLOOMS. YOUR TIMING IS IMPECCABLE.

Josh: IF THAT'S A MARRIAGE PROPOSAL, YOU'LL HAVE TO GIVE ME SOME TIME TO THINK ABOUT IT.

Erica: PONDER AT LEISURE.

Josh: OKAY, I'M DONE THINKING ABOUT IT. DO YOU WANT TO FIND THE CATERER OR SHOULD I?

Erica: I'VE ALREADY GOT A CALL IN TO DOMINO'S. UNLESS YOU PREFER MICKEY D'S.

Josh: I KNEW YOU WERE TOO CLASSY FOR ME.

Erica can hardly believe that she is nonsense texting with a man she spent one afternoon with. But it's just what she needs after last night's call with Greg. To feel desired. To be wooed. To smile. To admire a crazy-quilt bouquet on her desk.

Erica: GOTTA RUN. SOME OF US HAVE REAL JOBS.

Josh: AH-CHOO! THOSE TWO WORDS ALWAYS TRIGGER MY ALLERGIES. HOW ABOUT A LITTLE BOAT RIDE ON SATURDAY?

Erica: YOU HAVE A BOAT?

Josh: A REASONABLE FACSIMILE ANYWAY. WE'LL HEAD UP THE HUDSON. KIDS TOLERATED.

Erica: WE'RE THERE.

Josh: 79TH STREET MARINA AT 10 AM WORK FOR YOU?

Erica: BARRING THE UNFORESEEN.

Erica puts down her iPhone and picks up her office line and calls Mort Silver.

"I have three words for you, Erica: Through. The. Roof."

"That's great, but—"

"No, it's more than great. We're going to raise our advertising rates on your show."

Erica sees an opening and takes it. "Listen, Mort, I want to do in-depth profiles on the two presidential candidates. Maybe two or even three hours each, shown over consecutive nights. I want to visit their birthplaces, look at their childhoods, schooling, major influences, and mentors, really trace their growth and development. We're making history here with a Latino and a woman competing against each other."

"Erica, if it bleeds it leads. Your ratings have spiked because of a bombing and a murder-suicide. I don't think viewers will flock to see you traipse around Lucy Winters's elementary school and do a soft-focus interview with the principal, who has already been spewing out her Little Lucy Winters spiel every time she gets within ten feet of a microphone."

"I don't do soft focus, Mort, and you know it. I happen to think we have a crucial role to play in this election. There's a *lot* at stake. For this country and the world."

"There's a lot at stake for this network in keeping you number one in your time slot."

Time to put the screws on. Erica lowers her voice and speaks slowly. "Doing these profiles is *very* important to me, Mort."

There's a pause. "You're a force to be reckoned with, Sparks. Consider them green-lighted."

Erica hangs up and allows herself a moment of triumph. She'll have all the resources of the network behind her. "Inside Mike Ortiz" and "Inside Lucy Winters" will be hard-hitting investigative journalism. She'll follow the truth *wherever* it leads her. And she senses it may be down some very dark alleys.

Erica calls down to the Smart Room, the network's research center. It's staffed 24/7 by lawyers, accountants, scientists, and researchers. Throw them a question and they'll find the answer.

"Hi, Erica, this is Judith Wexler. What can we do ya this morning?"

"I need contact info for Robert DeNiro."

"Coming right up."

As Erica waits for Judith to call back, she Googles "Al-Qaeda in Iraq." She leans forward, avidly scanning the links—she's a dog with a new bone, ready to get into some serious chewing.

Her research is interrupted when Judith Wexler calls back with the number of DeNiro's office. She hangs up and calls.

"Yes?" a woman's voice answers.

"Hi, this is Erica Sparks."

"What can I do for you?"

"I was wondering if I could attend Mr. DeNiro's fundraiser for Mike Ortiz on Friday?"

"It's a closed event, no media. No pictures. No taping."

"I understand. I'm doing in-depth pieces on both presidential candidates and would like to attend as background. Just to soak up the atmosphere, see how Ortiz does in situations like this one."

There's a pause and then, "I'd have to run it by Mr. DeNiro."

"Of course."

Erica gives the woman her phone number and hangs up. Then she starts to work on her material for tonight's show. She'll be leading with the assassination and suicide, of course. Which is tough for her. To relive it so soon will be gut-wrenching, but that's her job. The fact that Tuttle flew in the night before the shooting, that his press credentials were so expertly forged, and that adhesive-tape residue was found under a bench in the courthouse all point to the man's not having acted alone. He and his cohorts, whoever they are, very much wanted to keep Markum from revealing his motives for the bombing. Erica keeps going back to the same questions: Who benefited the most from Buchanan's death? And who also has the means to engineer the crime and its follow-up? The answer never changes. Or becomes any less disturbing.

Erica's phone rings—the incoming number is blocked.

"This is Erica Sparks."

"Erica, it's Bob . . . Bob DeNiro."

Erica sits up straight and fights the urge to gush. It's a dead end with celebrities—it puts up a wall. If you come off as a foaming fan, you're immediately unequal. *Plus,* Erica thinks, *I ain't exactly chopped liver.* "Thanks for getting back to me."

"I understand you want to . . . ah . . . you know, show up on Friday. At my place. On Friday."

Erica quickly makes her pitch about her piece on Ortiz.

"He's one helluva interesting guy, isn't he?" DeNiro says.

"Fascinating. And I want to get up close and personal. I understand you're limiting the size of the fundraiser."

DeNiro laughs. "I think it's the price of the ticket that's the limiting factor here, Erica Sparks. Not every Joe Schmo on the street can . . . you know, shell out ten grand to la-di-da it at my pad."

"As a journalist, of course, I can't pay. But you'll be doing a service for our democracy."

"A service for our democracy, huh? That kinda language loses me. I do this for the people who are hurting. Here. Now. In my city. In my country."

"Well then, you should let me do this for them. They have a right to make an informed choice when they vote. And, to be blunt, you should do it for *me*. It will all be off the record; you have my word on that."

There's a pause and then, "All right, Erica. Come on down Friday. I'll put your name on the list."

"I need a plus one."

"Oh, now she needs a plus one." He laughs again and then says, like a perfect gentleman, "I look forward to meeting you. And your friend."

CHAPTER 23

ERICA IS DRESSED DOWN FOR DeNiro's fundraiser in a simple little black dress and a pair of clip-on sapphire earrings—she doesn't want to draw attention to herself. She's hired a car and driver for the evening, and she picks up Martin Vander at his apartment building in Chelsea. Vander cleans up pretty nicely for an academic—his beard is trimmed and his black suit fits well. He's also keyed up—eyes alight, gestures fidgety—eager to see his subject up close.

"I've become obsessed with Mike Ortiz. And his wife," he says as the car makes its way down to Tribeca. "I've been devouring every word I can read on them. And watching every video I can find."

"And?"

"I'm still not ready to make any definitive judgments, but I do think there's something, for lack of a better word, *unnatural* about them."

"Say more."

"If you study their body language, you can see that for every move one of them makes, the other makes a countermove. Their bond is extraordinary. And she seems to be the dominant player. He's submissive. It's subtle but, once you start looking for it, undeniable."

"This should be an interesting evening."

The car pulls up in front of an old factory that is now home to priceless loft condos. There's a small phalanx of security guards in front.

Erica and Vander get out of the car, and she walks up to a man with an iPad. He recognizes her, smiles, and ushers them both in. The elevator is manned and it lets them off directly into DeNiro's loft, which has high ceilings and banks of metal-mullioned windows and seems to stretch on forever. The place is crowded and buzzing with that electric New York energy that never fails to recharge and renew Erica.

There's Beyoncé. And Jay-Z. And Sarah Jessica Parker. And Anna Wintour. And George Clooney. And Taylor Swift. And Andy Cohen. And on and on. Erica doesn't have to worry about being recognized in this crowd. In fact, she feels almost B-list. That is, until Beyoncé waves and smiles. Erica manages a wave back, thunderstruck by the singer's beauty.

Vander seems completely nonplussed by the glittering crowd. He unabashedly devours the artful hors d'oeuvres being offered by the army of waitstaff. Erica scans the room and sees no sign of the Ortizes, but she knows from experience that the candidate often doesn't appear until after an introduction.

And then she sees DeNiro, looking handsome in a suit, chatting intently with a tall Chinese woman who is without a doubt one of the most striking women Erica has ever seen. She looks about five nine, lean as a pole, wearing a stunning black suit with bright-orange silk lapels. Her jet-black hair is slicked back, her skin as pale as a winter twilight, her glistening red mouth as bold as a dare.

Erica heads over to the two of them.

"Thank you so much for letting me crash your party," she says to DeNiro.

"My pleasure. Lily Lau, Erica Sparks."

Lily narrows her eyes and looks at Erica with a knowing smile. Then she extends her hand. "I watch you almost every day."

"You must love being bored."

"I love being informed. And you're never boring. In fact, you get more interesting all the time."

"Where is the guest of honor?" Erica asks.

"They're hiding out in my office," DeNiro says, indicating a hallway at one end of the loft. A security guard stands at the front.

"It's all about making an entrance," Lily says.

"I'll leave you two ladies while I go play host," DeNiro says, heading into the crowd.

"Do you know Mike Ortiz?" Erica asks Lily. Even though she knows the answer.

"I'm one of the campaign's chief fundraisers. I also advise the candidate. And I run Pierce Holdings. For Celeste Ortiz."

"So you know them well."

"Celeste and I met at Stanford. She's going to be an extraordinary First Lady."

Erica realizes that she's deep in the Ortiz camp and has to watch her words. But she would love to squeeze some information out of this Lily Lau. "Ortiz's story is so compelling. And Celeste has been by his side every step of the way."

"Their marriage is a great love story. He's her one and only."

"How does Celeste feel about giving up her own career in international finance?"

Lily takes a sip from her glass, which holds water. Erica can't imagine this woman taking even a whiff of an intoxicant.

"Celeste has never been about Celeste. She's a visionary who sees a better world ahead."

Erica's cliché alert sounds. Getting anything fresh, interesting, and revealing out of Lily Lau is going to be very tough. She changes tack.

"How did you end up at Stanford?"

"My father was the Chinese counsel to San Francisco. I grew up in the city. When he left the position and moved back to Beijing, I stayed in the States and became a citizen."

Over Lucy's shoulder Erica sees Martin Vander lingering near the entrance to the hallway that leads to DeNiro's office. When the security guard turns to answer a guest's question, he slips past him.

"And tell me, what brings you to Mike's fundraiser? Aren't you compromising your journalistic standards?"

"Hardly. I'm not endorsing Mike Ortiz. I'm doing research."

"For?"

"I'm putting together profiles of both candidates. I plan to go to a Lucy Winters fundraiser next."

"That should be dull."

"So you've known Mike Ortiz almost as long as Celeste?"

"She introduced me to him a month after they met."

"How do you think his time as a prisoner in Iraq affected him?"

Lily narrows her eyes before answering. "It strengthened him."

Just then there's a ripple in the room as DeNiro appears with Mike and Celeste Ortiz in tow. Behind them, Martin Vander slips out of the hallway and back into the throng. He looks perplexed, troubled, thoughtful—and even more keyed up.

DeNiro steps up onto a small makeshift stage and hushes the room. Mike and Celeste stand to the side. Her eyes sweep the room like a searchlight—when she reaches Erica she stops and gives her a warm smile and a little wave.

"I'm very happy to introduce you to a man who has proven he has guts and smarts and a big heart. Let's hear it for the next president of the United States, Mike Ortiz."

The crowd is so rich, so famous, so accomplished—it takes a lot to impress them, and their applause is polite but hardly rousing. The truth is this tribe will continue to thrive no matter who wins the White House. They live in Fat City and have an easy familiarity with each other—there are no strangers in the brotherhood of success—that even Mike Ortiz can't quite crack. In some ways, Celeste's fortune means more to them than Mike Ortiz's credentials. After all, at the end of the day, Washington, DC, is at their beck and call.

"I feel like I'm at the *Vanity Fair* Oscar party," Mike Ortiz cracks. It's a great opening line, and the crowd laughs and nods approval. "Some people may call you world-famous celebrities. I call you my base." More laughter. "Thanks for your support. I know this is an expensive ticket and some of you worked for a good five minutes to earn it."

Now he's got the crowd eating out of his hands. His performance is so smooth, so polished. Too smooth, too polished. Celeste is standing beside him, beaming. Erica wonders who his joke writer is.

As Ortiz goes into his boilerplate pitch, Erica makes her way over to Vander, who is watching Mike intently. She leans into him and asks, "Thoughts?"

"This has been very illuminating." His eyes are afire.

"I saw you slip down that hallway."

"I was just looking for a bathroom," Vander says, deadpan.

"And did you find one?"

"I thought I had. I opened the door and it turned out to be DeNiro's office."

"And you discovered Mike and Celeste inside?"

"I interrupted them. They were at the far end of the room. He was sitting. She was standing over him. She had a hand on his shoulder. They were repeating some sort of incantation. It was call and response. He was answering her."

"An incantation? What were they saying?"

"I don't know. They were speaking Chinese."

The party seems to disappear around Erica; all she sees is Martin Vander's face, all she hears are his words.

"What did they do when they saw you?"

"There was a moment of shock. And then they smiled. I acted like I hadn't heard a thing and then beat a hasty retreat. Listen, Erica, I have to gather my thoughts and write them up while they're still fresh."

"Wait. That's it?"

"For now, yes. I should have a better sense of things in a day or two. There's something I have to search for. That I *must* find. I'm going to call in all my contacts. It may take a trip to Chinatown." Then he turns and almost races through the throng and out of the party.

On the stage, Ortiz is finishing up. "When it comes to political speeches and a crowd like this, less is always more. Thanks for coming. Now let's have some fun." He and Celeste are so charming and convincing and casual that for a moment Erica wonders if Martin Vander misheard them. Or maybe they have some innocent Chinese affirmation they repeat before public appearances. Or maybe . . . maybe *what?*

Ortiz works the room as a disc jockey starts to spin records, and suddenly it's a party: the noise level soars; laughter rings out; people start to dance. Erica hasn't been to a lot of high-end political fundraisers, but she's been to enough to know that this one is different. It was orchestrated down to the last beat and is definitely more party than policy. Erica sees Lily Lau dancing with Katy Perry and wishes she could film it all for her profile.

Instead, she makes her way over to Celeste Ortiz, who is surrounded by a mix of celebrities and sycophants. But even as she chats and laughs, her eyes follow her husband as he makes his way through the crowd, glad-handing, laughing, hugging.

"Hi, Celeste," Erica says.

Celeste gives her a big smile and grasps her hand. "Erica, what are *you* doing here?"

"My job."

"I thought you were an investigative reporter, not a celebrity chaser."

"The two aren't mutually exclusive," Erica says.

Celeste laughs—it sounds like shards of ice.

"I'm doing an in-depth piece on your husband."

"Be careful, you don't want to get in over your head."

"You know, the tougher the assignment, the better I like it. If you don't believe me, ask Nylan Hastings."

Celeste laughs again. Then Julianne Moore approaches, and Celeste turns away from Erica and gushes, "Julianne!"

"Hi, Celeste. I actually wanted to meet Erica Sparks."

A look of anger, rage really, flashes across Celeste's face in the blink of an eye. But Erica didn't blink—and she and Celeste exchange a glance of mutual understanding. Just like they did that afternoon in Pacific Heights.

"What a pleasure," Erica says, shaking Moore's hand.

"Your reporting on the Buchanan bombing has been very moving. I actually think you're helping us all heal. Don't you agree, Celeste?"

"There's no doubt that Erica is very talented. Of course, we all know that talent isn't enough."

"You need luck," Julianne says.

"I believe we make our own luck," Erica says. "Now, lucky me has to go home and make sure my daughter has finished her homework."

"How's she doing at Brearley?" Celeste asks, suddenly all concern.

"She's doing just fine."

"Are you sure? I know those schools can be tough, especially for a girl coming from . . . *public* school."

"I am sure. She's fine."

"Well, if you and . . . is it Ashley?" Celeste says.

"Jenny."

"If you and Jenny ever have any issues or . . . *challenges*, do let me know. My cousin Joan is on the board."

As Erica walks over to the elevator she feels frustration bubbling in her veins—why does she still let girls like Celeste get to her? She's proven her worth a thousand times over. And yet they *do* get to her. They still have the ability to make her feel insecure, like an imposter, someone not quite good enough. As if, no matter how successful she becomes, she can never erase the stain of her childhood.

At the elevator, she turns and takes a last look at the party. The kitchen and dining area are in a corner, a relatively quiet space. She sees Celeste and Lily Lau huddled there together, deep in conversation. Then, just as the elevator doors open, both women turn and look over at Erica—and she can practically see their wheels turning.

As the elevator takes her down to the street she can't get that look out of her mind.

CHAPTER 24 —————————————————

IT'S SUNDAY MORNING, AND ERICA and Jenny have just boarded Josh Walters's cabin cruiser, docked at the romantic, even whimsical, Seventy-Ninth Street Boat Basin on the Hudson River. The boat's open stern is home to a picnic table—its benches are two huge, smile-inducing erasers.

"Welcome aboard!" Josh says with a boyish grin, looking adorable in beat-up khaki shorts, flip-flops, and a sort of hip-hop/Hawaiian shirt.

Erica has always been a little wary of rah-rah types, especially when they're over the age of twenty-five—news flash: life is hard—but Josh's exuberance feels completely unforced, as natural as breathing. And then there's that mop of curly ginger hair, that conspiratorial smile, and that compact muscular body.

Jenny and Lisa sit at the table and immediately take out their smartphones and start sharing vlogger videos.

"*Lee*-sa, you know the rules," Josh says. "Fork it over." Lisa reluctantly hands over her phone. "Jenny, this boat is a phone-free zone."

Jenny looks at Erica, who shrugs and smiles. "He's the captain."

"We're on one of the world's greatest rivers in the world's greatest city. Do you really want to keep your nose buried in a tiny electronic device cramming your brain full of useless information and the antics of narcissistic clowns, all of which will still be waiting for you when we get back? That's a rhetorical question."

Jenny hands Josh her phone.

"Grown-ups too," Lisa says.

"Actually, I kind of have to claim reporter's prerogative here," Erica says. She's been playing phone tag with Martin Vander since Friday night's fundraiser at DeNiro's. On his last message Martin said he was "very eager" to talk to her. "I'm expecting an important work call that I really have to take."

"What do you say, gang, should we make an exception?" Josh asks.

"I'd like to take her phone, her laptop, and *her job* and throw them all in the Hudson!" Jenny says.

There's laughter all around and then Josh says, "I'm sorry, no exceptions."

Erica *can't* give up her phone. Can she? It's only for a couple of hours, and there's something attractive and reassuring about Josh's adamancy. His boat. His rules. She looks around at the river, the boats, the sky, the day. Then she takes her phone out of her bag and hands it over to Josh. He stashes it with the others in a small box labeled *Freedom*.

Josh pilots the boat out into the river—Erica feels a surge of excitement and adventure—and in no time they're heading under the George Washington Bridge.

"Over there, on one of the highest points in Manhattan, you can see the Cloisters, the medieval monastery that was brought over from France in the late 1930s and turned into a museum." He points across the river to the sheer rock face that lines the other bank. "Those are the Palisades. The Rockefellers bought up the land to protect the Cloisters' viewscape from development."

Josh is a tour guide whose passion is infectious. Erica inhales every morsel of information about her adored adopted city and state. As they make their way upriver, she can't help but compare Josh to Greg. Sophisticated, ironic, hard-driving Greg. Intense, serious, *philandering* Greg. Josh is just so guileless, but not like some overgrown boy, like a man who has decided he's going to enjoy life. In some ways, the balance feels better than it does with Greg. After all, opposites not only attract, they complement.

Josh points out one landmark after another. After about a half hour, Erica hears Lisa mutter under her breath to Jenny, "Welcome to the snooze cruise." The two of them dissolve into giggles, but Erica can tell that Lisa adores her dad.

It's a warm day, but there's a breeze on the river and the homemade lemonade Josh has served is tart and refreshing. The world looks so different from the water—you get to see views and houses that are inaccessible by land. They pass a rambling, neglected Victorian that looks like Blanche DuBois's summer place, and then a midcentury modern glass house cantilevered out over the river. There are tiny bank-hugging hamlets that look unchanged from their founding two hundred years ago.

"We're now entering the Hudson Highlands," Josh says as mountains seem to rise straight out of the water on both banks, squeezing the river. "During the Revolutionary War, the British strung chain metal across from one side to the other in an unsuccessful attempt to stop Washington's navy."

They round a bend, and there, tucked into the highlands, is the fortress of West Point.

A little farther upriver a ruined castle comes into view, sitting on its own tiny island. It's towering and eerie, like something out of a nightmare—or maybe a Tim Burton movie.

"And that's Bannerman's castle, built by arms dealer Francis Bannerman in 1901 as a storage facility for his armaments. After he died in 1918, the island was essentially abandoned. It now belongs to New York State, which is trying to figure out what the heck to do with it."

Even the girls are mesmerized by this apparition, and Josh deftly maneuvers the boat to a large, flat onshore rock. Then he jumps onto the rock and ties the boat to a nearby tree. "Should we do a little exploring and have some lunch?"

First Lisa and then Jenny take his extended hand and hop ashore. Just as Erica is about to follow, she hears the muffled sound of her phone ringing. Her river reverie is broken.

"Can I just check and see who it is? If it's anyone but the important call, I promise I won't answer."

Josh smiles and nods. Erica retrieves the phone. "It's him . . . Hi, Martin."

"Erica, can we meet? I've made some disturbing discoveries." He sounds spooked.

"Can't you tell me on the phone? I'm forty miles up the Hudson River."

"I'd rather we met in person," Vander says. "Phones sometimes . . ."

"I'll be back this afternoon."

"How about we meet on the High Line at Twenty-Sixth Street at four?"

"See you then." Erica hangs up on the call—and on her carefree mood. She could tell by Vander's voice that he's deeply unsettled, even frightened, by what he has uncovered. Has he come to some sort of conclusion about Ortiz's mental and emotional state?

"Bad news?" Josh asks from shore.

"Possibly."

"Hey, why don't you girls explore the island while I get lunch set up?"

Jenny and Lisa eagerly take off. Josh steps back onto the boat. He's serious now and concerned. "Are you okay?"

"Yeah. I am. I should probably tell you right now that I have workaholic tendencies. When I'm investigating a story I turn into a single-minded, obsessive, exceedingly boring bulldog. You planned this lovely day, and I'm afraid I'm going to be distracted and pretty poor company for the rest of it."

"Erica, I'm not the kind of guy who's looking for Martha Stewart Lite. I love gutsy women who own their power. So I admire your work ethic and I'm wholly supportive. I'm also wildly curious as to what you're investigating."

Erica would love to open up to Josh, to tell him about Ortiz and Celeste and Lily Lau and her misgivings. She'd value his input—sometimes a fresh civilian eye can offer up helpful suggestions. But she knows from experience it's better to play her cards close to the vest, especially early on. "I can't talk about it at this point. It's in the early stages and I don't want to jinx things."

Josh studies her for a moment, then reaches out and gently runs his hand down her cheek. It's a tender gesture, a pledge of friendship, and Erica is touched by it. "You can still eat, though, can't you? We've got tuna fish, egg salad, potato chips, and pickles."

Josh is just a doll, one of those what-you-see-is-what-you-get great guys. Erica feels a real attraction toward him, his generosity, his kindness, his spontaneity, his easy physicality. And the lunch sounds delicious.

But the only thing Erica has an appetite for right now is Vander's information.

CHAPTER 25 ——————————

THE HIGH LINE IS ONE of New York's newest wonders—a former elevated railroad line that has been turned into a park that stretches some twenty blocks from the former meatpacking district up to Thirty-Fourth Street. It's gorgeously landscaped and offers a banquet of urban viewscapes. But today Erica is too tense to savor its charms. As she waits for Vander she paces, ignoring the surrounding sea of tourists and natives. She hears police sirens in the distance, followed by an ambulance's wail. She sits on a bench, crosses her legs, and watches the left one bouncing; she stands up, never taking her eyes off the staircase that leads up from the street below. It's 3:55.

Four o'clock comes. And goes. Now it's 4:10 and now it's 4:15 and now it's 4:20 and now Erica's anxiety is revved up into overdrive. The presidential election is just months away, the Democratic convention is weeks away, and if Vander has discovered something troubling about Mike Ortiz she needs to build her case quickly. A woman recognizes her in spite of her cap and sunglasses and gives her an encouraging smile. Erica tries to smile back but it comes out closer to a twitch. Thank God New Yorkers are blasé to celebrity; she's not sure she could handle a selfie assault right now.

At 4:30 she takes out her phone and calls Vander. His voice mail picks up, and she leaves a message. "Martin, it's Erica. I'm here at the High Line. Are you all right? Please call me."

At 4:50 Erica decides to go to Vander's house. She hates to disturb his wife and children, but she needs to make sure he's all right. And, of course, she's burning to hear his news. She races down the steps to Twenty-Sixth Street and heads east. At the corner of Ninth Avenue she sees what caused the police sirens and ambulance wails. A body, covered by a police tarp, lies in the avenue, a good ten feet from the curb. Erica feels a terrible sense of foreboding. She approaches a cop.

"What happened?" she asks. The cop looks at her skeptically and then recognizes her.

"Hit-and-run," he says.

"Who is the victim?"

"White male. Late middle age."

"Do you know his name?"

The cop shakes his head and then nods in the direction of a dark-suited Asian man. "Detective Hirata would."

Erica walks up to the detective, who is taking a statement from a witness. "I'm very sorry to interrupt, but have you identified the victim?"

Hirata shoots her a hard glance. "Sorry, but nobody jumps the line, not even Erica Sparks."

"I was supposed to meet Martin Vander on the High Line, and he never showed up. I just want to make sure he wasn't the victim."

Hirata turns to her with a resigned expression. "I'm sorry."

"It *is* him?"

The detective nods.

Erica takes two steps backward, is afraid she'll topple over.

"Were you friends with Vander?" Hirata asks.

"We were working together. What happened?"

"He was crossing the street with the light when that car"—he points to a late-model BMW—"ran him over. The driver jumped out of the car and fled on foot."

"There must have been a lot of witnesses."

"There were, but the perpetrator had on a ski cap and dark glasses, and I'm getting a lot of conflicting descriptions—white, Latino, Asian, a teenager, in his thirties, tall, not so tall. Whoever he was, he could sprint."

"What about the car?"

"Stolen two hours ago on the Upper West Side."

"Has his family been informed?"

The detective nods. "A hit-and-run in broad daylight is pretty rare."

Erica looks down at the cold, impersonal police tarp. Under it lies the mangled body of a man she respected and liked. A man who was helping her. A man who had something important to tell her. Gone. Dead. Murdered? *Was he murdered?* Murdered before he could tell Erica what he had learned? A man she had sought out and enlisted in her investigation. If he was murdered, she was responsible. Erica feels a crashing wave of guilt engulf her.

She gets the detective's card, tells him she'll be in touch, and raises an arm to hail a cab. As one pulls to a stop in front of her, her guilt is joined by determination—a fierce resolve to find out the truth about Mike and Celeste Ortiz. Is Vander's death a warning to back off? If it is, it backfired.

CHAPTER 26

THE FOLLOWING TUESDAY ERICA IS at her desk at GNN. She has a headache and her feet hurt. The last couple of days have been rough. She calls Detective Hirata three times a day, but there have been no leads in Vander's death. There were no fingerprints in the car, so identification of the perpetrator has been stymied. The police have released a sketch, and in it, the man looks . . . generic. Regular features, race indeterminate; the only thing witnesses agree on is that he's of medium build. The fact is the hit-and-run could easily have been an accident. But Erica highly doubts it. If only, if only, *if only* she could find out what it was Vander wanted to tell her.

Adding to her frustration is the lack of any major developments in the Buchanan bombing and subsequent murder-suicide. Although the police don't considerate it particularly significant, Erica is intrigued and troubled by the fact that the whereabouts of both Tuttle and Markum in the week before their respective crimes is unknown. They seem to have both disappeared into the ether. There are no credit card transactions, no sightings, no nothing. Where were they? And maybe more importantly, who were they with?

The only other piece of possibly significant information to come out is that Peter Tuttle had a large life insurance policy that named his wife as the sole beneficiary. She's due to receive three million dollars. Amy Tuttle has admitted that the family is thousands of dollars in debt, and that her husband worried obsessively about the burden it was causing her and their two young children.

It's just after lunch—Erica couldn't choke down anything more than a few bites of cold pizza—and she's going to leave in a few minutes to attend Martin Vander's memorial service. It's being held at the Ethical Culture Society on Central Park West, just a couple of blocks down from her apartment. She sent his widow flowers and a personal note, but she wants to go and honor his memory.

There's something else that's bothering her. Something so painful that she hates to admit it, even to herself. She crosses and recrosses her legs, shuffles some papers around, checks her e-mail. Then her phone rings. She dreads answering it—until she sees it's Moira.

"Hi, Moy."

"Boy, you sound down."

"Two words and you can tell?"

"Actually I can tell in half that. What's going on?"

"Vander, of course. I'm sad, shocked, guilty, frustrated. And the Buchanan case, which is going nowhere. Moy, I'm just feeling overloaded and having these terrible thoughts . . ."

"What terrible thoughts? Spit it out. This is me here."

Erica looks out her office window at the sunbaked city, the city of her dreams. *Beware of answered prayers.*

"Oh, Moy, I'm starting to think . . . to think that it was a bad idea for me to get custody of Jenny. I'm never home, I'm missing meals and school events, she's bonding like a house on fire with Becky, which I think is partly passive-aggression toward me, and I just feel . . ." Erica's throat tightens. "I feel like I'm failing at being a mother."

Moy lets the words hang there a moment before saying, "Oh, sweet baby girl, please know that you are loved. By me, of course, but also by Jenny. She's not expecting perfection from you. She's a smart kid—after all, she's *your* kid—and she knows you're trying your best."

"Am I, though? I could probably carve out more time for her if I really tried, but right now I'm consumed by my work. I feel like I can't let up or I'll lose whatever momentum I have."

"Your love for the job is part of the equation. Jenny understands that. She may not like it all the time, but she gets it. And she admires you."

Erica takes a deep breath and closes her eyes. "The truth is, Moy—oh, this is hard to admit—but sometimes I think *my* life would be easier if she went back and lived with her father."

"Of course your life would be easier, but it would also be lonelier, much lonelier. And less fun. And less fulfilling. You love that kid heart and soul, Erica Sparks, and she loves you and she is *so* proud of you. Do you mess up at times? Yes, you do. Welcome to motherhood."

Erica exhales with a soul-deep sigh. She sits up straight as glints of hope and promise flow into her veins like oxygen. Somebody was smiling on her when they sent Moira Connelly—the proud, smart, beautiful daughter of two Boston cops, one black, one Irish—into her life.

"You there, kiddo?" Moira asks.

"What do you know about motherhood? You don't have any kids."

"And believe me, it's not an accident," Moira says. "I took all that tuition cash and sprang for a Beemer."

Erica has to laugh at that. And then Moira laughs. And now the two of them are roaring like kids, laughing in celebration of motherhood and anti-motherhood and friendship and the crazy, complicated contradictory absurdity of it all.

And yes, you are trying your best.

When the laughter finally dies down there's silence, a silence filled with the love between two old friends.

"You're my guardian angel," Erica says finally.

"Oh please, you know I'm schmaltz-phobic. I just called to rave about these Louboutins I scored online for sixty bucks."

"Text a pic."

"It's been sitting in your box for ten minutes. Why do you think I called in the first place?"

As Erica hangs up, grabs her bag, and heads out to Vander's service, she thinks, *Saved by the shoe.*

CHAPTER 27 —————————————————

THE ETHICAL CULTURE SOCIETY IS located in a handsome redbrick and limestone building, built in 1910, on the corner of Sixty-Fourth Street and Central Park West. Erica makes her way to the meeting room. It's a soaring wood-trimmed space. She slips into a back pew. All the seats are filled and Vander's family is onstage. His wife, Margaret, is an attractive woman in her forties who looks like she's drowning in grief, but is dry-eyed, clearly marshaling her resources, determined to get through the service without breaking down.

Erica listens as one speaker after another talks about Martin Vander's integrity, his intelligence, his scientific mind leavened with wit and compassion. Sitting there, Erica is moved, but she can't shake her guilt. Would he still be alive if she hadn't enlisted him in her investigation? She pushes aside the futile conjecture. It won't bring him back, and he *agreed* to help her. He was excited by the prospect of exploring whether Mike Ortiz was somehow . . . *altered* after his time as a prisoner in Iraq.

The atmosphere in the room is sad, hushed, and comforting—it feels something like a sanctuary to Erica. Ever the journalist, she notes that there's little makeup on the women, lots of uncombed hair on the men, and that their clothes run to the understated, even dowdy. Erica is reminded that New York is home to scores of colleges and universities, including Columbia, Barnard, and NYU. This is a tribe of New Yorkers she rarely sees—intellectuals, humanists, academics—curious and caring, carrying on learning traditions that harken back centuries and speak to man's nobler pursuits. It's another world from the pressure-cooker atmosphere of GNN, and from the celebrity worship, ravenous ambition, and worship of wealth that seems to pervade so much of the city's zeitgeist.

The service ends with Vander's teenage son and daughter singing "Knockin' on Heaven's Door." When they finish there isn't a dry eye in the house. Erica remains seated as the mourners make their way up the aisle. She wants to say a few words to Margaret Vander, who is down in front of the stage accepting condolences.

When the room has almost emptied out, Erica makes her way to Margaret, who stands alone as the gathering ends and the future looms. Erica waits until Margaret sees her and smiles wanly.

"Thank you for coming," she says.

"I wanted to pay my respects. Your husband was such a lovely man."

"Wasn't he?"

"He was helping me with a project."

"Yes, he mentioned it to me. He was enjoying it, found it challenging. And Martin loved a challenge. So thank you for brightening his final days."

"He brightened mine."

"His enthusiasm was infectious, wasn't it?"

Erica nods.

"I thought you might come today, and I'm glad you did. I know Martin was on his way to meet you when he was killed. He had something for you in his briefcase. I brought it with me."

Margaret Vander takes a small package out of her bag. It's wrapped in brown paper and tied with a string. *For Erica* is written in marker on the outside. Margaret hands it to her.

"I have no idea what it is. But it's yours."

"Thank you. If there's anything I can do now, ever, please let me know." Erica grasps Margaret's hand just as tears start to roll down the widow's cheeks.

CHAPTER 28 ————————————

BACK AT HER DESK, ERICA gently unties the string on the package and opens the brown paper. There's a book inside. It looks ancient—the paper is foxed and brittle and looks like it could crumble into dust at any second. And the book is in Chinese. Erica gingerly opens it in a few places. The characters are graceful and beautiful, but of course she has no idea what they mean.

Why did Martin Vander want Erica to have this? What could it possibly have to do with Mike Ortiz? And what is the book *about*?

Erica Googles "Chinese languages," and several Chinese alphabets come up. She tries to match the characters on her screen with the ones on the book. It's hopeless. She knows China has many regional languages, and with a book this old she hasn't a clue where to begin. But clearly Martin Vander thought this text was important in understanding Mike and Celeste Ortiz.

Erica stands up and paces, feeling pressure to prepare for tonight's show—which is going to include segments on the drought in the West, the spread of the West Nile virus, and updates on the Buchanan bombing. But she feels a pulsing urgency to make some sense of this book. The nominating conventions are just around the corner. Once Mike

Ortiz is the official nominee, her investigation will only become more difficult. And Lucy Winters will be the only thing standing between Ortiz and the Oval Office.

Erica grabs her phone and calls Becky. "Listen, Becky, can you do some research for me?"

"That's what I'm here for."

"I need to find a scholar of ancient Chinese texts."

"Sounds fascinating. May I ask what for?"

Becky has become *so* inquisitive. *Of course she has, she's a budding journalist.* Still, some instinct tells Erica to hold back. "Oh, just a segment I'm considering about China's global economic clout. I want to tie it to their history, traditional financial customs, so forth."

"I see. So you need a scholar to explain their ancient customs to you."

"Ah . . . yes. Exactly. I'd like to find the best, of course."

"I'll get right on it," Becky says.

Erica hangs up and gets to work on her follow-up to the Buchanan bombing. She's growing obsessed with the missing week in both Markum's and Tuttle's chronology. They both disappear, and when they reappear they commit horrific crimes. Almost as if they were programmed to kill and then set loose. She could certainly discuss this theory on tonight's show, but she's hesitant. She wants to keep her suspicions sub rosa for now. The fewer people who know what she suspects, the safer she feels. Head down, one foot in front of the other, keep probing. But where? She walks into the kitchen for no reason and then walks back into her office, pacing, feeling stuck, stymied, stifled—buried under a barrage of questions whose answers seem out of reach.

Erica slips out of her dress, into yoga pants and a T-shirt, and does twenty minutes of strenuous Tae Kwon Do. When she finishes she feels stronger, more in control. Something will break open—and if not, she'll kick it open. The truth is her lodestar, and she won't rest until she reaches it.

Becky calls back. "Harvard's Department of East Asian Languages and Civilizations is considered one of the best in the world. There's a professor there who has written extensively on ancient Chinese texts. His name is George Yuan. From my research he's the tops in the country. I also have a half dozen backups if he doesn't work out. The full list, with all contact information, should be in your in-box."

"Good work, Becky, thank you. And I'm sorry so much of the job has been the care and feeding of Jenny."

"That's okay, really. In fact it's been, and continues to be, a total pleasure. But I am eager to prove my journalistic props."

"Of course you are." Erica hangs up and calls George Yuan's office at Harvard.

"This is George Yuan."

"Hello, Professor. My name is Erica Sparks. I'm a journalist."

"I know who you are, of course. And I'm George."

"I'm calling because I've been given a book, a book in Chinese. It looks very old. Of course I can't read Chinese so I have no idea what it's about. I was wondering if you had the time, or inclination, to take a look."

"Who gave you this book? Can't that person tell you what it is?"

"I got it from Dr. Martin Vander, who you may know."

"I know his work, yes. And I saw his obituary in the *Times*. Very sad."

"I have reason to believe the book is related to an investigation I'm conducting."

"Interesting. Can you text me a picture of the book?"

"Hold on a sec." Erica takes a picture of the cover and texts it to Yuan.

"Got it. Let me just take a look . . ."

There's a pause, a long pause.

"Are you there . . . George?"

When he answers, his voice is charged with excitement and gravity. "What exactly is your investigation centered on?"

"I would rather not get into that, especially on the phone."

"I see."

"Can you tell me what the book is about?"

"If you're worried about the phone, I should also keep my counsel. Can you come up to Cambridge and bring the book with you?"

"Of course. With my newscast, I can't come until the weekend. Does that work for you?"

"When something intrigues me, I make the time. And I am *very* intrigued."

"And I'm intrigued as to why you're so intrigued."

"Then we will be a good team. I can tell you that Dr. Vander uncovered an exceedingly rare—and important—manuscript."

Erica hangs up and books a seat on the Acela to Boston on Saturday. Then she remembers she promised Jenny a trip to the Cloisters that day.

CHAPTER 29

ERICA ARRIVES HOME TO FIND Jenny and Becky sitting on opposite living room couches, books in hand, intently if somewhat haltingly having a conversation in French. Both frequently pause to look up words, tenses, pronouns, and the thousand other idiosyncrasies of the language.

"*Je suis* impressed," Erica says.

Becky rolls her eyes and smiles. She's been losing weight and paying more attention to her posture and hair, and is starting to look markedly more attractive. "Don't be. Jenny is teaching *me*."

"Let's stop now," Jenny says, slapping her book shut with a frown. And Erica was already dreading this evening.

Becky stands up. "Good night, Jenny."

Erica walks Becky to the door. "Listen, what's your schedule like on Saturday?"

"I thought you were taking Jenny to the Cloisters?"

Erica grimaces. "I have to go out of town . . ."

Becky waits expectantly. Erica stops there.

"She's really looking forward to it. She was talking about it all night."

"I really didn't need that information."

"Of course you didn't. Stupid me. Will you be gone long?"

"Just the day. I'll be back Saturday night."

"So you're not going far . . . ?"

Erica exhales. "I'm going up to Cambridge to see George Yuan."

"Oh great. So that project is moving along?"

"Becky, when I'm involved in an ongoing story, sometimes I like to keep things to myself until I see what direction it's heading in. Does that make sense?"

Becky nods.

"When I'm a little further along, I'll bring you on board. You've already been helpful."

"I can work Saturday. I'll take Jenny up to the Cloisters."

Erica feels that familiar stab of jealousy. "Maybe not the Cloisters, I was looking forward to seeing it myself."

"Actually, she's doing a paper on the museum. She told her teacher about it."

Well, she hasn't told her mother. "Yes, of course . . . I knew that."

Becky looks at her doubtfully.

Why is she fibbing to this young woman? Because—when it comes to Jenny and motherhood—she's still a roiling bundle of insecurity, doubt, and guilt.

"By the way, Becky, you're looking terrific."

Becky smiles—has she had her teeth whitened too?—and leaves.

Erica finds Jenny in her bedroom—her neat-as-a-pin bedroom—laying out her clothes for school tomorrow.

"Hi, honey."

Jenny grunts a greeting.

"Can we talk for a minute?"

Jenny doesn't look at Erica but makes a great show of pulling out skirts and shirts to consider. "What about?"

"Well, about Saturday, first of all. But also about *us*, about where we're going."

Jenny wheels on her. *"What about Saturday?* Are you canceling again?"

Erica could kick herself—why did she start with the bad news? She's so inept. "I think I started on the wrong foot here, honey. Could we back up?"

"No. I need to know if you're canceling our trip. I have a paper on the Cloisters due! You care about that job ten thousand times more than you care about me."

Erica makes a quick decision—and this time there's no fibbing. "No, I am *not* canceling Saturday. Not if you think I shouldn't."

"I think you shouldn't."

"Can you at least hear me out for two minutes?" Erica sits on Jenny's bed. "Please, honey, just come sit for a minute and let's talk." She pats the bed.

Jenny hesitates, then comes over, sits on the edge of the bed, and crosses her arms, looking straight ahead.

"I'm working on a story that I think might be important. *Very* important. I think there might be something wrong with Mike Ortiz."

Jenny frowns, and Erica can see she's trying to stifle her curiosity, but out it comes. "What do you mean? Like, what wrong?"

"Well, that's just it, honey. I don't know exactly what. But when he came back from his time as a prisoner in Iraq, his affect seemed different, flatter. And he seems to be controlled by his wife, to an unnatural degree."

"Is that a crime?"

"It's not a crime, per se, but if something . . . unusual . . . did happen while he was a hostage, I think the American people have a right to know it. He could be our next president. I think the Buchanan bombing, the assassination and suicide that followed, and then the hit-and-run of Martin Vander might all be connected to the Ortizes."

"Really?"

"Yes. Right now I have ten questions for every answer. But there's so much at stake. I feel a real responsibility to follow this investigation. I may come up empty-handed, but I have to try."

"Do you have to try on Saturday?"

"I have a piece of potential evidence that needs to be examined by an expert up at Harvard. I feel very real time pressure. The nominating convention is coming up, and then it's only a couple of months before the election."

Jenny looks down and says nothing.

"My offer to cancel still stands."

"Oh sure, cancel—and then when President Ortiz turns out to be a robot, blame me."

"That *would* be a weight on your shoulders."

"If I can handle *you*, I can handle anything."

Erica can't stifle a laugh.

"There's one thing I want in return."

"What's that?"

"My allowance raised to thirty dollars."

"But that's emotional blackmail."

"Whatever it takes."

Since those three words are one of Erica's mantras when she's conducting an investigation, what can she say? "All right, thirty it is."

Jenny sticks out her arm, and mom and daughter shake hands.

"Do you have *any* idea how much I love you?"

"Please don't get all syrupy, Mom."

Without thinking Erica reaches out and grabs Jenny, pulls her tight to her breast, kisses the top of her head again and again, squeezes her, holds her, hugs her, now and for always.

Then she looks up and sees Becky in the doorway.

"Oh, I'm sorry to interrupt. I forgot my glasses. I knocked and rang the bell, but when there was no answer I tried the door and it was open and so I just came in and got them." She holds up the retrieved glasses. "Bye now." Becky disappears.

A shiver races up Erica's spine. She takes Jenny's hands in her own, looks her in the eyes, and says, in her most serious mother voice, "Listen, Jenny, don't mention *anything* to *anyone* about what I told you. Even Becky."

"Okay."

"Promise?"

"Promise."

Erica kisses Jenny one last time and then goes and locks the front door. Then she goes to the living room window and looks down. She watches as Becky leaves the building, crosses Central Park West, and then reaches into her bag, takes out her cell phone, and makes a call.

CHAPTER 30 ————————————————

AS HER TRAIN APPROACHES BOSTON'S South Station, Erica's baggage includes more than the briefcase on the seat beside her. She and Boston have a checkered history—this is the town where she first tasted success. And where she wound up in jail for DUI and reckless endangerment. But all that's behind her. Isn't it?

Erica usually finds train trips relaxing, but she's too filled with expectation, even foreboding, to enjoy this one. She's deeply unnerved by Vander's death, which she is growing convinced was murder, flawlessly planned and executed. She's almost afraid to learn what the frail manuscript that she has gingerly tucked into her bag is about.

She leans back in the seat and closes her eyes, hoping to grab a moment of peace—instead, she flashes on Becky standing there in the doorway of Jenny's room, silently watching them. How long was she there? How much did she hear? Was she lurking out of sight, listening, before she appeared in the doorway? Erica tries to quell her doubts about Becky. She's just a kid from the wrong side of the tracks who's trying to get a toehold in the big leagues. Erica remembers her own youthful missteps. And Becky *is* good for Jenny. If Erica replaced Becky it would be a big disruption in Jenny's life. Not to mention her own.

The train comes to a stop, and Erica gets off and heads to the cabstand. She's wearing cream slacks, a blue blouse, and sunglasses as protection against the world—she's in no mood for autographs or selfies or even understated Bostonian expressions of goodwill.

As her cab makes its way through the narrow streets lined with charming old buildings and a palpable sense of history, civility, and respect for tradition, she thinks, *America could use a little more Boston these days.*

They reach the Charles River and drive west to Cambridge. The water is sparkling, dotted with sculls and pleasure boats, the sky is blue, but all Erica sees is danger and malevolence, lurking, waiting. All the tradition in the world, all the civility, even all the lovely weather, none of it is protection in the end.

They drive through Harvard Square, jammed with tourists soaking up the Harvardness—sidewalk singers, buskers and magicians, bookstores and cupcake emporiums, clothing stores catering to fourteen-year-old social-media addicts. They reach the vast Harvard campus—passing gates that lead to grassy yards filled with students in the last blush of innocence. They come to Divinity Place, where the Department of East Asian Languages and Civilizations is housed in an undistinguished redbrick building.

Erica holds her bag close to her chest as she finds the office of George Yuan. The door is open, and when Yuan sees Erica he bounds up out of his chair.

"Welcome to Ye Olde Cambridge. What a pleasure!" Yuan is young, midthirties tops, lean, and bristling with energy, with thick black hair, eyes that beam out a restless intelligence, and a movie-star handsome face he tries to soften with a pair of hip-nerd black glasses. "Sit, sit, make yourself comfortable."

Erica sits in a chair, expectant—she meets a lot of dynamic people in her business, but they have nothing on George Yuan. He closes the office door, sits, rubs his hands together, and makes a pro forma stab at small talk. "So . . . you found us all right?"

"Yes. As you may know, I used to work in Boston."

"I do know. You were my favorite newscaster."

Erica is disarmed by his compliment. George Yuan is a generous guy who has managed to make her feel drawn to him within thirty seconds of meeting. "From what I've read it sounds like you do fascinating work."

"Oh, I'm just a musty academic. I've always admired people like you, out in the real world, making a difference." He rubs his hands together again. "So . . . you've brought the manuscript?"

Erica takes the brown-paper-wrapped book out of her bag and hands it to Yuan. He places it on his desk and gently unwraps it. The book sits there and he stares at it for a few moments before opening it at a couple of places—handling the pages as reverently as if it were a Gutenberg Bible. His focus is intense, and Erica's curiosity is becoming almost unbearable. Finally he turns from his desk to her.

"I don't know how much you know of the ancient Chinese texts, sometimes called the canonical texts."

"That would be somewhere between zero and zilch."

"They're called the Four Books and Five Classics. They were written before the Qin dynasty unified China in 221 BC, and cover history, philosophy, agriculture, medicine, mathematics, astronomy, religion, art, and literature. Together they provide a priceless record of that ancient neo-Confucian civilization. Probably the most famous in the West is the *I Ching*."

Erica knows a little bit about China's rich history, and she closely follows the extraordinary trajectory of modern China as it has become the world's economic superpower. But these texts are new to her, 221 BC. That's a long time ago—over 1,600 years before Columbus set foot in the New World. America was home to wildly scattered Native American tribes, while in China the foundations of a highly advanced civilization were being recorded.

"There is one classic text of which so few copies exist that some scholars consider it a fraud, an imposter written centuries later by generals and military scholars. Other experts, myself included, believe this so-called 'lost' text is wholly legitimate, but was suppressed at the time because its methodology was rejected by the leaders of the ascendant Qin dynasty."

"And *this* is that text?"

"Yes. Not an original, obviously. None of the original texts has survived. However, they were transcribed by ensuing generations. I would date this copy back to the late nineteenth century. This is the only time I have ever seen this manuscript outside a museum. It remains controversial, with few scholars taking it seriously. Do you know how Dr. Vander came to have it?"

"He told me he was going to visit Chinatown, but that was the only hint he gave."

"New York City is home to the largest Chinese population outside China. A lot of secretive commerce takes place there. He may have had a lead to a rare books dealer, perhaps one operating out of his apartment, under the radar. The important thing is, we have this now."

"You haven't told me what it's about."

"Well, it's a military text—but it's not about armies and grand strategies and battlefield tactics. No—it covers the philosophy, history, and methodology of a single and peculiar element of military tactics."

"Which is?"

"Well, the title is *How to Conduct Warfare of the Mind*."

CHAPTER 31

"YOU LOOK SHOCKED, ERICA," GEORGE Yuan says.

"I am shocked." Erica tries to gather herself, to make some sense of what she's just learned. "I don't know what I was expecting, but . . . well, it only heightens my suspicions."

"Which are?"

Erica is hesitant to open up to Yuan. He seems completely trust-worthy, and could possibly even be helpful, but she feels like she's playing with fire—a serious conflagration—and she wants to err on the side of caution.

"I'd rather not go into a lot of detail."

"Am I right to assume you believe the tactics described in this text are being used today?"

"Is there a translation of the text?"

"Ah, your evasions only add to *my* suspicions." They exchange a complicit glance. "In Chinese culture we value discretion. In American culture discretion is the better part of failure. I am caught in between."

"So am I. Has the text been translated?"

"Not that I know of. As I said, it was discredited for centuries and didn't generate a lot of interest. It's written in ancient Chinese, which is an obsolete language. Finding a translator will be difficult."

"But you know ancient Chinese?"

"I do." He leans back in his chair, locks his fingers behind his head, and stretches out his elbows—a gesture that shows off his lithe, toned body. "Okay, I'll take a stab at it."

"Seriously?"

"I'm up to my neck in my new book—but it will be nice to work on something relevant."

"I'm so appreciative."

There's a pause, and as the room goes quiet the mood shifts. Yuan grows serious, even somber, and he leans forward, elbow on knees. "Erica, from what I know of this book, it is dark. *Very* dark. It goes to places in the human soul that are pure evil. If you're dealing with people who are using it, you are in danger. Do you understand?"

Erica nods.

"Are you sure you want to move forward with this?"

"I am. I believe the arc of history bends toward justice. I want to add my weight, my strength, to bending it."

There's another pause as he considers her words. Then he says, "I am with you, Erica. As an ally. And as a friend." He reaches out and clasps her hand.

As Erica walks down the sidewalk to her waiting car, she is touched by Yuan's pledge, renewed and recharged. Up above her is the cobalt blue sky, and all around her, bright, idealistic young people walk and talk and laugh and play—there *is* decency and justice in the world, and she wants to make it more secure for those coming up behind her. For Jenny. Erica's spirits soar. Then she looks over her shoulder and sees a dark cloud bank sweeping in from the west.

And she didn't bring an umbrella.

CHAPTER 32 —————————————————

AS ERICA RIDES BACK TO South Station, she tries to put the pieces together. *How to Conduct Warfare of the Mind.* Is it a manual of brainwashing? Does it detail techniques to gain control of a victim's mind, to turn him into an automaton who will do what he is told, no matter how evil?

If so, was this mode of warfare, were these techniques, practiced on Ortiz? Vander saw him and Celeste chanting some call-and-response incantation in Chinese. And Celeste was in the lead, the dominant player. And what about Markum? And Tuttle? Is there some kind of conspiracy behind it all? Tuttle lived in Woodstock, New York, about three hours from Boston . . .

Erica leans forward and says to the driver, "Can you take me to the nearest car rental, please?"

———

As Erica drives west on the Mass Pike through the intermittent thunderstorms, she calls Moy and asks her to find Tuttle's address. It feels good to be alone, in a car, a compact car, driving, moving toward some answers. They recognized her at the Avis counter and wanted to give her a free upgrade, but she declined—she likes the ease and feel of smaller cars.

That's one of the ironies of being rich and famous—people are always throwing swag at you, upgrades and perks and gift bags filled with two-hundred-dollar sunglasses and Dr. Dre headphones, and at every turn there's a sumptuous lobster-laden buffet. Being rich and famous, of course, you can easily afford it all, while those who really need help are stretching their food-stamp budgets to feed their families and haunting the Goodwill to clothe them.

Erica reaches New York State. She drives over the mighty Hudson, wide and slow and serpentine. She remembers her day on Josh's boat. He's lively and warm and a little goofy, but she senses a rock-solid integrity under his boyish locks, and when he ran his fingers down her cheek after she got that troubling call from Vander, she was touched by his sincerity and concern. They've spoken a few times since and have a tentative date set for tomorrow, sans kids.

As for Greg, they haven't spoken since that terrible night when he de facto admitted to an affair with Laurel Masson. Of course she's burning with curiosity about its length and intensity. Was it a one-night tipsy fall into the sack? Or is it ongoing and developing into something serious? Or is it somewhere in between—a casual affair between two busy adults? Her feelings would change depending on where it fell on the scale, but the hurt is still so fresh, so raw, that Erica prefers just to push the whole mess out of her mind, out of her heart. Well, she can try anyway.

She drives south on the New York State Thruway and then exits and heads west to the village of Woodstock. The sky has cleared and she's charmed by the town's ragtag, albeit upscale, hippie vibe—there's a spontaneous musical celebration on the village green, complete with drummers and guitar players, latter-day hippie chicks, pony-tailed middle-aged men and near-naked toddlers all dancing with abandon, the scene watched over by day trippers clutching bags filled with boutique scores. It's all borderline satirical—spruce things up around the edges and this could be Hippieland, a new attraction at Disney World.

Moy got her Tuttle's address—it's right in the village—and so Erica decides to park in a town lot and walk. She puts on her shades and a cap and savors strolling unrecognized through the colorful streets. She makes her way to a neighborhood tucked away behind the village green, in a hollow beside a roaring stream. The houses are Arts-and-Craftsy, small but charming in a whimsical way. She finds Tuttle's house, which is small and neglected. The tiny front yard looks like the toy department at the Salvation Army, and there's a rusting wind chime that Erica finds deeply depressing.

It's almost a month since the murder-suicide, and the story has lost some of its urgency. No matter how big a story is, the world always moves on. Erica hopes Tuttle's widow, Amy, will have been out of the limelight long enough to gain some perspective. She was all over the news in the days following the crime, and she came across as lost, defensive, and overwhelmed. Erica thought about calling first, but decided a surprise visit would up the odds of getting unfiltered answers. She knocks on the front door. There's no response. She can hear the sound of a television from inside, so she knocks again.

"Yeah, coming." The door opens and Amy Tuttle stands there. She's in her midtwenties and looks wan and exhausted, with dark circles under her eyes and long scraggly hair, wearing a thin shift, barefoot. She takes one look at Erica and says, "Well, shut up, look who's here. Where's the camera crew?"

"It's just me," Erica says, extending her hand.

Amy Tuttle looks down at the proffered hand and finally shakes it. Hers is damp and limp. "What do you want?"

"Just a few minutes of your time, if possible. I'd like to ask you a couple of questions about your husband."

Amy tilts her head and narrows her eyes; for a moment a little smile plays at the corners of her mouth and Erica can tell that she enjoys the attention. Always a good sign for a reporter.

"Come on in."

Erica follows Amy into the house, which is so small it looks like it was built for a family of gnomes. The décor is over-the-hill-hippie— lots of low furniture, messy pillows, and swirly posters. Clearly none of her husband's life insurance payout has come through yet.

Amy plops down on what looks like a huge beanbag. "The kids are in school. Well, preschool."

Erica sits on a straight-back chair—it wobbles. "First of all, I'm very sorry about everything you and your family have gone through."

"It sucks."

"How are you and your children doing?"

Amy scoops up her unruly mane in her fingers and holds it over her head a moment before letting it cascade down. "We're getting by." Then she smiles. "I guess you could say I'm a lady-in-waiting."

"As you know, there's been very little progress in the Buchanan bombing case. I'm trying to find out why your husband did what he did."

"He did it to take care of me and Lucy and Corey. We've been living on mac 'n' cheese for three years."

"Most people would be incapable of committing murder and then suicide, no matter how much they wanted to take care of their family."

"You didn't know Peter . . ." Her voice softens. "He was a seeker. He didn't care about the material plane. Like jobs and stuff. He was searching for, you know, God and Nirvana and the meaning of the cosmos."

"Is that why he went away on retreats?"

"Yeah, he was always going away on his *quests*. Once he went to Costa Rica and climbed up into a tree house and took some jungle drug and didn't come down for three days."

"And didn't he go away in the weeks before . . . before he committed the crime?"

"Yeah, he did. He went out to Kripalu. You know, it's a big spiritualist yoga-y place over in Massachusetts."

"I've heard of it. Isn't it expensive?"

"Yeah, but he always did a work-study scholarship thing."

"What was the focus of the retreat?"

"I don't know . . . finding your inner light. Isn't that what they're all about?"

"And did he call when he was out there?"

"Now and then. He would get this all-natural high, he called it, and pretty much forget about us. He was supposed to be gone for a week. Then he stayed an extra week."

"Do you know why?"

"Yeah, he decided to sign up for some Chinese something or other."

Erica sits up straight. "Chinese what?"

"Some ancient Chinese spiritual quest workshop. He was all fired up about Confucius and Buddha and darma and karma."

"When he came back he was all fired up?"

"Well, really, when he got home he was kind of weird."

"Weird how?"

"Distant. Quiet. I thought it was because he was on a spiritual plane. Then a few days later he flew out to Detroit and . . . well, we all know what he did."

"Did he tell you who led the Chinese workshop?"

"He never told me stuff like that."

"And you never went with him?"

"Nah. The only thing I'm seeking is my kids' next meal."

"Well, when you get your insurance money, that will never be a problem again."

"Yeah. I went to a financial planner," she says, curling her legs up under her.

"So you're moving on?"

"Oh yeah, sure, I'm moving on. I'm moving on to waking up in a cold sweat in the middle of the night, seeing *you* standing there as Peter blows his brains out. I'm moving on to Lucy and Corey crying, screaming really, for no reason anytime day or night. I'm moving on to trying to know what to tell them when they ask me 'Why did Daddy do it?' for the five hundredth time." A dark, cynical expression settles on her face. "My husband killed a lot more than himself when he stuck that gun in his mouth."

"I'm very sorry."

Amy picks up a half-smoked joint from the table next to her and lights it. She takes a deep puff, holds it in, and exhales. Then she says, "Hey, it's all good."

On the drive down to the city on the thruway, Erica calls the Kripalu Center. She reaches Mindy Wilson, the head of enrollment.

"This is Erica Sparks with a couple of questions."

"Let me save you some breath. Peter Tuttle was here for a weeklong workshop called 'Spiritwalker—a Journey in Shamanic Empowerment.' When it was over he signed up for 'Rising Moon,' a five-day intensive in Chinese afterlife mythology. That ended on May 26 and he left campus that day. And, no, I don't know where he was between May 27 and June 2, when he returned home to Woodstock . . . I hope that didn't sound *too* rote."

"Can you tell me who led the Chinese afterlife workshop?"

"His name is Dave Brennan. Fascinating man. Former marine. He served in the Iraq War, suffered PTSD, and turned all his energies to spiritual growth. He says it saved his life."

"Do you have contact information for him?"

"We don't give that out. But you can find it on his website."

"Did you have any personal contact with Peter Tuttle?"

"I did, when he came into the office to sign up for the second workshop."

"What was your impression of him?"

"He was very anxious, was sweating profusely. Didn't look me in the eye. We get a lot of people who are missing something in their lives. They come here to try and find it. But even given that, he seemed like a young man at sea. Drowning. Desperate."

Ripe for the picking.

———

Erica arrives home close to midnight, exhausted physically and emotionally. And starving. She heads into the kitchen and finds a smoked salmon sandwich waiting for her on the counter, with a note in Becky's writing: *In case you need a little midnight sustenance.*

Erica sits at the kitchen table and takes a grateful bite. The sandwich is delicious, spiced with mustard and horseradish. She wonders what Becky made Jenny for dinner. Then she tries to piece together what she learned today—but her brain isn't up to the job. So she just savors the sandwich.

Then comes a soft cozy, "Hi."

Erica is momentarily startled. She looks up to see Becky standing in the doorway. She's wearing a nightgown and slippers.

"Thanks for the sandwich."

"We thought you might be hungry. I waited up to hear you come in."

"That's not necessary."

"I promised Jenny I would. She worries."

"How did homework go?"

"Well. How did things go up in Boston?"

"They went fine, Becky."

"Oh good. It sounds like you're on to something . . . ?"

"We'll see, won't we?"

There's a pause. Becky comes into the kitchen and absently wipes down the counter with her palm, then sweeps the stray crumbs into her other palm. It's a proprietary gesture, and Erica resents it.

"Big date tomorrow, huh? Jenny told me." Becky smiles. "She likes him."

"I'd like to keep my dates my business."

Becky frowns and pouts out her lower lip. "Message received." There's another pause. "Nighty-night," she says before padding off.

Erica tosses the rest of the sandwich. She's glad she's not wearing any makeup because she's too exhausted to even wash her face. As she enters her bedroom she notices that her bed has been turned down. She supposes it's a thoughtful gesture on Becky's part. Then why does it make her shudder?

CHAPTER 33 ———————————————

IT'S LATE SUNDAY MORNING AND Erica is sitting at her kitchen table savoring a cup of coffee. Jenny is spending the day with a school friend at her family's country house in Connecticut; she's going to sleep over and then drive straight to school with them in the morning. Which, if Erica is honest with herself, is an enormous relief. They've been getting along well, but having the apartment to herself feels like a great luxury. Jenny will be leaving for camp in the Adirondacks next week, and after that she'll spend three weeks at her father's in Massachusetts. Erica has mixed feelings about their summer apart, but it will certainly free her up to single-mindedly focus on her work.

As she waits for Josh to arrive for their "play date," she runs through where things stand with her investigation. There have been no leads in the hit-and-run death of Martin Vander, and the police are moving on to other cases. As they've told her numerous times, there's no evidence that it was anything more than a fleet-footed car thief who ran a red light. A terrible tragedy, but hardly a conspiracy. Erica thinks a breakthrough is more likely to come from the histories of Timothy Markum and Peter Tuttle. Both fit the profiles of troubled young men who are susceptible to programming or indoctrination of some sort.

Then there's Mike Ortiz, who, while hardly a troubled young man, was under severe psychological, emotional, and physical stress as a prisoner of war. She's beginning to wonder if a trip to Iraq—under the guise of research for her in-depth profiles of the two major party nominees—should be on her calendar.

Erica's phone rings. She doesn't recognize the incoming number, but she does recognize the area code—207. It can only be one person. Someone she hasn't spoken to in over a year. Someone her accountant sends three thousand guilt-assuaging dollars to every month. Someone she wants out of her life forever.

Her mother.

Unless . . . unless it's a hospital calling, or the police, to tell her some news—an overdose, a stroke, an arrest—news she needs to hear.

"Hello."

"Is that my little sweetie pie?"

It's not an emergency. It's *her*. The woman who spent Erica's childhood alternately taunting, ignoring, and abusing her. Still . . . she *is* her mother, sick, sad creature that she is, product of a rotten poverty-stricken childhood herself.

"Hi, Susan. What's up?"

"Gosh, pumpkin, can't a mommy call her little baby just to say hi?"

Yeah, right. So what's on sale at the supermarket?

"We haven't spoken in a year. I have a hard time believing this is just a little catch-up call."

As if they could ever catch up. Susan is incapable of an honest discussion, and any attempt to have one with her only leads to frustration, rage, and then terrible feelings of helplessness and sadness, a cosmic sadness.

"I just wanted to thank you, honey, for the checks you send. You know how much your ole momma needs them." Her voice is raspy and raw from decades of cigarettes and pot and booze and pills and screaming.

"You're welcome."

"I'm kind of a celebrity up here, on account of you being so famous.

I get my hair done every week, and you should see some of my new outfits."

"I'm sure they're lovely."

"Don't you take that high and mighty tone with me. Anyhow, I was thinking I might like to visit New York City. Everyone asks me when I'm going to see my famous daughter. And I've never met my granddaughter, little Jenny."

The last thing she wants is for Susan to meet Jenny. Erica's life is about breaking the chain of abuse and depravity. If she lets her mother in, she'll infect them with her pathology, her neediness, her sick head games, her narcissistic self-pity.

"I'm very busy right now. It's not a good time."

"Well, last time I checked you don't *own* the city. I could just come down, get a hotel room, see a show, and pop into your office. Unless, of course, you're ashamed of me."

Of course I'm ashamed of you. You should be ashamed of yourself.

And then Erica feels it. That guilt. That sadness. That yearning to make things better with Susan, to somehow move past some of the pain and ugliness, to build some semblance of a healthy relationship. With the woman who brought her into the world, who gave her life.

"When were you thinking of coming?" Erica asks, her voice tentative.

"Oh gosh, I don't know, honey. Maybe in a couple of weeks. I want to bring my new boyfriend. His name is Frankie."

"Hey there, Erica," Frankie calls in the background.

"You're going to love Frankie. He's smart. He worked a forklift but got injured on the job and now he's on permanent disability."

Erica pictures the two of them, loud, probably high, hygienically challenged, Maine yokels, showing up at GNN. Having dinner with Erica and Jenny. *No way.*

"I'm so busy with the election and my show, I'm always flying out of town on a moment's notice. Let's talk again after the election."

There's a pause and Erica hears her mother taking a deep pull on her cigarette. "Well, sweetie, I'm sorry you feel that way. As I said, there's no law against me and Frankie just hopping in his truck and heading down there."

"No, there isn't, is there? However, I might not be available."

"Well, that would be a terrible shame, pumpkin. Oh! One thing I forgot to tell you. The *National Enquirer* wants to do a story on me."

"What?!"

"Well, on me *and* you. On how we're estranged and all and have no contact."

"I send you a check every month and this is the thanks I get?"

"I'm sorry, sweetie pie, Frankie called them up. Truth is he likes the attention, doncha, hon? Why, he introduces me as Erica Sparks's mother. Like I don't even have a name of my own." She laughs, and the laugh makes her cough and hack and hock and suddenly Erica is hearing the soundtrack of her childhood.

This is nothing less than raw emotional blackmail. And it's not the first time it's happened.

"Do *not* talk to the *Enquirer*. If you do, the checks stop."

"Gosh, honey, that's harsh." And now Susan is crying, instantly bawling and blubbery. "I tried my best to be a good mommy. I tried and tried, but I guess I'm just a terrible person." She gulps air and the tears subside to a whimper. "You know there's two sides to the story. You were a hard child, always so moody, off reading and whatnot."

"Listen, I have to get off."

"The *Enquirer* asked for pictures of this crummy doublewide. We texted them some. Nobody can believe Erica Sparks's mother lives in a dump like this."

Suddenly it makes sense. "I bet you've got your eyes on a brand-new one, don't you?"

"How did you know that?"

Erica stands up and starts to pace. "How much is it?"

"Oh, it's so beautiful, honey. It has Corian countertops."

"How much is it?"

"Seventy-nine thousand dollars."

"I'll call my accountant."

The tears start again. "Oh, my sweet baby girl, you're my angel sent from heaven. I love you."

"I love you too," Frankie shouts.

Erica hangs up. There's a vase on the table and she'd like to pick it up and throw it against the wall. When your mother—*your mother*—is that messed up, that emotionally unstable, that creepy and manipulative, you can't escape feeling tainted. It's a stain that can never be removed, a scar that will never heal. Erica forces herself to do some deep breathing. She looks around the lovely living room and out to Central Park as her blood pressure returns to normal. She may be stained and scarred, but she's not going to let it stop her.

Her intercom rings. It must be Josh. Who is exactly the person she needs right now to pull her out of this dark mood. Josh is planning some kind of surprise and advised "knockabout clothes"—Erica is wearing shorts, a T-shirt, and sneakers, although she's not sure how she feels about being knocked about. "If that's Mr. Walters, tell him I'll be right down."

She walks out of her building to find Josh sitting on a bright-blue Vespa. "Good morning," he says with his warm, infectious grin.

"I've never ridden on one of these," Erica admits.

"It's the best way to get around Manhattan—zip-zip!" He hands her a helmet, and for a second she worries about what it will do to her hair. Josh gives her an encouraging grin and she puts it on. "Just put your arms around my waist and relax."

Erica complies and soon they're heading downtown on West Street with the Hudson River on their right. They pass the cruise ship terminal, the aircraft carrier *Intrepid* museum, and then the gracious Hudson River Park—it's filled with runners, dog walkers, blooming flowers, swaying grasses, skateboarders, and Rollerbladers—the rhythm of urban life. The bitter residue of her call with her mother fades away.

When they're stopped for a light, Josh turns his head and says, "Do you believe they wanted to turn this whole thing into a super highway? It would have cut the city off from the river. All the Powers That Be pushed for it."

"How was it stopped?"

"By a whole lot of little people getting together and fighting. Fighting hard."

"They're heroes, aren't they?"

"I sure think so. They changed the future of urban planning across the country. The whole focus moved from cars to people."

They zoom by the Chelsea Piers and then on the left the graceful twin glass Richard Meier apartment buildings. There's a wonderful sense of freedom in being on the Vespa—the open air, the wind, the water, the sun—it's exhilarating. They pull over in front of Pier 40, a massive, three-story structure. Josh hops off the Vespa and Erica follows.

"This is huge," Erica says.

"Yeah, it's a former marine terminal. We're just looking at the front; it's a square and the inside is a playing field. We're heading up there." Josh points to the roof—Erica looks up and sees trapeze apparatus, including two climbing platforms and a net.

"Whoa, Josh, I don't know."

"Just keep an open mind; that's all I ask."

They take an elevator up to the Trapeze School of New York and meet their instructor, a preternaturally fit young man with a toothy smile. He runs them through a warm-up and preliminary exercises on the ground, including how to grasp the bar with your hands, then pull your folded legs up to your head, grasp the bar with your knees, and let go with your hands. Josh's enthusiasm carries Erica through, though she keeps looking up at those platforms with trepidation.

And now she's standing on one—the trapeze bar in her hands, her safety harness secured, and the instructor behind her—while Josh is on the other platform, smiling across at her.

"Go!" the instructor says, and Erica does go—stepping off the platform into thin air as the bar swings her out and back. "Legs through," the instructor shouts, and she maneuvers her legs through her arms and her knees over the bar. "Let your hands go!" and now she's swinging by her legs with the greatest of ease! "Hands again" and she reverses the maneuver. "Drop the bar!" and she lets go and drops down into the net, bouncing in her harness. There's only one thing she wants: *more!*

She's back up on the platform and now Josh is swinging from the other platform and Erica swings out and gets her legs over the bar and releases her hands and swings by her knees and there's Josh, reaching out for her—reaching out his arms for her—and she grabs his hands and he pulls her off the bar and he's holding her and she's swinging free and then he says, "Gonna let you go," and he does and she bounces down into the net.

Erica hugs Josh when they're both down on terra not-so-firma, and she hugs the instructor and she looks up at the trapeze—*I can't believe I actually did that*. Then they're back on the Vespa, and now they're at Josh's townhouse on impossibly romantic Bank Street in the West Village.

"I live on the parlor and lower floor and rent out the top two floors. I mean, how much space does a bachelor need?" he says as he leads her in.

The parlor floor is a series of three large high-ceilinged rooms that ends in the kitchen, which overlooks a captivating rear garden. The walls are home to a striking collection of colorful folk art and old advertising signs. And, of course, there's a shoe the size of a canoe, a six-foot pencil, and a coffee cup that could double as a small lap pool.

"I made us a little crab salad for lunch," Josh says, opening the fridge. He sets out the salad, which looks delicious, sticks a baguette in the oven, opens a selection of cheeses and sets them out on a cutting board, and pours Erica a glass of his amazing homemade lemonade. Something about his ease, his manner, his compact physicality, his curly mop, his warm smile—and of course the trapeze—combine to make Erica feel tingly and alive. Her blood seems to be running a little faster; the world looks fresh. She's met her fair share of men in her life, but she's never met anyone quite like this exuberant iconoclast.

Yes, thoughts of Greg intrude on her idyll, but with each day the hurt lessens—and she gives Josh a lot of the credit.

They load up their plates and then head out the kitchen door and down a flight of steps to sit at the garden table surrounded by ivy, lilies, and grasses.

"Josh?"

"Yes?"

"That was a *blast*!"

They grin at each other—the attraction is snap-crackle-popping.

"Okay, so you know quite a bit about me. I'd like to know a little more about you," Erica says. "Like the basic hometown stuff."

"You asked for it. I was born and grew up in Bayside, Queens, a perfectly nice working-class neighborhood. Both of my parents were public school teachers; I have three sibs, so money was tight. We were a happy, even joyful family—but my folks made it clear from day one that they wanted us to get good educations and good jobs. It was unspoken, but they didn't mean as teachers—they wanted us to move up the financial ladder. So there was pressure there. I was a cut-up, in school plays, loved to sing and dance. I wanted to go into show biz, but boy, was that discouraged. I stuffed it and went to CCNY law school. You know the rest of the story. Miserable at work. Quit. Married a princess who lost interest the day I turned into a frog."

"Who's laughing last?"

"That's how I look at it. But I wish her well. She's Lisa's mother; she married some Wall Street guy; life goes on."

And they eat and laugh and chat and Erica feels a sense of perspective. Yes, she's involved in an important investigation that she has no intention of letting go of, but there's a danger that it could consume her, tie her in psychic knots, just about eat her alive. She has to remember that she has a life and a child and now maybe a nice guy. Sitting in his enchanting Greenwich Village backyard, she feels a tentative happiness.

"Okay, this is great, but I have to speak my piece," Josh says. His face grows serious and there's a hint of insecurity in his eyes. "I find you incredibly attractive, Erica, and I want to kiss you."

Erica can't contain the broad smile that spreads across her face. "Oddly enough, I feel the same way about you."

And they lean across the table and kiss. And it's the first of a dozen—oh, at least a dozen—and by the time Erica climbs into her Uber an hour later, she's walking on sunshine.

When she arrives at her building fifteen minutes later, Greg is standing on the sidewalk in front, waiting for her.

CHAPTER 34

ERICA STOPS COLD ON THE curb, not trusting her own eyes. Is it really Greg? Yes, it is. And seeing him—so handsome, so fit, his skin tawny and burnished by the Australian sun—instantly rekindles something inside her. Raw physical attraction, yes, but also a surge of tenderness. She was in love with this man. Is she still? Can they get back what they lost? Can she forgive him? Erica struggles to get her bearings.

Greg crosses the sidewalk to her. "You look shocked to see me."

"Sydney is a long way away."

"Too far." He reaches out to hold her, and an image of Laurel Masson flashes in her mind; she tenses up and takes a step backward.

They stand there with so much to say and nothing to say. Part of Erica wants to invite him up to her apartment to fall into his arms. Another part of her wants to slap him across the face.

"Can we talk?" he asks.

"Yes."

"Would you like to go to a café or . . . ?"

"How about the park?"

"The park is good."

They walk in silence, entering the park at Seventy-Second Street and finding a bench in Strawberry Fields, the garden dedicated to the memory of John Lennon, who was assassinated across the street in front of the Dakota apartment house. The centerpiece is the circular Imagine mosaic—and although it's only yards from the hustle and bustle of the city, there's a quietude here that Erica finds renewing. At this moment, however, quietude is the last thing she's feeling.

"Erica, I came back to apologize. I made a terrible mistake. But I can't face losing you."

She turns on him. "Maybe you should have thought of that *before* you slept with Laurel Masson."

"Don't I know it? I kick myself a hundred times a day. You have to believe me, Erica; she means nothing to me."

"You still work together, don't you?"

"We do. But I've made it very clear to her that it's over."

"You're going to go back to Sydney. You're going to get lonely. She's a beautiful woman . . ."

There's a pause, and then he turns and looks at her with those soulful green eyes. "Let's go down to City Hall on Monday morning and get married."

Erica jerks back on the bench, as if pushed by an invisible hand. They could be married in less than forty-eight hours. Man and wife. On second thought, it's the twenty-first century—let's make that "woman and husband." Husband who cheats. Within months of their being separated. Then she remembers their history—Greg's support during her early days at GNN, his bravery that fateful day in Miami, when he was shot and gravely wounded. His kindness and strength and bemused irony. The smell of his pine soap. Her confusion deepens. She's no longer sure what she feels.

"I'm not ready to take that step, Greg. You know I've been through this before. And Dirk at least had the excuse of my drinking for his affair."

"You can't forgive me?"

"I honestly don't know, Greg." She looks down at her hands: they're intertwined, curled and twisted together like a knot. "Trust is . . . it's easy to lose and hard to regain."

"Oh, come on now. I didn't commit a murder."

He doesn't get it.

They sit there in silence for what seems like a long time. Greg is sorry, but his apology feels perfunctory. It's as if by flying back and showing remorse and proposing a City Hall marriage, his affair would be erased. But it isn't. She feels betrayed and humiliated and deeply hurt. She remembers the night she realized he was sleeping with Laurel Masson, the way her stomach hollowed out, her world hollowed out. Trust doesn't come easy to her—how could it when she couldn't trust her own mother and father? To have it stomped on, publicly really, when you consider that tweet of Greg and Masson arm in arm. Erica feels a flash of anger. "I was on a date today," she says.

"I don't think I need to know that. But, lucky guy, okay, lucky guy. What more can I say?"

And now Greg looks a little lost, like a kid, a boy who has been hurt and doesn't understand why. And Erica, for the first time since she saw that tweet, feels a rekindling of her deep affection for him. He's a good man. The man she was going to marry. Her throat tightens. Being a grown-up is so complicated and so sad and sometimes we hurt each other when maybe we don't need to.

Greg leans forward, elbows on his knees. He takes a deep breath and says, "The network goes live in six weeks. I can't possibly get away before then. Will you at least wait until I come back before making any final decision?"

That's not really asking for very much. Goodness knows, Erica has a busy couple of months coming up. She nods. He smiles. The mood between them lightens. "You must have terrible jet lag," she says.

"It is awfully light for the middle of the night."

Erica puts her hand on his and squeezes. "I miss you at work."

"That's not where I want you to miss me, but I'll take what I can get. What are you working on?"

"Something important."

"Say more."

"Well, I'm hitting more walls than I'd hoped, so I may be on a wild goose chase, but in a nutshell? I'm not sure Mike Ortiz is fit to be president."

"You know, I've never been that impressed with him. He's wooden and rote, and doesn't seem like the brightest crayon in the box."

"His wife, on the other hand, is terrifying."

"Hey, I've got a couple of ears here if you want to avail yourself."

Erica realizes, with something of a jolt, that while she may not trust Greg with her emotions, she trusts him completely when it comes to work and her investigation. She gives him a quick overview.

When she's finished he's quiet for a moment and then says, "You know, where there are this many unanswered questions, there's usually fire." He turns to her, his animation growing. "It really sounds to me like something very creepy happened to Ortiz when he was a prisoner. It's the only explanation that makes sense. *What* was done, *who* did it, and *why* are three big unknowns. The stakes here really couldn't be higher. And when you're dealing with ambition on this scale, well, *ruthless* is a mild word for what people will do. You have to be very careful for your own safety, Erica. Assume they know *everything* you're doing. And call on me 24/7. You've got a tiger by the tail. And it's a rabid tiger."

Erica feels a fear rat scurry up her spine. But then again, danger is part of the job description. "Yeah, I think I should head home and do some more digging."

Erica and Greg walk out of the park and down two blocks to her building. They reach the entrance and turn toward each other.

"Thank you for coming," Erica says.

"I'm coming back."

Part of Erica still wants to fall into his arms. Part of her doesn't. It all feels unresolved, but looking at the vulnerability in his eyes, what she feels most strongly is tender regret.

Back in her apartment, Erica sits at her computer and Googles Dave Brennan, the former marine who led the workshop on Chinese afterlife mythology that Peter Tuttle took just before he killed Markum. Brennan has a website that details his spiritual growth and awakening after he returned from the Iraq War and suffered PTSD. Casting about for meaning and solace, he developed a profound interest in Chinese religion, spirituality, and mysticism. There's a phone number, and she calls and gets his voice mail. His voice is resonant and spectral, even hypnotic. Erica leaves a message.

CHAPTER 35

CELESTE TOOLS HER MERCEDES DEEP into the lush, wooded landscape of northwestern Marin County, past the tony suburbs of Ross and San Anselmo and Fairfax, through rustic Woodacre and into Nicasio, where the last vestiges of suburbia give way to vast stretches of undeveloped hills and forests and streams and curvy roads that lead to hidden shacks and castles tucked into the folds of the landscape. She turns off Nicasio Valley Road onto Old Rancheria and continues until she comes to a tall and imposing metal entrance gate.

She presses a button and smiles at a camera, and the gate swings open and she follows the serpentine track up and up, through brown hills dotted with stands of pine, oak, and eucalyptus, until she rounds a bend and there it is—revealed in all its beauty and strength and promise: Eagle's Nest.

Headquarters. Or, as the world knows it—Lily Lau's weekend house. Celeste feels that familiar surge of adrenaline as she enters the compound.

Rising power.

She parks in the spot reserved for her. Lily is so thoughtful that way. In every way, really. Celeste gets out of her car and looks around, inhales the fresh country air, approvingly notes the discreet coming and going—at the periphery, of course, never in the sanctum sanctorum—of several black-clad Chinese men and women, unsmiling, laser-focused, knowing how great their responsibility is to the future.

She looks at the view west, out toward the Pacific—it just keeps going, past Hawaii, to the future.

Rising power.

There's the main house, surprisingly not massive—Lily is too classy for one of those nouveau monstrosities—designed in the timeless style of Frank Lloyd Wright, wood and glass, long and low, at one with the land. It's cantilevered over the ridgeline, and evokes an eagle about to take flight—in search of prey. And then, arrayed around a graceful central courtyard, are the three "guesthouses." Guesthouses indeed.

Celeste stands there in the cool northern California sunshine feeling as if she is on the cusp of greatness, as if all this—Eagle's Nest, the sun, the sky, the breeze, *Lily*, their work together—is part of her destiny, her charmed and dappled life, a life that will earn her not only unimagined power but a unique place in the history books.

To the naked eye, of course, all this looks like nothing more than evidence of Lily Lau's success, drive, and professionalism. She's so clever: to provide cover and give her an excuse to spend time away from the Ortiz headquarters in the city, Lily has set up a satellite campaign and fundraising office in one of the guesthouses.

Rising power.

Celeste can sense, can *feel* the hum of history being written, right here, right now, and each time she visits and the election grows closer, the hum is slightly higher pitched—as the dawn breaks and the new world order begins.

Rising power.

Celeste strides into Lily's house—*Lily, oh Lily!* The inside is open and immaculate and lined with redwood planks, the grain perfectly aligned piece-to-piece to form a continuous pattern—the painstaking workmanship evokes the ancient traditions of the Chinese temples. The house is a work of art. But everything Lily creates is a work of art. Including the future.

Rising power.

How foolish America is, squandering its moral authority and trillions of dollars fighting unwinnable wars in the vast messy sandbox of the Middle East. While China keeps its head down, sticks to its knitting—*how Mummy loved that expression!*—and spends its billions buying influence in every developing country on the planet. But Beijing is after a bigger prize. The biggest prize of all.

Where is Lily? The house stretches out in front of Celeste, one vast room that ends in a wall of glass that looks out on the sculpted evergreen garden—another work of art—and then the infinity pool that hangs off the edge of tomorrow.

There she is; there's Lily, outside, on a chaise, reading something on her iPad. Celeste's pulse quickens, as it has quickened every single time she has seen Lily since that first time—that fateful Silicon Valley day twenty-five years ago—when she spotted her across the classroom in Introduction to Chinese History.

"Lily!" she calls, unable to keep the urgency, the excitement, out of her voice. Lily turns and smiles and raises her hand in a small wave. Celeste joins her in the garden. Lily's wearing a geometric black shift that looks like it was designed by an architect. She's so chic. And it comes to her so effortlessly, not like all those straining SF socialites drowning in tulle and tooth whiteners. "What are you reading?"

"Stephen King. I want him on a stamp."

"That shouldn't be hard to arrange. When and if."

"If?" Lily narrows her eyes.

"I mean *when*, of course, *when.*"

There's a pause, and it's filled with Lily's expectation. Celeste reaches into her bag and takes out a small jewelry box. She hands it to Lily and holds her breath as she opens it. It contains an Art Deco ring—two rectangular rubies surrounded by black jade. Lily examines it and Celeste waits—still, after twenty-five years—for her approval. Lily slips it on her finger and holds it up to the light.

"It's lovely, Celeste. Thank you."

"It was my aunt's. Cartier. She left it to me. Red and black are your colors."

Lily stands up and looks at Celeste. Then she lifts the shift over her head and drops it on the chaise. She's wearing a sleek one-piece molded to her tall, lean lithe body. She really is a goddess among us.

Lily does a couple of slow sensual stretches and then she walks over to the pool and dives, a perfect dive—sheer grace, another work of art. She does a half dozen laps and climbs out of the pool and smooths back her inky hair and stands there looking out toward the Pacific. Then she turns and smiles at Celeste, crosses to her, and takes her face in her hands; her long, cool fingers cup Celeste's cheeks. And she leans in . . . close . . . closer . . . and whispers, "Let's get to work."

CHAPTER 36 ———————————————

THE SLAVE—OH, SHE'S NOT *REALLY* a slave, silly (or is she?)—is a young Chinese girl who is forbidden to look Lily in the eye. She brings out their green tea, grown on a tiny organic farm high in the Himalayas, and then bows and leaves.

"I'm a little bit worried about this Erica Sparks," Lily says.

"What's the latest?" Celeste asks. She's glad that Lily has put on a robe, it makes it easier to concentrate.

"Well, the cow"—that's their nickname for pathetic Becky—"overheard Erica telling her spawn that she had to go up to Harvard to meet with a professor about a book. It was the ancient text."

"And do we know where Martin Vander got the book?"

"We hacked into his computer. He found it at a rare book dealer's in Queens. Using an Internet search. So sloppy of us not to have found it first. The person responsible for that oversight has been disposed of."

"Vander's death was a terrible tragedy—in that it didn't happen *before* he found that text," Celeste says.

The two women smile at each other—small, appropriate smiles—and the air between them crackles with their shared secret, their twisted bond. Ordering the death of another human being is a special kind of magic. The rush is indescribable. Why, it's almost addictive.

"It's really Becky's fault that the manuscript made it to Harvard. She should have searched Erica's briefcase. It's part of her job," Lily says.

"She was probably too busy polishing the bottom of Erica's shoes."

They smile again. They have so much *fun* together. And their best years are ahead of them. The day after the election, President-elect Ortiz will name Lily Lau his chief of staff. Then Celeste will be working alongside Lily every day. When all is said and done, that's what drives her. They both understand that.

"Do you think Erica is a real danger?" Celeste asks.

"Not at this point. We've done our homework. But we can't be too careful. And of course, we need her. And want her. As an ally in the months and years ahead. She has a lot of power. The American people trust her. However, right now I'm not sure *we* can."

"The spawn is going away to camp. So Becky won't be in the apartment as much. We may miss things."

"Good point." Lily picks up a tiny sliver of a phone and presses a button.

"Hello," comes Becky's quivery voice through the speaker.

"Have you been a good girl?"

"Yes."

"We need live-feed cameras in Erica's apartment—living room, bedroom, office."

"Oh, you do? Okay, okay."

Lily mutes the phone and says to Celeste, "We can't have a tech put them in, tradesmen have to sign in downstairs at Erica's building." She unmutes. "You will get a call from a man. He will come to your apartment with the equipment and will instruct you how to install it. Do you understand?"

"Will I be able to do it?"

"I hope that's a rhetorical question."

"Oh . . . ah, yes, of course, ha-ha," Becky blubbers.

"Because if you *aren't* able to do it, well, there *will* be consequences. Let me know when they're up and running."

"Yes, yes, of course I will."

Lily gives Celeste one of her mischievous smirks before adding, "Oh, Becky, put one in her shower too."

"In her shower?"

"Yes, you never know what Erica might be up to in the shower."

CHAPTER 37 ————————————

ERICA AND JENNY HAVE JUST arrived at the corner of Seventy-Ninth Street and Fifth Avenue, where the bus is loading to take Jenny up to Camp Woodlands on St. Regis Lake in the Adirondacks. Erica wanted to drive Jenny, but the camp recommends the bus—it gives the girls a chance to bond on the six-hour trip and minimizes teary good-byes.

Still, there are plenty of tears, especially from younger first-time campers. Jenny is being very grown-up. Maybe that's one of the unintended benefits of a rocky childhood—you don't sweat the small stuff like saying good-bye to your mom for six weeks of fun. Erica holds back and watches as Jenny hands her duffel bag to the driver, who slides it into the luggage compartment.

Jenny looks around at her fellow campers. She recognizes a couple of fellow Brearley students and waves. Then she notices a shy, tear-stained girl whose parents have just departed. She walks over to the girl and says, "Hi, I'm Jenny. This should be interesting. Want to sit next to me? I've got a stash of chocolate-covered cashews."

The girl sniffles and gives Jenny a grateful smile. Erica's pride could just about burst. And then she lets herself claim a little of that pride for herself.

Jenny comes over to Erica, who hugs her and kisses her again and again. "I think you're going to have a blast, young lady."

"If I can stop worrying about you."

"Your old mom can take care of herself."

They look at each other, and Erica's eyes well up.

"Cut that out," Jenny says. "We Sparks girls don't cry."

"You're darn right we don't," Erica manages as a tear runs down her cheek.

"Maybe you'll come for parents' weekend."

"I'm planning on it."

They hug one last time, and Jenny climbs onto the bus. She gets a window seat, and as the bus pulls away from the curb, she and Erica exchange one last wave. Then Jenny turns to her seatmate.

Erica decides to walk home through Central Park. As she passes Cleopatra's Needle—the towering ancient Egyptian obelisk covered with hieroglyphics—her cell rings. It's Dave Brennan, the former marine who led the Chinese afterlife workshop Peter Tuttle took just before he killed Timothy Markum and then himself.

"Hi, Dave, this is Erica. Thanks for getting back to me."

"I'm afraid I'm not going to be much help. Just ask the FBI." He has a friendly, matter-of-fact voice, with none of the ethereal woo-woo of his voice mail. That must be a marketing tool.

"Can you tell me your impressions of Tuttle?"

"You know, these workshops I run are tricky. They attract a lot of sincere curious people. And they attract some . . . marginal people. I would put Tuttle firmly into that second category. He was needy, a little dirty, moody, attention seeking. He would laugh—this barking laugh—at inappropriate times. I would go so far as to say he was maybe borderline schizophrenic."

"Did he hook up with anyone in the class? There are days between the end of your workshop and his return home that are unaccounted for."

"He started sleeping with this older woman in the workshop. She was another marginal. Way marginal."

LIS WIEHL WITH SEBASTIAN STUART

"How so?"

"She was a large woman. Who believed in exposing as much of her pulchritude as possible. She said it was her 'pagan prerogative.' She also claimed to speak Mandarin—and that she used it in her conversations with Confucius."

Erica stops walking. "Do you know her name? Where she lives?"

"Diane Novotny. She lived in Brattleboro, Vermont."

"Lived?"

"She killed herself the day after Tuttle did."

"Oh no. How?"

"She drank antifreeze. Tore her guts apart."

"Thanks for the information. Listen, what attracted you to Chinese afterlife mythology?"

"I think it's because I'm an optimist."

"An optimist?"

"Yeah—there's got to be something better than this."

172

CHAPTER 38

ERICA OPENS HER FRONT DOOR. As she walks down the long entry hall a wave of loneliness washes over her. Jenny's gone and the apartment is so big and there are no voices, no laughter, no music—just the echoes of her footfalls.

As consumed as she is with her investigation, she does have a day job. A demanding one. She'll hunker down in her office and do some prep work for the conventions—the Democrats kick theirs off next week in Chicago. She heads down to her bedroom to get her reading glasses off her bedside table.

Just as she walks into her bedroom, Becky walks out of her bathroom.

The girl's mouth falls open and she stops dead in her tracks. Then she flushes red.

"What are you doing in my bathroom?"

"I thought Jenny's bus was scheduled to leave at noon."

"Would it be all right to be snooping in my bathroom if it *had* left at noon?"

"I wasn't snooping, Erica, I swear. I was just making sure everything was clean and the way you like it. I know Yelena will only be coming in once a week to clean now that Jenny's gone, and I thought maybe the towels needed to be washed or—"

"Do they?"

Becky smiles, a twitchy little smile. "No. If they had, they'd be in my arms. Everything looks fine in there."

"Okay then, you can head out. And with Jenny gone, you won't be in the apartment much either, so we'll see each other at the office."

"Don't you think you might want me to run errands and stuff, drop things off, that kind of thing?"

"Maybe. But why don't you give me your keys."

"But how will I get in?"

"I'll call downstairs and have them let you in. That way there will be a record of your visits."

Becky looks as if she might start to cry. "They're out in my bag."

"Well, let's go get them then."

They walk out into the living room and Becky hands over her keys. Erica escorts her to the front door.

"Would you like me to help you prepare for the convention? Or even come to Chicago with you?" Becky asks hopefully.

"I think everything is under control."

"Okay, see you at GNN tomorrow."

"No doubt," Erica says.

As she locks the door behind Becky, she thinks that with Jenny gone she really won't be needing a personal assistant for a while. She heads back down to her bedroom to get her glasses. That's when she notices that her lingerie drawer is open.

CHAPTER 39 ⸻

ERICA LOOKS OUT THE WINDOW as her plane banks down for its arrival in Chicago, host of the Democratic convention. Erica hasn't spent a lot of time in the city, but she's spent enough to know that she loves it—the way it's set against the curve of Lake Michigan, the incredible architecture. But it's the people that really win her over—they're friendly and fun and soulful and smart and even their swagger has a sly edge.

GNN producers, directors, and technicians have been in the city for weeks setting up. Erica will be reporting from a skybox at McCormick Place; the rest of the operation is housed in a series of trailers outside the arena.

The convention itself holds no surprises. What little suspense there is concerns who Mike Ortiz will pick as his running mate. Even there, it's pretty much a done deal that Governor Alice Marshall of Missouri will get the nod—the Dems need a Midwestern woman to try and offset Lucy Winters's appeal.

Erica is much more concerned—make that obsessed—with getting inside the heads and hearts of Mike and Celeste Ortiz. Every instinct in her body tells her there is something strange and dangerous going on. But without proof, any accusation she might make would get her laughed right out of a career. She's a journalist. She needs facts. And she keeps hitting brick walls. And antifreeze-swigging New Age freaks.

She arrives at her suite at the Four Seasons and unpacks, feeling anxious and frustrated. Her requests for an interview with Ortiz have been turned down. He's also turned down every other cable network, choosing to speak only to Diane Sawyer, in another savvy nod to the gender dynamics of the race. But what is Erica going to do for the next three days—report on the tedious speeches, celebrity sightings, and hyperpartisanship that will define the overblown confab? Although they were before her time, she yearns for the days when nominees were actually picked at the parties' conventions, where they were filled with horse-trading, rumors, smoky rooms, and real suspense.

Erica sits at the suite's desk and goes over her schedule—she's due at McCormick Place in an hour for a walk-through—but she has a hard time concentrating. She calls Moy.

"Hey there."

"I'm in Chicago, trying to figure out how to get close to the Ortizes. He's being kept under wraps."

"Listen, Erica, this is a two-way street. You host the go-to show on cable news. They need you almost as much as you want them. She may be easier to get to than him. Get ahold of her schedule. She's bound to be doing some parties or fundraisers. Show up."

"Show up and what? Ask her if she's controlling her husband? She'll laugh me off with, 'Well, I certainly hope so.' Moy, look at the body count—the Buchanans and the bystanders, Markum, Tuttle, Vander, Tuttle's Vermont lady friend. Everyone who could possibly help answer my questions has been offed."

"Are you afraid for your own life?"

"Yeah, I am."

"Good. Stay that way."

Erica hangs up and heads over to the arena. It's barely controlled pandemonium as final preparations are made—lights, sounds, seating, special effects, balloons, the thousand details large and small that translate to a seamless show for the folks at home. Erica begins to feel her juices flowing. Canned, overproduced, predictable—say what you will—this is democracy in action. It matters. A lot.

Her sky booth has a great view of the floor and the stage—the stage on which, in two nights, Mike Ortiz will be making the most important speech of his career, formally introducing himself to the American people and asking them to elect him president.

As Erica checks out her seat, her desk, her mic, she has a moment where she wonders if her suspicions are all wrong—the product of an overactive imagination and a little understandable paranoia, in light of the evil Nylan Hastings turned out to be up to. After all, Ortiz is well-spoken, has demonstrated leadership in the Senate and proven his appeal—the people of California elected him by a landslide. Could he really be some kind of brainwashed human robot? The fact is she has no *evidence* that he is. Is she chasing a chimera down a dead-end street? She could fold up her tent right now. Her life would be so much easier.

As she heads back to her hotel, Josh calls. Their trapeze date was two weeks ago and they've only spoken once since, and she didn't return his last call. She debates whether to answer this one. The truth is she's still tangled up in blue about Greg. His surprise visit stirred up all her old feelings and left her torn. Josh is a really great guy, but . . . but . . . does he stir her soul the way Greg does? And if he doesn't yet, might he later? And as for Greg, she still feels once bitten, twice not ready to trust again.

She decides not to pick up and listens as he leaves his message: "Erica, it's Josh. Listen, if I'm being a pest, too bad. Until I get my marching orders I'm moving forward. I had so much fun the last time we were together. Please call me, I can't help but worry about you. This is your pal, Josh."

His concern touches her. But right now her romantic complications are one complication too many. She texts him: IN CHICAGO BUSY WITH CONVENTION PREP. TALK SOON.

Back at the hotel, Erica gives herself three days to come to a decision to either curtail or double down on her investigation. She orders a light dinner from room service, does a little work, and is in bed by ten. Just as she's dozing off, her phone rings.

"Erica, it's Celeste Ortiz. Can we talk? Off the record?"

CHAPTER 40 —————————————

AT TEN THE NEXT MORNING Erica walks into the soaring Palmer House lobby—it's one of the country's classic old hotels, but she has no time to admire it. As she walks over to the elevators and heads up to the presidential suite for her meeting with Celeste Ortiz, she reminds herself to play her cards close to the vest. She has no doubt that Celeste has an agenda. Well, so does she.

She knocks on the door of the suite, and Celeste answers it herself. "Erica, welcome," she says in a low-key way, smiling warmly, ushering her in. Like they were a couple of old friends.

Celeste is wearing a white T-shirt, khaki shorts, no makeup, and her hair is up in a wide elastic band. Talk about dressing down . . . She looks like she just stepped off the elliptical at the gym. Erica is surprised to see that there are no staff bustling around. It's just the two of them.

Celeste shows her over to a cozy seating area in front of a fireplace. "I ordered us some tea."

"I'm good, thanks."

Celeste is silent for a moment and then says, "Isn't it nice to be in a quiet place for a few minutes?"

Erica nods.

"Sometimes I just want to walk away from the whole thing." Celeste pours herself a cup of tea and takes a sip. "But I think the country needs my husband. Speaking of our families, how's Jenny?"

"She's fine. Off at camp."

"What fun. And your lucky fiancé?"

This is getting awfully personal awfully quickly. Erica doesn't answer.

"Distance can be tricky in a relationship. Sometimes it's the best thing. When my husband was a prisoner in Iraq, I felt closer to him than I ever had . . ." Celeste puts down her teacup and clasps her fingers together. "It was difficult . . ."

Erica sees an opening and jumps discreetly, matching Celeste's low-key manner. "Did you get any reports or updates when he was in captivity? Was he able to communicate with you personally?"

"No, I was in the dark. I would get reports from the CIA, but they weren't verified. I never could be sure if he was even still alive."

Erica knows enough about war to know that if enough cash changes hands, information is available. "Did you make any back channel attempts to reach him?"

"I'm not sure what you mean."

"In the fog of war, money can work miracles."

Celeste turns and looks out the window, takes a sip of tea, and then says, "Yes, I did try. Of course. What wife wouldn't? But even my money proved useless against jihadism." She exhales and sits up straight. "Do you *ever* take off your reporter's hat?"

"No. I even swim in it."

"That might be unwise. It could block your sightlines."

"I'm a strong swimmer."

"What if you get caught in a riptide?"

"I always make it back to shore."

"Watch out for rogue waves." Celeste gives her a tight smile that slowly morphs into a warm one. "Listen, I wanted us to meet like this for a couple of reasons. First of all, both Mike and I thought your piece on us at home was terrific. You captured our love for each other and our commitment to the nation. And, by the way, you handled poor Jasper's death pitch-perfectly that day."

"You lost a family member."

"If only we could care about *people* as much as we do our pets." She tucks her legs under her, which only adds to the informal, welcoming vibe.

But it's a casual old-money pose—curled up in an armchair—that for a moment ignites Erica's social insecurities. Do prep schools teach courses in casual confidence?

"My husband feels very at ease with you. As do I."

"That's always nice to hear."

"You showed us kindness; we would like to return it." Celeste gives Erica a flitting look, but there's no mistaking the proffered quid pro quo. "Politics is such an awful business, isn't it? There's so much backbiting and petty payback. *Threats*. People are always looking for ways to tear you down."

"It's important to question power."

"Yes. But not to engage in character assassination. To go looking for dirt under every rug. If my husband should have the honor of serving as president, he's going to change that culture."

"It won't be easy."

Celeste looks Erica in the eye. "He won't tolerate it. Neither will I."

Well, you're not in the White House yet, Celeste, and I'm going to keep looking under every rug.

Erica is burning with curiosity about the "kindness" they want to bestow on her, but she doesn't want to appear overeager. "How confident are you of winning?"

"The polls are looking good. But you never know until the last vote is counted. Something unexpected could come up, but we're working to minimize that possibility."

"Are you? How?"

"Vigilance." She looks Erica in the eye. "By monitoring my husband's enemies. Staying one step ahead."

"If your husband has nothing to hide, his enemies will come up empty-handed."

"Well, sometimes people make reckless charges. Their imaginations run away with them." She lets the words hang in the air a moment, then switches gears. "In any event, we do have a little surprise up our sleeve to create some excitement here in Chicago . . ."

"Which is?"

"The chattering class assumes that Mike to going to name Alice Marshall as his running mate." She takes another sip of her tea. "Well, they assume wrong."

The kindness is revealed. And it's a real scoop. In spite of any misgivings Erica may have about the Ortizes, announcing his VP pick would be a real coup for Erica and GNN. Mort Silver would be over the moon. Erica leans forward. Celeste smiles and leans back in response—the fish is on the line.

"Can you tell me who he *is* going to pick?"

Celeste lowers her voice, *très intime.* "I can't. Not just yet. I hope you don't think I'm being coy."

"A tease maybe."

"Why don't I ask Mike? If he agrees, we'll give the scoop to our favorite reporter."

"She would be happy to have it. Providing it comes with no strings attached."

"Strings are for puppets. You look to me like you're made of flesh and blood. Speaking of flesh, I better get my face on. I'm delivering welcoming remarks to a women's luncheon in an hour."

In the elevator heading back down, Erica replays the scene. They're trying to co-opt her. Keep your friends close and your enemies closer.

Her phone rings. It's Knut Ludlow, her building's superintendent. What on earth could he be calling about?

"Hello, Knut, this is Erica."

"I'm sorry to disturb you, Ms. Sparks, but there's been a burst pipe in the master bathroom two stories up from you. We've got the leak under control, but there was damage in the apartment above yours. I'd like to give your place a quick check. I need your permission to enter the apartment."

"I'd appreciate it."

"I'll call you back with a report."

"Where exactly was the leak above me?"

"In the shower stall."

CHAPTER 41

AS SHE'S IN THE ELEVATOR heading up to her room, Knut Ludlow calls her back.

"We made a disturbing discovery in your bathroom, Ms. Sparks."

"Oh dear, is there terrible water damage?"

"No, there's no water damage. But the plumber saw what he thought was a small water bug in the upper corner of the shower stall. He only saw it because he was on a stepladder doing a thorough check for leaks. He reached up to squish it, but it wasn't an insect. It was a tiny camera."

Erica feels the blood drain from her head. She puts a hand on the elevator railing.

"Ms. Sparks, are you there? Are you all right?"

"Yes, I'm here. Can you please text me a picture of the camera immediately?"

"Of course."

By the time Erica reaches her suite, she has the picture. The camera is tiny. But its size is the least of her concerns. She flashes back to Becky coming out of her bathroom. The girl is troubled, but is she so creepy and twisted that she would actually put a camera in Erica's shower? The implications are too disturbing to dwell on. If there's one camera, are there more? Erica needs help and she needs it now.

She texts the picture to Greg and then calls him. It's around midnight in Sydney. Hopefully he's up. And not in the arms of another woman.

"Erica, I just got your text."

"That camera was planted in my shower."

"Whoa. Do you know by who?"

"I'm pretty sure it was Becky Sullivan, my personal assistant. But I want the whole apartment searched by a security expert. Do you know any?"

"There's a fantastic private security firm—Firewall Partners. We used them a couple of times when I was at GNN. Do you want me to call them?"

"I'll do it."

"Keep me posted."

There's a moment of silence between them. They both realize how seamlessly they connected just now, getting right to the heart of the problem and taking the right action to address it. Erica feels a swelling of emotion. "Thank you, Greg."

"*Any*time."

Erica Googles Firewall Partners, gets their number, calls, and speaks to president Gary Goldstein. She quickly explains the situation.

"I'm very sorry you're facing this threat. We'll be there within the hour."

"I'll call the superintendent and tell him you're on the way."

Erica hangs up and collapses onto a couch, reeling. She's been hit by a rogue wave.

CHAPTER 42 ———————————

BECKY IS JUST COMING HOME from work. It's past nine and dark, but she was glad she stayed so late, tying up every loose end she could find for Erica, who is out in Chicago. She wants to be *helpful*; she needs to be, to make amends for what she did. What she *had* to do. What they *made* her do. But it's all right now. Erica won't know. She believed Becky when she said she was in the bathroom to check that everything was in tip-top shape. Becky was a cool customer. Erica still likes her, Jenny *loves* her. Everything is going to be fine.

Becky is on Seventy-Eighth Street between Second and Third. It's a quiet block at this time of night. Her building is right around the corner on Second. Home. Her mind turns to dinner. She'll just call out for a pizza—that's what she loves about New York, the fingertip living. She hugs her bag to her chest. Secreted in the bottom—carefully wrapped in tissue—is her latest trophy and talisman to add to the Erica collection that sits under her bed in the vintage suitcase, calling to her. She'll wait until after she's eaten and washed her hands, and then she'll pull out the suitcase, slowly, and open it. There's Erica's scarf that holds traces of her Chanel No 5; there's the soap from her shower, the strands of her hair. She'll place the tissue-wrapped treasure beside them and then slowly, gently, she'll unwrap Erica's soft silk slip.

Becky quickens her pace, nearing the corner, and then there's a man on either side of her. They're both in dark suits and they smile at her and each one takes an arm—they're wearing black gloves—and they turn her toward the curb where there's a black car waiting with its back door open.

"We're just going to go for a little ride," one of the men says. Becky pulls back, but the men are strong and they steer her toward the car, and there's a couple up ahead but they don't turn around.

Now she's in the back of the car between the two men. The driver, another man in a dark suit wearing black gloves, pulls away from the curb.

"Who are you?! Where are we going?"

"We're just going for a little drive," one of them says.

Becky feels fear rising up in her stomach, her throat. Suddenly she's freezing but she breaks out in a sweat. *"Who are you? Where are you taking me?"*

The men ignore her, and she feels panic flood over her. She has to get out of this car; she has to get out. She lunges across one of the men and grabs for the door handle—*it's gone!*

"Let me out. Please let me out!"

"Calm down, Becky; we're not going to hurt you. We're from the government." When he says that, all three of the men smile.

"You are? From the government? Oh, okay. *Which government?"*

The men smile again.

"Why is the government taking me? Where are you taking me?!"

Now they're farther uptown, on a street Becky's never been on before. She sees a sign: *Morningside Drive.* It's a nice quiet street, so quiet, with no shops, just apartment buildings on one side and an old stone wall on the other. It looks like there's a park down below the stone wall, way down below. Maybe they really are from the government; they're nice men who are taking her to meet someone in the government who lives in one of the nice buildings. There are so few people on the street, there's no one to help her. Should she scream?

The car pulls over.

"We're just going to go and meet someone down in the park. He wants to talk to you, you have nothing to be afraid of."

But she is afraid; she's never been so afraid in her life. She's sweating and shaking and it's hard to breathe. And now she's outside the car and the men lead her over to the wall.

"See that man down there?" one of the men says.

Becky looks down. The drop is so steep and there's a big rock outcropping at the bottom. And then she does see a man. Down in the park, sitting on a bench in the dark, smoking. "I see him," she says, but her mouth is quivering and it's hard to talk.

"He wants to see *you*," one of the men says. And then he laughs. A mean laugh.

And then Becky is lifted off her feet and now she's tumbling, tumbling through the air toward the rocks below, and she opens her mouth to scream—but nothing comes out.

CHAPTER 43 ———————————————

ERICA IS IN GNN'S BOX at McCormick Place, anchoring the network's coverage. It's all pretty dull, with one speaker after another spouting party-line pabulum. The only piece of suspense is: Who will Ortiz pick as his running mate? Erica has been slipping hints that there may be a surprise pick, but without knowing who it is, she can't go too far out on a limb.

The energy in the hall is pretty subdued and there are hundreds of empty seats. Everyone is waiting for the main event—Mike Ortiz's acceptance speech tomorrow night. Luckily, Erica can throw coverage to the half dozen reporters GNN has down on the floor, where they do one-on-ones with elected officials of all ranks who spout more same old same old.

If Fred Buchanan had lived, this convention would have had true drama. But he was blown into a thousand pieces by a bomber seemingly without a motive, or even a life. And in many ways the country has moved on. Not Erica. She *needs* to feel that she is doing everything she can to find answers and bring some kind of closure to the Buchanan family, to herself, and to the nation. If Tuttle was acting alone, so be it. If not, then his coconspirators must be brought to justice.

During a commercial break Eileen McDermott comes over. "Celeste Ortiz is out in the hallway and would like to see you."

Erica feels her adrenaline spike. "This could be the news I've been waiting for. Throw it to the floor if I'm not back in time."

"Erica!" Celeste is glowing like a Christmas tree; she looks like she's just back from a week at a spa. She's carrying a woven picnic basket and she greets Erica effusively, moving toward her to do the air-kiss thing. Erica takes a step back.

Celeste opens one side of the basket—it's filled with gourmet treats. "I threw together a few little goodies for you and your hard-working people."

I bet you did, Celeste, with your own two hands.

"That was thoughtful of you."

Celeste smiles like the Cheshire cat. "So . . . the next vice president of the United States is going to be . . . Sally Carpenter!"

Carpenter wasn't on anyone's list of possible picks. She's a two-term congresswoman from northern Florida, dynamic, smart, a real mover, but young and untested. This is big news.

"Can I consider that confirmed?"

"Don't you trust me?" Celeste asks, wide-eyed.

"I'm a journalist."

"It's a done deal. Can you think of a more exciting ticket? The youth, the energy, the charisma! She's whip smart. PhD from Princeton. She was one of the people we vetted, of course, and then she and Mike met and just clicked. They sat and talked for three hours. Why, I'm *almost* jealous."

"Celeste, I appreciate this."

Celeste grasps one of Erica's hands. "We appreciate *you*."

Erica turns to go back into the skybox.

"You forgot your goodies," Celeste exclaims, pressing the picnic basket onto Erica.

She goes back into the booth and puts it on the crafts services table. On the air, one of the floor reporters is interviewing a congressman, giving Erica a chance to grab a few sips of water before breaking the VP news. Her phone rings—it's Firewall Partners.

"This is Erica."

"Gary Goldstein, Erica. In addition to the one found in your shower, we found cameras in your bedroom, living room, and office."

"What about my daughter's room?"

"Clean. As are the kitchen, dining room, and guest room."

"Can you tell me anything more?"

"These cameras are the best, state-of-the-art, German made."

"Do they record sound?"

"Yes."

"Any idea how long they've been there?"

"Well, they're pristine, no dust or grease on them, so I would say not long."

"And is there any way to find out where they transmit to?"

"That's the million-dollar question. No. Untraceable."

Erica hangs up and stands there stunned, horrified, and angry. She feels violated and vulnerable. It's high-tech rape. She calls Becky Sullivan and gets her voice mail.

"Becky, it's Erica, call me as soon as you get this message."

"You're on in thirty," comes Eileen's voice though Erica's earpiece.

"Listen, run the *Breaking News* banner. I know who the VP pick is—and it's a surprise."

Erica returns to the anchor desk, and as she gets ready to deliver the biggest scoop of the convention, she looks into the camera, the camera . . .

. . . the cameras . . . in her office and bedroom and shower . . . the cameras . . .

CHAPTER 44 ——————————————————

BACK IN HER HOTEL ROOM, Erica tosses in bed, the sheets twisted and knotty. Despite a rigorous bout of Tae Kwon Do, a dozen hands of solitaire, and a hot bath, sleep eludes her. She's left two more messages for Becky. What kind of game is that girl playing? Erica is ticked off, although she still finds it hard to believe that Becky is responsible for the cameras. She may be a troubled young woman who is obsessed with her boss, but would she really engage in such sophisticated surveillance? Doubtful. She's too needy and insecure. So if she did plant the cameras, somebody must have put her up to it. *But who?*

There's an elephant in Erica's psychic room and she can't ignore it any longer. Her denial is crumbling. She's being pulled into something dark and dangerous, just as she was when she investigated Nylan Hastings. She almost lost her life that time. Will her luck hold? How much responsibility does she have to Jenny? To herself? She wishes she could say it's just a job, but it's not. It's so much more. Something evil is going down. Something on a scale that might even dwarf Nylan's sick, vainglorious scheme. So . . . her responsibility is transcendent.

Oh, just forget about it!

In a sudden fury, she throws off the covers and bolts out of bed.

She's not Joan of Arc or Mother Teresa. She's just a hardworking kid who had a lousy childhood, and she has every right to walk away from this. She could get a gig on *Sixty Minutes* and still do some hard-hitting journalism. And be safe. For her daughter, her baby, her still-vulnerable baby. And for *herself*. She has *no* interest in being a martyr. A dead hero.

Yeah right, Erica, like you could let it go now.

She looks at the bedside clock: 3:12. The witching hour. She needs to turn off her brain and get some sleep or she'll be in terrible shape in the morning. And tomorrow is a big day, culminating in Ortiz's acceptance speech. She has a Xanax prescription, but she hates to take a pill; she just hates it. It feels like defeat, almost like a character flaw, an admission of weakness, the first step on the road to a drink.

Get over it—you're not taking the lousy pill to get high. You need sleep!

And so she does take the pill, and falls into grateful if fitful sleep.

The next morning, feeling semi-human, she calls Becky and leaves another message. Then she decides to head down to the hotel's dining room for breakfast. She craves a little hubbub, a little humanity, a little distraction to quell the loneliness and fear. And she'll no doubt run into some colleagues and maybe pick up some hot skinny. As well as congrats for her Sally Carpenter scoop.

The dining room is expansive, bustling and buzzing with politicians, aides, donors, media, political junkies, celebrities—all of them schmoozing, laughing, gossiping, networking. Everyone looks well fed, well dressed, pampered, and buffered in this plush cocoon.

Erica is led to a table for two. She orders coffee and a vegetable omelet and then surveys the room. People smile and wave at her, and she recognizes most of them. A senator from Oregon comes by to pay his respects, then several colleagues from GNN and the other cable news networks. It's all pretty convivial until you look closely and notice the whispered confabs, the intense expressions, the shrewd darting eyes. Make no mistake—this is the big time, where deals are cut, alliances formed, plans hatched.

It all comes down to two words: *power* and *money*. Money and power. Put them in either order; they are the drugs of choice for this tribe.

Then Erica notices an older Latino couple standing tentatively at the entrance to the room. They're modestly dressed and look like tourists who are splurging on a fancy hotel for their anniversary. They seem a bit uncomfortable, as if they're calculating how much breakfast in this posh birdcage will cost them. The man picks up a menu off the hostess stand and they quickly peruse it. The hostess appears and greets them profusely. The man shakes his head and they turn and leave arm in arm. There's something touching about them; they're so clearly still in love.

Then Claire Wilcox, an old colleague from Erica's first days at GNN, walks by her table. Claire is a raven-haired, Stanford-bred beauty and a first-class rhymes-with-rich.

"Those are Ortiz's parents. Do you *believe* they'll be sleeping upstairs at the White House if he wins? I wonder if they'll put in a taco stand."

"Nice to see you too, Claire."

"Kudos on your Carpenter scoop. What'd you have to do to get that one?"

Erica pulls forty dollars out of her purse and leaves it on the table. Then she follows the older couple across the hotel lobby and out onto East Delaware Place. They reach the corner of Michigan Avenue, turn north, and head into the Oak Tree restaurant, a far more modest affair than the Four Seasons. Erica follows them in.

The place is large and modern, filled with conventioneers from around the country, most bedecked with hats and ribbons and signs announcing their allegiance to the Ortiz/Carpenter ticket. There's already a sense of building excitement about tonight's acceptance speech.

The older couple go unrecognized and are shown to a table. Erica heads into the bakery section and checks out the carbs while keeping an eye on her quarry. They seem like such soft-spoken, decent people—it's hard to imagine them having Christmas Day dinner with their daughter-in-law. Erica takes out her phone and Googles to find their names.

This is the part of her job that she hates, but it *is* part of her job. She walks over to the couple. "I'm sorry to interrupt your breakfast. But aren't you Alberto and Miranda Ortiz?"

"We've been discovered," Alberto says good-naturedly to his wife—they both smile.

"And we know who *you* are," Miranda says. She's a buxom woman with smooth coffee-colored skin who—in her seventies—still radiates an earthy sensuality. "We enjoy watching your show."

"It makes me very happy to hear that. Would you consider coming on as guests sometime?"

Alberto and Miranda exchange glances. "We're pretty private people," Alberto says.

"It may be difficult to stay that way," Erica says. "May I sit down and join you for five minutes?"

"No cameras?"

"No cameras," Erica says, laughing.

"Please," Alberto says, standing and holding out a chair for her. This man has more class in his pinky than Donald Trump will have in five lifetimes.

"How do you plan to handle the onslaught of attention?" Erica asks.

"Firmly," Miranda says.

"Nobody asked us to run for parents of the president. We have no interest in that world."

"We are proud of Mike, but I was happy with him staying in the Senate."

"He says that his time as a prisoner in Iraq convinced him to run for the presidency," Erica says.

Both Alberto and Miranda grow silent; their faces darken. "If that's what he says, then we support him," Miranda says.

"His wife is a strong woman," Erica says.

Miranda takes a sip of her coffee. Alberto looks out the window.

"Do you think she had a great deal of influence on his decision?"

The Ortizes remain silent.

Finally Alberto says drily, "Celeste is very generous. She has helped many charities in our community."

"His time in captivity must have been very difficult for you."

"I never expected to see my son alive again," Alberto says.

"The worse part was imagining his treatment. My boy, being beaten and filthy and no food or water sometimes. I had to go on medication to control my anxiety and fear," Miranda adds.

"But he came home," Erica says.

There's another silence, and then Alberto says slowly, "Yes, he came home."

"Was he different?"

Miranda puts down her fork, looks at Erica, and says with finality, "He is my son."

"I understand. And I hope I haven't disturbed your breakfast. Just one last question: Do you know Lily Lau?"

Both Alberto and Miranda stiffen, almost involuntarily. They try to disguise it, but their distaste for Lau comes through loud and clear. There's a long pause.

"When my son was in Congress and then the Senate, he worked to help families who were struggling to make better lives. If he wins, we only hope he will remember those people," Alberto says.

Erica is moved by his simple words. After a moment she says, "I'm sure he's very proud of you."

"You see, honey, I told you she was a good woman," Miranda says.

Erica stands up. "And if you ever change your mind about appearing on my show, the door is always open."

As Erica walks back to the hotel her phone rings. It's George Yuan from Harvard.

"Hi, George."

"I'm making slow but steady progress on the translation. The text is extraordinary. It's basically a how-to manual in brainwashing and psychological warfare."

"Written in 200 BC."

"Yes! It's books like these that make scholarship so exciting."

"What have you learned so far?"

"There are five core steps to gaining control of someone's mind: Isolation. Sensory Deprivation. Fear. Indoctrination. Love."

"Love?"

"Yes. They wanted their subjects to love them as well as fear them. The combination led to complete submission."

"Fascinating."

"Numbers were very important to them. Nine was considered the most sacred number. It was dictated that the mind-control process should take exactly nine months and nine days."

"Interesting."

"Here's a passage: 'The subject, upon release, should be able to fit into society with no one suspecting that they are being controlled.'"

"Sort of like a Trojan horse."

"Exactly. I took several courses in the history of covert action. The CIA has employed many of these same tactics in its intelligence work."

The CIA. Erica knows something of the CIA's methods, of course, but this is the first she's heard of overt brainwashing. She ducks into a doorway. "Say more."

"In Nicaragua, Chile, Vietnam, and countries in the Middle East, the CIA was and is known for 'creating' infiltrators out of local officials. Sometimes it pays off their families. Then it removes them, voluntarily or not, to secret camps, brainwashes them, and then sends them back out as spies and assassins."

"Do you think the CIA could have operatives in Al-Qaeda?"

"That question is out of my wheelhouse. But I don't see why not. They are the best in the world. And they are absolutely merciless."

Erica's mind is spinning like a pinwheel in a wind tunnel. Could the CIA be working to put Mike Ortiz in the White House? Peter Tuttle had a life insurance policy, which is much more legit than cash, which is traceable. And it makes perfect sense that the CIA would want Vander out of the picture. In fact, they would want anyone out of the picture who stood in the way of their goal. And Erica knows the CIA is a brilliant killing machine when it wants to be. It never leaves a trace. It's all-seeing, all-knowing.

All-seeing, all-knowing. Even in the shower.

Erica feels herself start to sweat.

"Erica, are you there?"

"I'm here, George. I can't thank you enough. Stay in touch."

As Erica rides back up to her suite to change into her work outfit, she can barely contain her excitement. Or her fear.

CHAPTER 45 ─────────────

NO SOONER HAS ERICA WALKED into her suite than she gets a call from Shirley Stamos.

"Hi, Shirley, what's up?"

"I have some terrible news, Erica."

"What?"

"Becky Sullivan either killed herself or was murdered last night."

Erica is stunned into silence. Then a terrible foreboding grips her and she feels her body temperature drop. "How?"

"She either jumped or was thrown off a wall on Morningside Drive, down into the park."

"There were no witnesses?"

"No. It's quiet up there at night."

"She didn't know that part of town; she hasn't been in New York long enough. She was a small-town girl."

"I had those same thoughts."

"I'm stunned. It's so sad. She was a good kid, a little troubled, but I'm sure she would have worked it out."

"She certainly worshiped you."

"Jenny adored her. I've got to call and tell her."

"That's going to be a tough call. Erica, I'm here for you. If there's anything I can do to help, *anything*, please let me know."

"Can you send flowers to her family back in Ohio? Send two bouquets. One 'from all her friends and colleagues at GNN' and one 'from Jenny and Erica.' And get me their phone number."

"Of course."

Erica sits down and tries to compose herself. Becky is gone. Becky who spent many evenings at Erica's, who *was* terrific with Jenny. Her poor parents, to lose a child so young—and so violently. And poor sad, insecure Becky. Could it have been a suicide? If Becky had been responsible for the hidden cameras, the fact that they were discovered could have driven her over the edge. Still, why would she have headed uptown to Morningside Heights to do it? She could have leapt out her apartment window.

And if it was murder? Was Becky doing someone's bidding when she hid the cameras? And once she was unmasked, did she represent a security risk that had to be taken out?

Erica takes a deep breath and exhales with a sigh, pushing her speculation aside and turning her focus to Jenny. No point postponing the inevitable. She calls Jenny's camp and reaches the director, Meg Winston, who promises to track down Jenny and bring her to the office.

Shirley texts Becky's home number in Ohio, and Erica calls it.

"Yes?" comes a woman's voice, sounding numb and drained.

"This is Erica Sparks. Is this . . . ?"

"Yeah, I'm Mary Sullivan. Becky's mom."

"I just wanted to call to say how sorry I am. Becky was a lovely young woman."

"She was a good kid. She wanted to make something of her life." The poor woman sounds so beaten down.

"She *did* make something of her life. My daughter adored her. She was very helpful to me."

"That's nice to hear. She was talking about coming back home."

"She was?"

"I think New York was too much for her. I think it scared her. Last time she called she told me she felt trapped."

Erica wants to ask more questions, but the woman's sadness is just too much. So Erica says, "Again, I'm so sorry."

She hangs up and remembers Becky's overeager face. Then she sees Fred and Judy Buchanan and the innocent bystanders to the bombing, some of whom will never walk or see again. The names and faces tumble out—Markum, Tuttle, Vander.

And Mike Ortiz. The man who changed somehow while in Al-Qaeda custody. Is he now the Trojan candidate, a stalking horse for . . . who? The CIA? They certainly have the resources and the expertise. And the motive. If Ortiz won, America's shadowy intelligence agency could take control. And who controls the CIA? The military-industrial complex that President Eisenhower, in his final speech to the country, warned posed the greatest threat to Americans' liberty. In the face of the global terrorist threat, democracies around the world are taking away freedoms, imposing curfews, curtailing free speech, and banning demonstrations. Could America be next?

Erica's phone rings, and she starts. She pulls herself back to the here and now.

"Jenny?"

"Yes, Mom?"

"I have some very sad news."

"What is it?"

"Becky died, honey."

"What?"

"I'm so sorry, honey."

Jenny starts to cry. "She was my friend."

"I know she was, sweetheart, and you were a good friend to her."

"What happened?"

Should she tell her the truth? It will be so disturbing. But she will find out eventually and resent being lied to. Erica decides to split the difference. "She fell off a high wall. It may have been an accident."

"Becky was afraid of heights, she told me that."

"I know it's hard to accept, but that's what happened, honey."

"I don't think she fell; she would never get up on a high wall. What if she was pushed?"

"They're investigating everything."

"I think she was murdered."

"It's really too soon to say, honey."

"It's not too soon to say. You know it and I know it. She was murdered."

"Let's let the police do their work."

"No, I don't need to wait. Becky was probably killed because she was connected to you."

Erica runs her fingers through her hair and slumps down in the chair—she's had the same thought.

"Please don't say that, Jenny. It makes me feel terrible."

"Good! I think you're selfish. You don't care about me! What if you get killed next? And please don't tell me it's your *stupid job*!"

Erica feels like her emotional toolbox is empty. There's nothing left. What can she say? How can she make this better? There's a long pause filled with Jenny's anger and tears.

Finally Erica says, "I sent flowers to her family, from both of us. And I spoke to her mother."

Jenny says nothing; there's just faint phone static between them.

"I'm sorry about Becky, honey."

"I'm sorry about *everything*. I wish I was still living with Dad and Linda."

These are the words Erica most dreads. She closes her eyes and takes a deep breath. "I don't want you to leave me, Jenny. It would break my heart. But if you honestly feel that way, we can discuss it."

"By the way, don't come for parents' weekend."

"Honey, I'm planning on it. I took that Friday off work."

"Dad and Linda are coming."

"I wish you had told me sooner."

"I guess we both wish things."

"Jenny, I can't let you go when things are like this between us. I just can't. It would tear me up. I'm your mother and I love you more than anything in the world. You can talk to me about anything, anytime. I will stand with you and stand behind you, now and always . . . We'll keep talking?"

There's a pause and then Jenny says a halfhearted, "Okay."

Erica grabs that *Okay* like a life preserver.

CHAPTER 46

ERICA IS DUE OVER AT McCormick Place in an hour. But she picks up the hotel's landline and calls Greg in Sydney, where it's ten at night.

"Erica, don't you have a busy day ahead of you?"

"I do, but I need to talk."

"All ears here."

She quickly gives him an update on her investigation, the murders so far, Becky's death, the cameras discovered in her apartment, her suspicions about mind control, and then George Yuan's pointing out how the ancient text seems to perfectly describe some of the tactics the CIA uses. The words tumble out of her in an urgent rush, and when she's finished there's a pause.

"Erica, you're in deep on this."

"Do you think I'm off on a wild goose chase?"

"No! I wish you were. Your instincts are sharp, and at this point we're way beyond instinct. Someone is committing systematic killings. And it's certainly within the realm of possibility that the CIA would want to control the presidency. It would give it the ability to dictate American foreign policy. Not to mention domestic."

"Listen, we've all seen what the CIA is capable of. It has engineered the overthrow of more than one legitimate government," Erica says.

"The time Ortiz spent as a hostage is basically unaccounted for," Greg says. "The CIA could have come in with suitcases of cash and bought control of him from Al-Qaeda. And then brainwashed him. Sounds farfetched at first blush, but look at Nylan Hastings. That seemed beyond the realm of possibility."

"Exactly. Do you have contacts I could *absolutely* trust who might be helpful?" Erica asks. "A former CIA agent would probably be best. Or maybe someone who dealt with them over in Iraq?"

"You know, when I was a photographer in the Middle East, I did meet a guy, Anwar Hamade. He's an Iraqi journalist. Upstanding guy and incredibly knowledgeable. His specialty was covert action, by his own and other governments. He spent a lot of time studying the CIA."

"Do you have contact information on him?"

"I can find it. Erica, you've taken on another biggie."

"They find me."

"That's not true and you know it. Can you handle this?"

"I think I'm past the point of no return."

"You can't be too careful."

"Listen, I've got to get over to McCormick Place. Big night tonight."

There's a pause. Greg lowers his voice and says, "I wish I were there with you."

"So do I, Greg."

CHAPTER 47 ——————————————

"THERE YOU HAVE IT, SALLY Carpenter's speech accepting the vice presidential nomination. The mood here at the McCormick Center is joyous and festive, rocking with anticipation."

As Erica looks down at the arena, she gets goose bumps. In spite of everything that she's juggling, she is moved by the sight of so many of her fellow Americans—of all races and faiths, straight and gay, young and old, wealthy and working class—actively engaged in *democracy*. And to think that it's been working for 240 years. There's a lot of cynicism in the news business, understandably to some extent—journalists are witnesses to lies and vanity and greed—but Erica doesn't share it. In fact, she *hates* cynicism. It's a dead end, a surrender, the enemy of unity, inspiration, and progress.

Watching her fellow Americans exercising their basic rights, she feels a renewed energy for taking on the CIA—or *whoever* is responsible for the Buchanan bombing and its deadly aftershocks.

"That's Senator Bob Frankel of New York who has just walked out on the stage to introduce Mike Ortiz. Let's listen to his speech."

GNN cuts to Frankel, and with each word out of his mouth, more people are standing on chairs and waving banners, yelling and screaming their approval at the senator's description of Ortiz's strength and character. His voice rising, Frankel finishes with, "It is with great pride that I ask you to join me in welcoming the next president of the United States of America, Mike Ortiz."

Ortiz strides onstage to a roar that feels like it might blow the roof off the arena. He looks like a movie star, fit and handsome, yes, but he also has that intangible quality—"it"—that makes it impossible to take your eyes off him. He stands at the podium letting the adulation wash over him, waving, smiling, looking confident but not arrogant.

After five minutes of pandemonium, Ortiz quiets the arena and begins his speech. In rising cadences he recounts his life story and talks about his vision for America. The crowd is eating out of his hand, breaking into thunderous applause at every cue. Of course there's an element of performance, but is Erica the only one who thinks it goes beyond that, that it's too perfect, that Ortiz looks and acts programmed, as if he were the world's most amazing trained seal? He nails all the rhetorical tricks, hits all the high notes, but to Erica something is missing—there's no *soul* behind it.

Now Ortiz is talking about his time as a prisoner. "I learned the meaning of real hardship and true grit. Some days I fell into a pit of despair. But I always found a way to climb out. Why? Because I was determined to come back to the country I love and make a difference. I methodically planned my escape. And after exactly nine months and nine days, I took my fate into my own hands and—"

Those are the last words Erica hears.

George Yuan's voice echoes in her head: *The mind-control process should take exactly nine months and nine days.*

Erica pushes away from her desk and stands up, sucking air, shivering in the chill that's sweeping over her body. Her colleagues turn and look at her with concern.

An associate producer comes over to ask, "Erica, are you all right?"

Erica takes a step back. The well-meaning woman looks like she's a million miles away—in another world, a better world.

CHAPTER 48

SOMEHOW ERICA GETS THROUGH THE rest of the night, finally signing off at a little after eleven. The first thing she does is call Mort Silver.

"I need to talk to you, Mort."

"You seemed a little off your game tonight, Erica." From the sound of his voice, it's been a liquid evening.

"Thanks for the vote of confidence."

"Just calling it like I see it."

"Well, I need to see you."

"I'm in my suite; come on up."

Erica heads back to the Four Seasons and right up to Mort's suite, where he has been hosting a watch party. He opens the door himself and exclaims with a big smile, "The one and only Erica Sparks!" Yes, he's definitely been tippling.

Erica walks into the expansive suite. There are several dozen guests including politicians, network executives, newscasters, and buttoned-down business types. There's a lavish if picked-over buffet and a bartender who has clearly had a busy night. The guests greet Erica's arrival as a big deal. Good. It gives her a little leverage.

"Forgive me, but I'm going to steal Mort away for a couple of

minutes," Erica says, steering him toward what looks like an unoccu-
pied bedroom. She shuts the door behind them.

"Well, someone's got something on her mind," Mort says, a little
put out by her initiative.

"Listen, Mort, I want to go to Iraq to research my in-depth profile
on Mike Ortiz."

"Erica, I don't think that's necessary. There's lots of stock footage
of that country and of Al-Qaeda."

"It's not the same thing as being there."

"No, it's not. Which is a very good thing." Mort starts to pace, and
Erica can see him sobering up, putting on his boss cap. "Do you know
what kind of shape Iraq is in right now? It's a mess. ISIS controls about
a third of the country. The Shiites and Sunnis are blowing each other
up. It's a *very* dangerous place. You think I'm going to let GNN's most
valuable asset put herself at that kind of risk? I'm sorry, Erica, but it's a no."

"We're talking about creating compelling television. I want the
American people to see what Ortiz went through. I want to bring it to
life, viscerally."

"Good instincts. Bad plan. Do you know what it would *cost* to provide the kind of security you would need?"

"I want to slip under the radar, Mort, make the trip unannounced.
Which will make it a news story in itself when I come back. I'll need
minimal crew and light security. Anything more would only draw
attention to me."

"I'm sorry, but the risk and costs outweigh the benefits. McCain
was a prisoner of war; it didn't get him elected."

"I'm not trying to get Ortiz elected, I just want the American
people to understand the man who may be our next president. I'll go
just as in-depth on Lucy Winters."

"You mean about the years she spent in a 4H camp?" He laughs
mirthlessly. "I don't think you're going to find much of anything juicy
on *her*. In fact, I can hear her campaign squawking about our bias if we
make too much of Ortiz's prison ordeal."

"This is going to be the furthest thing from a puff piece, I assure you."

"Erica, you're going to be playing up the most compelling part of Ortiz's narrative. It could come across like a campaign ad."

"I don't do that kind of journalism and you know it."

"You seem very keyed up. Does this have to be settled right now? Tonight? I've got guests out there."

"It kind of does, Mort."

"Why?"

"Listen, Mort, my ratings have been high lately. I'm number one every night."

"True."

Erica looks him in the eye. "I want to go over to Iraq," she says, an iron will in a velvet voice.

Mort shakes his head, and a little bit of the fight goes out of him. "For goodness' sake, when do you want to go?"

"ASAP."

"And for how long?"

"Two or three days should be enough. And I want as few people as possible to know I'm going. We can announce it as a vacation or just say 'Erica Sparks has the week off.' Downplay it across the board. And absolutely no mention of Iraq."

"It may be impossible to keep it a secret once you arrive."

"We'll deal with that when I get there. I want to start things in motion first thing on Monday. I'll ask Greg Underwood to help me find a local producer who knows the lay of the land. He can set up lodging, escorts, security, a local crew."

Mort shakes his head in acceptance and looks at Erica with real concern. "Are you *sure* you want to put yourself at this kind of risk?"

"One hundred percent."

"I suppose it could pay off."

More than you know, Mort, more than you know.

CHAPTER 49

ERICA GETS UP EARLY THE next morning, picks up her iPad, and starts reading *The Call of Freedom* by then congressman Mike Ortiz. She skips to the section on his time as an Al-Qaeda prisoner and his escape from the primitive jail in which he was held.

It was June 2010 and he was on a congressional humanitarian mission in Baghdad. The focus of the trip was education, with the ultimate goal being to convince Congress to fund dozens of elementary schools in the city. Ortiz believed it was not only the right thing to do but that it would be a powerful antiterrorist tool. It was late afternoon, and he and the three other members of the mission were just leaving a school they had toured. They had ample security, but as they walked to their armored vehicles, a car screeched to a halt on the sidewalk. Five masked and heavily armed men leapt out. A gunfight broke out, a congresswoman from Nevada was shot in the leg, and two Iraqi soldiers and one of the gunmen were killed. Ortiz was picked up by two of the gunmen and shoved into the trunk of the car, which then sped away.

Ortiz sweltered in the dark cramped space for hours, in shock and afraid, with no idea where he was being taken or who his captors were. Finally the car stopped, the trunk was opened, he was lifted out, roughly walked into a small, one-story adobe building, and shoved into a dark cell. This was where he stayed until his escape.

The conditions were horrific—food was erratic and basically inedible, his toilet was a bucket that was emptied once a week, and he had one thin blanket to get through the frigid desert nights. He lost forty pounds, suffered through extreme intestinal illness, insect bites that became infected, bleeding gums, fevers, and delirium. He was subjected to torture in an effort to get him to reveal military secrets and to renounce the United States, and was repeatedly threatened with beheading.

Back home in the States, his capture was front-page news. Al-Qaeda demanded that the US stop its bombing campaign in return for Ortiz's release. The president refused to negotiate with the jihadists. As the days turned into weeks, the story lost its urgency and the country's attention turned elsewhere.

Over the ensuing days, weeks, and months, Ortiz was able to make some sense of his surroundings. He was being held in a makeshift prison somewhere north of Baghdad. His fellow prisoners were a mix of thieves, adulterers, and other infidels. The prison held fewer than a dozen inmates and was guarded by three Al-Qaeda soldiers who spent a lot of time smoking, praying, and tormenting their captives.

During it all, Ortiz's love for his wife, family, and country sustained him. Sitting in his cell at night, he planned his escape. Al-Qaeda interrogators and officers would come every week, take him from his cell into a small room, and see if he had changed his mind about spilling secrets or denouncing the US. Ortiz saw these sessions as his best opportunity for escape. An armed soldier stood guard. If Ortiz could neutralize the guard, get his AK47, and shoot his interrogators and the prison guards, he could then flee, commandeer their vehicle, and drive south to Baghdad. It was a risky plan, brave and brazen. But Ortiz was determined.

Finally, after those fateful nine months and nine days, he put it into action. He was led from his cell into the interrogation room and, as usual, sat across a table from his interrogators. No sooner had he sat down than he shoved the table over onto them, momentarily stunning them. He kicked the armed guard in the stomach, grabbed his AK47, and took out the guard and the two interrogators. The three regular guards rushed into the room, but he was ready. He killed two of them and wounded the third before fleeing to Baghdad in an Al-Qaeda truck.

Once again, Congressman Mike Ortiz was front-page news, a hero whose courage and bravery propelled him right to the Senate. And beyond?

Erica turns off her iPad. The story is well told and undeniably stirring. But she is struck by the fact that there were no witnesses to any of the events and no corroborating evidence. The prison was emptied and abandoned soon after Ortiz's escape.

Erica is going to have her work cut out for her in Iraq.

———

It's time to start packing for her return flight to New York, but first there's a call she has to make. She dials Meg Winston, the director of Woodlands Camp.

"I'd like to fly up and see Jenny on Tuesday, just for a couple of hours, maybe take her out to lunch."

"I'm sorry, but that violates camp rules," Winston answers firmly.

Erica loves the camp's discipline—the fact that all electronic devices are forbidden, that no candy-laden "care packages" are allowed. But this is a different matter entirely.

"Can you possibly stretch the rules a little, just this once?"

"We're a camp, not a piece of salt water taffy. If we stretched for one we'd have to stretch for all, and that would leave us very stringy."

Erica has a feeling Winston has used that line before.

She wonders how deeply she should get into specifics. The fact is she *has* to see Jenny before she leaves for Iraq. "I'm going away on assignment, and I can't make parents' weekend. This will be my only chance to see my daughter."

"Ms. Sparks—"

"Please . . . Erica."

"Erica, we have a lot of prominent parents with busy schedules. CEOs, movie stars, et cetera. The rules apply evenly and fairly to all."

"Meg, I really can't get into the details, but it's important."

"Erica, Jenny was traumatized by your last call. By the death of that young woman, Rebecca Sullivan. She's been moody and withdrawn. She has expressed her anger toward you to several of her counselors. This kind of attitude can infect other campers. And if we pulled her out of activities for lunch with you, it would only escalate the situation. I'm not sure a visit from you is in the camp's best interest right now."

Erica wants to scream at this woman: *She's my daughter, for goodness' sake, and I'm going to come and see her!* Instead, she sits on the edge of the bed and takes a deep breath. "I completely understand your concerns. But I hope you can understand mine. Things are somewhat unsettled between us at the moment. Before I leave on assignment, I simply must talk to my daughter in person."

What Erica doesn't say—and doesn't really want to admit to herself—is that she will be heading over to the most dangerous region of the world. And she may not come back.

Winston exhales with an exasperated sigh, and then her tone warms up. "I'm reading between the lines a little here, but I think I get it. Why don't you arrive at noon, and that way you can take Jenny out to lunch and have her back for her first afternoon activity. That seems the least disruptive plan."

Erica hangs up and realizes that in some ways, visiting Jenny feels like as much of a minefield as visiting Iraq.

CHAPTER 50 ———————————————

IT'S MONDAY MORNING AND ERICA is in her office organizing her trip. She's awaiting a call from a freelance producer, Bob Ruggio, who is based in Tel Aviv and whom Greg has worked with before. Greg has also gotten in touch with Anwar Hamade, the Iraqi journalist, and he's agreed to meet with Erica when she's in Baghdad. She flies out on Thursday.

As she goes over her checklist, she calls Nancy Huffman. Nancy was the head of wardrobe at GNN when Erica first arrived, and she became an immediate ally and then a friend. Nancy designed clothes in her off hours, and after Erica wore one of her dresses to the White House Correspondents Dinner, the designer was deluged with so many orders that she left GNN and now has a shop and atelier in the East Village. Erica often buys from her and consults with her, and the two friends meet for lunch or dinner every couple of months.

"Erica, how goes it?"

"Ah, mixed bag. Things are a little rough with Jenny."

"When have they not been a little rough with Jenny? It's the nature of the beast. That kid adores you and don't you ever forget it."

"Thanks. Listen, off the record I'm heading over to Iraq."

"What for?"

"I'm researching an in-depth piece I'm doing on Mike Ortiz."

"Okay. Can't say I feel warm and fuzzy about the guy. And please be careful over there. How can I help?"

"I'm not sure what to wear."

"Are you going to be reporting from Iraq?"

"Not live. And not from a studio. It's a stealth trip."

"Okay. Why don't I throw a few things together? I'll be up there in an hour or so."

Erica hangs up and says a silent blessing for Nancy, and for all her friends. Including Greg. Who, no matter where their relationship stands, has proved himself again and again.

The call comes in from Bob Ruggio.

"What a pleasure to meet you, Erica."

"Greg speaks very highly of you."

"Every gig is a new challenge. But I've been busy. You'll be staying at the Al Rasheed Hotel. Which is in the Green Zone, which is heavily fortified, no doubt the safest part of town. I've lined up a cameraman who also does sound. It's going to be bare-bones, and the footage won't be pristine."

"That might make it more compelling."

"My feeling exactly. The prison where Mike Ortiz was held is near the city of Baiji, about 120 miles north of Baghdad, on the main route between the capital and ISIS-controlled Mosul. This is one of the most volatile and dangerous parts of Iraq, although it has a lot of competition. ISIS and the Iraqi government have been engaged in a fierce battle over Baiji for years, and control has seesawed back and forth at least a half dozen times. Right now the Iraqi government has the upper hand. The good news for us is that the prison—which is abandoned—is twenty miles south of the city, in an area that's definitely under government control. Still, ISIS has made forays that far south. Any way you look at it, Erica, this is a dangerous mission."

"I need to find out what went on in that prison. Do you think we could find any Iraqis who worked there? Or were prisoners there at the same time as Mike Ortiz?"

"Doubtful. It was just a makeshift prison, a former rope factory that Al-Qaeda commandeered. There were only a handful of prisoners. However, I've heard from a reliable source that there is one surviving guard. He lives in a tiny town north of the prison."

"He's the person I want to talk to."

"We'll do our best to make it happen. I've got your flight number, you're coming via Dubai. I'll meet you at Baghdad airport. I've hired a driver for the duration. You've got my phone number and my backup number?"

"Yes."

"Let's check in on Wednesday. Call me anytime before then with any questions."

"I will. And thank you."

"Oh, and I've got a flak jacket for you."

———

After the call, Erica sits quietly at her desk. This is the first time in her life that she's traveled to a war zone. Hardly a week goes by without a bomb killing civilians in Iraq. ISIS claims religious justification for the systematic rape of girls as young as twelve. Erica has seen more than one beheading video. Capturing her would be a propaganda coup for ISIS. How would they treat her if they did capture her? As a publicity bonanza to be paraded in front of the world? As a hostage used to make demands on the American government? Or would they simply behead her and post the footage on social media? Erica imagines that happening—she's kneeling on the ground, her masked assassin stands over her, holding his sword, and . . . she closes her eyes but sees it all.

Then, sitting at her desk with the sunlight pouring in the floor-to-ceiling windows, she feels a strange new emotion descend on her. The world around her looks both hyperreal and not quite real at all.

It's almost as if she's disassociating from her surroundings, her job, her trip to Iraq, herself. Watching herself from up above. Is it a defense? To protect herself from the tsunami of fear that's building inside her? Is she having a premonition of her own death? Whatever she's feeling, it's deeply unsettling. She stands up, fighting off the cosmic dread, the claustrophobic panic. Is she signing her own death warrant?

"Knock, knock."

Erica whirls around. Nancy Huffman is standing in her office doorway.

"Are you all right, Erica? You look seriously spooked."

Erica lets out a deep exhale. She's pulled back to earth, to the here and now, by Nancy's voice and presence. "I think I'm okay. A little rattled by this trip, but I'll be fine." Erica realizes, with dark finality, that turning her back on this mission isn't an option. She'd never be able to look in the mirror again.

Nancy crosses the office and gives Erica a hug. "You're smart and tough, Erica, and you're going to find what you're looking for over there."

Erica can feel her internal systems returning to something close to normal. "And how are you?"

"Too busy, but it beats the alternative."

Nancy is without a doubt the chicest woman Erica knows. She's a little older, with a tight Afro and gorgeous black skin. Today she's wearing black leggings, black flats, and a simple white oxford shirt worn out with the sleeves and collar up. A parade of silver bracelets marches up her right forearm.

"Let's get down to work," Erica says, thankful for the prosaic demands of the trip.

"So, here's what I'm thinking," Nancy says, opening a garment bag. "Safety first for my friend. Women are much more vulnerable in that culture. Especially Western women. Especially blond Western women. So . . . I want you to look like a man from ten paces." Nancy takes out two pairs of men's cargo pants, two oversize work shirts, two floppy men's sun hats, and a pair of work boots.

"My first foray into cross-dressing."

"Hey, you're on trend. And whatever it takes."

"I think this is a smart idea."

"Every little bit helps. Listen, I have a long-scheduled fitting with one of my best customers."

"Go, go. And thank you for this."

Nancy looks at Erica, and her face fills with concern. She grasps Erica's hands in her own. "Hurry back."

With Nancy gone, Erica takes another look at the clothes. They make perfect sense. She holds up her hair, puts on one of the hats, and checks herself in the full-length mirror on the inside of her closet door.

Are you really ready for this, Erica? No. But you're as ready as you'll ever be.

Erica walks to the window. She looks out at the city—the towers, the traffic, the surging sea of humanity—and with a jolt she realizes that she's never felt more alive.

CHAPTER 51 ——————————————

ERICA PEERS OUT THE WINDOW as the plane begins its descent to Lake Placid Airport. She's never been to the Adirondacks before, and she's amazed at how vast the region is—it seems to go on forever, dense forest punctuated by seemingly endless lakes, a tapestry of deep greens and shimmering blues.

The plane lands and Erica disembarks into the dry, pine-scented air. The car she ordered is waiting to take her to Woodlands Camp, a forty-minute drive.

When they arrive at the camp Erica gets out and surveys the scene. Woodlands sits on the shore of St. Regis Lake, and its buildings and cabins are constructed in classic Adirondack style—unfinished logs atop stone foundations highlighted with whimsical porch railings, benches, and columns made of roots and twigs and branches. She can see down to the beach where campers are getting swimming lessons and playing volleyball. The girls all seem so athletic, with thick shiny hair and lithe bodies, crying out with delight, charging for the ball or slicing through the water.

She can't help but compare the scene to her own summer child-hoods when she would get on her bike and ride and ride and ride, alone and lonely, anything to get away from that stifling, soggy doublewide filled with pot smoke, six packs, black-market pills, rage, and despair. Watching the campers' carefree cavorting, she feels a tinge of envy toward these girls—and toward Jenny.

She finds the administrative building, and Meg Winston bounds out to greet her. She's early middle-aged and radiates common sense. She extends a hand to Erica. "Welcome to Woodlands."

"It's lovely."

"Isn't it? Jenny's in ukulele class. We're two minutes to the lunch bell."

Erica feels a sudden wave of anxiety. "She's going to meet us here?"

"Yes."

"How's she been the last couple of days?"

"She's a resourceful girl. But she's got a full plate. A lot of our campers are second- and third-generation, or have been coming for years, so it can be a little tough on the newcomers. But all in all, I think she's doing well."

And there she is, coming around the side of a building, looking tawny and healthy. She sees Erica and breaks into a run. Then she catches herself and slows to a walk. Erica wants to run to her, but knows that would embarrass her.

Erica hugs Jenny, and she smells like the pines and the lake and like . . . privilege. *Erica, this is what you wanted for her. You can't have it both ways. Stop torturing yourself.*

"Oh, honey, it's so good to see you. You look wonderful. How's your uke playing?"

"I killed 'Blue Skies.'"

Erica puts her arm around Jenny and leads her to the car.

———

The town of Tupper Lake is a strange mix of busted lumber town and tourist haven. There are funky bars and pizza parlors and hairdressers and then shops selling Adirondack furniture, fancy balsam soap, and antler coat racks. Erica and Jenny land somewhere in the middle, at a clean and homey coffee shop. As they scoot into a booth, Erica feels a zap of happiness—she and Jenny are together in a fun new place.

"How's the food at camp?" Erica asks as they look at their menus.

"It's good. They try not to use any processed food."

"That must be hard."

"It's not hard, Mom. Do *you* want to eat poison?"

Ouch. "We eat well at home, don't we?"

"We did when Becky was alive. You can't cook."

"You're right. I can't. And I have no desire to learn. Does every mother have to be a great cook?"

"I hope I will be."

Okay. "How you feeling about Becky?"

"Oh, just wonderful."

"Jenny, if you're going to be nothing but sarcastic—"

"Why did you come up here?"

"Because I wanted to see you." Erica wants to reach across the table and kiss Jenny, hold her, hold her tight. She's not going to tell Jenny about her trip—it would only add fuel to the flames. But the truth is fear is gnawing at her gut, she hasn't been sleeping, and she's haunted by the image of her own beheading.

The waitress comes over, and Jenny orders a bacon cheeseburger with fries. Erica bites her tongue—and orders the same thing. "Split an order of onion rings?"

Jenny nods.

"I was hurt that you asked your father and Linda up for parents' weekend without telling me."

"We have to talk, Mom."

"I'm listening."

"I want to move back to Massachusetts."

Erica nods, trying to control her response—but she suddenly feels like she's on a roller coaster perched on the edge of a precipitous drop.

She failed. She failed as a mother. The legacy continues. Her throat tightens.

"Okay," she manages.

Jenny winces. "Don't look so sad, Mom. It's not about you."

Of course it's about me. She's just being kind. Jenny *is* kind—and knowing *that* brings a measure of solace.

"Who is about then?"

"It's about *me*, Mom. This camp is nice, Brearley is nice. But I don't fit in. I don't belong. My dad's a teacher, not a plastic surgeon or a banker or a tech billionaire. I like public school."

"There are public schools in New York."

"This is hard. Please don't make it harder."

"And what about your mom? She's a television journalist who worked really hard to get where she is."

"Which is never home."

Erica fiddles with the salt and pepper shakers. "Is your decision final?"

Jenny nods.

All Erica wants to do is cry. But that's the one thing she can't do. It wouldn't be fair to Jenny. "We'll make it work, honey." It brings some comfort to know that if something happens in Iraq, Jenny will be in a safe place, with a father who loves her and a caring stepmom.

Jenny takes a napkin and dabs at the corner of Erica's left eye.

"It's not like I'll be in Sydney," Jenny says.

Greg. If only Greg were here with her. Instead, there's just loneliness.

"That's right, honey, you'll just be a few hours away. And you'll still have your room, so you can come down and stay anytime you want, for special occasions and Broadway shows and—"

"Mom?"

"Yes?"

"Can I ask you a question?"

"Of course."

"How come you never talk about *your* mother?"

Just when Erica thought this lunch couldn't get any more painful. She looks out the window, then fiddles with the salt and pepper, then takes a deep breath. "Well, honey, my mother and I have always had a . . . difficult relationship. I've told you how poor I was growing up. There's more. My mother was, well, she was an addict and sometimes she was . . . she was abusive."

"Did she hit you?"

"Jenny, do you think we could have this conversation when you're a little bit older? I think you have every right to ask, and every right to know, but it's just . . . it's just . . . I don't know, too much for me. Right now. Today. With everything else."

Jenny nods gravely, and suddenly she's the parent and Erica is the child. "I understand."

Their food arrives. It looks disgusting. But Erica smiles at Jenny and forces herself to take a big bite.

CHAPTER 52

IT'S WEDNESDAY NIGHT AND ERICA has just finished *The Erica Sparks Effect*. She could have taken the night off, but she knew the demands of the show would keep her dread at bay. She's washed off her makeup and is sitting at her desk. She leaves for Iraq tomorrow, and it seems like most of her loose ends are tied up—at least the practical ones.

"Hi there!" Josh says, appearing at her office door.

Oh no, they had an after-work date tonight!

"Josh!" Erica says, standing up.

"Did you forget?"

"Oh no, of course not, don't be silly . . . *Yes*, I forgot."

"This is where you see my bruised-male-ego pout."

"I've been waiting for that to appear. You've taken longer than most men I've dated. Listen, I have been crazy, crazy busy—convention, Jenny, and I'm going out of town on assignment tomorrow."

"I forget my own birthday. Are you still up for it?"

Erica looks down at her desk. No, she's not up for it. She's come to realize that no matter what happens with Greg, she's emotionally bruised and needs time without any entanglements. You couldn't ask for a nicer guy than Josh, but that may be part of the problem too. Erica

225

is an adrenaline junkie. She needs to feel challenged, to push herself to the edge. Josh lives by a whole other credo. A lovely one, in some ways an inspiring one, but Erica is growing to believe that it would leave her unfulfilled. She's just not sure that Josh understands her in the same way Greg does.

He holds up a small shopping bag. "I picked us up a little picnic. Whaddaya say?" He looks so touching and tentative.

"I think we should talk," Erica says.

"Okay. Do you want to eat while we talk?" he asks hopefully.

Food is the last thing on her mind. "Sit down," Erica says, managing a wan smile. Josh does. They look at each other. Erica has a hard time holding his gaze and shuffles some papers on her desk. "So . . . after our day on the trapeze, I came home and found Greg Underwood waiting outside my building."

"Oh, okay. Now things are starting to make sense."

"As you know, we were engaged."

"Were or are?"

"That hasn't been formally settled. But the point is, well, there're still a lot of feelings between us. Plus, he's been helping me with a work project."

"Unless I'm wrong, he's also been sleeping with another woman."

"How did you know that?"

"Never underestimate the power of a Google search."

That ticks her off a little.

"Don't get bent out of shape, Erica. When you're infatuated with someone, you take what you can get."

"I don't think it's anyone else's business."

There's a silence and Josh looks down, as if he's surprised and disheartened by their pointed tone. Erica feels a wave of sadness sweep over her.

"I'm going to make this easy for you," Josh says. "And for me." He stands up and gives her a rueful smile. "I've enjoyed every minute— except the last ten—of our time together."

"So have I."

"I think we should just leave it at that then."

Erica nods and stands up. There's an awkward moment—should they hug? They both take tentative steps toward each other and stop. The distance is too great.

Josh leaves. Erica paces, feeling hollow and lonely. She's lost Jenny. She's lost Josh. Has she lost herself?

CHAPTER 53

ERICA IS SITTING IN DUBAI Airport waiting for her connecting flight to Baghdad. Outside the massive wall of plate glass, the temperature is hovering at 125, and heat mirages dance over the runways. She's never been to Dubai before, and even though all she's seeing up close is the airport, she's in no hurry to come back. It just feels like the most artificial place on earth—a gleaming, glossy monument to extravagance sitting in the baking blistering sun, its very existence made possible by the all-seeing, all-knowing God of Air Conditioning.

And now she's onboard the jet for the two-and-a-half hour flight to Baghdad. Her fellow passengers are a mix of businessmen—both Western and Arab—and women in burkas lugging shopping bags from posh boutiques. Where do they wear their Chanel suits and Lauren belts and Hermes perfume? At clandestine dress-up parties? Or do they simply hang them in their closets and hope the day arrives when they can proudly flaunt their wealth on the streets?

They land, and Bob Ruggio is waiting to meet her. He's in his forties with a slight paunch, bald on top, half glasses hanging on a cord around his neck.

"Welcome to Baghdad."

"I'm psyched to be here."

"You must be exhausted."

"I could use a shower and a nap."

After getting Erica's suitcase, they step out into the furnace-like air and get in the waiting car. Erica is fascinated by what she sees. Her first impression is that everything is so . . . sandy. The streets, the buildings, the land, even the air. The architecture is a mix of ancient turreted mosques rising gracefully to honor Allah, and more recent and far less graceful office and apartment buildings. The scars of war are everywhere—empty lots, pockmarked houses, broken windows, rusting hulks of burned-out cars, concrete barriers. This is a nation that has been at war for decades now, and it shows. The streets have little foot traffic, and the few people who are out hurry along. She sees children playing, though, running down streets, throwing balls, laughing. They've lived with war their entire lives and they won't let it stop them from being kids, although when they glance at her car their eyes look wary.

"Here's a phone for you, and here's a backup," Ruggio says. "We're due to drive up and look at the old jail tomorrow. Then we'll head to the village where the one surviving guard lives."

"He's key here. I just hope he has the information I need and is willing to part with it."

"We'll bring cash. It has a way of loosening lips."

"And the area is currently under government control?"

"Yes, but ask me again in ten minutes."

"It's that bad?"

"It's worse."

They're silent for the rest of the drive. They enter the gated and heavily fortified Green Zone. Rows of steel-reinforced concrete barriers guard the front of the Al Rasheed hotel. It's a long hulking building, and the lobby is decorated in shades of dated and tacky. Erica checks in, thanks Bob, tells him she'll be waiting in the lobby at eight in the morning, and heads up to her suite.

Before she opens her suitcase she calls Anwar Hamade, the journalist Greg put her in touch with.

"It's Erica Sparks."

"Welcome to my beautiful country," he says with an ironic edge.

"Everyone I've met at the hotel has been very nice."

"That's a good random cross section."

"So any chance I could lure you over here for dinner?"

"Of course. I've been looking forward to meeting you."

Erica takes a long shower and tries to grab a short nap. No chance. So she does twenty minutes of Tae Kwon Do. She dresses down—though not in the I'm-a-man camo Nancy brought her—and heads down to the restaurant. Hamade is at a table, and he stands and waves her over.

"Greg speaks very highly of you," he says as they shake hands.

"And of you."

Hamade is around fifty, with thick black hair going gray at the temples, knowing restless eyes, and a half smile that reads as bemusement-as-a-defense. Erica likes him immediately.

"Greg tells me you're an expert on covert action."

"As an Iraqi journalist, I hardly have a choice."

"This may be a stupid question, but has the CIA been very active in Iraq?"

"The CIA has been very active in the entire Middle East for many decades. The region is still crawling with CIA agents, operatives, and informers. In fact . . ." His eyes scan the room.

"Seriously?"

"Count on it. And they know you're here."

Erica looks around. Several diners quickly avert their eyes. Suddenly the restaurant, the hotel, doesn't feel like a safe place.

"Do you think it's possible the CIA had something to do with Mike Ortiz's capture, imprisonment, and escape?"

"It's very possible. You know, there are still a lot of unanswered questions about Ortiz's case."

Erica leans forward. "Say more."

"First, why was *he* taken, and not one of the other three congressmen? From what I have been told, he was not the easiest target. The congresswoman who was shot was the logical choice—closest to the gunman and least able to resist. But they went straight for Ortiz. So clearly they had orders to take him and him alone. This is an issue the American authorities have never raised. Why not?"

The question hangs there as they order. The waiter is inscrutable, unsmiling. When he has left, Erica asks, "Do you have any theories?"

"They are only theories. But Ortiz, after his own tour in Iraq as a marine and his subsequent election to Congress, became a fierce opponent of the war and its architects in the Bush administration. Perhaps the CIA was engaged in a little payback. After all, his capture neutralized his criticisms of the war."

"Are you saying his own government had him kidnapped?"

"As I said, it is only a theory. But stranger things have happened in this region. And many can be traced back to the CIA."

"And his escape?"

"A little too neat. A little too easy."

"So you think he had help?"

Hamade shrugs.

"But who?" Erica asks.

"Look at how it has benefited his campaign for president."

"Yes, but surely the CIA doesn't want him in the White House. He's a critic of American involvement in foreign wars. He advocates for diplomacy."

"Yes, that is my thinking. And that is what makes this case so fascinating. There are many questions. Perhaps tomorrow we can find some answers."

"If you're right about his capture and escape, Ortiz isn't a hero at all. He's a pawn."

"As I said, nothing has been proven. But there have been rumors all along. You know, Iraq is a nation in crisis. We take one step forward and two back. It's heartbreaking on many levels. The Iraqi people have suffered so much; the country has so many problems . . . We don't devote too much time and energy to Mike Ortiz."

"But he may become president on the basis of lies."

"Well, he would hardly be the first leader to accomplish that."

Hamade's cynicism is showing. It's understandable. But if this was all a setup, Erica is not going to let the American people be fooled. Ortiz will be the most powerful man on the planet, capable of molding the course of history. And if he's under the control of the CIA or some other unknown entity, the American people have to know it. *Before* election day.

"I'm going to head up to Baiji tomorrow. I need to see the jail where he was kept. And my producer has tracked down the village where the one guard who survived Ortiz's escape lives. I'm going to try and find him and get his version of events."

Now Hamade leans forward. "Are you taking an Arabic speaker?"

"My producer knows some Arabic."

"Would you like me to come? I can translate. I would like to see the jail myself and hear what the guard has to say."

"Of course. You know it's a very dangerous area."

"This hotel is a very dangerous area."

After dinner Erica goes up to her room. She tries to piece together what Hamade has just told her, but she is so tired that her synapses aren't firing. Her exhaustion is physical, emotional, and psychic; she can barely keep her eyes open. She undresses and slips between the sheets. But sleep won't come. Her mind is racing from thought to thought, from fear to terror. According to Hamade, the CIA knows she's in Iraq. And he implied it wasn't just the CIA; it was any number of clandestine agencies or even terrorist groups. Erica feels sweat break out over her body—she's being watched; the room is probably bugged; she's in danger.

She throws off the covers, leaps out of bed, and starts to pace. The implications of what Hamade has told her about Ortiz are staggering.

She goes to the window. Baghdad looks ominous. Patches are lit by streetlamps, but great swathes of the city are dark—dark streets and dark houses. How can she *prove* Ortiz's capture and escape were premeditated, a setup, a fraud, designed to propel him to the White House? How can she *prove* that he was subjected to mind control, to brainwashing? And what if she's wrong about all of it?

The darkened room feels like a prison cell. Erica can't go outside, doesn't even feel safe going down to the lobby. She races into the bathroom and splashes cold water on her face again and again. She goes back out to the room, leans against the wall, and then slowly slides down it. That's when she notices something moving on the rumpled bedsheets. At first she thinks her eyes are playing tricks on her. Then slowly it comes into focus—first two claws, then the head and body and the creeping movement as the huge scorpion makes its way to her pillow.

Erica jumps up and freezes, watching the scorpion with wide, petrified eyes. Then, not taking her eyes off it, she slowly makes her way across the room to where she's put the work boots Nancy gave her. Grabbing one by the toe, she moves toward the bed. When she's close enough she brings the heel down on the scorpion again and again and again, until it's nothing but a twisted mass of glistening guts and smashed shell.

Erica pulls a wad of tissues out of the box, picks up the mess, walks into the bathroom, and flushes it down the toilet. Then she goes back out into the room and turns on every light and conducts a thorough search, including pulling off the mattress and all the bedding. The room is clean. Of scorpions at least.

Erica *has* to sleep. If she doesn't, she'll be incoherent in the morning. She takes out her cards and plays a half dozen games of solitaire. Then she pushes through the wall of her fatigue and forces herself to do an hour of vigorous, even punishing Tae Kwon Do until she's sweating and aching and literally unable to remain standing. And finally it comes, a restless sleep that brings no answers and no solace.

CHAPTER 54 —————————————————

ERICA STANDS IN FRONT OF the full-length mirror in her hotel room at seven thirty the next morning. She's exhausted and out of sorts, but edgy and eager to get going. She's wearing the men's clothes Nancy brought her and the flak jacket from Bob Ruggio. With her hair pinned up and the hat's brim pulled down, she could pass for a man, at least from a distance. It's a strange and disconcerting feeling. And a little bit heady. In the Arab world—not to mention the rest of the world—the rules are different for men. They have freedom to come and go without worrying about being sexually assaulted or raped, freedom to look like crap some days, freedom to seize power without apology or explanation, to be full-out jerks. Erica smiles ruefully and walks around a little bit, almost clomping in her boots.

You know what? I'd still rather be a woman.

But Nancy was right—she feels more secure and anonymous in these clothes.

As she walks through the lobby, no one gives her a second glance. She joins Bob Ruggio and the cameraman at their table in the dining room. The room is pretty full, and even at this hour there are a lot of sidelong glances and huddled whispers. Erica scans the faces—who can be trusted? Who is an enemy? She feels slightly nauseous, uneasy, a stranger in a strange land, a place where scorpions crawl across bed-sheets and ISIS kills innocents in the name of God.

"This is Riley Smith," Bob says.

Riley is young and eager, handsome and sun-burnished with a hip-ster beard, clearly a young adventurer.

"Thank you for signing up," Erica says.

"I'm juiced," Riley says, inhaling a plate of eggs and sausage and potatoes.

"Smart outfit, Erica," Bob says. "Are you anxious?"

"Yes. You?"

"I've been doing this for a while, and I always try to stay anxious. I've located the jail on GPS; we'll go there first. It may be full of squat-ters, but we'll see. Then we'll drive to this tiny village and look for the guard."

"Hamade will be here at eight."

"It's fantastic that he's coming. He's considered one of the country's best journalists. He may be very helpful both in finding the guard and getting him to talk. My Arabic is passable but . . ."

The men eat, but Erica is just too queasy to get down anything but half a banana. She's having a hard time sitting still. Eight o'clock comes—and goes. So do eight fifteen and eight thirty. The mood at the table grows ever more apprehensive.

"I'm going to go call," Erica says. She heads out of the restau-rant, filled with prying ears, and finds a quiet lobby alcove. She calls Hamade's house. A woman answers.

"This is Erica Sparks. I'm trying to reach Anwar Hamade."

"This is his sister-in-law. Anwar is dead." She sounds very sad and very angry. Erica can hear sobbing in the background.

"Oh no. *No!*"

"Yes."

"What happened?"

"When he turned on his car, it exploded."

"I am so sorry."

"Maybe you should be. Maybe you are the reason he is dead."

Erica feels a massive wave of guilt pummel her. Her mind goes blank for a moment. It just flatlines. What can she possibly say? There is more wailing in the background. Erica starts to rock on her feet, at a loss. Thankfully, Hamade's sister-in-law hangs up. Erica stands there, numb. She remembers Hamade from last night—serious, ironic, helpful. Clearly a man of the greatest integrity. A fellow journalist. Who would want her to move forward with her investigation. To quit now would dishonor him and his death.

She returns to the table. "His car was rigged, he's dead."

"Oh, sweet mercy," Bob says.

Riley goes silent and Erica knows that both of them are rethinking today's trip. She isn't. Horrific as it is, Hamade's death confirms her suspicions that someone is very threatened by her investigation. And that she's closing in on some answers.

Erica leans across the table and lowers her voice. "Listen, Bob, Riley, if you want to back out, I'll understand. But this isn't some puff piece about the horrors Mike Ortiz endured as a hostage and how brave his escape was. I wouldn't put us in danger for a story like that; I'd rely on stock footage. I believe Ortiz underwent some sort of brainwashing in that jail and that he came back to the States a different man, under control of some outside entity, maybe the CIA. Hamade felt that the whole thing—Ortiz's capture, imprisonment, and escape—may have been a setup. If Ortiz wins the presidency, he will be a fraud and maybe a puppet. And who knows what dark agenda his puppet masters have."

There's a long pause and then Riley says, "Whoa."

"I'm in," Bob says simply.

"Me too," Riley says.

Erica stands up and says, "Let's do this."

CHAPTER 55 ——————————————————

THEIR DRIVER, STOIC IF PROFESSIONAL, heads north out of Baghdad
with Riley riding shotgun and Erica and Bob in back. The city gives
way to unkempt suburbs, and then they're in the countryside. The land
and sky are vast and unforgiving. How does anyone survive in this brutal landscape? But they do. And have for thousands of years.

Erica is hyperalert, looking for any signs of trouble or ambush.
She scans the landscape, often turning to look behind them. As they
continue north they pass small villages with gas stations and car repair
shops, restaurants, general stores with their wares piled out front, and
children playing, families walking. These people are far enough away
from the cities and towns to feel somewhat safe from the worst of war,
and Erica gets a sense of life going on as always. It's really all anybody
wants, isn't it, no matter where they live—the chance to raise a family, earn a living, snatch some good times. And yet their leaders seem
to prefer bombs and bloodshed. Eternal bloodshed. If Mike Ortiz is
elected president, she wonders, will he lead the country back into war?
Will his time as a prisoner give him political cover? Is that *why* the
CIA—or whoever—wants to control him?

The traffic is steady—buses jammed with passengers, their suitcases tied to the top and sides, small trucks loaded with crates of squawking chickens, old American cars with their colors faded, military transports. And all around them the sun and heat, heat and sun. Erica feels disoriented. It's all so foreign and forbidding, she feels like they could be swallowed up by the sand and sky and never heard from again.

"We're about halfway there," Bob says, his voice tense.

"You want a little establishing footage?" Riley asks. Clearly he's eager to put his nervous energy to use.

"Wait until we get closer," Erica answers.

The miles pass in expectant silence. And then the driver turns right onto a dirt road.

"Where are you going?" Bob demands in Arabic.

The driver doesn't answer but his jaw is set, his eyes unreadable behind dark glasses. And then up ahead, in the distance, they see a van.

"It's a setup," Erica says, her pulse rocketing up.

As they approach, the van's back door flies opens and two men with machine guns leap out. Bob pulls out a pistol and slams it down on the driver's skull. He cries out but keeps driving.

Erica reaches over the front seat and grabs the driver's door handle and pushes his door open, crying to Riley, "Kick him out!"

Riley braces himself against his door and kicks, hard. The driver grips the wheel like a vise, and they're getting closer to the men with the machine guns. Erica fights to pry his hands off the wheel, and they loosen a little. Bob brings the pistol down on his skull again and blood spurts out as Riley kicks and kicks. And then, with a piercing cry, the driver lets go of the wheel and is ejected from the car. Riley scrambles into the driver's seat, grabs the wheel and turns it hard, kicking up dust, executing a tight screeching turnaround. Then he floors it.

As they speed away, Erica looks back to see their driver struggling to his feet and the two assailants growing smaller and smaller. The only sound in the car is the three of them gulping air. They reach the main road and Riley turns right, heading north toward the prison.

"Is that the best they can do?" Erica asks finally. And they laugh. But the laughter is hollow, and the day takes on a darker cast. Erica thinks of Greg, of his years as a war photographer—traveling into dangerous territory like this was just another day on the job. How did he do it? Live with the fear, all day and all night, every day and every night? The man has true courage. If only he were with her now.

They drive deeper into the countryside, and settlements grow few and far between. If they get into trouble out here, they're on their own.

"There should be a road coming up on the left," Bob says.

Sure enough, they reach a rutted, torn-up paved road. Riley turns and the car rattles along.

"We should be coming to a small settlement. According to my sources, it's been abandoned. Still, I think we should stop and do some reconnaissance before we drive in."

And then there it is, up ahead, a small collection of one-story buildings that look like a Middle Eastern ghost town. Riley stops and turns off the engine. Almost instantly the car turns into a sauna. Bob takes a pair of binoculars out of his bag and looks through them.

"No signs of life as far as I can tell. You check." He hands the binoculars to Riley, who looks and then hands them to Erica. She scans the landscape—there are about a dozen small structures, and the ground is littered with dented oil barrels and a couple of dead vehicles. There's something eerie and malevolent about the scene. It's too quiet. As quiet as death. She scans the perimeter and sees—nothing. Just endless sky and endless desert. And eternity—implacable and indifferent.

"Judging from the pictures I've seen, I'd say the structure on the left was the jail," Bob says.

Erica scans the jail. It's beat-up, has a few high horizontal windows. Like the rest of the settlement it looks long-deserted.

"Let's go in. Riley, how about I drive and you shoot our approach?" Erica says.

She gets out, opens the driver's door, and gets in as he moves over and hefts up his camera to start shooting through the windshield.

Behind her, Bob leans out a window, his gun at the ready. Erica turns on the engine and taps the accelerator, driving no more than five miles an hour, practically rolling toward the spectral settlement. Then they've arrived. She turns off the engine and that deathly quiet settles over them. They get out of the car and walk over to the jail as Riley shoots more establishing footage.

The door to the jail is ajar; Erica pushes it open and they all step inside. It takes a moment for their eyes to adjust to the sudden dark, pierced only by the shafts of light from the doorway and the narrow horizontal windows set high in the far wall.

Then the smell hits them—it's some rank combination of tobacco and sweat and urine and excrement and fear. They're at one end of a corridor that runs down the center of the jail. Erica slowly walks down it. There are three cells on each side, enclosed by mortar walls, with a small window in each door for food to be passed through. She pushes open the door to one of the cells and steps inside. It's tiny, no more than four feet by four feet, smaller than most kennel cages, with a dirt floor and no window, no room to lie down, no room to think or dream or plan. But more than enough room to go insane.

Erica feels a wave of claustrophobia and steps back into the corridor. She reaches the room at the back, the interrogation room. There are several straight-back chairs and an old table. There's no sink, no toilet, no running water, no electricity. And the air is so hot and dense that Erica feels as if it has substance and shape—moving through it takes effort. Sweating in her heavy clothes and flak jacket, made slightly dizzy by the heavy air, she feels alive and alert. Something happened to Mike Ortiz in this jail, and she feels she is moving toward the truth of what it was.

"What a place," she says quietly. "Riley, let's go outside and get some footage."

Erica stands about twenty feet in front of the jail as Riley shoots. "Behind me—here in the middle of the blistering Iraq desert—is the jail where Mike Ortiz was held captive for nine months and nine days.

The jail is part of this unnamed and abandoned settlement. Let's take a look inside."

Riley trails Erica as she walks back into the jail, his camera's light on, throwing the creepy interior into stark light and shadow. Bob stands beside Riley, checking the small monitor on the side of the camera, nodding encouragement to Erica.

"One of these six identical cells housed Ortiz," Erica says. "This is where he slept, ate, and exercised. Food came once a day, if that, and was usually a slimy gruel. Ortiz lost forty pounds. There was no toilet, only a bucket that was emptied by his captors when they felt like it. Ortiz had no books, no writing implements or paper, no contact with the outside world." She moves down to the office. "This is the room where he was interrogated by Al-Qaeda officers. At first they wanted him to divulge intelligence and to renounce the United States, but when he refused, they tortured him, almost for sport. He was whipped and threatened with beheading. Standing here, in air that is so hot and thick that breathing is difficult, it's hard to imagine how Ortiz survived with his sanity intact. And yet he took this hell and turned it into strength and will." She exhales and tells Riley, "That's good for now."

Riley turns off the camera and Bob says, "Looks strong, Erica."

"I think we've got what we need here. Now let's go try and find that guard." As they leave, Erica takes one last look behind her at the dark dank prison.

Isolation. Sensory deprivation. Fear. Indoctrination. Love.

CHAPTER 56

WITH BOB RUGGIO NOW DRIVING, they continue north through the sandblasted landscape. After twenty minutes, Bob turns down a paved road. "The village should be a couple of miles up here." The three of them go on high alert as they put more distance between themselves and any possible escape.

And then there it is. Bob stops the car when they're still several hundred yards away, and they look for signs of trouble. The village is tiny; there couldn't be more than a couple of hundred residents, but it's tidy and benign looking. There's a small food store, children playing, a man is plastering the outside of a house, and in the central square a woman is drawing water from a well using a hand pump that looks like something out of an old Western.

"You'll often find these villages around a dependable well," Bob says. "And they have power." He nods to the overhead line running in from the main road.

"And we're sure Ortiz's former guard lives here?" Erica asks.

"I trust my source. I've got the guard's name, Akram Kouri. So we should be able to find out, one way or the other."

Several villagers notice their car and stop what they're doing to stare. "Places like this don't get a lot of visitors. Remember, they don't want trouble any more than we do," Bob says. "Let me go break the ice."

He walks into the village square. A middle-aged man comes out of the food store; he has a paunch and carries himself with authority. He greets Bob and they shake hands and talk. After a few minutes Bob waves to the others to join him. By the time Erica and Riley—carrying his camera—reach Bob, a small crowd has gathered. They're curious and wary, but there's no hostility. Still, Erica knows that ISIS could be hiding anywhere—even in a tiny village like this one—and her heart is pounding in her chest.

"How do you do?" the man says. "I am Ahmet and this is my village and my shop. You are welcome. We do not have war here. Are you hungry?"

While Ahmet seems trustworthy and peaceable, Erica wants to find Kouri as quickly as possible. "We're fine, thank you. What we would like is to speak to Akram Kouri."

"Ah . . . Akram. He is . . . ah . . ." Ahmet makes a circular gesture with his index finger beside his ear.

"Was he a guard at the prison where Mike Ortiz was held?" Erica asks.

"Yes. He see bad things. It is sad. Come."

Ahmet leads the three of them through the village—they pass small houses, gardens, and yards home to chickens and goats. They reach the house farthest from the square. There is a walled front yard with dusty chickens pecking at the dusty earth. An elderly woman is sitting in a plastic-webbed lawn chair that looks like it was picked up at Lowe's a decade ago. Her face is crisscrossed with a crazy quilt of deep wrinkles and she's shucking a bowl of peas. As they enter the yard she frowns at them. When she sees Erica she leans back in surprise; then she narrows her eyes, sneers, and looks away.

"She is Akram's mother," Ahmed explains.

Bob hands the old woman some bills, and she nods her head toward the front door. They walk inside—the house is just one room, small and dark and at least ten degrees cooler than outside. The place smells like sweat and rancid cooking oil overlain with cheap air freshener. There are two single beds at one end and a rudimentary kitchen at the other. There's an old man sitting at a small table covered with oilcloth. No, wait, he's not old. He's middle-aged, but his face is so haunted, so ravaged and sunken, that he looks as old as his mother.

There's a tiny tinny radio on the table. The BeeGees are singing "Stayin' Alive" and the man is making jerking gestures in response to the beat. He is definitely off in his own private Idaho.

Ahmet greets him, and the man looks at them blankly. Then he recoils. Ahmet speaks to him calmly, soothingly, and the man relaxes a little.

"Can you tell him we want to find out about what happened in the prison?" Erica says.

Ahmet speaks to Kouri, loudly and slowly. A look of abject fear comes over his face and his body shrinks in on itself. Riley stays in the background, quietly filming.

Ahmet continues to question him, and Kouri grows more and more agitated and begins to speak in a fevered rush. Then he leaps out of his chair, eyes wild, words spewing, and he mimics strangling someone, now a blindfold is going on, now he's screaming in someone's ear, now he's tying them down in a chair, now he's whipping them. He's in a frenzy, a fit, talking, babbling, flailing.

And then, like a switch was flipped, he stops and goes completely still. But his eyes remain wide with fear and agitation.

"Ask him who did it," Erica whispers.

"Who?" Ahmet asks.

The man remains silent, sits back down, and a bizarre calm settles over him.

"Please, try again. I need to know," Erica says.

Ahmet squats down so he's level with the man. He puts a hand on his thigh, lowers his voice, and asks again. There's a pause and time stops and Erica feels suspended over a great chasm, the chasm of truth.

Then Kouri mouths an almost inaudible answer. Ahmet brings his ear close to Kouri's mouth and asks him to repeat it. He does.

"What did he say?" Erica implores.

Ahmet turns to her. "He said they were Chinese."

In the pounding desert heat Erica feels her blood run cold. She needs to be sure. She asks, in a slow somber tone, "You are sure the men who came and tortured Ortiz were Chinese?"

Ahmet asks and Kouri nods.

"How often did they come?"

"He says they came all the time."

Then the old man's body starts to shake and he starts to cry and blabber.

"What's he saying?" Erica asks.

"He's afraid the men are coming for him. Today."

CHAPTER 57 ———————————

ON THE FLIGHT BACK TO New York that night, Erica is still reeling from what she learned in that tiny Iraqi village. It was the Chinese who were spending all that time just torturing Mike Ortiz. His book is full of lies. It wasn't just torture. It was systematic brainwashing.

Isolation. Sensory deprivation. Fear. Indoctrination. Love.

Erica can imagine it all going down in that sweltering jail hidden from the world. Ortiz kept isolated, blindfolded, his ears plugged, caged in that tiny cell, his will wearing down. And then hauled out for the long sessions of torture, beaten, threats made to him and his family, and more torture until he's thrown back into the cell, where he cowers in the corner, trembling with fear. Then, when he's broken, desperate and terrified, the mind games begin, the propaganda, programming, paranoia. And finally, when Ortiz is reduced to a quivering subhuman mass, deranged with confusion and want and fear—the love. The love that is his if he obeys. Love. Always and forever. Of course he'll obey. Any edict. Any order. Just keep loving me and not hurting me. Please. Please don't hurt me.

All hail. But all hail *who*?

Erica is beginning to doubt her theory that the CIA was behind the plot. Surely they wouldn't have enlisted the Chinese to help them. From what Hamade told her, the CIA had more than enough Iraqi operatives to pull it off themselves had they wanted to.

Erica's mind goes back to Lily Lau and Celeste Ortiz. Lau is the daughter of a Chinese diplomat. Celeste was a banker specializing in China. Who recites incantations in Chinese with her husband before public appearances. China is the world's greatest economic power and is spreading its global web of influence in cunning ways. Like all empires, it wants to keep expanding. How brilliant it would be if China could gain control of the White House through the means of a subservient, compliant, brainwashed Mike Ortiz.

All hail . . . *Lily Lau?*

No, it's too crazy. Too grandiose. Too bizarre. Or is it? She remembers Nylan Hastings's plan to gain control of global media and communication and turn himself into some kind of twenty-first-century messiah. And how close he came to pulling it off.

Erica turns to her laptop and Googles Lily Lau. She devours a profile that ran in *San Francisco* magazine several years ago. From a family that has been prominent in Chinese politics for generations, the article details her cosseted childhood as the daughter of Chen Lau, then Chinese counsel general to San Francisco. The article touches on the deep ties between the city and China, dating back two hundred years to when San Francisco was the entryway for tens of thousands of Chinese seeking work. Today the city is still home to a vast Chinese population. It goes on to discuss Lily's years at Stanford and her friendship with Celeste Pierce, which morphed into an extraordinarily lucrative business alliance. There's a picture of Lily as maid of honor at Celeste's wedding to Mike Ortiz at a Napa vineyard, another by the pool at her stunning country house in northern Marin County, and another of Lily in the compound's courtyard, which is dotted with three guesthouses. Lily explains that she needs them for her extended Chinese family.

Really? Three guesthouses? And the estate is so isolated.

The article ends with Lily praising Celeste and Mike Ortiz and talking about how honored she is to be a part of all their good works, which she hopes will only multiply in the years to come. All in all, Lily comes across as smart, driven, charming, and caring, with a touch of becoming modesty. In other words, it's a total puff piece. Lily may as well have written the article herself. The woman is a master of image manipulation.

Next Erica Googles Chen Lau, Lily's father. She reads about his distinguished lineage and career, that he is considered shrewd and ruthless, that he is an undefeated chess master known for his ability to plan a dozen moves ahead of his opponents. When Lily was at Stanford, he moved back to China. Finally the article states that today he heads the Ministry of State Security, the Chinese intelligence agency—its equivalent of the CIA.

Erica is glad she's in a private first-class seat. Otherwise, her fellow passengers might wonder why her whole body suddenly quivered like a leaf in an icy gust.

CHAPTER 58

ERICA WALKS IN THE DOOR of her apartment, drops her suitcase, and heads straight for her office, where she keeps several prepaid phones. She calls Mark Benton, the former GNN IT wizard who helped her crack the Nylan Hastings case. For his efforts Mark was assaulted, beaten, and left for dead on a Greenwich Village sidewalk. He survived, but it's been a long haul back to physical and emotional health. By his own admission he's still suffering from PTSD, although he's functioning and even finding pleasure in life.

Mark left New York and moved out to Portland, Oregon, in part to live in a more low-key city, in part because he's a passionate wind-surfer. He found a good job in IT at Nike, which has much less of a pressure cooker culture than GNN. Erica is happy for him. The man has proved himself above and beyond.

"Hi, Mark, it's Erica Sparks."

"Erica, how goes it?"

"There's no short answer to that question at the moment. Listen, I need your help."

"Uh-oh."

"If you don't want to get involved, I will understand completely."

"To be honest, I am getting a little bored by sneakers."

"I'm working on a story about Mike Ortiz, an in-depth profile. As you may know, his wife is a billionaire and she is *very* secretive about how she manages her money. It's all done through a company called Pierce Holdings, which is headquartered in San Francisco. I'm not at all sure things are what they seem. Hypothetically, is there any chance you could get into their system?"

"Hypothetically that would be breaking the law."

Erica lowers her voice and gives him a broad-strokes overview of her investigation. When she's done there's a pause, and then Mark says, "Let me look into it."

"Mark, there aren't words."

"Erica, my adrenaline is pumping. In spite of everything, that's a good thing."

They hang up. Erica trusts Mark with her life. The question is: Does she trust herself with his?

CHAPTER 59

ERICA IS SITTING IN HER broadcast booth at Houston's NRP Park, better known as the Astrodome. Down below, the center is filled with thousands of delegates to the Republican convention, who are listening to yet another speech. There's even less drama here than at the Democratic convention, because presidential nominee Lucy Winters has already announced her pick for vice president, Senator Clark Hobbs of Tennessee. Erica is fidgety and fighting to stay focused, basically running on automatic pilot. The only story that interests her is unfolding out in San Francisco.

The energy here is a pale shadow of what it was in Chicago. Lucy Winters just doesn't inspire the same fervor as Mike Ortiz. In the course of putting together her piece on Winters, Erica has come to like and admire her. She may not be a show horse, but she's a real workhorse, well versed in policy, with a raft of solid ideas. Erica believes her low-key, methodical manner would serve the country well in these overheated times. Especially since Winters shows no hesitation in standing up to the far right, almost bloodthirsty ideologues in her party. In the primaries, her moderation almost cost her the nomination. In the general election it should help her, although she's still behind in the polls.

The speech ends and Erica goes live, introducing yet another speaker, some governor, does it really matter? What matters is that Mike Ortiz is months away from becoming the most powerful puppet on the planet.

GNN cuts away to a panel of gasbags who will rehash what just happened—and bore the pants off any viewer not addicted to predictable "in-depth analysis" that any sixth grader is capable of. One of the producers comes over and tells Erica she has fifteen minutes. Erica goes to the craft services table and tries to pretend she has an appetite. Her prepaid rings and she goes out into the hallway.

"Erica, it's Mark."

"Hey there."

"Listen, I've gotten partway into Pierce Holdings. A lot of firewalls here, it's going to be very tough to get through. But I have discovered something very interesting. The company seems to have two servers."

"Meaning?"

"They basically have two sets of computer systems."

"Could it just be a backup system?"

"When an organization does that, it backs up the original system as a fail-safe. It doesn't create an entirely new system. That's what we have here."

"Don't some companies have one system for management and then a general system for all employees?"

"Yes, but that's not what this looks like. Pierce Holdings is a *very* lean machine. One hundred percent owned by Celeste Pierce Ortiz. It has enormous assets in just about every sector of the global economy. Considering the size of their assets, the number of employees is strikingly low. And there seems to just be one system for all of them. So this second system appears to be a discreet entity."

"What would the motive be to have two systems?"

"One may be a cover."

"You mean the main system is a front for activities not related to Pierce Holdings?"

"Basically, yes. Although Pierce Holdings is obviously a very real and successful entity. But I believe something else is going on at the same time. To get into this second system, you have to go through Pierce Holdings, which acts like a potent firewall. Without it, this second system would be much more vulnerable to hacking. You could be a Pierce Holdings employee and not know this second system exists. It's basically hidden in plain sight."

"It sounds like an incredibly smart setup."

"I've never seen anything quite like it before."

Erica feels a terrible sense of responsibility toward Mark. Helping her out almost cost him his life once. "Listen, Mark, thanks so much. I'd like you to stop working on this now. You've already given me very valuable information. I'll take it from here."

"Erica, once I get started, well, it's tough for me to stop. This is a fascinating configuration they have set up. My curiosity is raging."

"I don't want to put you in any danger."

"You're not holding a gun to my head. I trust you that if this wasn't really important you wouldn't have called me."

"Please don't do *anything* that will let them detect your cyber-presence. If you sense they have, *stop immediately*. And that's a gun to your head talking."

"Gotcha."

Erica puts a call in to Celeste Ortiz, who gets back to her within two minutes.

"Erica. You must be bored out of your skull there in Houston." Her voice is both warm and cold.

"I'm strictly nonpartisan."

"You could belong to the Birthday Party and be bored by that convention."

"I wanted to thank you for all your cooperation with my piece on your husband."

"I sense an ask coming."

"You must be psychic."

"I can predict trouble. What's up?"

"The piece is coming well, but to be honest, Celeste, there's a tremendous amount of interest in your finances."

"I've released my tax returns. Isn't that enough for the vultures?"

"Mort Silver and my producers are pressuring me to delve a little deeper. You know that people are fascinated by wealth and privilege. I'm not interested in an exposé, but I do think it's a legitimate topic to explore."

"Out of the question. Pierce Holdings is a privately held company. I'm the sole owner. Besides, do you know how many pieces have been done on me and my money? *Fortune*, CNN, FOX Business, Politico, you name it. My finances have been turned inside out. Yes, I was born to privilege, but I sure didn't rest on it. I *made* the bulk of my money and I'm proud of it. There's more than enough public information for you to cobble together a segment on my holdings."

Erica waits before answering. *Let her sweat.* "You know, I'll have no choice then but to make your refusal part of the segment. In fact, it will probably be the *focus* of it. It may look as if you're hiding something."

"Erica, I gave you the biggest scoop of the Democratic convention and this is how you repay me."

"We agreed that came with no strings attached. I took you on your word."

"Don't you know how the world works?"

"I know how I work."

"This is blackmail."

"It's nothing more or less than a journalist going after a story."

"I'd call it a journalist *creating* a story."

"You can take that up with Mort. For my piece to be well-rounded, I have to cover the issue. You know it could come back to bite you. Remember Romney's fatal 47 percent remark."

"My husband is *not* Mitt Romney."

"But he is a one-tenth of one percent-er. Lucy Winters grew up on a farm. That her father later lost to bankruptcy. I've heard whispers that the Winters organization is going to make the contrast a lynchpin of their campaign, just as Obama did so effectively with Romney."

There's a pause, and Erica can practically hear Celeste's wheels turning.

"What do you want?"

"What are you offering?"

Now Erica can almost hear Celeste's teeth grinding. "Well, *I'm* certainly not going to give you an interview. That would only create the wrong impression in people's minds. Besides, I'm not involved in the day-to-day operations. I have more important things to do."

"Who would you suggest?"

"How about our operations manager, Paul Court? He's articulate."

"I'm not sure an operations manager is the right choice. We need someone with real authority."

"You drive a hard bargain, Erica." There's a pause, and then Celeste says, "I suppose you could do a *short* interview with our CEO, Lily . . . Lily Lau."

Yes! "We met in New York. I remember her well."

"She's a memorable woman."

"Please tell her I'll be calling to set a date."

There's a frosty pause before Celeste says, "You know, Erica, playing hardball can be dangerous."

"Batter up."

CHAPTER 60 —————————————————————

IT'S LATE MORNING ON THE Monday after the Republican convention, and Erica has just arrived at the Huntington Hotel in San Francisco. Since coming back from Iraq she's been keyed up, anxious, sensitive to any sudden sound or movement. Sleep is elusive and the early-morning hours are filled with demons. She worries about Jenny and is confused by her feelings about Greg, but forces herself to concentrate on the task at hand. She's going to interview Lily Lau at the offices of Pierce Holding this afternoon; Eileen has hired a local crew to go with her. She wants to try and break through Lily Lau's cool, rattle her a little, get her to tip her hand—without tipping her own.

After unpacking, Erica takes out her cards, sits at the suite's desk, and deals a couple of hands of solitaire. The game usually helps to center her, calm her runaway mind. These days it's not enough. Only the truth will really bring her any peace. There's a window in front of her, and she looks out at the view—Grace Cathedral, the Union Club, the charming park. San Francisco is just *too* beautiful, she decides. No wonder it has one of the country's highest suicide rates. If you can't be happy here in Shangri-La, why not just pack it in? At the end of the rainbow lies the abyss.

Erica stands up and starts to pace, trying to tamp down her anxiety. She feels lonely and afraid, as if she's going into battle alone, unarmed, and outmanned.

She gets a call from Mort Silver. "I've got some great news."

"I could use it."

"The debate commission is going to name you moderator for the third and final debate. It's being held in Seattle one week before the election. This is *huge*, Erica."

It is huge. Her surge of triumph, however, is quickly followed by one of duty. More weight on her shoulders. Still, she wanted this. Badly. And now she has it. "Do you know how it happened?"

"Well, this is where things get a little delicate. And this is strictly off the record. I got a phone call from someone I'm not at liberty to name. The Winters camp wanted you all along. The Ortiz people resisted, but then apparently Celeste Ortiz stepped in and okayed you."

"That's a little bit strange."

"However, the Ortiz camp wants to convey its expectation that your piece on him will not contain any 'surprises.'"

"In other words, they want a puff piece in return for okaying me."

"That's awfully strong wording, Erica. Remember, these are power players operating at the highest levels. I include both of us in that assessment. You know there's a lot of quid pro quo. Moderating this debate is going to take your career to a whole new level."

"I'm just going to pretend I didn't hear any of that and move forward with my piece."

"Erica, both sides reserve the right to change the moderator up until two days before the debate. We have to tread lightly here. This debate will be a coup for you, but also for GNN and its bottom line. We're less than three years old, and this would put us right up there with the more established networks. I told them that we didn't anticipate your piece containing any surprises."

"In other words, you spoke for me."

There is a pause, and then Mort says with finality, "You work for me."

"Last time I checked, I was the only number one show on GNN. If you think I'm going to compromise my integrity in service of your bottom line, well, you better start looking for my replacement."

"Now, now . . ."

"Don't 'now, now' me, Mort. Every other network on television would leap to hire me and you know it. Why? Because I *deliver*. And I don't deliver puff pieces."

When Mort speaks, his tone is conciliatory. "Are you anticipating any surprises in your story?"

"I'm anticipating an honest, in-depth look at Mike Ortiz's life and career." She takes a deep breath. "Listen, Mort, I want the moderator gig. I want it *a lot*. So let's you and I work together on this. When you get that follow-up call from your unnamed source, just tell them that Erica has assured you the report will be fair and honest and will show-case Ortiz's many strengths."

"Good. Good, Erica. That's exactly what I'll do."

Erica hangs up. She has no time to savor her win. In fact, she feels like she's racing against the clock. She concentrates on Lily Lau. Her father, Chen Lau, is the head of the MSS. The men who tortured Mike Ortiz were Chinese. Were they MSS agents?

Isolation. Sensory deprivation. Fear. Indoctrination. Love.

Erica sees that baby, gurgling with happiness, as Judy Buchanan holds it up and makes a funny face. A second later both of them were shredded into pieces by the bomb Tim Markum planted. And then that horrific day in Detroit when she was splattered by bits of Markum's brains and blood and bone when Peter Tuttle shot him in the face before killing himself. Martin Vander plowed down in broad daylight. Becky Sullivan thrown onto the rocks of Morningside Park. Anwar Hamade's car exploding when he turned the ignition. All of these crimes were seamlessly planned and executed. No doubt the MSS, with its resources and smarts, was as adept as the CIA in the art of killing.

Erica remembers the look that Celeste and Lily—huddled in a

corner—gave her as she waited for the elevator at the New York fund-raiser. It was chilling. If Ortiz wins the White House, they'll be the most powerful women in the world. Is Lily Lau a stalking horse for Beijing putting its pawn in the White House? But she couldn't be doing it alone. The MSS must have operatives in this country, just as surely as the CIA has them in China.

Erica sits down at her laptop and brings up the *San Francisco* magazine piece on Lau. She takes another look at her country compound with its three guesthouses. She searches real estate records and finds the address. Then she goes to Google Earth and zooms in on it. Much of the estate is obscured by trees. Then there is its isolation, up a two-mile driveway. There would be no one to hear you scream. One of those guesthouses could be the perfect location for—

Isolation. Sensory deprivation. Fear. Indoctrination. Love.

CHAPTER 61

ERICA AND HER POD—SOUNDMAN AND cameraman—arrive at the stately old office building on Market near the Embarcadero where Pierce Holdings is headquartered. As they ride up in the elevator, Erica says, "I'd like you two to wait outside while I have a brief pre-interview talk with Lau. I'll come and get you when I'm ready to start taping."

The elevator doors open to a reception area that looks like it hasn't been renovated since the 1950s. The lettering of the Pierce Holdings sign, the furniture, the dull prints on the walls, all give the impression of an old-money company that has nothing to prove.

The receptionist smiles and informs Lily that Erica has arrived. Within moments she strides out, even more striking and glamorous than Erica remembered. She smiles in an approximation of warmth.

"Erica, how lovely to see you again. Come in. Bring your crew." She's going through the motions, but she seems distracted, preoccupied, anxious, as if she has something far more pressing on her plate.

"I thought we could talk for a couple of minutes alone, in preparation."

Lily looks thrown, for just a nanosecond. "Whatever you prefer."

They walk down a hallway lined with more generic art and into Lily's relatively modest office. The art in here is in a whole different league—three striking black-and-white abstract paintings. Lily sits behind her desk and Erica sits facing her. Lily's mouth is drawn tight. Erica takes a deep silent breath. Lily glances down at her phone.

"I'm hoping this won't take too long," Lily says. "As you know, Pierce Holdings is a private company. We don't divulge much. It's not good business."

"Do you worry about people looking into your inner working?"

"I don't *worry* about. I simply make sure they can't." She glances down at her phone again.

"Isn't that difficult in this day and age? Hackers are very sophisticated."

"I thought you were here to talk about where Pierce Holdings was invested. And perhaps we could discuss the work of the Pierce Foundation. We gave away thirty-five million dollars last year." She drums the desktop with her fingertips.

This chick is wound tight. Good. Push your advantage.

"We can certainly touch on the Foundation. But as the campaign heats up there is a great deal of interest in exactly where Celeste Pierce Ortiz's money is invested. Do you have holdings in fossil fuels? Companies that employ child labor? It could become an issue."

"It's no and no to both those questions."

"Do you have a lot of overseas holdings?"

"Erica, Pierce Holdings is not a nonprofit. I'm in the business of making money. I go where that's likely to happen. Last time I checked that wasn't a crime. Politics is so ugly."

"It is, isn't it? People will do *anything* to get elected."

"It's been going on for millennia." Another glance at her phone. "In fact, things are tame today compared to what our ancestors engaged in."

"You mean like murder?"

"Listen, I'm pressed for time."

Erica doesn't move. "Interesting art."

"Pierce Holdings has one of the world's best collections of contemporary Chinese art."

"How prescient. That might be a good opening for us. We could sit in front of one of the paintings."

"I'm not sure middle America is interested in Chinese art."

"I'm interested in *everything* Chinese."

"Are you?"

"Yes. Your country's history is so rich."

"It is, isn't it?" Another glance at her phone.

"They were early masters in so many fields. Including warfare."

Lily stands up. "Are you ready to shoot your piece?"

Erica remains seated. She's hit a nerve. Time to hit another one. "I've been researching Mike Ortiz's time as a hostage. His body was subjected to some brutal abuse. So was his mind."

"Mike Ortiz is an extraordinary man who is going to be a great president."

"If he wins, will you be joining his administration?"

"I never count my chickens."

"We're not talking about chickens."

"Then let's talk about geese. I spoke to Celeste this morning. About the debates." She gives Erica a thin smile. "Only a fool would kill a goose that lays golden eggs."

"Geese are nasty animals. And some things are more valuable than gold."

"Such as?"

"The truth." Erica looks Lily in the eye and holds her gaze. "I saw some amazing pictures of your weekend house. It's quite a spread."

For a second Lily's eyes turn into burning ice cubes. Then she turns away with a look of vague dismissal.

Too late, Lily, I saw that look.

Lily gets a call. Still feigning nonchalance, she says, "Would you excuse me for just a moment?"

"Of course."

Lily walks out into the hall. Erica immediately decides it's the perfect time to go get her crew. She silently walks to the open office door—she can hear Lily's urgent whisper, "Well, *were* we breached?"

Erica steps out into the hallway and Lily whirls on her. Erica says, "Just going to get my crew," and walks down to the reception area.

In their taped interview, Erica and Lily continue their taut tango. Lily is guarded and stingy with information about Celeste's wealth. Erica presses her, but not hard. After all, facts about Celeste's fortune aren't what she came for.

When Erica gets back to the hotel she calls Mark on her prepaid.

"Listen, Mark, I think they may have detected you. Pull back *now.*"

"Just when things are getting interesting?"

"I'm serious. I want you to shut down your work. You're at risk. Do you understand me?"

"All right, Erica, I will. But I have learned something that might interest you. While I haven't been able to get into their second system, I have been able to discern a location for a lot of its activity."

"Is it in China?"

"No, it's in northern Marin County."

Erica hangs up with Mark, opens her laptop, and pulls up the Ortiz campaign schedule provided to the press. The candidate and his wife are flying out of town first thing in the morning, and they'll be criss-crossing the country all week. Lily Lau is listed as accompanying them.

Next Erica finds a helicopter rental agency and gives them a call.

"Hi, this is Erica Sparks. I'm interested in real estate in northern Marin. I'd like to do a flyover to get a good look at several properties."

"We can certainly accommodate you."

"Do you have a copter available tomorrow morning?"

"We do, yes. We leave from the Signature Flight Support Terminal at SFO."

"I'll be there at nine."

CHAPTER 62 —————————————————

THIRTY THOUSAND FEET IN THE sky above Florida, the Ortiz campaign jet is slicing through the ether on its way to a fundraiser and rally in Miami. Celeste is in the plane's salon room having her hair done by Sylvie, who is the only woman she lets touch it and who travels with her everywhere. Celeste looks at herself in the mirror as Sylvie works. She's never looked better and it goes beyond Botox and La Prairie; she is just radiant and glowing—and she knows why. Because she has never felt so alive, so full of energy and drive and excitement. She smiles to herself. How brilliant it all is. If only the world knew. That beneath each guest-house at Eagle's Nest is a secret bunker in which a select few are toiling. In the first house, information is mined 24/7 from the Pentagon, the CIA, the FBI, the whole dark beating heart of American intelligence. Codes are broken, movements are tracked, the unseen is made visible. In the second house, preparations for the transition are being made—demonstrations and even civil unrest might ensue, but Lily will always be two steps ahead. To those who say America has never used its military on its own people, she answers—*"And?"* In the third building is the propaganda machine, ready to twist the tiny minds of the masses until they think black is white, up is down, and that the new administration cares about their pathetic little lives.

On the surface the Ortiz administration will be as Go-Go-USA as every other presidency. Everything will be methodical. Ordered. Patient. First the warming of Chinese-American relations, the cultural exchanges, academic alliances, business partnerships, leadership visits, the ever-growing reach of China's tentacles into every aspect of American life. Then the trade agreement between the two countries. And then, perhaps two years into President Ortiz's first term, the historic military pact between the two great nations, the pact that will make NATO look like the wimp on the beach, that will usher in the most powerful alliance the world has ever seen. One controlled, of course, by Beijing—and Lily Lau from her perch by the president's side in the Oval Office. She and Celeste will ascend to the fiery Parthenon.

"All done," Sylvie says.

"Thank you, dear," Celeste says.

She gets up and walks down the hall and into the plane's private office. Lily, Mike, a speechwriter, and a speech coach sit around the large table. Celeste knows they've been prepping for an interview with Anderson Cooper, with the writer standing in for Cooper. Mike does well with large crowds and at fundraisers, and he's surprisingly good at debates, where he can slot in his prepared answers as called for. But he tends to falter at town halls and in one-on-ones, where he has to think on his feet and make direct human contact. He's not great at human contact. But, honestly, Celeste thinks, human contact is so overrated.

Celeste sits down just as he stumbles on an answer to a question about pre-K education, and he looks at her sheepishly. She loves the look of supplication, although right now she wishes he'd just rise to the occasion. Tending to her candidate is becoming a bit of a bore. She reminds herself that it will all be over in a matter of weeks. Mike just has to keep his mojo going. He's really doing awfully well. She's proud of him. Poor thing.

Celeste is more worried about Lily, who is definitely distracted. She has her face buried in her phone and her shoulders are hunched. She barely acknowledged Celeste when she came into the room. Celeste isn't sure she has ever seen her this out of sorts. There's something black and icy in Lily's eyes. She seems coiled and ready to strike. They haven't had a chance to talk privately, but they will as soon as this tutorial is over. Still, it's disconcerting. Celeste lives and dies by Lily's moods—and this one is ominous.

"Remember to maintain eye contact," the coach says.

"Yes, darling, *eye contact*," Celeste seconds.

"When you get an education question, talk about *children*, mention that they're the *future*. Bring up *Tajari*, the six-year-old homeless girl you met in Detroit. Or *Michael*, the ten-year-old foster child in Denver," the speechwriter says.

"Children. The future. Tajari. Michael," Mike repeats.

"Remember how they touched you, darling? How you want them to have the same chance every other child in America has?" Celeste says.

Mike nods.

The writer repeats the education question, and Mike looks at Celeste before leaning forward and making eye contact with his questioner. "You know, Anderson, children are more than statistics; they're our future. I'll never forget the look in the eyes of Tajari, a six-year-old homeless girl I had the privilege of meeting in Detroit. She was living in a shelter. I asked her what she needed most of all, and she answered, 'A desk to do my homework on.' I was deeply moved by her plea. If I'm elected president, I *will not rest* until Tajari and every child like her has a desk."

In spite of everything she knows, Celeste is moved by Mike's words. She's really done an amazing job, hasn't she, molding him into this presidential figure. She knows how Michelangelo must have felt, taking a lump of marble and turning it into a brilliant work of art. It's immodest of her to think that, but modesty is for losers. She looks to Lily for her reward, but all she sees is a set jaw and those burning eyes. Something is terribly wrong. In spite of Mike's progress, Celeste feels her anxiety level skyrocket.

She stands and crosses to Mike, leans down, and kisses the top of his head. "That was marvelous, darling." Mike beams. "Do you feel like a nice workout?" Mike nods. "Wonderful. I'll join you in a few minutes. We can have a private spinning class."

Mike *needs* his daily workouts. It's the only way he can work off all that excessive energy. *Well, there is one other way,* Celeste thinks with a little smile. But she's been withholding that—just once a week, when the man wants it three times a day—with the promise that they'll make up for lost time after he wins the election. It's the proverbial sex on a stick.

As soon as they're alone, Celeste asks Lily, "What's the matter?"

Lily stands and starts to pace. "Erica Sparks is wrong, for one thing." Even as she says the name, Celeste can hear grudging respect in her voice.

"And after we agreed to let her moderate the final debate! We may have to pull that plug. What has she done now?" Celeste asks.

"I think she knows too much."

"Knows or suspects?"

"Either way is bad news. She was very aggressive in questioning me *before* the filmed interview. She told me that she's looking into Mike's days as a hostage. She brought up China. And she brought up hacking. Our people have detected suspicious activity."

"You didn't tell me that."

Lily turns on her. "I'm telling you now!"

Celeste feels a terrible pang of hurt. She can't handle it when Lily gets short with her. All she said was one simple sentence and Lily bit her head off. "Were we hacked?"

"Didn't I just say they have *detected suspicious activity*? If we were hacked, wouldn't I have just come out and said *we've been hacked*? Honestly, Celeste, sometimes I think you're as slow as your husband."

Celeste can feel hot tears welling up behind her eyes. Lily knows how hurtful she's being; she knows.

"I'm only trying to be helpful."

"By asking me a lot of third-grader questions?"

"How am I supposed to know what's happening if I don't ask questions? You're being horrid to me, and it's not fair!" Celeste is quivering and she can't stop herself.

Lily laughs in derision. "*Horrid?* I'm being *horrid* to you? 'Oh, Mummy, Mummy, Lily is being horrid to me. Make her stop it, Mummy. Make her stop!'"

Since the day they met, Lily has teased Celeste about her upbringing, needling her mercilessly at times, imitating her country club manners and speech. But before it's always been in fun. This *isn't* in fun. Something has shifted.

And then it hits Celeste like a thunderbolt: *Lily is afraid.* She's never seen her afraid before. Erica Sparks is getting too close for comfort. And Lily can't handle it. She needs help. She needs *Celeste*, more than she's ever needed her before.

Celeste feels a combination of succulent warmth and gushing empathy. Poor Lily. Poor dear, vulnerable Lily. Celeste calmly takes a breath. "We'll get through this," she says in a smooth soft voice. Then she goes to Lily and squeezes her hand. "The same way we get through everything. *Together.*" She smiles in reassurance.

Lily pulls her hand away. "Of course we'll get through it. You don't think I'm *worried*, do you? Please. I could crush that Erica Sparks like a bug if I wanted to. Just like I crushed all the others. Like little bugs underfoot. I love that sound they make as their shells shatter and you grind them into oblivion."

Oh, how touching!—Lily can't *admit* that she's afraid. It's her fierce pride, of course. The Chinese are so proud. Celeste is so sensitive, so attuned to Lily's every mood and inflection. What Lily needs most is a concrete plan—she's always best when she feels in control.

"Has there been any more suspicious activity on the system?" Celeste asks.

Lily shakes her head.

"It sounds as if the suspected breach may have simply been a false alarm."

"Perhaps," Lily says, somewhat begrudgingly.

Oh, she's coming around, poor thing. "As for Erica Sparks mentioning China, and even Mike's time as a prisoner, she was just on a fishing expedition. There's nothing there. We made sure of that. And China *is* on everyone's minds these days. Sparks is just a clever reporter looking for a way to make news in a campaign that—thanks to your brilliance and that insipid Lucy Winters—doesn't seem to be holding any surprises."

"The latest polls are good," Lily says.

"Better than good when you look at the electoral college. We worked hard with Mike today. That's the best path forward. Heads down, do the work, keep our eyes on the prize."

Lily nods, her jaw relaxes.

Then Celeste says, almost casually, "There is one other thing we should do."

"What's that?" Lily asks, a little too quickly. She just revealed that she's hanging on Celeste's every word.

Celeste takes a long pause to savor the dynamic. She's taking care of Lily, protecting her, mothering her. What a beautiful thing.

"I'm angry at Erica Sparks too," Celeste says. "She was disrespectful to you. Who does she think she is? She grew up in a trailer. She's a common drunk. Arrested for reckless endangerment. Sometimes this country gives opportunities to people who shouldn't have them."

"She really has overstepped the bounds, hasn't she?" Lily says.

"She has."

"I think it's time to deal with her once and for all," Celeste says.

"But we have to be very careful. She's a public figure. There will be *a lot* of interest if something unfortunate should happen to her. And we don't have much time."

"Can't we just turn it over to the team? They've been so effective so far."

"They're extraordinary. But we're mere weeks from bringing this whole thing home. We want to be very smart," Lily says.

"You're right, of course. The final solution could cause unwanted attention, be a distraction. And we don't know who she's been talking to. They could come out of the woodwork."

Lily stands up and starts to pace again, but she's no longer anxious or distracted. She's thinking, focused, that razor-sharp brain of hers is at work—clicking-clicking—it's thrilling to see. Then she stops cold. A little smile plays at the corners of Lily's mouth, her beautiful, perfect mouth, and she says, almost casually, "I've got it."

Their eyes meet and ignite and they sit down next to each other at the table and lean in, shoulders touching, their voices bare whispers—fevered whispers charged with malice and electricity.

CHAPTER 63

THE HELICOPTER BANKS OVER THE sweeping hills and valleys of northern Marin County. Inside the chopper Erica is filming with her iPhone—it's a stunning landscape, but she wouldn't care if it looked like Gary, Indiana. She's only after one thing.

"You thinking of buying a place?" the pilot—handsome, starstruck—asks.

Erica nods.

"A lot of celebrities have places up here. You can have real privacy."

"You could almost hide away in these hills," Erica says.

"A lot of people do," he says.

Then Erica sees the long, low wood-and-glass house that swoops out over the ridgeline, its infinity pool seeming to float on air. And there's the courtyard surrounded by the three guesthouses.

"Let's take a look at that place. But don't get too close, I don't want to disturb anyone."

"Sure thing."

The pilot is expert and he hovers a distance away from the compound while Erica films, zooming in, making sure she gets the periphery, the wooded hills that surround the estate.

"Sweet spread. I bet somebody powerful lives there," the pilot says.

"No doubt."

"Maybe some tech billionaire. Or it could be Chinese money. There's a whole lot of that pouring in."

And then Erica notices a car on the road that leads to the estate. It pulls up to the gate, and a moment later the gate swings open. The car speeds up the long drive. Maybe it's the caretaker. But would a caretaker drive a Porsche? The car pulls into the courtyard and a man gets out. Erica zooms in as tight as she can—he's dressed in a black suit and he looks Asian, but she won't be sure until she studies the footage. She expects the man to head into Lily's house, but he turns toward one of the guesthouses. Another man in a black suit comes out of the guesthouse. They shake hands and then look up toward the sky, toward the helicopter.

"Let's head back," Erica says.

"Will do."

"It's gorgeous up here."

"God's country," the pilot says.

As the helicopter heads south back to SFO, Erica turns, takes a last look at the estate, and thinks, *That depends on who your god is.*

CHAPTER 64

ERICA IS IN HER ROOM at the Huntington the next morning. She's wearing jeans, a blouse, a light Windbreaker, and hiking sneakers. She's studied the footage of Eagle's Nest and the surrounding countryside a dozen times. Her rental car is waiting downstairs. She's keyed up, but as long as she's moving forward her anxiety stays in check. There's one last thing before she sets off. She sits down and writes an e-mail to Greg, Moy, and Mark, telling them what she's about to do. If something happens to her, they'll know where to look. She hits Send and then closes the computer before checking to see if the e-mail went through.

As Erica drives down to Lombard Street to pick up Route 101, she looks in her rearview mirror and sees a black sedan behind her. The visor is pulled down and she can barely make out the driver in the shadow. Male. Wearing dark glasses. Unshaven. She turns on Lombard, and so does the sedan. Erica changes lanes, it follows. She gets on the Golden Gate Bridge, the sedan stays on her tail. She can feel her pulse quicken and sweat break out on her brow. She crosses the bridge and heads through the tunnel and into suburban southern Marin. She changes lanes several times, the sedan is right with her.

Erica gets off 101 at Sir Francis Drake Boulevard. So does her eager suitor. Now her heart is thumping in her chest. She follows Sir Francis Drake into the rich suburb of Ross. She's in the middle of the shopping district, there's a stoplight up ahead, it turns from green to yellow, and Erica sees a chance. At first she slows, then when the light turns red—at the last possible second—she swings a fast left onto Lagunitas Road. She looks in her rearview—her tail is stuck at the red light. She races up two blocks and comes to Ross Common, where she takes a left and then pulls over in front of a parked SUV, which hides her car. She sits frozen, her eyes glued to the side-view mirror, which shows the traffic behind her on Lagunitas. The black sedan drives by and she can just make out the driver's head frantically twisting left and right. The car behind him honks. Erica executes a tight U-turn, goes right on Lagunitas, and then left on Francis Drake. She checks the rearview. There's no sign of her tail.

Suburbia fades out as she drives through San Anselmo and Fairfax and reaches rustic Woodacre, where she turns right and heads north on Nicasio Valley Road, into the undeveloped reaches of northwest Marin. She turns right and heads up Old Rancheria Road. After six miles she reaches the gate to Eagle's Nest. She keeps going past the gate for about a quarter of mile and then turns on the overgrown, barely visible dirt road she found on Google Earth. She drives up about a quarter of a mile, pulls in behind a copse of trees, and gets out of her car.

Erica is sweating and she's scared. But there's no way she's turning back. She starts to make her way through the woods. There's not a lot of underbrush to hide in, and she stays hyperalert for any movement or sound—the crunch of shoes on the leaves, a cough, a shadow behind a tree. She moves steadily, to the beat of her thumping heart. After a half hour she reaches the base of Eagle Nest's hilltop. She's approaching from behind the guesthouses, which are partially built into the slope, made of stacked stone. They look as solid as death. The whole compound has a secretive, forbidding air. Even though she isn't moving, Erica is now sweating profusely and she feels dizzy with fear.

She begins to move closer, slowly, deliberately, looking down before each step, landing as silently as she can. Now she's just below the guesthouses, ready to make the final climb. She searches for any sign of activity. It's a still, blue day, and all she can hear is the wind rustling the leaves and an occasional birdcall. It's quiet. Too quiet. Then she feels a mosquito bite her neck. She reaches up and slaps it, but there's no bug. Then everything goes black.

CHAPTER 65 ————————————————

CELESTE IS IN SOME DREARY backstage holding room at a Mike Ortiz rally in Des Moines. At least she thinks it's Des Moines. They all blur together, these rallies in dead-end cities Celeste wouldn't be caught alive in at any other time. She can hear the muffled screams and cries from the masses in response to Mike's rising cadences. Women, of course, go crazy for her husband, in his shirtsleeves, his muscles straining against his shirt.

Scream all you want, ladies, he's mine. Not that I really want him. Well, occasionally. Just to keep him happy and in line. Oh, all right, I enjoy it too, but the most exciting part for me is the head game. The fact that I control him. He's in my power. He worships me. And my body. But he'll never be numero uno. *That spot was taken twenty-five years ago.*

Celeste is bored. She looks around at the minions—the sweaty aides and pollsters and volunteers and speechwriters and strategists. The whole apparatus. She wishes she could just apply the accelerator to Father Time and speed up the next two weeks. Yes, it's just two weeks until election day. Until she and Lily accomplish the seemingly impossible. Celeste shivers at the thought. At how brilliantly they've engineered the whole thing and dealt with every obstacle. They're one of history's great teams. Why, they make Franklin and Eleanor and Ron and Nancy look like minor leaguers. Books will be written about them, movies made, statues built, schools named.

There's only one possible speed bump and that's the last debate, which is in three days. But it will be fine. Celeste and her tight team have tutored and nurtured their star pupil until he glows with confidence and sincerity, with thoughtful answers to a hundred possible questions at his fingertips.

There are several television sets on in the room. One of them is turned to GNN, and suddenly there's that urgent pulsing sound and a headline scrolls across the bottom of the screen *Update: The Disappearance of Erica Sparks.* Celeste moves closer to the set.

Anchor Patricia Lorenzo is saying, "It's now been two days since journalist and GNN host Erica Sparks's car went off a cliff on Highway 1 just north of San Francisco." Footage plays of Erica's rental car, smashed on the wave-lashed rocks below a sheer cliff.

"The search for her body continues in the frigid waters of the Pacific." Footage of scuba divers in the surf.

"Investigators have said it's likely that Sparks was ejected from her car on impact and that her body was carried out to sea by the strong currents in the area. Her fiancé, television producer Greg Underwood, arrived from Australia the day after the accident to supervise the search. He is also looking for answers to the mystery of what Sparks was doing in Marin County that day. He has been joined by Sparks's oldest friend, Moira Connelly, a newscaster on KTLA in Los Angeles. They have set up a command center in the Huntington Hotel in San Francisco, where Erica was staying on the day she disappeared."

Footage of an earlier interview with Greg appears on-screen, with Moira standing beside him. They both look haggard, stunned, and sad. Greg says, "This makes no sense to me. Why haven't we found Erica's body? And why was she on Highway 1? It's the slowest route back to San Francisco, and Erica was a woman in a hurry. Why didn't she inform anyone of her plans for that day? This is completely unlike her. And frankly, I'm not sure she was in that car when it went over the cliff." Footage of the car being hoisted up the cliff face is shown.

Lorenzo continues, "Adding to the mystery of Sparks's disappearance is the fact that her computer, which she left in her hotel room that day, was completely scrubbed. The computer has been analyzed by experts from the FBI, and they have confirmed that there is nothing on it. Everything was erased."

Shots appear of a distraught Jenny being escorted out of school. "Sparks's eleven-year-old daughter, Jenny, is with her father in Framingham, Massachusetts. Dirk Sparks has asked the country to please respect his family's privacy.

"All that is known for sure is that Erica Sparks left her hotel at approximately ten thirty on the morning of October 26 and got into a rented gray Honda Accord. According to the odometer and the records from Hertz, she drove 104 miles that day, meaning that she did not simply drive north to the vicinity of where the car went off the cliff, which is about fifteen miles from San Francisco. The accident occurred at approximately 2:40 that afternoon, just past a very sharp turn, with no witnesses." Footage of the vertiginous stretch of road is shown.

Patricia Lorenzo pauses for a moment and her face fills with emotion. "On a personal note, all of us here at GNN are deeply shaken by Erica's disappearance. She was part of our family. Our thoughts go out to Greg and Jenny. Erica had millions of fans, and we have been inundated with messages of love and support. We will, of course, keep you updated on any developments in the story."

Celeste walks away from the television set. Out in the arena, the screaming crescendos as her husband reaches the climax of his speech. Erica made a fatal mistake—*Well, not fatal,* Celeste thinks with a smile. Not yet anyway. She made a *major* mistake in messing with Lily Lau. What happened to her is her own fault. They were so good to her, feeding her scoops and green-lighting her as debate moderator. And in return she was sticking her nose where it didn't belong. Foolish girl. Life is so much easier if you just go along to get along.

But Erica will change. Of course she will. The change has already started. When Lily is finished with her, Erica will be one of *them*. She'll be much happier. She's such a complex woman. Too complex for her own good. Soon she won't have all those awful conflicts that bedevil her. She'll be free.

CHAPTER 66 ─────────────────────────────────

MRS. MORRIS WAS ERICA'S KINDERGARTEN teacher. She was about thirty-five, tall, at least five feet nine, with shoulder-length auburn hair. She wore running shoes every day. She had an unconscious habit of scratching her chin with her index finger when she was thinking about a question from one of the kids in class. The other kids gave her little presents at Christmas. Erica didn't have any money for a present, but she did make her a card out of red construction paper and she cut out letters from old magazines that spelled out *Mary Christman!* Mrs. Morris said, "This is my favorite card, Erica!" That made Erica so happy and proud.

Mrs. Brullette was her first-grade teacher. She was older, chubby, probably in her forties, and she had short dark hair that she held off her face with a barrette. She was strict and she sighed a lot. One day Erica raised her hand—

Oh no, an itch!

On the bottom of her left foot. A fierce itch. Erica tries to squirm. But she can't. She can't move her feet. Or her legs or her torso or her arms or her head. She can't see. She can't hear.

But she can feel. Something is in her arm. It must be an IV. And she's catheterized. And she can feel the air coming in through her nostrils.

But she can feel more than that. She can feel like she's going insane. But she won't go insane. Because that's what they want.

This is the tenth time she's worked her way through all of her teachers from kindergarten through Yale. She's also gone through every job she ever had. And every man she ever went out on a date with. And any place she has ever lived. And every birthday present she ever gave Jenny.

Jenny! Where is Jenny? Is she safe? Her mommy is gone. They took her mommy. Oh, Jenny, oh baby, my baby, please stay strong, stay strong for Mommy. And Mommy will stay strong for you. My life. My child.

Erica struggles to move, to move anything, she marshals everything she's got and desperately tries to move—but it's useless and she knows it . . . She's struggled a thousand times before over the last . . . the last . . . *what* . . . She has no idea how long she's been here. Like this. The last thing she remembers is the quiet in the woods, the eerie quiet and then the mosquito that wasn't a mosquito. It's been days, she knows that much. What time is it? Noon? Midnight? She feels as if she's hurtling through time and space, through infinite blackness, untethered and alone.

If only she could scream, she'd feel so much better if she could scream. Just scream and scream and scream. But she can't. Her mouth is taped shut. Tight.

And suddenly Erica wants to cry because all she wants to do is scream and she can't. And Jenny has no mother. Tears well up and seep out from her eyes, but she can't move her eyelids, which are covered with something thick and suffocating.

She's suffocating. Suffocating. She's dead and she's in hell. No, she's in a nightmare. They drugged her and put her into a nightmare. It's all real. It's a real nightmare. And she's in it. Forever.

Then a beautiful thought breaks through: Jenny's not in the nightmare. Jenny is free. Jenny is laughing and happy. She's on green grass and the sun is shining. Oh, look how pretty she is. Erica can handle the nightmare—sure she can—as long as Jenny stays on the green grass in the sunshine.

And then, with a sharp inhale through her nostrils, Erica knows that it isn't working. All the cataloging of teachers and boyfriends and jobs isn't working anymore. She is going crazy. Is she crazy already?

And the tears keep seeping out of her eyes. And she tries to blink, to blink them away. And she can't. But she keeps trying. Because the tears remind her that she's in a nightmare and she wants to forget it. As she keeps trying to blink, to blink away the tears, she asks herself where she left off. Then she remembers. Second grade. Yes, second grade. Mrs. Nealy. She was older, in her fifties, and she smelled like the cigarettes she pretended she didn't smoke, and Erica's tears keep coming and she keeps trying to blink and . . .

She blinks!

Not a full-fledged blink, not even close, but her eyelids opened a little, they opened and tears escaped. And it feels like she just won the US Open or an Olympic gold medal or leapt a tall building in a single bound.

CHAPTER 67

CELESTE AND LILY ARE WATCHING Erica. They're on the Ortiz campaign plane flying to the great city of Whocares. They're sitting at the desk in the conference room watching the live feed from what they call The Spa—*ha-ha!*—and Erica seems to be in the throes of an epic panic attack. Poor thing! Of course it's hard to tell exactly, she's so tightly bound to the bed, but she's trying to writhe and the expression on her face—what you can see of her face under the tape and bandages—looks awfully anxious. Terrified, really.

"Maybe she's doing her Tae Kwon Do," Celeste suggests.

The girls laugh. Their secret, giddy laugh. Why is it *so* much fun to watch Erica? What does it say about Celeste? She must ask Oprah next time she sees her. The thought of asking Oprah makes Celeste laugh again.

And the election is approaching like a steamroller and nothing can stop them now. They neutralized the only obstacle. Not only neutralized her—*claimed* her. She belongs to them now. And when they're finished with her, she'll always belong to them. Just like Mike does.

Of course, who has nine months and nine days these days? The world is operating much too fast for that. And so Lily, brilliant Lily, working with a Chinese neurologist at Eagle's Nest, has come up with a breakthrough that cuts the time down to nine days. Nine days to gain control of a mind. And a heart. Only six more days to go, and Erica will be theirs.

Isolation. Sensory deprivation. Fear. Indoctrination. Love.

Just add electroshock, that's all. Celeste smiles—it sounds like a commercial for a cleaning product. *Just add PineSol, that's all.*

Electroshock really *is* like a cleaning product. It sanitizes the brain, declutters, sweeps up all that messy, unnecessary information, dissolves all those useless memories, melts away all that emotional baggage. After a few sessions Erica Sparks will have a virgin mind, a blank blackboard onto which Lily can imprint . . . *Lily.* It's like teaching a child, really. No great mystery. Just repetition, reinforcement, *learning.* Erica will understand who her friends are, whom she can trust, whom she loves and who loves her. Because that's the beautiful part. When Lily and Celeste control someone, they love that person. Look at Mike. When they're finished with her, Erica will feel safe. She'll be ready to go back out into the world. Parts of her memory will come back. She'll work again. Will she be the old Erica? Of course not, thank God. She'll be the new Erica. The new, improved Erica Sparks. Just like the new, improved Tide! Celeste laughs again.

Lily is still focused on watching Erica. Celeste knows it excites Lily to see Erica—who really is quite beautiful, whose body really is quite lovely—tied and trussed and helpless.

And it excites Celeste to see Lily excited.

What a wonderful world.

"What's she up to now?" Celeste asks casually.

Lily answers in a charged whisper, "I think she's screaming."

"For ice cream?"

They look at each other and break into peals of laughter. *Such fun!*

And then Mike walks into the conference room. He frowns a little to see them laughing. Sometimes he feels left out. Even gets a little jealous. Poor thing. He's like a child that way. "What's so funny?" he asks.

"Oh, we're just looking at Kristen Wiig videos from old *SNLs*," Celeste says, getting up and going to Mike, kissing him on the cheek. "How was your nap?"

"Good. I'm ready for the next stop."

Celeste and Lily exchange a glance, and Lily says, "Your crowds have been huge. The latest polls show you holding your lead at about six points. Only one more debate to get through. We're getting close. We just have to maintain."

"American loves you, honey."

Mike smiles, that big boyish smile. "And you love me," he says with that touching glint of insecurity in his eyes.

"Of course I love you, darling. Always and forever. And so does Lily."

"Listen, Mike, I have to go back to California for a couple of days," Lily says.

"Oh, I thought you were going to be with us all week," Mike says, disappointed.

"I wish I could. But there are a couple of big new donors—Johnny-come-latelies, but never mind—who I want to reel in."

"That's exciting," Mike says.

"Oh, it should be electrifying," Lily says. Then she looks at Celeste. Their eyes dance with glee.

CHAPTER 68

SHE WAS WRONG. THIS ISN'T a nightmare. It's hell. She's in hell. She died and was sent to hell for being a bad mommy. A terrible mommy who put Jenny in danger. More than once. In danger of being killed. Killed dead. Erica's not in danger anymore because she *is* dead. That's one good thing. So there are good things in hell. If she's going to be here forever, which it looks like she is, she might as well look for the silver lining. With Erica dead, Jenny isn't in danger anymore. That's wonderful news. Can you have wonderful news in hell? *Wonderful news in hell*. Sounds like a song title. An Elton John song.

I know. I'll write it. In my head. I can hear the beat—a little jangly in that Elton John way and very up-up-up.

Erica smiles. *She* feels up. Yes, she does. This is okay. Where she is. Now that she knows Jenny is safe.

Oh no, another itch! Itches are the worst. This one is on her scalp. It's excruciating. *A scratch, a scratch, my kingdom for a scratch.*

And the itch makes the curtain part and the illusion fall away and Erica knows with crushing certainty that she isn't in a nightmare and she isn't in hell, she's in some terrible place where evil people have total control over her. And she feels so cold. As cold as death. And she's so afraid. She's never been so afraid.

And then the molecules in the room rearrange themselves. Erica can feel the molecules. When you're trapped in blackness, you feel every minute little change; it washes over you. Someone is near her. Very near. She tenses.

And then one of the bandages around her head is loosed, just a little, over her left ear. And then something is taken out of her ear and she can hear. Just the drip of her IV, but it sounds like clanging cymbals—*drip/clang drip/clang drip/clang.*

"Erica . . . ?"

It's a sweet, soft voice. She recognizes it. From a long time ago. When she was a real person.

"It's me, Erica, your friend . . ." A cool hand strokes her forehead. ". . . your friend Lily. I want you to hear something. Something beautiful . . . something that's happening right now . . ."

There's a pause, and then Erica hears Jenny's voice: "I don't want to do my stupid homework. My mother is missing and you want me to write some dumb book report! I didn't even really read the stupid book! I hate you, Dad; *you're* stupid. You can go to hell!" Now she's crying. "Leave me alone!" Now a door slams. And all Erica can hear is whimpering. Her baby whimpering. Then she can make out faintly, so faintly . . . , "Mommy, Mommy . . ."

"Oh, Erica, I'm sorry . . . That wasn't beautiful. It was *sad,* wasn't it? It was sad *and* beautiful. Your little girl misses you. I hope she gets to see you someday. Maybe she will. Maybe she won't . . ."

Erica feels that cold, smooth hand on her neck.

"You have such a pretty neck, Erica." Then the hand squeezes her neck. It tightens its grip . . . again . . . then again . . . and Erica can feel her windpipe narrowing and she can't breathe . . .

And now Erica is trying to fight, to thrash; she's never tried so hard and she feels a tiny bit of give on her restraints . . . just a tiny bit . . .

STOP THRASHING! Pretend to thrash. So nothing moves. And stop blinking because with every blink the blindfold moves a tiny minuscule little bit. Just wait. Try and wait . . .

And Erica tries to wait, but then she starts shivering, shivering uncontrollably.

"Oh, Erica, you're afraid . . . You're afraid you might die. You might. Or Jenny might. That would be so sad. Of course, it happens to everyone. Death. It's just a matter of how and when . . ."

And now Erica feels a blade on her neck, a sharp, cold blade, and it traces its way from one ear to the other. "*Oh!* . . . I'm sorry. I drew a little blood . . ." And now a finger traces the blade's path. ". . . Mmm, even your blood tastes pretty . . . Pretty lady, pretty blood. I have to go now, Erica. But don't worry. I'll be back. I'm going to help you. I'm going to give you something that will make you feel better. It won't hurt. I promise. And when it's over you'll be a brand-new Erica. A *better* Erica." And now she's so close that her lips graze Erica's ear. "You probably wonder what I want, don't you . . . ? I want *you.*"

CHAPTER 69

CELESTE HAS JOINED LILY AT Eagle's Nest, just for an afternoon. It's so good to get away, away from it all, and to be up here with Lily, even if only for a few snatched hours. They're sitting at a large table in the guesthouse that Lily uses as an on-site campaign war room.

Celeste's mind wanders for a moment, wanders down two stories below them, down to the bunker, where Erica Sparks awaits the final phases of her transformation. The one that will turn her from a threat into an ally. When she's ready, they'll drive her up to Mt. Tamalpais and lead her deep into the woods. She'll stumble out of the forest, dehydrated, disoriented, hungry—she'd gone on a hike and gotten lost, slept on the mountain. As for her car, it must have been stolen. She'll believe every word of the story. Because that's the way her mind will work. Then, after the election Erica—with her clout and gravitas and popularity—will become a leading mouthpiece of the New Order.

Celeste looks over to the built-in bookcases that line one wall. No one would ever suspect that behind one panel lies an elevator. An elevator that can transport you down to . . . heaven.

Rising power.

"A new poll from Georgia shows us pulling ahead," Lily says, poring over real-time data on her laptop.

"No Democrat has won Georgia since Clinton in 1992," Celeste says.

Lily picks up a phone. "Frank, flood Georgia with television and social media advertising. Buy everything available. Pull as much staff and as many volunteers as possible from Alabama, which is a lost cause, and get them into Georgia. We're going to win it."

After Lily hangs up, there's a moment of silence. The two women look at each other. What they set in motion twelve years ago—when they searched the political landscape for the perfect vehicle for their ascent and found Mike Ortiz—is about to come to full fruition.

Then there's a firm knock on the door. Odd. They haven't summoned any staff. Who could it be?

Lily gets up, crosses to the door, and opens it. A man and a woman in dark suits stand there.

"Lily Lau?" the man asks.

"Who's asking?" Lily answers.

"Kevin Marcus. This is my partner, Carol Norton. FBI." They both flash their badges.

Celeste notices Lily's whole body tense.

"May we come in?"

Celeste feels her pulse start to race. She and Lily exchange a glance.

"Of course. Welcome," Lily says with a smile, standing back.

"Could I get you a cup of coffee or tea? Water or a fresh juice?" Celeste asks.

"We're good, thanks," Agent Norton answers.

"To what do we owe the pleasure?" Lily asks.

"We'd like to ask you both a few questions," Agent Marcus says.

"About?" Lily asks.

"The disappearance of Erica Sparks."

Celeste feels a sudden chill at the back of her neck; goose bumps break out on her arms. *Cool it. Follow Lily's lead. Say as little as possible.*

"I'm afraid we're not going to be much help," Lily says. "We've obviously been consumed with the campaign and aren't paying a great deal of attention to the story . . . But please, have a seat. Ask away."

The four of them sit at the table. Celeste looks at the agents with concern and a touch of bewilderment.

"A security camera in Fairfax recorded Sparks's rental car driving northwest on Francis Drake Boulevard at 11:17 on the morning of her disappearance, October 26," Marcus says, watching the two women intently.

Celeste wills herself not to react as a bead of sweat rolls down from her left armpit. But her breathing grows shallow.

"An eyewitness saw the car on Nicasio Valley Road shortly thereafter," Norton says.

Celeste feels slightly dizzy. The world is suddenly so quiet, so quiet and still. All she can hear is her heart thumping in her chest. Can the agents hear it? Both of them are expressionless. Now sweat is running down from both her armpits and she's blinking. *Stop blinking.*

Lily, on the other hand, seems completely blasé. She picks up her phone and scrolls through. "We were in St. Louis on the twenty-sixth. None of my staff has told me that Erica Sparks made an appearance here. And they certainly would have. But you're more than welcome to question them yourselves."

"She was finishing up pieces on both my husband and his opponent. She was in San Francisco to interview Lily for that story," Celeste says, forcing her voice to stay steady. "But I don't understand why she would come up here."

"She interviewed me at the office of Pierce Holdings on October 24. I haven't heard from her since," Lily says.

"I admired her integrity so much. It's a real loss to journalism," Celeste says.

"So neither of you has any knowledge or information concerning Sparks's whereabouts on the twenty-sixth?" Marcus asks.

"No," Lily tosses off.

"None," Celeste seconds.

There's a long pause. The agents are still eyeballing them. Finally Norton says, "We'd like to search the houses and grounds."

"Of course," Lily says. "I'll have my caretaker show you around."

There's another long pause. The agents just sit there. It feels like a game of chicken.

"I certainly don't mean to be rude, but we are *very* busy," Lily says.

Marcus and Norton look at Lily. She holds their glance. After what seems like an eternity, they look away and seem to shrink a little.

Lily looks at Celeste, and Celeste's confidence sparks; she decides to press their advantage. "Unless you have any more questions . . . ," Celeste says. Then she gently caresses her hair with one hand, summoning up the might of her money and privilege and upbringing. She's the next First Lady. These agents are government employees. In effect, they work for her. They're little people, dazzled by her $800 haircut and fame and the chic outfit she put on this morning to please Lily, clothes that cost more than they make in a month.

For the first time the agents look around at the expansive, luxurious room.

"May I ask what precipitated your visit?" Celeste asks.

"We've gotten a number of calls from interested parties who don't believe Sparks died in that car accident on Route 1. They think she was either murdered or is still alive," Marcus says. "They believe that she was investigating some sort of conspiracy that was responsible for the Buchanan bombing and the subsequent murder-suicide."

"And who are these interested parties?" Lily asks casually.

"We're not at liberty to answer that question."

"I still don't understand what this has to do with us," Celeste says.

"It's our job to explore every possibility," Norton says.

Lily walks over to the bookcase, to the panel that conceals the elevator, and places one hand on one of the shelves and the other on her hip. "That's completely understandable."

"I think it would be fitting for my foundation to establish a journalism scholarship in Erica Sparks's memory," says Celeste.

"She's officially missing, not dead."

"In her *honor*, then. Please do tell the interested parties of my plan." Celeste feels a wave of elation—she handled this so well, she can tell Lily is proud of her. She leans forward on the table and smiles a warm, sorrowful smile, saying, "We're all in this together." Then she adds, "Are you *sure* I can't tempt you with a little lunch?"

CHAPTER 70

HER UNIVERSE IS TINY, NARROW, and weightless. It's moving up and down. Up and down. That's all that exists. All that matters. Up and down. Up and down. Ever since Lily left. And that was days ago. Wasn't it? Or was it hours ago? Or minutes ago? Up and down. Up and down.

And with each blink she's brought closer to Jenny. And so she blinks for hours and hours and more hours. And yes, the bandage is moving, it's moving up. She can feel it. Because that's all she can feel. All she cares about. All that exists.

She's tired and scared, but there's no room for fear or fatigue. Only fight. *Fight!* Up and down. Up and down.

There is no thought. No emotion. No lists of old teachers or old boyfriends or books read or jobs held. There is just this. Up and down. Up and down.

And then there was light!

Faint, so faint . . . fainter than faint . . . just a trace . . . just a shadow of a trace . . .

Faster. Up and down. Up and down. Fight. Fight.

And now it's hours and hours and then . . . There's more light . . . Now the trace is a glimmer . . . and now the glimmer is a sliver . . .

A sliver of the room.

And the world is revealed in a tiny horizontal sliver at the bottom of her eye bandage. And the room is brightly lit, like a laboratory. And through the sliver Erica can see down her body, her trussed-up body, to the foot of the bed and the blank wall beyond. And she inhales sharply. Inhaling strength.

They're watching you! They're always watching you!

And then gently, so gently, imperceptibly, she begins to clench and unclench her muscles. She starts with her feet, then up to her calves, her thighs, her butt, her stomach, her chest, her arms. Clench and unclench, from feet to chest, then chest to feet, up and down, down and up, feel the blood flow, the strength flow. And now make a tiny rolling motion, side to side, so slight, *invisible.* And then she twists, tiny undetectable twists. She keeps clenching and rolling and twisting.

Fight!

And then the molecules in the room rearrange themselves. *Go still.* Now she feels a slight tug on her arm. They must be changing her IV. Good. She needs the strength. But suddenly she feels so weak. And sleepy . . . so sleepy.

No! Stay awake!

But she can't stay awake . . . she's overpowered . . . pulled down . . . down . . . and sleep comes. A dreamless sleep. A sleep as deep as death.

CHAPTER 71 ──────────────────────

ERICA WAKES UP IN A cold sweat, gripped by a wildfire of fear. A fear so deep it's burrowed into her bones. For Jenny. And for herself.

And then the molecules rearrange themselves again. There's someone in the room. And through the sliver of an opening at the bottom of her eye bandage she sees a machine wheeled down to the foot of the bed. Then the person leaves. The machine is medium-size, atop a pole. It looks cold and sinister. An instrument? To perform a procedure? On Erica's body? Then she sees the two electrodes attached to the machine—wires with circular patches at the end of them. And on top of the machine there's a plastic mouth guard.

Oh, it's an electroshock machine, Erica realizes with odd detachment. How shocking! And then it hits her—*they're going to use it on her*. And under her bandages a thousand fear rats bloom and race up and down her flesh and she recoils involuntarily, and her restraints give just a little bit, but she doesn't notice because she's gripped by obliterating terror.

They're going to fry my brain. Fry my brain. Fry my brain. And then, when it's fried and shriveled, they're going to fill it with lies. Sick lies. And sick love.

Just like they did with Mike Ortiz.

Time is running out. She runs through what she knows. She's in a room—she can see a sliver of it out the bottom of her eye bandage. It's empty now. She's been here for days, probably three or four. She's been isolated and immobilized, subjected to sensory deprivation. And fear.

Isolation. Sensory deprivation. Fear. Indoctrination. Love.

She's still in the fear stage, but she's nearing indoctrination. It all makes sense. They'll erase her brain with electroshock and then imprint it with their agenda. She'll become a puppet in service of their plan to control of the government under President Mike Ortiz. She'll be their ally, with her huge platform on GNN. A mouthpiece for their agenda.

Erica begins her regimen of imperceptible clenching and rolling and she quickly realizes something. Her bonds have loosened, just a bit, just a little bit. The weight she's lost on the IV diet is helping.

And then the molecules rearrange themselves again. And now her left ear is uncovered and the plug is removed and Lily's mouth is so close to her ear she can feel her hot breath. It makes Erica's skin crawl. She wishes she could plunge a knife into her back.

"Did you miss me? Because I missed you. I have some good news and some bad news. Which do you want first?" She runs her cool, smooth palm over Erica's forehead. "Oh, Erica, try not to frown so much. You'll grow wrinkles. Okay, I'll give you the good news first. Tomorrow is a big day. It's the last debate. The one *you* were going to moderate. You blew that chance. Big mistake. Oh well. And the day after *that*, you start your treatments. The ones that are going to be so helpful. That will make you feel so much better."

Erica looks through the slit, down at the machine, sitting there, waiting, cold and malevolent.

"So! That's the good news. I almost hate to tell you the bad news. It's about Jenny. And it's very bad. And sad. Poor Jenny. She needs help. She needs a mother. And, if you're good, she'll have one . . ." And now Erica can hear Jenny sobbing, right beside her ear, loud sobbing, blubbery hysterical sobbing. "I'm glad you can't see what I see, Erica. She's cutting herself. There's blood on her dress and on her bedspread. What a terrible mess."

And now Erica hears a door fly open and Dirk's voice, "Oh no, Jenny, no, what are you doing? Linda, get the car, we have to get Jenny to the ER! I have you, baby, don't worry. Daddy has you, you'll be all right."

And Jenny starts to scream, to scream at the top of her lungs, and Erica hears footfalls and screaming and yelled orders and doors slamming. And then there is silence.

And then all that Erica can hear is the sound of her own weeping.

CHAPTER 72 ─────────────────

IT'S NOON ON THE NEXT day, the day of the final debate. Megyn Kelly has replaced Erica as moderator. The atmosphere in Mike Ortiz's expansive suite at the Fairmont Olympic Hotel in Seattle is tense. There are dozens of aides and staff on phones and laptops, everyone is poised on the precipice. Ortiz's lead in the polls has been holding, all he has to do is make no mistakes tonight—and then he can coast through the final week until the election. Early voting has started in a number of states, and turnout is high in Democratic precincts and through the roof among Latino voters.

Celeste is in one of the suite's bedrooms. She can't sit still. *Where is Lily? Her flight should be in by now.* She's tried on no fewer than eight different outfits. Some are too swanky. Some too casual. She finally settles on a simple blue sleeveless midthigh dress. She's pacing around the room. She can't relax, not without Lily here.

She's got Mike on the rowing machine in the other bedroom. Don't let him overthink things. They've got him prepared for every possible question. He's worked like a dog. First to get the answers down pat. Then to make it look like they're not down pat, that he has passion and spontaneity. He's memorized personal anecdotes about a dozen people he's met on the stump. He knows to take a deep breath before answering. To be respectful of Lucy Winters. There's really nothing more they could do to prepare him. He's a well-oiled machine. *But where is Lily?*

Hair and makeup will be here later this afternoon. Celeste wants to look her best, but she doesn't want to go full out. Not the time and place. Wait for the first state dinner. She has *big* fashion plans as First Lady. Forget Jackie Kennedy and Michelle Obama. She's going to reset the bar.

Her phone rings—her untraceable, unbugable, only-for-Lily phone—and she almost leaps for it.

"Where are you?"

"We just landed."

Celeste exhales with a sigh. "Get over here as soon as possible. How did it go?"

"Well. It went well. We have her right where we want her. I just sent you the mobile link to the live feed. See you soon."

Celeste hangs up and then uses the phone to access their untraceable e-mail account. She clicks the link. And there she is, the high and mighty Erica Sparks, tied up like a stuck pig. Celeste feels a moment of sympathy for her. The moment passes. She's getting exactly what she deserves. Sticking her pretty blond head where it doesn't belong.

Still, watching Erica—is she wriggling ever so slightly? No, that's just the camera—Celeste feels a tinge of unease, of foreboding. As if the whole enterprise is a house of cards that could tumble down at any minute. She starts to pace again. They're in so deep. They're about to stage a bloodless coup. The federal government will in essence be run from Beijing. Every decision will be made at the command of Chen Lau and his superiors. They've built the ultimate Trojan horse, and in eight days he'll be president-elect of the United States.

Celeste feels like she's going to jump out of her skin. Dark thoughts start to bubble up. Lily was so mean to her on the flight, when she was afraid they might have been hacked. And she's been distant lately. Will Lily change once power is hers? Has Lily been manipulating Celeste to get what she wants? Is brilliant Lily the ultimate user? And is Celeste just one more pawn?

Celeste couldn't stand it if anything changed between them. She loves Lily. She needs her. She wants to make her proud. The future belongs to Lily, to her father, to China. And Celeste wants to be by Lily's side, part of that future.

The door opens—and there she is!

Celeste rushes across the room. "Lily!"

Lily is not a hugger, but she kisses Celeste on the cheek. Celeste feels her anxiety and fear evaporate. They're together. A team. What silly thoughts she had! It's an equal relationship. Has she forgotten that Lily needs *her*?

She does need her. Doesn't she?

CHAPTER 73

ERICA IS WAITING. LIKE A leopard. Like a hungry leopard.

He'll be in soon. Or is it a she? The one who changes her IV. The one who changes her IV will be in soon. And then . . . she doesn't know. She doesn't even know where she is. The lay of the land. What it would take to get out. But she knows that she can wriggle her hands and the restraints on her arms have some give. And that she's going to fight.

It's clammy in the room. It must be underground. Like the Underground Railroad. She needs to be free. Like the slaves on the Underground Railroad. Freedom is a beautiful thing . . . There are still beautiful things in the world . . .

And then she hears Jenny's screams and she knows there are no beautiful things in the world. She was just kidding herself . . . The world is a sick, evil place filled with sick, evil people . . .

Stop it, Jenny, please stop it; please stop screaming!

And then she feels it; the molecules in the room rearrange themselves and she knows that he/she is approaching the bed, the IV, and then she feels that slight tug on her IV port and then she gathers every bit of her strength and will, like a mom whose kid is trapped under a car—*Jenny!*—and her right arm flies up and grabs, grabs at air. Then she finds hair and grabs it—it's a woman—and yanks, *yanks hard*, and the woman tumbles forward and her head slams on the bed railing and Erica slams it again and again and again, skull on metal, and now there's gurgling and the body goes limp and falls to the floor . . .

Erica rips off her blindfold. *Ahhhh*—the light is so bright! She tears at the restraints on her left arm and gets it free, and she takes the plugs out of her ears and reaches down and frees her torso and legs, working feverishly—*there's the camera in the corner.* She has no time, *no time* . . .

She stands up and stumbles—her legs are weak and all she's wearing is a blue hospital gown. The nurse is on the floor with blood streaming from her forehead and mouth and ears, and her eyes are rolled up. Erica reaches into the nurse's pants and finds her keys.

Erica opens the door. She's in a windowless hallway. A bunker. There's an elevator. A keyed elevator. She rifles through the keys and finds the right one. She presses the button.

You're being watched!

Erica presses herself against the wall and the elevator door opens and a man steps off and he has a gun and he brings it up and Erica kicks his hand just as he fires and the gun goes flying and the bullet ricochets off the wall and grazes Erica's leg and she winces in pain as blood oozes down her leg. Then she crouches and executes a flying kick to his head and his neck snaps back with a grisly sound and he drops to the floor. She gets in the elevator. There are just three buttons—1, 2, and 3. She presses 1 and the elevator rises. As they pass 2, she can hear yells of alarm, shouted orders.

The elevator doors open, revealing a white wall. She pushes it open. It swings back and she steps out into a beautiful, large room. Through the windows she can see the courtyard—she's in one of the guesthouses at Eagle's Nest. She keys the elevator so the door stays open, immobilizing the car. She can hear faint shouts from down below.

Get out. Get out!

Erica runs out the front door. There are half a dozen cars parked nearby, and she desperately searches the keys. There's one for a Honda and she presses the key and an Accord blinks its light and honks and she runs over and jumps in and turns it on and tears off down the long drive—then she remembers the impenetrable metal gate at the end of the drive. She waits until she can see the gate, then she pulls over and leaps out of the car and runs into the woods, toward the road. A shot rings out behind her. She trips and falls, scraping her right forearm; blood oozes out, her bare feet are getting scratched and cut. Pain shoots through her, but who cares.

She hears more shots behind her as she runs and runs, reaching the road. She turns west, toward Nicasio Valley Road, and runs and sucks air and her lungs burn and her gown is bloody and pain shoots through her leg and arm and feet and she runs and runs—*please let there be a car*—and runs and runs . . .

And then, behind her, she hears an engine and she turns and a blue pickup truck is heading toward her and she stands in the middle of the road and waves her arms and yells, "*Stop, please, I need help! Please, stop!*"

And the pickup does stop and the driver is a nice-looking young man with a beard and Erica races to the passenger side and leaps in and chokes out the words, "Drive, please drive, quickly; they're after me. *They're after me!*"

And the bearded young man looks at her in concern and says, "Are you all right there, lady? Just *who* is after you?"

Erica's whole body is heaving. "Please just drive, please, please. I'll explain . . ."

"You look a little raggedy, lady. Slow down there, just slow down. Take it easy . . ."

Then the nice young man tilts his head and smiles a small smile and makes a U-turn and Erica realizes that he's not a nice young man— *he's one of them!*

And Erica punches him in his right temple so hard that his head bounces off his window—"Ahhhh!"—and he reaches down and picks up a pistol and she punches him again and his head bounces again and he drops the gun on the seat and Erica grabs it and pulls the trigger again and again, shooting him in the torso and chest and head. Then she grabs the steering wheel with her right hand and reaches over his body and pushes open his door and shoves him out of the pickup with her left leg. She hits the brakes, puts the truck in park, and jumps out, kneels beside his dead body, frantically searches his pockets and finds his cell phone.

She jumps back in the pickup and pulls away, hitting sixty miles per hour on the curvy road, checking the rearview, racing, racing, sucking air, dialing . . . desperately dialing . . . Now there's ringing . . .

"Who is this?" comes Moira's voice.

"Oh, Moy," and then Erica starts crying and can't talk, she can't talk . . .

"*Where are you?!* Keep talking, you have to keep talking. We're with you, we love you! Where are you?!"

And Erica struggles to talk through her sobbing and heaving. "Please call Jenny. Tell her I'm alive and I love her . . ."

"*Where are you?!*"

"I'm heading to . . . Francis Drake Boulevard . . . in Marin . . ."

"*Come on, Greg, she's in Marin!* We're on the way, Erica. We're both in San Francisco; we'll be there in no time. Just keep driving. Just keep talking."

"Greg? Is Greg with you?"

"Yes, he came back from Australia the day after you disappeared."

Oh, Greg . . .

Erica can hear sounds of running and then car doors slamming. "Call Jenny. Tell her I love her, tell her to stay strong . . ."

"Greg is calling her right now. We're on our way; we're heading toward the Golden Gate Bridge. Keep talking, baby, keep talking and keep breathing . . ."

"I'm afraid, Moy. They're still after me. They drugged me and kept me tied up in blackness and they were going to use electroshock on me and . . ."

"*They? Who is they?*"

"Lily Lau."

"Oh no . . . ," Moy says. "I'm handing you over to Greg now, baby. We'll be together soon."

"Erica . . ."

"Greg . . ."

"I spoke to Dirk; he's going to tell Jenny."

"Poor Jenny. I'd call her but I'd just break down . . ."

"Where are you now?"

"I'm on Francis Drake. There's traffic but I'm still afraid . . ."

Then Erica reaches Fairfax and there are shops and people and it's a sunny day and she's back, back in a world where people go about their daily business, where they smile and are kind to one another. They are kind. Aren't they? Erica sees a teenager duck around a corner. A dark corner. He ducked around a dark corner. She sees dark corners everywhere she looks.

"We're over the bridge; we're on the way toward you," Greg says. "Moy, I think we should call the police. They can escort—"

"*No!* Please. Not yet. I . . . I can't face it all yet . . . I just want to be with you and Moy and to talk to Jenny, please . . ."

"Erica, this story is going to blow wide open. You've been missing for four days. A lot of people thought you were dead."

"Well, I'm not dead. I'm *alive!*" And just saying the words brings Erica strength. She reaches Ross, bustling with people, and with each passing mile her breathing slows, her shaking diminishes. She looks in the rearview mirror—her hair is clumped and plastered to her head, her skin is pale and blotchy, and there are dark circles under her eyes. But she *is* alive. And she *is* going to bring down Lily Lau and the Ortizes.

"I don't care about the media. I need a little time, I need to talk to Jenny. I just need a couple of hours."

"All right, Erica, all right, we'll come back to the hotel and then we'll call the FBI . . . Moy just found a Starbucks in Greenbrae. It's in the Bon Air shopping center right off Francis Drake. Meet us in the parking lot."

"Okay. Listen, what's happening with the election?"

"Ortiz has kept his lead. Tonight is Lucy Winters's last chance."

"Tonight?"

"Yes, the final debate is tonight."

Erica breath catches. "I didn't realize it was tonight."

"Yes, in about six hours. In Seattle. Megyn Kelly has replaced you."

Erica struggles to make sense of this information. And then she sees that sweet baby being held aloft in Judy Buchanan's arms, gurgling with delight . . .

Oh sweet thing, sweet baby. I was a baby once. An innocent baby.

And Erica feels some life force swelling insider her, some intangible, inexplicable cosmic strength, the strength to make this harsh, crummy world at least a slightly better place.

"Are you there, Erica?"

"Yeah, I'm here, Greg. I'm definitely here."

"You suddenly sound stronger, Erica."

"Listen, Greg, book us a private plane to Seattle for this afternoon."

"What?"

"Just do it. I'm going to hang up now, but one more thing—can you text me Megyn Kelly's phone number?"

CHAPTER 74

THE MASSEUSE IS BRILLIANT, HER magic hands bringing Celeste that most elusive of feelings—relaxation. Lily is just a couple of feet away, on a second table, with her own set of magic hands. They're in Lily's suite at the Liberty, just down the hall from Mike and Celeste's. Celeste booked the massages as a little surprise for Lily, a little *je ne sais quoi* that will leave them refreshed and radiant, ready to glide through the night ahead, the big beautiful night. Nothing is more flattering than a wholesome glow on a wholesome girl. And who could be more wholesome than little Celeste Pierce and her BFF Lily Lau? Celeste smiles at the thought and for a giddy moment she's a bright beautiful young debutante again—San Francisco's *It* Girl. *Well, Mummy, I think your little girl has done pretty well.*

They're both on their stomachs, and Celeste turns her head and gives Lily a warm smile. Lily returns it. And then Lily's private cell—which lies at the ready beside her—makes a funny noise Celeste has never heard before. Lily's eyes widen and she checks the screen. Then she bolts upright, shocking the masseuse, who takes a step backward.

"You can go, ladies. Pick up the tables later," Lily says. She stands up and slips into a robe.

"Lily, what is it?"

The masseuses beat a hasty retreat. Lily is in a far corner of the room, huddled over, talking in a fevered whisper.

"Lily, what is it, what's wrong?" Celeste cries, rushing over to her.

"Find her, get her, *kill* her," Lily hisses into the phone. Then she turns the phone to Celeste, who sees the empty bed where Erica lay.

"She escaped?"

Lily nods. Celeste feels all that wholesome blood drain from her face. Then her teeth start to chatter. "What are we going to do?"

"Nothing. This is being handled at the highest level. Erica Sparks won't live to see the sun set."

CHAPTER 75

ERICA IS IN THE BEDROOM of her suite at the Huntington. Megyn Kelly couldn't have been more gracious. She readily agreed to let Erica reclaim her post as moderator of the debate. She did insist on having an exclusive on Erica's first post-debate, post-rescue interview—she didn't get to be Megyn Kelly by accident.

Erica took a shower and now, in a hotel robe, she's sitting on the edge of the bed. She dials.

"Hello?"

"Hi, Dirk, it's Erica."

"I'm glad you're still with us."

"Thank you. Listen, your house is bugged."

"What?"

"I know. I'm very sorry. Call Gary Goldstein at Firewall Protective Services in New York. Tell him I'll pay whatever it costs for them to come up and sweep it. Now, may I talk to Jenny?"

"She's been in very rough shape."

"I know."

"She's been through the wringer with this. We all have. Hang on."

"Mom . . . ?"

"Hi, baby, I love you."

Then Jenny starts to cry quiet, exhausted tears. And Erica starts to cry quiet, exhausted tears. And they both let the tears flow and under the tears is a river of love.

"Can I come and see you? Tomorrow?"

"Yes."

"We have a lot to talk about."

"Yes, we do."

"See you then, sweet baby."

"Times a-wasting," Greg calls.

Erica jumps into jeans and an oxford and goes out into the living room. Greg and Moira are grave and tense.

"We're going to leave through the hotel basement. We've got a jet standing by at SFO. It'll get us to Seattle in two hours," Greg says. "The debate commission and NBC want to go public with you taking over. They think it will lead to a ratings bonanza."

"Ask them to hold off for a couple of hours," Erica says. "The longer we can keep this quiet, the better."

"When it breaks it's going to break big."

"I put together a little prep for you," Moy says, handing Erica a folder. "It covers breaking stories, the latest poll numbers, some suggested questions." Then she picks up a light-green suit. "I've been texting pics with Nancy Huffman. She thinks you should go with this suit. And how about these emerald clip-ons? I've got hair and makeup people meeting us at the airport."

Erica nods. "Let's hit the road. We've got work to do."

CHAPTER 76

CELESTE AND LILY ARE IN Mike's suite at the Liberty, along with his closest advisors and some select members of the media, including a producer, reporter, and pod from CBS that is recording the historic night. There are several television sets on; it's wall-to-wall coverage of the debate, most of it live from Meany Hall at the University of Washington. Mike is relaxed, bantering with a couple of reporters. Celeste and Lily are pacing around on a razor's edge.

Suddenly on NBC there's throbbing music and the banner *Breaking News*. Everyone turns to the set.

Lester Holt announces, "We have breaking news on both the Erica Sparks disappearance and tonight's debate. Erica Sparks has been found. I repeat: Erica Sparks has been found. She is alive and apparently well. No details of her whereabouts for the last four days have been disclosed. However, she is currently in Seattle and she, not Megyn Kelly, will be moderating tonight's debate."

The room falls into a stunned silence. Celeste is sure that her heart has stopped beating. She looks over at Lily. She's staring at the set, as still as a statue. Within moments all the other networks have gotten the news, and suddenly the coverage is wall-to-wall.

The CBS producer is on his headset. "*Go live! Go live! We've got Ortiz right here.*" He listens and then says to the reporter, "You're on!"

"This is Bill Condon reporting live from Mike Ortiz's suite at the Liberty Hotel in Seattle. Mike, what is your reaction to the news that Erica Sparks has been found and will be moderating tonight's debate?"

Mike looks blank. Then he looks over to Celeste. She freezes for a moment and then races over to him, fighting to control her voice. "I think my husband is in a little bit of shock, *good* shock. As we all are. Isn't that right, Mike?" She squeezes his arm and gives him an imploring look.

Mike nods his head and says, "I'm going out there to debate the issues with Lucy Winters."

Lily is huddling with a campaign aide, who comes over and whispers to the producer, "The man has to prepare. No more live coverage."

Celeste feels panic rising inside her. She takes Lily's hand—it's so cold—and pulls her into a bedroom and shuts the door.

"*What are we going to do, what are we going to do?*" she pleads, close to tears.

"Will you cool it!" Lily barks. "We're going to proceed as planned. We have no idea what happened with Erica. We're just happy she's safe."

"We're just happy she's safe," Celeste mimics in a singsong.

"We have no idea what shape she's in, or even how much she knows about what she went through."

Celeste's lower lips starts to quiver.

"Will you please pull it together! You're going to be the First Lady of the United States—and you're acting like a sniveling child."

"Please don't be mean to me, please."

"*Please don't be mean to me, please.* Where's the *pretty please?*"

"I'm sorry, Lily. I try to be strong for you. I try so hard, but sometimes I get scared. I'm sorry." Celeste collapses on the edge of the bed and starts to cry.

"You *are* sorry. Now pull yourself together and get in that bathroom and clean yourself up. I have to go over to my suite and pick something up. The cars are leaving for the arena in ten minutes. I want your game face on. You understand me?"

"Please don't leave me; please don't leave me alone."

Lily looks down at Celeste in disgust. Then she slaps her across the face.

Lily's slap eases all Celeste's anxiety and fear. Her cheek throbs with a tingly pain. She likes the feeling. Lily's in control. Everything will be fine.

CHAPTER 77

BY THE TIME THEY LAND in Seattle the story has broken and the start of the debate is only an hour away. They've been able to keep Erica's location a secret, so there's no press waiting at the airport. On the flight up, hair and makeup made Erica look presentable while she studied the prep folder.

In the car on the way to the University of Washington with Greg and Moy, Erica ignores her faint dizziness, the weakness in her limbs, her hollow stomach. She's digging deep, calling up everything she's got, and she feels her adrenaline spiking—she's keyed tight, running at a fever pitch, almost jumping out of her skin. The next couple of hours are the most important in her life.

They arrive at the hall with little time to spare. The scene outside is raucous and rowdy, with thousands of partisans holding signs for Ortiz or Winters. The scene triggers another flashback to the night of the Ortiz-Buchanan debate. And the bomb going off with a deafening boom and then blackness and then the mangled bodies and the girl with her leg blown off and . . . and . . . Erica tries to push the images— and the fear they ignite—out of her mind.

"Take us to the back entrance," Greg says.

The driver nods and finds his way to the rear of the building. She, Greg, and Moy make their way to a holding room. There's a television tuned to GNN, and Patricia Lorenzo is reporting from New York over live shots of the audience in the hall.

"As you can see, Meany Hall at the University of Washington is filled to capacity." The camera zooms in on Lucy Winters's family—her husband and three teenagers. "Here we see Jeff Winters and the three Winters children. Just two rows in front of them is Celeste Ortiz, sitting with Alberto and Miranda Ortiz, the candidate's parents." The camera pans to Celeste, with Alberto and Miranda on one side of her and Lily Lau on the other. "We can see in their faces the tension and nerves that everyone is experiencing, as we are just minutes away from the start of the final debate of the campaign. With Ortiz leading in the polls, there is general agreement that Lucy Winters needs a breakthrough performance tonight to shake up the race."

The camera pans to the stage, where there are two podiums for the candidates and a desk facing them downstage, where Erica will sit.

Erica is half watching the screen, half going over her notes one last time. Now that they're actually in the hall, minutes away from starting, she's finding it hard to concentrate, to formulate her questions. She's so exhausted, in some realm beyond exhaustion; she's afraid she might collapse or faint or be unable to get out a coherent sentence. She feels sweat break out under her arms and on her brow.

An associate producer pokes her head in the room. "You're on."

Greg and Moy give her smiles of encouragement as Erica stands up—did she wobble slightly?—picks up her notes, and walks toward the stage. It feels like a mile-long trek, and in the distance she can see the bright lights and hear the tense murmurs of the crowd. And now the announcer says, "Host of GNN's *The Erica Sparks Effect*, debate moderator Erica Sparks." And she walks onstage and there is applause and Erica tries to smile, but her facial muscles feel like they aren't working right and then she sees Celeste Ortiz and Lily Lau sitting side by side, taut smiles on their faces, and a wave of fear floods over her and she wants to turn and run away, run away from all this forever and be free. Can she ever be free? Will she ever be free?

And Erica looks away from the two women and wills herself to *focus*, to be a pro. She sits behind the desk and makes a show of checking her notes, but when she looks down at them the letters look jumbled and random, the words don't make any sense.

And now the announcer is saying, "Please welcome Minnesota senator Lucy Winters and California senator Mike Ortiz." As they walk onstage the audience applauds and shouts, each side's partisans trying to outdo the other's.

Mike Ortiz's smile is somewhat muted, but he looks relaxed and confident and toned; his suit hugs his muscular body. At the same time he is clearly trying to project some of the gravitas that Americans want in their president. Lucy Winters is no slouch in the charm department herself; attractive and fit and outdoorsy, she smiles a warm smile that complements her natural dignity and purpose.

Erica and the candidates exchange nods. Ortiz seems guileless, and for a moment she wonders if the last four days were all a dream, a nightmare, and now she's awake. And the whole world is watching. Can she pull this off?

"Good evening to you both," Erica says. "You each have three minutes for your opening statements." After both candidates have recited their boilerplate spiels, she says, "I'd like to start by asking you both the same question: Who has been the most influential person in your life? Senator Winters?"

"My mother. Growing up on a farm I saw that she not only pitched in with all the chores, she also ran the household budget, cooked, cleaned, took care of her three children, was active in our church, and volunteered at the library and food pantry. When we lost the farm, my dad went into a depression. My mom went back to college, earned a teaching degree, got a job, and held our family together. My whole life has been dedicated to honoring her legacy."

"Senator Ortiz?"

"I would have to say my wife, Celeste." He smiles at Celeste. "She has taught me that we all have a responsibility to the common good. She's the smartest woman I've ever met—my best friend and my confidante. Her heart and her wisdom guide every decision I make."

Boy, both those answers feel canned. In spite of their smiles, the candidates are nervous. Time to make one of them *a lot* more nervous.

"This is a question for Senator Ortiz. You've written and spoken a great deal about your time as a hostage in Iraq. In an effort to get you to divulge military intelligence, you claim you were subjected to torture by Al-Qaeda operatives."

"That's correct. I was."

"What sort of torture?"

"They tried to break my spirit—but they only strengthened it."

"How? What were the *specific* means of torture?"

Ortiz looks at Celeste and Lily, who have looks of concern and empathy plastered on their faces.

"It's all in my book."

"Yes, your recounting is in your book. Not every voter has read the book. You're asking the American people to elect you their president. One of the lynchpins of your campaign has been your time as a hostage. As you know, many soldiers return from war emotionally and psychologically damaged. I think the nation deserves an exploration of your experience." A murmur ripples through the audience, along with some muffled boos from Ortiz supporters. "So, can you tell us some specifics about the torture you were subjected to?"

Ortiz shoots another glance at Celeste. Is there a beseeching edge to it? Celeste nods in encouragement, an almost imperceptible nod.

"Well, I was restrained. Tied up. Blindfolded. My mouth was taped shut. My ears were plugged up. I was whipped and choked and told I was going to be killed if I didn't cooperate."

"Told by *whom?*"

"Whom?"

"Yes, who told you this?"

Another murmur courses through the audience. Celeste and Lily Lau are having a hard time maintaining their poker faces.

"The Al-Qaeda operatives."

"How many were there?"

"How many?"

"Yes. How many Al-Qaeda operatives took part in the torture?"

"Two. Three. I was blindfolded."

"Was it the same two or three people every time?"

"Ah . . . yes. I think so."

"You *think* so?"

"I just said I was blindfolded."

"You couldn't recognize their voices?"

"They were the same. I think. Mostly the same. I was under a lot of duress. Hungry and dirty and scared and sick."

"And what did they say to you besides the threats?"

"Beside the threats? Um . . . um . . . they told me propaganda and stuff."

"Propaganda and *stuff*? What kind of *stuff*?"

"Um, things like America was bad and they were good and I had to obey them. Stuff like that." Sweat breaks out on Ortiz's brow. The boos have stopped and the audience sits rapt.

"Anything else?"

"Else?" Ortiz tries to smile—which is totally inappropriate—but his mouth twitches.

"Yes. Did they tell you anything else?"

"Oh, okay. Okay, okay. They told me I was being groomed to do great things for the world."

"What kind of great things?"

"That if I followed them I could be a savior."

"A savior of what, of whom?"

"Of mankind."

"So first these men tie you up; then they torture you; then they tell you that you're going to be a savior of mankind?"

319

Mike Ortiz's eyes keep darting to Celeste. She looks frozen. "Yes, yes," he blurts out, looking totally at sea. Sweat drips down his temples.

"And were these men from Al-Qaeda?"

"Um . . . yes," he mumbles unconvincingly.

"Did they tell you they were from Al-Qaeda?"

"Tell me?"

"Yes, Senator Ortiz, did the men who tortured you and told you you would be a savior tell you they were from Al-Qaeda?"

The arena has fallen into absolute pin-drop silence.

"Why does it matter?"

"*Why does it matter?* Because you're asking us to elect you president, Senator; *that's* why it matters. Who were they?"

"I don't remember." Ortiz looks around wildly, as if for a way to escape.

"*You don't remember?* Well, I just spent four days with some of those same men." There's a gasp from the audience. "Would you like me to refresh your memory about what the men looked like?"

"Leave them alone!"

"Leave who alone?"

And now something close to rage fills Ortiz's face. He clenches his jaw and spits out, "The men! They were my *friends*! They took *care* of me. They *helped* me. They *loved* me! *They still love me!* Just like my wife loves me! And Lily Lau loves me! You don't love me. So stop it!"

There's a gasp of shock and incomprehension from the audience, followed by agitated murmurs.

"Who were the men, Senator? Tell the American people who they were! We have a right to know! They took control of your mind. Who *were* they?"

Mike looks like a trapped rat, his eyes bulging, his jaw grinding. *"Chinese! They were Chinese!"*

CHAPTER 78 ⎯⎯⎯⎯⎯⎯⎯⎯⎯⎯⎯⎯⎯⎯⎯⎯⎯

CELESTE LEAPS UP IN HER seat. "Stop it! Stop it right now! Leave my husband alone!"

Lily grabs Celeste's wrist and yanks her down to her seat. People are staring at them, staring in shock. But they all recede to the periphery. All Celeste cares about is Lily.

"What's going on, Lily? What's happening to us? What's happening here?"

Lily sits there, preternaturally calm. "Erica Sparks outsmarted us. She won."

"But, Lily, we still have each other. I still love you. Do you still love me?"

"*Still* love you? I *never* loved you."

Celeste's face starts to spasm and crumble. *"Don't say that; please don't say that. You told me you loved me . . ."* Tears gush from her eyes as she slips into hysteria.

Lily opens her bag and takes out a pill vial. "And you believed me, you stupid cow."

"Please don't call me that, Lily. I love you. I love you so much!"

All around them people are buzzing and standing and moving but it all blurs for Celeste, who is lost in her own world, her own collapsing world, falling, falling into a black bottomless pit . . .

Lily opens the vial and shakes out a pill. She puts it in her mouth and bites down. Within seconds she turns sheet-white and grasps her chest and gasps for air, then slumps down in her chair, motionless.

"Nooooo!" Celeste wails, and now people are racing toward them, and someone lifts Lily's body up and places it on the floor in the aisle. A man puts two fingers on her neck, on her pulse, and then shakes his head.

And Celeste wants to die. She wants to die with Lily, to be with Lily, always and forever, and the vial is on the floor and she lurches for it and grabs it and there's another pill in it and she takes the pill in her hand. And a woman grabs her wrist and shakes it and the pill drops to the floor and rolls away and Celeste falls to the floor and crawls for it under the seat—*she needs to be with Lily!*—and now she's being lifted up, restrained, but she's screaming, screaming and flailing, screaming from the bottom of her soul and then . . . Mike is there, looking at her with concern and fear.

"Celeste, what's happening? Please tell me what's happening?"

She looks at his face, his sincere, handsome, stupid face, and says, "It's over."

CHAPTER 79 —————————————————————————

ERICA SITS AT THE MODERATOR'S desk as the mayhem swirls around her and she feels strangely . . . calm, detached, almost as if she's disassociating again. Across the stage, Lucy Winters is surrounded by aides trying to contain their stunned jubilation. She has just been handed the keys to the White House.

Erica is also surrounded by colleagues, journalists, bloggers, political operatives, all shouting questions at her. It all blurs together into a meaningless cacophony. She doesn't even try and answer. She's not sure if she's in a state of shock or a state of grace, or some combination of the two. But it is over. She was right. There was a Chinese-led conspiracy to take control of the presidency. She brought the truth to light.

It was all worth it. *Wasn't it?* Only Jenny can answer that question. *Please forgive me, dear baby girl. Please try and understand your poor old mom.*

Erica stands up, still ignoring the pleas and shouts and questions. She walks across the stage, glancing down at the audience to see Celeste and Mike Ortiz surrounded by police, FBI agents, and freaking-out aides. Lily's dead body is being loaded onto a stretcher by two EMTs.

On some level Erica understands that this is a fateful moment.

That she has written herself a place in the history books. But all she wants to do is see Greg.

And there he and Moira are. And they each take one of Erica's arms and lead her through the pack of people and back to the holding room. Greg closes the door. Suddenly they're enveloped in a silence that feels like pure luxury.

Moira hugs Erica so tightly that their hearts are beating as one. And Erica inhales Moy's fresh, sweet smell and knows that it's what love smells like.

They come apart and Moy takes Erica's face in her hands. "You did it." And now tears are streaming down Moy's face, but Erica isn't going to cry. She hears Jenny's voice: *We Sparks girls don't cry.*

Then there's a moment of silence as Greg and Erica look at each other and thoughtful Moy says, "I'm going to go make a fool of myself in private. I'm also going to make a reservation at the best restaurant in town. We need to get some meat back on your bones, young lady."

And now Erica and Greg are alone.

"You were there for me, Greg."

"That's where I always want to be. I quit my job. I'm coming home."

Erica goes to him and lays her head on his chest and his arms enfold her, and Erica thinks, *I'm already home.*

EPILOGUE ———————————————————————

IT'S A TUESDAY EVENING THE following May, and it's a lovely evening:
the cerulean sky is flecked with wispy, fast-moving clouds, and a breeze
ripples through the blooming apple, cherry, and dogwood trees that
dot the park. The sky and clouds and blooms are reflected in the waters
of the lake outside the boathouse as lovers in rowboats glide across its
surface. *It's like a Monet*, Erica thinks—*or is it Manet?* Either way, it's
almost *too* romantic. Erica has learned to never take anything at its face
value. Even love.

Jenny looks lovely in her blue maid-of-honor dress. And Erica feels
radiant and chic in the striking silk cream dress with metallic silver
threads running through it. Nancy, dear Nancy, made both of their
dresses.

It's all very low-key, which is what both Erica and Greg insisted on.
A few dozen guests, Reverend-for-a-day Moira Connelly performing
the ceremony, some great food, a good DJ. Simple. They've tried to
keep the wedding under wraps, but of course someone leaked it to the
press, and there are paparazzi and a few film crews outside. Greg and
Erica are going to slip out early and catch their flight to Nairobi for

their honeymoon safari. And from there, Erica is heading straight to Davos for a summit on climate change. There's no rest for those who have no desire to rest.

Erica doesn't believe in superstition—or even tradition, for that matter—but Jenny wants to walk her down the aisle, and so they're waiting in a private dining room until the music starts.

"Moy and I are going to see *Hamilton* tonight," Jenny says.

"I want a full report."

"And then I'm heading back to my boring life in Framingham, Massachusetts," Jenny says with a smile.

"Now you're venturing into dangerous territory. But I guess it's working out."

"It kind of is. I get the best of both worlds."

"I do miss you."

"I'm sorry if I went a little crazy last fall, Mom. I was just so worried about you."

"I know you were, honey. And I love you for it."

"I hope you don't put me through it again."

"I hope I don't put either of us through it again. But you never know."

"Oh, you're impossible!" Jenny cries, throwing her arms around Erica's neck and giving her a big kiss.

There's a rap on the door and Moy enters.

"I'm going to go see how my future stepdad is holding up," Jenny says, heading out.

"Hey there, my friend," Erica says.

"Well, here we are."

"Another adventure together."

"Do you want your big day to be unsullied by news updates?"

"I'm a junkie. Sully away."

"Celeste Pierce Ortiz tried to hang herself in her prison cell this morning."

"Jeez."

"I guess when you're the most reviled woman in American, doing six life terms for treason and accomplice to murder, oblivion looks pretty attractive."

"Ironically, I heard through back channels yesterday that Mike Ortiz is in much better shape. The deprogramming seems to be working. But he's still a broken man," Erica says.

"That man was in *way* over his head. So the saga is winding down. You must be so relieved."

"I'm relieved that Chen Lau was expelled from the Chinese government and that the MSS was forced to take responsibility for the Buchanan bombing and all the murders that followed. President Winters brought Beijing to heel. She's tough."

"Just imagine if Ortiz had won," Moira says. "The MSS would have been running the country."

"Through Lily Lau."

"I still can't believe she got to take the shortcut to hell."

"Look at it this way—she saved the taxpayers millions of dollars," Erica says.

"It's true. Her trial would have made the Simpson case look like Judge Judy on a slow day. She was a fascinating psychopath."

"Power is such an intriguing thing. I'm never sure if *having it* or *getting it* is what turns people into monsters."

"Which came first, the chicken or the evil? Say, listen, my station agreed to send me to Davos to cover the climate summit."

"Such great news. We'll get to hang. Between reporting on the planet's slow death," Erica says.

"Let's hope it *is* slow. There are going to be a lot of heavyweights there. A lot of power."

"By the way, have you met George Yuan yet?"

"I have. He introduced himself."

"And . . . ?"

"Some definite chemistry there."

"*Yes!* I sat you next to him at dinner."

"Thank you, Dolly Levi."

The two old pals smile at each other, and Erica half wishes she could blow off this Popsicle stand and spend the afternoon walking around the park with Moira, talking and laughing.

And then the music starts and Erica's heart leaps into her throat and it hits her—*This is really happening. I'm marrying Greg.*

Jenny races in and grabs Erica's hand. "Come on!"

"Wait a minute, you can't start without the minister!" Moy cries, rushing out ahead of them.

Now Erica and Jenny are walking down the aisle, past Nancy Huffman, Eileen McDermott, George Yuan, Mark Benton, Josh Walters and Lisa, and Josh's lucky new girlfriend, Greg's family—everyone is beaming at Erica, and she realizes she's beaming back and there's Greg, standing, waiting, looking impossibly handsome with his smile that holds so much love and promise . . . love and promise.

She reaches him and they look into each other's eyes, and Erica's happiness is leavened with just a touch of trepidation. Is happiness, lasting happiness, even possible in the age and world they live in? In any age, in any world?

Then she looks out at the gathering and over at Jenny, who is beaming like a searchlight, and she realizes that fleeting happiness may have to be enough.

Moy begins the service. "Friends, we are gathered here today—"

Then, from the back of the room, there's a small commotion. Moy pauses and heads turn—a woman has just arrived. She's blowsy and overly made-up, squeezed into a too-tight red satin dress, tottering on high heels. As she makes her way to a seat in the back row, she starts to cry.

Moy continues, "—for a joyous reason. Two wonderful people met, fell in love, and are sealing their commitment to each other with this ceremony."

The crying from the back row grows louder. People shift in their seats and take quick looks backward. Erica shuts her eyes for a moment, squeezes them tight, hoping that when she opens them the ghost will be gone. But she's still there. She gives Moy a tiny but firm nod: *Keep things moving.*

"If anyone thinks this couple should not be joined in marriage, keep your mouth shut."

The laughter drowns out the crying and Erica feels a moment of relief.

Greg takes out a small piece of paper and starts to read, "Erica, today I truly feel like the luckiest man alive. You are a life force who brings out the best in me. I just plain adore you and want to spend the rest of my life by your side."

Erica takes a small piece of paper out of her bodice and then—

"I'm just so proud of her, so darn proud," the woman says in a weepy stage whisper to the man sitting next to her, a cousin of Greg's. He squirms, and people glance backward. She addresses the group. "I'm sorry. Pay me no mind; keep going. I'm just here because I love my baby. This is *your* day."

Jenny tugs on Erica's hand and whispers, "Mom, is that—?"

Erica leans down to Jenny's ear and says, "Yes, honey, that's your grandmother."

DISCUSSION QUESTIONS ————————

1. What are the similarities between the presidential campaign in *The Candidate* and a real campaign for the White House?
2. It's been said that power is the greatest aphrodisiac. How does that play out in *The Candidate*?
3. How far would you go to get something you wanted? What is the furthest you've gone?
4. Celeste Ortiz is heiress to a great fortune. How has that privilege molded her character?
5. Erica isn't sure if Greg, her fiancé, is having an affair with a colleague in Australia. Would you forgive your betrothed an affair? If you suspected he or she was having an affair, would you confront them or seek confirmation without telling them?
6. No matter how much success she achieves, Erica is haunted by the demons of her past. What are those demons and why are they so hard for her to overcome?
7. Erica, a recovering alcoholic, has a slip and drinks in *The Candidate*. How do you feel about this? Is it a sign of character

weakness? Is it understandable considering the stress she's under? Do you forgive her?

8. Erica's relationship with her daughter Jenny remains volatile at times. Why is Erica so insecure in her mothering skills? Do you think she is a good mother? Does our culture put too much pressure on mothers to be "perfect"? What do you think is the most important attribute of a good mother?

ACKNOWLEDGMENTS ────────────

Dear Reader,

I acknowledge and thank you for bringing Erica Sparks and her adventures into your life. I love Erica's strength of character and fortitude. Stay safe, Erica.

Thank you to all my friends at Fox, who continue to encourage and support my love of writing a good mystery. Thank you O'Reilly, from Wiehl. And Roger Ailes, for hiring a certain legal analyst and bringing me in to the world of cable news at the highest level. Thank you, too, to Dianne Brandi. And continued thanks to bestselling thriller author, Steve Berry. It is an honor to be your friend. You gave me the tools to combine the worlds of cable news and mystery in this novel. For invaluable editorial advice and insight, thank you Stephen McCauley.

I love this publishing team! They "got" the idea of putting Erica right in the midst of the 2016 presidential campaign. Something is amiss. Erica is on the hunt. Her life is in danger. And off we go. As "real world" events unfolded during the writing of this work of fiction, I was amazed by how many things struck me as coincidentally similar. This team "got" it and ran with it. Daisy Hutton, Amanda

Bostic, LB Norton, Becky Monds, Becky Philpott, Jodi Hughes, Karli Jackson, Kristen Ingebretson, Samantha Buck, Kristen Golden, and Paul Fisher.

Special thanks to Todd Shuster, my book agent and friend for many years. *The Candidate* would simply not have happened without your guidance.

Thank you Sebastian, my collaborator and friend. I love your energy and spirit. Onward!

And always, thank you Mom and Dad. You are always my role models for following my moral compass.

All the mistakes are mine. All the credit is theirs. Thank you!

Lis

ABOUT THE AUTHOR

LIS WIEHL IS A *NEW York Times* bestselling author, Harvard Law School graduate, and former federal prosecutor. A popular legal analyst and commentator for the Fox News Channel, Wiehl appears weekly on *The O'Reilly Factor*, *Lou Dobbs Tonight*, *Imus in the Morning*, *Kelly's Court*, and more.

Enjoy Lis Wiehl's series as e-book collections!

AVAILABLE IN E-BOOK ONLY

AVAILABLE IN E-BOOK ONLY

LIS LOVES TO HEAR FROM HER READERS!

Be sure to sign up for Lis Wiehl's newsletter for insider information on deals and appearances.

Visit her website at LisWiehlBooks.com
Twitter: @LisWiehl
facebook.com/pages/LisWiehl

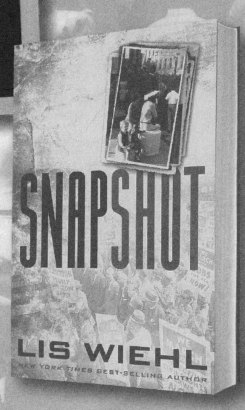

TWO LITTLE GIRLS, **FROZEN IN** BLACK AND WHITE. ONE PICTURE WORTH **KILLING FOR.**

SNAPSHOT

LIS WIEHL

NEW YORK TIMES BEST-SELLING AUTHOR

AVAILABLE IN PRINT, AUDIO, AND E-BOOK